THE PIRATE ISLAND

A STORY OF THE SOUTH PACIFIC

THE PIRATE ISLAND

A STORY OF THE SOUTH PACIFIC

Harry Collingwood

Contents

THE WRECK ON THE GUNFLEET

It was emphatically "a dirty night." The barometer had been slowly but persistently falling during the two previous days; the dawn had been red and threatening, with a strong breeze from S.E.; and as the short dreary November day waxed and waned this strong breeze had steadily increased in strength until by nightfall it had become a regular "November gale," with frequent squalls of arrowy rain and sleet, which, impelled by the furious gusts, smote and stung like hail, and cleared the streets almost as effectually as a volley of musketry would have done.

It was not fit for a dog to be out of doors. So said Ned Anger as he entered the snug bar-parlour of the "Anchor" at Brightlingsea, and drawing a chair close up to the blazing fire of wreck-wood which roared up the ample chimney, flung himself heavily down thereon to await the arrival of the "pint" which he had ordered as he passed the bar.

"And yet there's a many poor souls as has to be out in it, and as is out in it," returned the buxom hostess, entering at the moment with the aforesaid pint upon a small tray. "It's to be hoped as none of 'em won't meet their deaths out there among the sands this fearful night," she added, as Ned took the glass from her, and deposited his "tuppence" in the tray in payment therefor.

A sympathetic murmur of concurrence went round the room in response to this philanthropic wish, accompanied in some instances by doubtful shakes of the head.

"Ay, ay, we all hope that," remarked Dick Bird—"Dicky Bird" was the name which had playfully bestowed upon him by his chums, and by which he was generally known—"we all hopes that; but I, for one, feels uncommon duberous about it. There's hardly a capful of wind as blows but what some poor unfort'nate craft leaves her bones out there,"—with a jerk of the thumb over his shoulder to seaward,—"and mostly with every wreck there's some lives lost. I say, mates, I s'pose there's somebody on the look-out?"

"Ay, ay," responded old Bill Maskell from his favourite corner under the tall old-fashioned clock-case, "Bob's gone across the creek and up to the tower, as usual. The boy will go; always says as how it's his duty to go up there and keep a look-out in bad weather; so, as his eyes is as sharp as needles, and since one is as good as a hundred for that sort of work, I thought I'd just look in here for a hour or two, so's to be on the spot if in case any of us should be wanted."

"I've often wondered how it is that it always falls to Bob's lot to go upon the look-out in bad weather. How is it?" asked an individual in semi-nautical costume at the far end of the room, whose bearing and manner conveyed the impression that he regarded himself, as indeed he was, somewhat of an intruder. He was a ship-chandler's shopman, with an ambition to be mistaken for a genuine "salt," and had not been many months in the place.

"Well, you see, mister, the way of it is just this," explained old Maskell, who considered the question as addressed more especially to him: "Bob was took off a wrack on the Maplin when he was a mere babby, the only one saved; found him wrapped up warm and snug in one of the bunks on the weather side of the cabin with the water surging up to within three inches of him; so ever since he's been old enough to understand he've always insisted as it was his duty, by way of returning thanks, like, to take the look-out when a wrack may be expected. And, don't you make no mistake, there ain't an eye so sharp as his for a signal-rocket in the whole place, see's 'em almost afore they be fired—he do."

"And did you ever try to find his relatives?" asked the shopman.

"Well, no; I can't say as we did, exactly," answered old Bill, "'cause you see we didn't rightly know how to set to work at the job. The ship as he was took off of was a passenger-ship, the Lightning of London, and, as I said afore, he was the only one saved. There were nobody else as we could axe any questions of, and, the ship hailing from London, there was no telling where his friends might have come from. There was R.L. marked on his little clothes, and that was all. So we was obliged to content ourselves with having that fact tacked on to the yarn of the wrack in all the papers, in the hope that some of his friends or relations might get to see it. But, bless yer heart! we ain't heard nothing from nobody about him, never a word; so I just adopted him, as the sayin' is, and called him Robert Legerton, arter a old shipmate of mine that's been drowned this many a year, poor chap."

"And how long is it since the wreck happened?" inquired the shopman.

"Well, let me see," said old Bill. "Blest if I can rightly tell," he continued, after a moment or two of reflection. "I've got it wrote down in the family Bible at home, but I can't just rightly recollect at this moment. It's somewheres about fourteen or fifteen years ago this winter, though."

"Fourteen year next month," spoke up another of the company, decidedly. "It was the same gale as my poor brother Joe was drowned in."

"Right you are, Tom," returned Bill. "I remember it was that same gale now, and that's fourteen year agone. And the women as took charge of poor little Bob when we brought him ashore reckoned as he was about two year old or thereaway; they told his age by his teeth—same as you would tell a horse's age, you know, mister."

"Ay! that was a terrible winter for wrecks, that was," remarked Jack Willis, a fine stalwart young fellow of some five-and-twenty. "It was my first year at sea. I'd been bound apprentice to the skipper of a collier brig called the Nancy, sailing out of Harwich. The skipper's name was Daniell, 'Long Tom Dan'ell' they used to call him because of his size. He was so tall that he couldn't stand upright in his cabin, and he'd been going to sea for so many years that he'd got to be regular round-shouldered. I don't believe that man ever knowed what it was to be ill in his life; he used to be awful proud of his good health, poor chap! he's dead now—drowned—jumped overboard in a gale of wind a'ter a man as fell off the fore-topsail-yard while they was reefing; and, good swimmer as he was, they was both lost. Now, he was a swimmer if you like. You talk about young Bob being a good swimmer, but I'm blessed if I think he could hold a candle to this here Long Tom Dan'ell as I'm talking about. Why, I recollect once when we was lyin' wind-bound in Yarmouth Roads—"

At this point the narrator was interrupted by the sudden opening of the door and the hurried entry of a tall and somewhat slender fair-haired lad clad in oilskin jumper, leggings, and "sou'-wester" hat, which glistened in the gaslight; while, as he stood in the doorway for a moment, dazzled by the abrupt transition from darkness to light, the water trickled off him and speedily formed a little pool at his feet on the well sanded floor.

This new-comer was Bob Legerton, the hero of my story.

"Well, Bob, what's the news?" was the general exclamation, as the assembled party rose with one accord to their feet. "Rockets going up from the 'Middle' and the 'Gunfleet,'" panted the lad, as he wiped the moisture from his eyes with the back of his hand.

"All right," responded old Bill. Then drawing himself up to his full height and casting a scrutinising glance round the room, he exclaimed—

"Now, mates, how many of yer's ready to go out?"

"Why, all of us in course, dad," replied Jack Willis. "'Twas mostly in expectation of bein' wanted that we comed down here to-night. And we've all got our oilskins, so you've only got to pick your crew and let's be off."

A general murmur of assent followed this speech, and the men forthwith ranged themselves along the sides of the room so as to give Bill a clear view of each individual and facilitate a rapid choice.

"Then I'll take you, Jack; and you, Dick; and you; and you; and you;" quickly selecting a strong crew of the stoutest and most resolute men in the party.

The chosen ones lost no time in donning their oilskin garments, a task in which they were cheerfully assisted by the others; and while they were so engaged the hostess issued from the bar with tumblers of smoking hot grog, one of which she handed to each of the adventurers, saying—

"There, boys, drink that off before you go out into the cold and the wet; it'll do none of you any harm, I'm sure, on a night like this, and on such an errand as yours. And you, Bill, if you save anybody and decide to bring 'em into Brightlingsea, send up a signal-rocket as soon as you think we can see it over the land, and I'll have hot water and blankets all ready for the poor souls against they come ashore."

"Ay, ay, mother; I will," replied old Bill. "Only hope we may be lucky enough to get out to 'em in time; the wind's dead in our teeth all the way. Now, lads, if ye're all ready let's be off. Thank'ee, mother, for the grog."

The men filed out, Bill leading, and took their way down to the beach, a very few yards distant, the dim flickering light of a lantern being exhibited from the water-side for a moment as they issued into the open air.

"There's Bob waitin' with the boat; what a chap he is!" ejaculated one of the men as the light was seen. "I say, Bill, you won't take Bob, will you, on an errand like this here?"

"Oh, ay," responded Bill. "He'll want to go; and I promised him he should next time as we was called out. He's a fine handy lad, and old enough to take care of himself by this time. Besides, it's time he began to take his share of the rough work."

Reaching the water's edge they found Bob standing there with the painter of a boat in his hand, the boat itself being partially grounded on the beach. They quickly tumbled in over the gunwale; Bob then placed his shoulder against the stem-head, and with a powerful "shove," drove the boat stern-foremost into the stream, springing in over the bows and stowing himself away in the eyes of the boat as she floated.

It appeared intensely dark outside when the members of the expedition first issued from the hospitable portal of the "Anchor;" but there was a moon, although she was completely hidden by the dense canopy of fast-flying clouds which overspread the heavens; and the faint light which struggled through this thick veil of vapour soon revealed a small fleet of fishing smacks at anchor in the middle of the creek. Toward one of these craft the boat was headed, and in a very few minutes the party were scrambling over the low bulwarks of the Seamew—Bill Maskell's property, and the pride of the port.

The boat was at once dragged in on deck and secured, and then, without hurry or confusion of any kind, but in an incredibly short time, the smack was unmoored and got under weigh, a faint cheer from the shore following her as she wound her way down the creek between the other craft, and, hauling close to the wind, headed toward the open sea.

In a very few minutes the gallant little Seamew had passed clear of the low point upon which stands the Martello Tower which had been Bob's place of look-out, and then she felt the full fury of the gale and the full strength of the raging sea. Even under the mere shred of sail—a balance-reefed main-sail and storm jib—which she dared to show, the little vessel was buried to her gunwale, while the sea poured in a continuous cataract over her bows, across her deck, and out again to leeward, rendering it necessary for her crew to crouch low on the deck to windward under the partial shelter of her low bulwarks, and to lash themselves there.

It was indeed a terrible night. The thermometer registered only a degree or two above freezing-point; and the howling blast, loaded with spindrift and scud-water, seemed to pierce the adventurers to their very marrow, while, notwithstanding the care with which they were wrapped up, the continuous pouring of the sea over them soon wet them to the skin.

But the serious discomfort to which they had voluntarily exposed themselves, so far from damping their ardour only increased it. As the veteran Bill, standing there at the tiller exposed to the full fury of the tempest, with the tiller-ropes pulling and jerking at his hands until they threatened to cut into the bone, felt his wet clothing clinging to his skin, and his sea-boots gradually filling with water, he pictured to himself a group of poor terror-stricken wretches clinging despairingly to a shattered wreck out there upon the cruel sands, with the merciless sea tugging at them fiercely, and the wind chilling the blood within their veins until, perchance, their benumbed limbs growing powerless, their hold would relax and they would be swept away; and as the dismal scene rose before his mental vision he tautened up the tiller-ropes a trifle, the smack's head fell off perhaps half a point, and the wind striking more fully upon the straining canvas, she went surging out to seaward like a startled steed, her hull half buried in a whirling chaos of flying foam.

Old Bill, the leader of this desperate expedition, was a fisherman in winter and a yachtsman in summer, as indeed were most of the crew of the Seamew on this eventful night. Many a hard-fought match had Bill sailed in, and more than one flying fifty had he proudly steered, a winner, past the flag-ship; but his companions agreed, as they crouched shivering under the bulwarks, that he never handled a craft better or more boldly than he did the Seamew on that night. One good stretch to the eastward, until the "Middle" light bore well upon their weather quarter, and the helm was put down; the smack tacked handsomely, though she shipped a sea and filled her deck to the gunwale in the operation, and then away she rushed on the other tack, with the light bearing well upon the lee bow.

In less than an hour from the time of starting the light ship was reached; and as the smack, luffing into the wind, shaved close under the vessel's stern with all her canvas ashiver, Bill's stentorian voice pealed out—

"Middle, ahoy! where a way's the wrack?"

"About a mile and half to the nor'ard, on the weather side of the Gunfleet. Fancy she must have broke up, can't make her out now. Wish ye good luck," was the reply.

"Thank'ee," roared back Bill. "Ease up main and jib-sheets, boys, and stand clear for a jibe."

Round swept the little Seamew, and in another moment, with the wind on her starboard quarter, she was darting almost with the speed of her namesake, along the weather edge of the shoal, upon her errand of mercy.

All eyes were now keenly directed ahead and on the lee bow, anxiously watching for some indication of the whereabouts of the wreck, and in a few minutes the welcome cry was simultaneously raised by three or four of the watchers, "There she is!"

"Ay, there she is; sure enough!" responded old Bill from his post at the tiller, he having like the rest caught a momentary glimpse under the foot of the main-sail of a shapeless object which had revealed itself for a single instant in the midst of the whirl of boiling breakers, only to be lost sight of again as the leaping waves hurled themselves once more furiously down upon their helpless prey.

As the smack rapidly approached the scene of the disaster the wreck was made out to be that of a large ship, with only the stump of her main-mast standing. She was already fast settling down in the sand, the forepart of the hull being completely submerged, while the sea swept incessantly over the stern, which, with its full poop, formed the sole refuge of the hapless crew.

"Now, boys," remarked old Bill when they had approached closely enough to perceive the desperate situation of those on the wreck. "Now, boys, whatever we're going to do has got to be done smart; the tide's rising fast, and in another hour there won't be enough of yon ship left to light a fire wi'. Are yer all ready wi' the anchor?"

"Ay, ay; all ready," was the prompt response.

The helm was put down, and the smack plunged round head to wind, her sails flapping furiously as the wind was spilled out of them. There was no need for orders; the men all knew exactly what to do, and did it precisely at the right moment. Jib and main-sail were hauled down and secured in less time than it takes to describe it; and then, as the little vessel lost her "way," the heavy anchor—carried expressly for occasions like the present—was let go, and the cable veered cautiously out so that the full strain might not be brought to bear upon it too suddenly. Old Bill, meanwhile, stood aft by the taffrail with the lead-line in his hand, anxiously noting the shoaling water as the smack drifted sternward toward the wreck.

"Hold on, for'ard," he shouted at last, when the little Seamew had driven so far in upon the sand that there was little more than a foot of water beneath her keel when she sank into the trough of the sea. "Now lay aft here, all hands, and let's see if we can get a rope aboard of 'em."

The smack was now fairly among the breakers, which came thundering down upon the shoal with indescribable fury, boiling and foaming and tumbling round the little vessel in a perfect chaos of confusion, and falling on board her in such vast volumes that had everything not been securely battened down beforehand she must inevitably have been swamped in a few minutes. As for her crew, every man of them worked with the end of a line firmly lashed round his waist, so that in the extremely likely event of his being washed overboard his comrades might have the means of hauling him on board again.

Nor wore these the only dangers to which the adventurers were exposed. There was the possibility that the cable, stout as it was, might part at any moment, and in such a case their fate would be sealed, for nothing could then prevent the smack from being dashed to pieces on the sands.

Yet all these dangers were cheerfully faced by these men from a pure desire to serve their fellow-creatures, and without the slightest hope of reward, for they knew at the very outset that there would not be much hope of salvage, with a vessel on the sands in such a terrible gale.

The wreck was now directly astern of the smack, and only about one hundred feet distant, so that she could be distinctly seen, as it fortunately happened that the sky had been steadily clearing for the last quarter of an hour, allowing the moon to peep out unobscured now and then through an occasional break in the clouds. By the increasing light the smack's crew were not only enabled to note the exact position of the wreck, but they could also see that a considerable number of people were clustered upon the poop of the half-submerged hull, some of them being women and children. The poor souls were all watching with the most intense anxiety the movements of those on board the smack, and if anything had been needed to stimulate the exertions of her crew it would have been abundantly found in the sight of those poor helpless mothers and their little ones clinging there to the shattered wreck in the bitter winter midnight, exposed to the full fury of the pitiless storm.

A light heaving-line was quickly cleared away, and one end bent to a rope becket securely spliced to a small keg, which was then thrown overboard and allowed to drift down toward the wreck, the line being veered freely away at the same time.

The crew of the wreck, anxiously watching the motions of those on board the smack, at once comprehended the object of this manoeuvre, and, as the keg drifted down toward them, made ready to secure it. But the set of the tide, the wash of the sea, or some other unexplained circumstance caused it to deviate so far from its intended course that it passed at a considerable distance astern of the wreck, notwithstanding the utmost endeavours of those on board to secure it; in consequence of which it had to be hauled on board the smack again, and thus valuable time was lost. The smack's helm was at once shifted, and the tide, aided by the wind, gave her so strong a sheer in the required direction that it was hoped a repetition of the mischance would be impossible. The keg was again thrown overboard, the line once more veered away. Buoyantly it drifted down toward the wreck, now buried in the hissing foam-crest of a mighty breaker, and anon riding lightly in the liquid valley behind it. All eyes were intently fixed upon it, impatiently watching its slow and somewhat erratic movements, when the smack seemed to leap suddenly skyward, rearing up like a startled courser, and heeling violently over on her beam-ends at the same moment; there was a terrific thud forward, accompanied by a violent crashing sound, and the Seamew's crew had barely time to grasp the cleat or belaying-pin nearest at hand when a foaming deluge of water hissed and swirled past and over them, the breaker of which it formed a part sweeping from under the smack down toward the wreck in an unbroken wall of green water, capped with a white and ominously curling crest. The roller broke just as it reached the wreck, expending its full force upon her already shattered hull; the black mass was seen to heel almost completely over in the midst of the wildly tossing foam, there was a dull report, almost like that of a gun, a piercing shriek, which rose clearly above the howling of the gale and the babel of the maddened waters, and when the wreck again became visible it was seen that she had broken in two amidships, the bow lying bottom-upward some sixty feet farther in upon the sand, while the stern, which retained its former position, had been robbed of nearly half its living freight. And, to make matters worse, the floating keg had once more missed its mark.

This repeated failure was disheartening. The tide was rising rapidly; every minute was worth a human life, and it began to look as though, in spite of all effort, the poor souls clinging to the wreck would be swept into eternity before the Seamew's crew could effect a communication with them.

"Let's have one more try, boys," exhorted old Bill; "and if we misses her this time we shall have to shift our ground and trust to our own anchor and chain to hold us until we can get 'em off."

Risky work that would be, as each man there told himself; but none thought of expressing such a sentiment aloud, preferring to take the risk rather than abandon those poor souls to their fate.

The line and keg were rapidly hauled on board the smack once more, and Bill was standing aft by the taffrail watching for a favourable moment at which to make another cast, when Bob exclaimed excitedly—

"'Vast heavin', father; 'taint no use tryin' that dodge any more—we're too far to leeward. Cast off the line and take a turn with it round my waist; I'm goin' to try to swim it. I know I can do it, dad; and it's the only way as we can do any good."

The old man stared aghast at the lad for a moment, then he glanced at the mad swirl of broken water astern, then back once more to Bob, who, in the meantime, was rapidly divesting himself of his clothing.

"God bless ye, boy, for the thought," he at length ejaculated; "God bless ye, but it ain't possible. Even if the water was warm the breaking seas 'd smother ye; but bitter cold as 'tis you wouldn't swim a dozen yards. No, no, Bob, my lad, put on your duds again; we must try sum'at else."

But Bob had by this time disencumbered himself of everything save a woollen under-shirt and drawers; and now, instead of doing his adopted father's bidding, he rapidly cast off the line from the keg, and, making a bowline in the end, passed it over one shoulder and underneath the other arm. The next instant he had poised himself lightly upon the taffrail of the wildly tossing smack, and, a mighty breaker sweeping by, with comparatively smooth water behind it, without a moment's hesitation thence plunged head-foremost into the icy sea.

The broken water leaped and tossed wildly, as if in exultation, over the spot where the brave lad had disappeared; while all hands—both those on board the smack and the people on the wreck—waited breathlessly for his reappearance on the surface. An endless time it seemed to all; and but for the rapid passage of the thin light line out over the smack's taffrail, indicating that Bob was swimming swiftly under water, old Bill Maskell would have dreaded some dreadful mishap to his protégé; but at last a small round dark object appeared in bold relief in the midst of a sheet of foam, which gleamed dazzling white in the clear cold light of the moon.

It was Bob's head.

"There he is!" was the exultant exclamation of every one of the smack's crew, and then they sent forth upon the wings of the gale a ringing cheer, in which those upon the wreck faintly joined.

"Now, boys," exclaimed old Bill, "clear away this here line behind me, some of yer; and look out another nice light handy one to bend on to it in case we wants it."

The old man himself stood on the taffrail, paying out the line and attentively watching every heave of the plunging smack, so that Bob might not be checked in the smallest degree in his perilous passage, nor, on the other hand, be hampered by having a superabundance of line paid out behind him for the tide to act upon and drag hint away to leeward.

The distance from the smack to the wreck was but short, a mere hundred feet or so, but with the heavy surf to contend against and the line sagging and swaying in the sea behind him, it taxed Bob's energies to their utmost limit to make any progress at all. Indeed, it appeared to him that, instead of progressing, he was, like the keg, drifting helplessly to leeward with the tide. The cold water, too, chilled him to the very marrow and seemed to completely paralyse his energies, while the relentless surf foamed over his head almost without intermission, so that he had the utmost difficulty in getting his breath. Nevertheless he fought gallantly on until, after what seemed to be an eternity of frightful exertion, he reached the side of the wreck, and grasped the rope which its occupants flung to him. He was too completely exhausted, however, to mount the side at that moment; and while he clung to the rope, regaining his breath and his strength, a mighty roller came sweeping down upon the sands, burying the smack for the moment as it rushed passed her, and then surging forward with upreared threatening crest toward the wreck.

There was a warning cry from those on board the wreck, as they saw this terrible wall of water rushing down upon them, and each seized with desperate grip whatever came nearest to hand, clinging thereto with the tenacity of despair. Bob heard the cry, saw the danger, and had just time to struggle clear of the wreck and pass under her stern when the breaker burst upon them. Blinded, stunned, and breathless, he felt himself whirled helplessly hither and thither, while a load like that of a mountain seemed to rest upon him and press him down. At last he emerged again, considerably to leeward of the wreck, but with the rope which they had thrown him still in his hands. As he gasped for breath and shook the salt water out of his eyes, something swayed against him beneath the surface—something which he knew instantly must be a human body. In a second he had it in his grasp, and, dragging it above water, found it to be the body of a child, apparently about two years old. At the same moment a powerful strain came upon the line which he held in his hand, and he had only time to take, by a rapid movement, two or three turns of it round his arm when those on the wreck began to haul him on board.

In less time than it takes to tell of it, he was dragged inboard, and lay panting and exhausted upon the steeply inclined deck of the wreck, with a curious crowd of haggard-eyed anxious men and women gathered round him. A man dressed in a fine white linen shirt and blue serge trousers (he was the master of the ship, and had given his remaining garments to shield the poor shivering, frightened children) was in the act of kneeling down by Bob's side, apparently intending to question him, when a piercing shriek was heard, and a woman darted forward with the cry "My child! my child!" and seized the body which Bob had brought on board and still held in his arms.

This incident created a diversion; and Bob speedily recovering the use of his faculties, and rapidly explaining the intentions of those on board the smack, a strong hawser was soon stretched from the Seamew to the wreck, a "bo'sun's chair" slung thereto; and the transport of the shipwrecked crew and passengers at once commenced.

The journey, though short, was fraught with the utmost peril; for it being impossible to keep the hawser strained taut, the poor unfortunate wretches had to be dragged through rather than over the surf; and when all was ready the women, who were of course to go first, found their courage fail them.

In vain were they remonstrated with; in vain were they reminded that every second as it flew bore mayhap a human life into eternity with it; the sight of the wild surf into which the hawser momentarily plunged completely unnerved them, and they one and all declared that, rather than face the terrible risk, they would die where they were.

At last Bob, who knew as well as, if not better than, anyone on board the importance of celerity, whispered a word or two in the captain's ear. The latter nodded approvingly; and Bob at once got into the "chair," some of the ship's crew rapidly but securely lashing him there, in obedience to their captain's order. When all was ready the skipper, approaching the terrified group of women, took one of their children tenderly in his arms, and, before the unhappy mother could realise what was about to take place, handed it to Bob.

The signal was instantly given to those on board the smack, who hauled swiftly upon the hauling-line; Bob went swaying off the gunwale, with his precious charge encircled safely in his arms, and in another moment was buried in a mountain of broken water which rushed foaming past. Only to reappear instantly afterwards, however; and in a very brief space of time he and his charge had safely reached the smack. The little one was handed over to the rough but tender-hearted fishermen; but Bob, seeing that he could be useful there, at once returned to the wreck.

There was now no further difficulty with the women. The mother whose child had already made the adventurous passage was frantic to rejoin her baby, and eagerly placed herself in the chair as soon as Bob vacated it. She, too, accomplished the journey in safety; and then the others, taking courage once more from her example, quietly took their turn, some carrying their children with them, while others preferred to confide their darlings to Bob, or to one of the seamen, for the dreadful passage through the wintry sea.

The women once safe, the men made short work of it; and in little over two hours twenty-five souls—the survivors of a company of passengers and crew numbering in all forty-two—were safely transferred to the Seamew, which, slipping her cable, at once bore away with her precious freight for Brightlingsea.

The Betsy Jane

Once fairly out of the breakers the fishermen—at great risk to their little craft—opened the companion leading down into the Seamew's tiny after-cabin, and the poor souls from the wreck were conveyed below, out of the reach of the bitter blast and the incessant showers of icy spray. Bob and two or three others of the smack's crew also went below and busied themselves in lighting a fire, routing out such blankets and wraps of various kinds as happened to be on board, and in other ways doing what they could to ameliorate the deplorable condition of their guests. Fortunately the wind, dead against them on the way out, was fair for the homeward run, and the Seamew rushed through the water at a rate which caused "Dicky" Bird to exclaim—

"Blest if the little huzzy don't seem to know as they poor innercent babbies' lives depends on their gettin' into mother Salmon's hands and atween her hot blankets within the next hour! Just see how she's smoking through it."

Very soon the "Middle" lightship was reached, and as the smack swept past old Bill shouted to the light-keepers the joyful news of the rescue. A few minutes afterwards three rockets were sent up at short intervals from the smack, as an intimation to "mother" Salmon that her good services were required; and in due time the gallant little smack found her way back to her moorings in the creek.

The anchor was scarcely let go when three or four boats dashed alongside, and "Well, Bill, old man, what luck?" was the general question.

"Five-and-twenty, thank God, men, women, and children," responded old Bill. "Did ye catch sight of our rockets, boys!"

"Ay, ay; never fear. And 'mother' ashore there, she's never turned-in at all this blessed night. Said as she was sure you'd bring somebody in; and a rare rousing fire she's got roaring up the chimbley, and blankets, no end; all the beds made up and warmed, and everything ready, down to a rattlin' good hot supper; so let's have these poor souls up on deck (you've got 'em below, I s'pose), and get 'em ashore; they must be pretty nigh froze to death, I should think."

At Bill's cheery summons the survivors from the wreck staggered to the smack's deck—their cramped and frozen limbs scarcely able to sustain them—and the bewildered glances which they cast round them at the scarcely ruffled waters of the creek glancing in the clear frosty moonlight, with the fishing smacks and other small craft riding cosily at anchor on either side, the straggling village of Brightlingsea within a stone's throw—a tiny light still twinkling here and there in the cottage windows, and a perfect blaze of ruddy light streaming from the windows of the "Anchor," and flooding the road with its cheerful radiance—the bewildered glances with which they regarded this scene, I say, showed that even now they were scarcely able to realise the fact of their deliverance.

But they were not left very long in doubt about it. As they emerged with slow and painful steps from the smack's tiny companion, strong arms seized them, all enwrapped in blankets as they were, and quickly but tenderly passed them over the side into the small boats which had come off from the shore for them. Then, as each boat received its complement, "Shove off" was the word; the bending oars churned the water into miniature whirlpools, and with a dozen powerful strokes the boat was sent half her length high and dry upon the shore. Then strong arms once more raised the sufferers, and quickly bore them within the wide-open portal of the hospitable "Anchor," where "mother" Salmon waited to receive them.

"Eh, goodness sakes alive!" she exclaimed, as the first man appeared within the flood of light which streamed from the "Anchor" windows. "You, Sam; you don't mean to say as there's women amongst 'em."

"Ah! that there is, mother," panted Sam, "and children—poor little helpless babbies, some on 'em, too."

The quick warm tears of womanly sympathy instantly flashed into the worthy woman's eyes; but she was not one prone to much indulgence in sentiment, particularly at a time like the present; so instead of lifting up her hands and giving expression to her pity in words, she faced sharply round upon the maids who were crowding forward, with the curiosity of their sex, to catch a first glimpse of the strangers, and exclaimed—

"Now then, you idle huzzies, what d'ye mean by blocking up the passage so that a body can get neither in nor out? D'ye want these poor souls to be quite froze to death before you lets 'em in? You, Em'ly, be off to Number 4 and run the warmin' pan through the bed, and give the fire a good stir. Emma, do wake up, child, and take a couple of buckets of hot water up to Number 4, and put 'em in the bath. Run, Mary Jane, for your life, and see if the fire in Number 7 is burning properly; and you, Susan, be off and turn down all the beds."

The maids rushed off to their several duties like startled deer, while the mistress turned to Sam and directed him to convey his burden to Number 4, herself leading the way.

A number of women, the mothers and wives of the fishermen, had gathered at the "Anchor" as soon as it was known that the smack had gone out to a wreck, in order that they might be at hand to render any assistance which might be required. They were all collected in the bar-parlour; and two of them now rose, in obedience to "mother" Salmon's summons, and following her upstairs, took over from Sam their patient; and, shutting the door, lost not a moment in applying such restoratives and adopting such measures as their experience taught them would be most likely to prove beneficial.

The rest of the survivors speedily followed; the women and children being promptly conveyed to the rooms already prepared for them; but the men, for the most part, proved to be very little the worse for their exposure, seeming to need for their restoration a good hot supper more than anything else; and this contingency also having by "mother" Salmon's experience and foresight been provided for, the rescued and their rescuers were soon seated together at the same table busily engaged in the endeavour to restore their exhausted energies.

One man only of the entire party seemed unable to do justice to the meal spread before him, and this was the master of the wrecked ship. He seated himself indeed at the table, and made an effort to eat and drink, but his thoughts were evidently elsewhere. He could not settle comfortably down to his meal, but kept gliding softly out of the room, to glide as softly back again after an absence of a few minutes, when he would abstractedly swallow a mouthful or two, and then glide out once more. At length, after a somewhat longer absence than before, he returned to the room in which the meal was being discussed, the look of care and anxiety on his face replaced by an expression of almost overwhelming joy, and, walking up to Bob, somewhat astonished that individual by exclaiming—

"Young man, let me without further delay tender you and your brave comrades my most hearty thanks for the rescue of my passengers, my crew, and myself from a situation of deadly peril, a rescue which was only effected at very great hazard to yourselves, and which was successfully accomplished mainly—I am sure your comrades will join me in saying—through your indomitable courage and perseverance. The debt which I owe you is one that it will be quite impossible for me ever to repay; I can merely acknowledge it and testify to the overwhelming nature of my obligation, for to your gallant behaviour, under God, I owe not only the deliverance of twenty-five human lives from a watery grave, but also the safety of my wife and only child—all, in fact, that I have left to me to make life worth living. As I have said, it will be quite impossible for me ever to cancel so heavy a debt; but what I can do I will. Your conduct shall be so represented in the proper quarter as to secure for you all the honour which such noble service demands; and, for the rest, I hope you will always remember that Captain Staunton—that is my name—will deem no service that you may require of him too great to be promptly rendered. And what I say to you especially, I say also to all your gallant comrades, who will, I hope, accept the grateful thanks which I now tender to them."

Poor Bob blushed like a girl at these warm outspoken praises, and stammered some deprecatory remarks, which, however, were drowned by the more vigorous disclaimers of the rest of the fishermen and their somewhat noisy applause of the shipwrecked captain's manly speech; in the midst of which commotion "mother" Salmon entered to enjoin strict silence and to announce the gratifying intelligence that all the women and children were doing well, including the skipper's little daughter, the apparently lifeless body of whom Bob had recovered when first he boarded the wreck. A low murmur of satisfaction greeted this announcement, and then all hands fell to once more upon their supper, which was soon afterwards concluded, when old Bill and his mates, shaking hands heartily all round, retired to seek the rest which they had so well-earned, while the shipwrecked men were disposed of as well as circumstances would allow in the few remaining unappropriated bed-rooms of the hospitable "Anchor."

By noon next day the shipwrecked party had all so far recovered that they were able to set out on the journey to their several homes. Captain Staunton sought out old Bill and arranged with him respecting the salvage of the wrecked ship's cargo, after which he handed the veteran fisherman, as remuneration for services already rendered, a draft upon the owners of the Diadem, which more than satisfied the smack's crew for all their perils and exertions of the previous night. He then left for London to perform the unpleasant duty of reporting to his owners the loss of their ship, mentioning, before he left, the probability of his speedy return to personally superintend the salvage operations. In bidding adieu to Bob, who happened to be present while the final arrangements with old Bill were being made, Captain Staunton remarked to him—

"I have been thinking a great deal about you, my lad. You are a fine gallant young fellow, and it seems to me it would be a very great pity for you to waste your life in pursuit of the arduous and unprofitable occupation of fishing. What say you? Would you like to take to the sea as a profession? If so, let me know. I owe you a very heavy debt, as I have already said, and nothing would afford me greater pleasure than to repay you, as far as possible, by personally undertaking your training, and afterwards using what little interest I possess to advance you in your career. Think the matter over, and consult with your father upon it"—he was not then aware of poor Bob's peculiar position—"and let me know your decision when I return. Now, once more, good-bye for the present."

The weather having moderated by the next day, the Seamew's crew commenced salvage operations at the wreck, and for more than a week all hands were so busy, early and late, that Bob had literally no time to think about, much less to consult with old Bill respecting, Captain Staunton's proposal.

On the third day the chief mate of the Diadem appeared at Brightlingsea, having been sent down by the owners to superintend the work at the wreck. He announced that he had been sent instead of Captain Staunton, in consequence of the appointment of the latter by his owners to the command of a fine new ship then loading in the London Docks for Australia. It appeared that Captain Staunton stood so high in the estimation of his employers, and possessed such a thoroughly-established reputation for skill and sobriety that, notwithstanding his recent misfortune, there had been no hesitation about employing him again. A few days later a letter came from the captain himself to Bob confirming this intelligence, and stating that he had then a vacancy for his young friend if he chose to fill it.

Bob, however, as has already been remarked, was at the time too busy to give the matter proper consideration, so he wrote back saying as much, and hinting that perhaps on the return of the ship to England he might be glad to have a repetition of the offer.

To this letter a reply soon came, announcing the immediate departure of the ship, and containing a specific offer to receive Bob on board in the capacity of apprentice on her next voyage.

The idea of taking to the sea as a profession was so thoroughly novel to Bob that he had at first some little difficulty in realising all that it meant. Hitherto he had had no other intention or ambition than to potter about in a fishing smack with old Bill, living a hard life, earning a precarious subsistence, and possibly, if exceptionally fortunate, at some period in the far-distant future, attaining to the ownership of a smack himself. But a month or two later on, when all had been saved that it was possible to save from the wreck, and when nothing remained of the once fine ship but a few shattered timbers embedded in the sand, and showing at low water like the fragment of a skeleton of some leviathan; when Bob found time to fully discuss the matter with old Bill Maskell and his mates, these worthies painted the advantages of a regular seaman's life over those of the mere fisherman in such glowing colours, and dwelt so enthusiastically upon the prospects which would surely open out before our hero under the patronage of a man like Captain Staunton, that Bob soon made up his mind to accept the captain's offer and join him on his return to England.

Having once come to this decision the lad was all impatience for the time to arrive when he might embark upon his career. As it is with most lads, so it was with him, the prospect of a complete change in his mode of life was full of pleasurable excitement; and perhaps it was only natural that, now he had decided to forsake it, the monotonous humdrum fisher's life became almost unbearably irksome to him. Old Bill Maskell was not slow to observe this, and with the unselfishness which was so eminently characteristic of him, though he loved the lad as his own soul, he decided to shorten for him as far as possible the weary time of waiting, and send him away at once.

Accordingly, on the first opportunity that presented itself, he remarked to Bob—

"I say, boy, I've been turnin' matters over in my mind a bit, and it seems to me as a v'yage or two in a coaster 'd do you a power o' good afore you ships aboard a 'South-Spainer.' You're as handy a lad as a man need wish to be shipmates with, aboard a fore-and-aft-rigged craft; but you ought to know some'at about square-rigged vessels too afore you sails foreign. Now, what d'ye say to a trip or two in a collier brig, just to larn the ropes like, eh?"

Note: "South-Spainer"—A term frequently employed by seamen to designate a foreign-going ship, especially one sailing to southern waters.—H.C.

Life on board a collier is not, as a rule, a condition of unalloyed felicity; but Bob was happily, or unhappily, ignorant of this; the suggestion conveyed to his mind only the idea of change, and his face lighted joyfully up at his benefactor's proposition, to which he at once eagerly assented.

Bob's slender wardrobe was accordingly at once overhauled and put into a condition of thorough repair; Bill, meantime, employing himself laboriously in an effort to ascertain, through the medium of a voluminous correspondence, the whereabouts of an old friend of his—last heard of by the said Bill as in command of a collier brig—with a view to the securing for Bob a berth as "ordinary seaman" under a "skipper" of whom Bill knew something, and who could be trusted to treat the lad well.

Old Bill's labours were at length rewarded with success, "Captain"—as he loved to be styled—Turnbull's address in London being definitely ascertained, together with the gratifying intelligence that he still retained the command of the Betsy Jane.

Matters having progressed thus far satisfactorily, old Bill's next business was to write to "Captain" Turnbull, asking him if he could receive Bob on board; and in about a month's time a favourable answer was received, naming a day upon which Bob was to run up to London and sign articles.

Bob's departure from Brightlingsea was regarded by his numerous friends in the village quite in the light of an event; and when the morning came, and with it the market-cart which was to convey him and his belongings, together with old Bill, to Colchester, where they were to take train to London, nearly all the fishermen in the place, to say nothing of their wives and little ones, turned out to say farewell.

The journey was accomplished in safety and without adventure; and shortly after noon Bill and Bob found themselves threading their way through the narrow crowded streets to the "captain's" address, somewhere in the neighbourhood of Wapping.

On reaching the house the gallant skipper was found to be at home, in the act of partaking, together with his wife and family, of the mid-day meal, which on that occasion happened to be composed of "pickled pork and taturs." Old Bill and Bob were gruffly but cordially invited to join the family circle, which they did; Bob making a thoroughly hearty meal, quite unmoved by the coquettish endeavours of Miss Turnbull, a stout, good-tempered, but not particularly beautiful damsel of some seventeen summers, to attract the attention and excite the admiration of "pa's handsome new sailor."

"Captain" Turnbull proved to be a very stout but not very tall man, with a somewhat vacant expression of feature, and a singular habit of looking fixedly and in apparent amazement for a full minute at anyone who happened to address him. These, with a slow ponderous movement of body, a fixed belief in his own infallibility, and an equally firm belief in the unsurpassed perfections of the Betsy Jane, were his chief characteristics; and as he is destined to figure for a very brief period only in the pages of the present history, we need not analyse him any further.

After dinner had been duly discussed, together with a glass of grog—so far at least as the "captain," his wife, and old Bill were concerned—our two friends were invited by the proud commander to pay a visit of inspection to the Betsy Jane. That venerable craft proved to be lying in the stream, the outside vessel of a number of similar craft moored in a tier, head and stern, to great slimy buoys, laid down as permanent moorings in the river. A wherry was engaged by the skipper, for which old Bill paid when the time of settlement arrived, the "captain" being apparently unconscious of the fact that payment was necessary, and the three proceeded on board. The brig turned out to be about as bad a specimen of her class as could well be met with—old, rotten, leaky, and dirty beyond all power of description. Nevertheless her skipper waxed so astonishingly eloquent when he began to speak her praises, that the idea never seemed to occur to either Bill or Bob that to venture to sea in her would be simply tempting Providence, and it was consequently soon arranged that our hero was to sign articles, nominally as an ordinary seaman, but, in consideration of his ignorance of square-rigged craft, to receive only the pay of a boy.

This point being settled the party returned to the shore, old Bill and Bob going for a saunter through some of the principal streets, to enjoy the cheap but rare luxury, to simple country people like themselves, of a look into the shop windows, with the understanding that they were to accept the hospitality of the Turnbull mansion until the time for sailing should arrive on the morrow.

Bob wished very much to visit one of the theatres that evening—a theatre being a place of entertainment which up to that time he had never had an opportunity of entering; but old Bill, anxious to cultivate, on Bob's behalf, the goodwill of the Betsy Jane's commander, thought it would be wiser to spend the evening with that worthy. This arrangement was accordingly carried out, the "best parlour" being thrown open by Mrs Turnbull for the occasion. Miss Turnbull and Miss Jemima Turnbull contributed in turn their share toward the evening's entertainment by singing "Hearts of Oak," "The Bay of Biscay," "Then farewell my trim-built wherry," and other songs of a similar character, to a somewhat uncertain accompaniment upon a discordant jangling old piano—the chief merit of which was that a large proportion of its notes were dumb. Their gallant father meanwhile sipped his grog and puffed away at his "church-warden" in a high-backed uncomfortable-looking chair in a corner near the fire, utterly sunk, apparently, in a fit of the most profound abstraction, from which he would occasionally start without the slightest warning, and in a most alarming manner, to bellow out—generally at the wrong time and to the wrong tune—something which his guests were expected to regard as a chorus. The chorus ended he would again sink, like a stone, as abruptly back into his inner consciousness as he had emerged from it. So passed the evening, without the slightest pretence at conversation, though both Bill and Bob made several determined efforts to start a topic; and so, as music, even of the kind performed by the Misses Turnbull, palls after a time, about eleven p.m. old Bill hinted at fatigue from the unusual exertions of the day, proposed retirement, and, with Bob, was shown to the room wherein was located the "shakedown" offered them by the hospitable skipper. The "shakedown" proved to be in reality two fair-sized beds, which would have been very comfortable had they been much cleaner than they were, and our two friends enjoyed a very fair night's rest.

Bob duly signed articles on the following morning, and then, in company with his shipmates, proceeded on board the Betsy Jane. Captain Turnbull put in an appearance about an hour afterwards, when the order was given to unmoor ship, and the brig began to drop down the river with the tide. Toward evening a fine fair wind sprang up, and the Betsy Jane, being only in ballast, then began to travel at a rate which threw her commander into an indescribable state of ecstasy. The voyage was accomplished without the occurrence of any incident worth recording, and in something like a week from the date of sailing from London, Bob found himself at Shields, with the brig under a coal-drop loading again for the Thames.

Some half a dozen similarly uneventful voyages to the Tyne and back to London were made by Bob in the Betsy Jane. The life of a seaman on board a collier is usually of a very monotonous character, without a single attractive feature in it—unless, maybe, that it admits of frequent short sojourns at home—and Bob's period of service under Captain Turnbull might have been dismissed with the mere mention of the circumstance, but for the incident which terminated that service.

It occurred on the sixth voyage which Bob had made in the Betsy Jane. The brig had sailed from the Tyne, loaded with coals for London as usual, with a westerly wind, which, however, shortly afterwards backed to S.S.W., with a rapidly falling barometer. The appearance of the weather grew very threatening, which, coupled with the facts that the craft was old, weak, and a notoriously poor sailer with the wind anywhere but on her quarter, seemed to suggest, as the most prudent course under the circumstances, a return to the port they had just left. The mate, after many uneasy glances to windward, turned to his superior officer, who was sitting by the companion placidly smoking, and proposed this.

The skipper slowly withdrew his pipe from his mouth, and, after regarding his mate for some moments, as though that individual were a perfect stranger who had suddenly and unaccountably made his appearance on board, ejaculated—

"Why?"

"Well, I'm afeard we're goin' to have a very dirty night on it," was the reply.

"Umph!" was the captain's only commentary, after which he resumed his pipe, and seemed inclined to doze.

Meanwhile the wind, which had hitherto been of the strength of a fair working breeze, rapidly increased in force, with occasional sharp squalls preceded by heavy showers of rain, while the threatening aspect of the weather grew every moment more unmistakable. The brig was under topgallant-sails, tearing and thrashing through the short choppy sea in a way which sent the spray flying continuously in dense clouds in over her bluff bows, until her decks were mid-leg deep in water, and her stumpy topgallant-masts where whipping about aloft to such an extent that they threatened momentarily to snap off short at the caps. It was not considered etiquette on board the Betsy Jane for the mate to issue an order while the captain had the watch, as was the case on the present occasion; but seeing a heavy squall approaching he now waived etiquette for the nonce and shouted—

"Stand by your to'gallan' halliards! Let go and clew up! Haul down the jib."

"Eh!" said the skipper, deliberately removing his pipe from his mouth, and looking around him in the greatest apparent astonishment.

Down rushed the squall, howling and whistling through the rigging, careening the brig until the water spouted up through her scuppers, and causing the gear aloft to crack and surge ominously.

"Let fly the tops'l halliards, fore and main!" yelled the mate.

The men leapt to their posts, the ropes rattled through the blocks, the yards slid down the top-masts until they rested on the caps, and with a terrific thrashing and fluttering of canvas the brig rose to a more upright position, saving her spars by a mere hair's-breadth.

Captain Turnbull rose slowly to his feet, and, advancing to where the mate stood near the main-rigging, tapped that individual softly on the shoulder with his pipe-stem.

The mate turned round.

Captain Turnbull looked fixedly at him for some moments as though he thought he recognised him, but was not quite sure, and then observed—

"I say, are you the cap'n of this ship?"

"No, sir," replied the mate.

"Very well, then," retorted the skipper, "don't you do it agen." Then to the crew, all of whom were by this time on deck, "Bowse down yer reef-tackles and double-reef the taups'ls, then stow the mains'l."

"Don't you think we'd better run back to the Tyne, afore we drops too far to leeward to fetch it?" inquired the mate.

The captain looked at him in his characteristic fashion for a full minute; inquired, "Are you the cap'n of this ship?"

And then, without waiting for a reply, replaced his pipe between his lips, staggered back to his seat, and contemplatively resumed his smoking.

The fact is that Captain Turnbull was actually pondering upon the advisability of putting back when the mate unluckily suggested the adoption of such a course. Dull and inert as was the skipper of the Betsy Jane, he was by no means an unskilled seaman. The fact that he had safely navigated the crazy old craft to and fro between the Thames and the Tyne, in fair weather and foul, for so many years, was sufficient evidence of this. He had duly marked the portentous aspect of the weather, and was debating within himself the question whether he should put back, or whether he should keep on and take his chance of weathering the gale, as he had already weathered many others. Unfortunately his mind was, like himself, rather heavy and slow in action, and he had not nearly completed the process of "making it up" when the mate offered his suggestion. That settled the question at once. The "captain" was as obstinate and unmanageable a man as ever breathed, and it was only necessary for some one to suggest a course and he would at once adopt a line of action in direct opposition to it. Hence his resolve to remain at sea in the present instance.

Having finally committed himself to this course, however, he braced himself together for the coming conflict with the elements, and when the watch below was called at eight bells all hands were put to the task of placing the ship under thoroughly snug canvas before the relieved watch was permitted to go below. The brig was normally in so leaky a condition that she regularly required pumping out every two hours when under canvas, a task which in ordinary weather usually occupied some ten minutes. If the weather was stormy it took somewhat longer to make the pumps suck, and, accordingly, no one was very much surprised when, on the watch going to the pumps just before eight bells, an honest quarter of an hour was consumed in freeing the old craft from the water which had drained in here and there during the last two hours. Their task at length accomplished the men in the skipper's watch, of whom Bob was one, lost no time in tumbling into their berths "all standing," where they soon forgot their wet and miserable condition in profound sleep. Captain Turnbull, contrary to his usual custom, at the conclusion of his watch retired from the deck only to change his wet garments and envelop himself in a suit of very old and very leaky oilskins, when he resumed once more his favourite seat by the companion, stolidly resolved to watch the gale out, let it last as long as it might.

Note: "All standing" in this case means without removing any of their clothing.

A gale in good truth it had by this time become; the wind howling furiously through the brig's rigging, and threatening momentarily to blow her old worn and patched canvas out of the bolt-ropes. The dull leaden-coloured ragged clouds raced tumultuously athwart the moonlit sky; now veiling the scene in deep and gloomy shadow as they swept across the moon's disc, and anon opening out for an instant to flood the brig, the sea, and themselves in the glory of the silver rays. The caps of the waves, torn off by the wind, filled the air with a dense salt rain, which every now and then gleamed up astern with all the magical beauty of the lunar rainbow; but though the scene would doubtless have ravished the soul of an artist by its weird splendour, it is probable that such an individual would have wished for a more comfortable view-point than the deck of the Betsy Jane. That craft was now rolling and pitching heavily in the short choppy sea, smothering herself with spray everywhere forward of the fore-mast, filling her decks with water, which swished and surged restlessly about and in over the men's boot-tops with every motion of the vessel, and straining herself until the noise of her creaking timbers and bulkheads rivalled the shriek of the gale.

At four bells the Betsy Jane gave the watch just half an hour of steady work to pump her out.

This task at length ended, the men, wet and tired, sought such partial shelter as was afforded by the lee of the longboat where she stood over the main hatch, the lee side of the galley, or peradventure the interior of the same, and there enjoyed such forgetfulness of their discomfort as could be obtained in a weazel-like surreptitious sleep—with one eye open, on watch for the possible approach of the skipper or mate. All of them, that is, except one, who called himself the look-out. This man, well cased in oilskin, stationed himself at the bowsprit-end—which being just beyond the reach of the spray from the bows, was possibly as dry a place as there was throughout the ship, excepting, perhaps, her cabin—and sitting astride the spar and wedging his back firmly in between the two parts of the double fore-stay, found himself so comfortably situated that in less than five minutes he was sound asleep.

Captain Turnbull, meanwhile, occupied his favourite seat near the companion, and smoked contemplatively, while the mate staggered fore and aft from the main-mast to the taffrail, on the weather side of the deck, it being his watch.

Suddenly the mate stopped short in his walk, and the skipper ejaculated "Umph!"

The attention of both had at the same moment been arrested by something peculiar in the motion of the brig.

"Sound the pumps," observed the skipper, apparently addressing the moon, which at that moment gleamed brightly forth from behind a heavy cloud.

The mate took the sounding-rod, and, first of all drying it and the line carefully, dropped it down the pump-well. Hauling it up again, he took it aft to the binnacle, the somewhat feeble light from which showed that the entire rod and a portion of the line was wet.

"More'n three feet water in th' hold!" exclaimed the mate.

"Call the hands," remarked Captain Turnbull, directing his voice down the companion as though he were speaking to some one in the cabin.

The crew soon mustered at the pumps, and manned them both, relieving each other every ten minutes.

After three-quarters of an hour of vigorous pumping there was as little sign of the pumps sucking as at the commencement.

They were then again sounded, with the result that the crew appeared to have gained something like three inches upon the leak.

The men accordingly resumed pumping, in a half-hearted sort of way, however, which seemed to say that they had no very great hope of freeing the ship.

Another hour passed, and the pumps were again sounded.

"Three foot ten! The leak gains on us!" proclaimed the mate in a low voice, as he and the skipper bent together over the rod at the binnacle-lamp.

Shortly afterwards the wheel was relieved; the man who had been steering taking at the pumps the place of the one who had relieved him.

A hurried consultation immediately took place amongst the men; and presently one of them walked aft to where the skipper was seated, and remarked—

"The chaps is sayin', skipper, as how they thinks the best thing we can do is to 'up stick' and run for the nearest port."

The skipper looked inquiringly at the man for so long a time that the fellow grew quite disconcerted; after which he shook his head hopelessly, as though he had been addressed in some strange and utterly unintelligible language, and, withdrawing his pipe from his mouth, pointed solemnly in the direction of the pumps.

The man took the hint and retired.

The mate, who had witnessed this curious interview, then passed over to the lee side of the deck, and steadying himself by the companion, bent down and said in a low voice to his superior—

"After all, cap'n, Tom's about right; the old barkie 'll go down under our feet unless we can get her in somewheres pretty soon."

Captain Turnbull, with his hands resting on his knees, and his extinguished pipe placed bowl downwards between his teeth, regarded his mate with the blank astonishment we may imagine in one who believes he at last actually sees a genuine ghost, and finally gasped in sepulchral tones—

"Are you the cap'n of this ship?"

The mate knew that, after this, there was nothing more to be said, so he walked forward to the pumps, and, by voice and example, strove to animate the men to more earnest efforts.

Another hour passed. The pumps were again sounded; and now it became evident that the leak was rapidly gaining. The general opinion of the men was that the labouring of the brig in the short sea had strained her so seriously as to open more or less all her seams, or that a butt had started. They pumped away for another hour; and then, feeling pretty well fagged out, and finding on trial that the leak gained upon them with increased rapidity, they left the pumps, and began to clear away the boats. The mate made a strong effort to persuade them to return to their duty, but, being himself by that time convinced of the impossibility of saving the ship, he was unsuccessful. Seeing this, he, too, retired below, and hastily bundling together his own traps and those of the skipper, brought them on deck and placed them in the stern-sheets of the longboat. The men had by this time brought their bags and chests on deck; and finding that the brig had meanwhile settled so deep in the water that her deck was awash, they lost no time in getting their belongings, as well as a bag or two of bread and a couple of breakers of water, into the boat. The Betsy Jane was then hove-to; and as she was rolling far too heavily to render it possible to hoist the boat out, the men proceeded to knock the brig's bulwarks away on the lee side, with the intention of launching her off the deck. This task they at last accomplished, aided materially therein by the sea, which by this time was washing heavily across the deck. The crew then passed into her one by one—Bob among the rest—and made their final preparations for leaving the devoted brig.

Seeing that all was ready the mate then went up to the skipper, who still maintained his position on his favourite seat, and said—

"Come, skipper, we're only waitin' for you, and by all appearances we mustn't wait very long neither."

Captain Turnbull raised his head like one awakened from a deep sleep, glanced vacantly round the deserted decks, pulled strongly two or three times at his long-extinguished pipe, and then two tears welled slowly up into his eyes, and, overflowing the lids, rolled one down either cheek. Then he rose quietly to his feet and, with possibly the only approach to dignity which his actions had ever assumed, pointed to the boat and said—

"I'm cap'n of this ship. You go fust." The mate needed no second bidding. He sprang to the ship's side and stepped thence into the boat, taking his place at the tiller. Captain Turnbull, with his usual deliberation, followed.

He was no sooner in the boat than the anxious crew shoved off, and, bending to their oars, rowed as rapidly as possible away from their dangerous proximity to the sinking brig.

The short summer night was past, day had long since broken; and though the gale still blew strongly, the clouds had dispersed, and away to the eastward the sky was ablaze with the opal and delicate rose tints which immediately precede the reappearance of the sun. A few minutes later long arrowy shafts of light shot upward into the clear blue sky, and then a broad golden disc rose slowly above the wave-crests and tipped them with liquid fire. The refulgent beams flashed upon the labouring hull and grimy canvas of the brig, as she lay wallowing in the trough of the sea a quarter of a mile away, transmuting her spars and rigging into bars and threads of purest gleaming gold, and changing her for the moment into an object of dream-like beauty. The men with one accord ceased rowing to gaze upon their late home as she now glittered before their eyes in such unfamiliar aspect; and, as they did so, her bows rose high into the air, dripping with liquid gold, then sank down again slowly—slowly—lower and lower still, until, with a long graceful sliding movement, she plunged finally beneath the wave.

"There goes the old hooker to Davy Jones' locker, sparklin' like a di'mond—God bless her! Good-bye, old lass—good-bye!" shouted the men; and then, as she vanished from their sight, they gave three hearty cheers to her memory.

At the same time Captain Turnbull rose in the stern-sheets of the boat, and facing round in the direction of the sinking brig, solemnly lifted from his head the old fur cap which crowned his somewhat scanty locks. He saw that her last moment was at hand, and his lips quivered convulsively for an instant; then in accents of powerful emotion he burst forth into the following oration:—

"'Then fare thee well, my old Betty Jane,
Farewell for ever and a day;
I'm bound down the river in an old steamboat,
So pull and haul, oh! pull and haul away.'

"Good-bye, old ship! A handsomer craft, a purtier sea-boat, or a smarter wessel under canvas—whether upon a taut bowline or goin' free—never cleared out o' the port of London. For a matter of nigh upon forty year you've carried me, man and boy, back'ards and for'ards in safety and comfort over these here seas; and now, like a jade, you goes and founders, a desartin' of me in my old age. Arter a lifetime spent upon the heavin' buzzum of the stormy ocean—'where the winds do blow, do blow'—you're bound to-day to y'ur last moorin's in old Davy's locker. Well, then, good-bye, Betsy Jane, my beauty; dear you are to me as the child of a man's age; may y'ur old timbers find a soft and easy restin' place in their last berth? And if it warn't for the old 'oman and the lasses ashore there, I'd as lief go down with thee as be where I am."

Then, as the brig disappeared, he replaced the fur cap upon his head, brushed his knotty hand impatiently across his eyes, flung his pipe bitterly into the sea, and sadly resumed his seat. A minute afterwards he looked intently skyward and exclaimed, "Give way, boys, and keep her dead afore it! I'm cap'n of this boat."

The men, awe-stricken by the extraordinary display of deep feeling and quaint rugged eloquence which had just been wrung from their hitherto phlegmatic and taciturn skipper, stretched to their oars in dead silence, mechanically keeping the boat stern on to the sea, and so regulating her speed as to avoid the mischance of being pooped or overrun by the pursuing surges.

About mid-day—by which time the gale had broken—they sighted a schooner bound for the Thames, the master of which received them and their traps on board. Four days afterwards they landed in London; and upon receiving their wages up to the day of the Betsy Jane's loss, dispersed to their several homes.

Hurrah, My Lads! Were Outward-Bound!

Bob returned to Brightlingsea just in the nick of time; for on the day following his arrival home, a letter reached him from Captain Staunton announcing that gentleman's presence once more in England, and not only so, but that his ship had already discharged her inward cargo, and was loading again for Australia. He repeated his former offer, and added that he thought it would be a good plan for Bob to join at once, as he might prove of some assistance to the chief mate in receiving and taking account of their very miscellaneous cargo. Bob and old Bill consulted together, and finally came to the conclusion that there was nothing to delay the departure of the former, as his entire outfit could easily be procured in London. Bob accordingly replied to Captain Staunton's note, naming the day but one following as that on which he would join; and on that day he duly put in an appearance.

Bill, as on the occasion when Bob joined the Betsy Jane, accompanied the lad to London. The ship was lying in the London Dock; and the first business of our two friends was to secure quarters for themselves, which they did in a comfortable enough boarding-house close to the dock-gates. They dined, and then sallied forth to take a look at the Galatea, which they found about half-way down the dock. She was a noble craft of sixteen hundred tons register, built of iron, with iron masts and yards, wire rigging, and all the most recent appliances for economising work and ensuring the safety of her passengers and crew. She was a beautiful model, and looked a regular racer all over. Her crew were comfortably berthed in a roomy house on deck forward, the fore part of which was devoted to the seamen, while the after part was occupied by the inferior officers. Captain Staunton and the chief mate had their quarters in light, spacious, nicely fitted cabins, one on each side of the foot of the saloon staircase; while the apprentices were berthed in a small deck-house just abaft the main-mast. The saloon was a splendid apartment, very elaborately fitted up in ornamental woods of several kinds, and with a great deal of carving and gilding about it. The upholstering of the saloon was of a kind seldom seen afloat except in yachts or the finest Atlantic liners; the stern-windows even being fitted with delicate lace curtains, draped over silken hangings. Eight berths, four on each side of the ship, afforded accommodation for sixteen passengers. These were located just outside the saloon, and the space between them formed a passage leading from the foot of the staircase to the saloon doors.

Bill and Bob had to find out all these things for themselves, the mate, at the moment of their arrival on board, being the only person present belonging to the ship, and he was so busy receiving cargo that he could scarcely find time to speak to them. On being told who they were, he simply said to Bob—

"All right, young 'un; Captain Staunton has told me all about you, and I'm very glad to see you. But I haven't time even to be civil just now, so just take a look round the ship by yourselves, will you? I expect the skipper aboard before long, and he'll do the honours."

In about half an hour afterwards Captain Staunton made his appearance, and, hearing that Bill and Bob were down below aft somewhere, at once joined them in the saloon. He shook them both most heartily by the hand, and, in a few well-chosen words, expressed the gratification he felt at renewing his acquaintance with them, and at the prospect of having Bob with him.

"I have spoken to my owners concerning you," he said to Bob, "and have obtained their permission to receive you on board as an apprentice. You will dress in uniform, and berth with the other apprentices in the after house; your duties will be light, and it will be my pride as well as my pleasure to do everything in my power to make a gentleman as well as a thorough seaman of you, and so fit you in due time to occupy such a position as the one I now hold, if not a still better one." He suggested that Bob should sign his indentures on the following day, and then proposed that they should go at once, in a body, to see about our hero's uniform and outfit, the whole of which, in spite of all protestation, he insisted on himself presenting to the lad.

On the following day Bob signed his indentures as proposed, and joined the ship, assisting the chief mate to receive and take account of the cargo. Four days of this work completed the loading of the vessel and the taking in of her stores; and a week from the day on which Bob first saw her, the Galatea hauled out of dock and proceeded in charge of the chief mate down the river as far as Gravesend, where her captain and passengers joined her.

It is now time to say a descriptive word or two concerning the various persons with whom our friend Bob was for some time to be so intimately associated.

Captain Staunton, as the head and chief of the little community, is entitled to the first place on the list.

He was a tall, handsome man, in the very prime of life, being about thirty-five or forty years of age. His features were finely moulded, the lines about the firmly closed mouth indicating great decision and fixity of purpose, while the clear steadfast grey eyes beamed forth an assurance of the kindly and genial disposition of their owner. Light auburn hair, in short-cut but thickly clustering curls, crowned his shapely head, and a closely cut beard and moustache shaded the lower part of his deeply bronzed face. For the rest, his broad massive shoulders indicated unmistakably the possession of great strength; whilst his waist, slim almost as that of a woman, his lean muscular lower limbs, and his quick springy step, told of great bodily activity. His disposition was exactly what one would, from a study of his externals, judge it to be—frank, generous, genial, kindly, and sympathetic to his friends, but a fearless and formidable foe to any who might be so ill-advised as to constitute themselves his enemies.

Mr Bowles, the first mate—or "chief officer" as he preferred rather to be termed, thinking this title sounded more dignified than the other—was a big, burly, loud-voiced individual; a thorough seaman, a strict disciplinarian, and possessed of a general disposition to "stand no nonsense" from anybody, but particularly from the seamen, who, as a class, were regarded by him with an eye of great suspicion. He was, however, scrupulously just and straightforward in his dealings with all men, and, if a seaman proved himself to be capable and willing, he had nothing to fear from "Bill Bowles," as this individual was in his more genial moods wont to style himself; if, however, on the other hand, a man proved lazy, or incapable of executing the duties he had undertaken to perform, let him "look out for squalls."

The second mate was in every way a marked contrast to the "chief." He was a tall thin sallow-complexioned man, with straight black hair, thick eyebrows, and thin feeble-looking whiskers, the latter very lank and ragged, as he seemed never to trim them. His eyes were believed to be black, but no one seemed to be at all certain about this, as he would never look any man long enough in the face to allow the question to be decided. His glances were of a shifting stealthy description, and his face habitually wore a morose dissatisfied expression, with a dash of malice thrown in, which made those who were brought into contact with him eager to get away from him again as speedily as might be. It need scarcely be said that, with these characteristics, he soon made himself universally unpopular. This was his first voyage under Captain Staunton. His name was Carter, and it was understood that he was distantly related to one of the members of the firm owning the Galatea.

The third mate was a young fellow named Dashwood, formerly an apprentice. He had been out of his time rather more than a year, and the present was his second voyage with Captain Staunton. He was a smart young fellow, anxious to get on in his profession, and very good-natured.

There were three other apprentices, or "midshipmen" as they called themselves—Ralph Neville, John Keene, and little Ned Edwards, the latter being Bob's junior by a year, while the others were his elders respectively by three years and one year. It is not necessary to minutely describe these youths, as they are destined to perform only a very unimportant part in this narrative.

Then there were the passengers, of whom the ship took out her full complement.

First among these must be placed Mrs Staunton, the captain's wife; though she could scarcely be called a passenger since she paid no fare, the owners allowing their captains the privilege of taking their wives to sea with them. That the captain should have his wife with him was regarded indeed by the owners as a decided advantage, for, in the first place, she could conveniently act the part of chaperone to young and unprotected lady-passengers when there were any; and, in the next, they were justly of opinion that the captain would take extra care of the ship if she held a being so dear to him as his wife.

Mrs Staunton was considerably younger than her husband, being (if one may venture to disclose such a secret) about twenty-eight years of age. She was a very beautiful woman, rather above medium height, of a very amiable and affectionate disposition, and in all respects a worthy mate to her noble-hearted husband. She always went to sea with Captain Staunton, and made his private cabin a very palace of elegance and comfort for him. Their little daughter May, now three years old, the same little creature who had been so happily saved by Bob from a watery grave on the night of the wreck on the Gunfleet, was also on board.

There were three other lady-passengers, all unmarried, on board on the present occasion. The elder of the three, a Miss Butler, was a lady "of a certain age," with a quiet subdued manner, and nothing remarkable about her, either in character or appearance.

The two others were cousins, both of them being young and very pretty. The younger of the twain, Blanche Lascelles, was making the voyage on the recommendation of her physician, her health having been somewhat delicate of late. "There are no very alarming symptoms at present, my dear madam," was the doctor's assurance to Blanche's mother; "and a good long sea-voyage, say out to Australia and back, will be more beneficial than a whole pharmacopoeia of drugs." In accordance with which opinion Blanche's passage had been taken out and home on board the Galatea; and her fair self especially confided to the care and protection of Captain and Mrs Staunton. This young lady was eighteen years of age, fair-haired, blue-eyed, petite, very merry and light-hearted, and altogether exceedingly attractive and lovable.

Her cousin, Violet Dudley, aged twenty-two, was a tall and stately brunette, with a wealth of dark sheeny chestnut hair, almost black in the shade, magnificent dark eyes, which flashed scornfully or melted into tenderness according to the mood of that imperious beauty, their owner, and a figure the ideal perfection and grace of which are rarely to be met with out of the sculptor's marble. The rich healthy colour of her cheeks and full ripe lips, and the brilliant sparkle of her glorious eyes showed that it was not for health's sake she had undertaken the voyage. She was on board the Galatea in order that her cousin Blanche might have the benefit of her companionship, and also because a favourable occasion now presented itself for her to visit some friends in Sydney, whither the Galatea was bound.

The rest of the passengers, thirteen in number, were gentlemen. Of these it will be necessary to describe three only, namely, Mr Forester Dale, Mr Fortescue, and Mr Brook. Messrs Dale and Fortescue were partners, being contractors in a rather large way; and Mr Brook was their general manager and right-hand man. The trio were now going out to Australia on business connected with a large job about to be undertaken in that colony, for which they were anxious to secure the contract.

Mr Dale, or Mr Forester Dale as he preferred to be styled, was a somewhat querulous individual, with an unhappy knack of looking at the dark side of everything. Add to this the fact that he entertained a very exalted idea of his own (imaginary) excellences, and believed himself to be almost, if not quite, infallible, and it will be seen that he was not likely to prove a very desirable travelling companion.

Rex Fortescue, on the other hand, was so thoroughly good-tempered that it had grown to be a tradition among the employés of the firm that it was impossible to "put him out." He was never known to lose his temper, even under the most exasperating circumstances; he took the worries of life easily, and would seriously inconvenience himself to help others. He was as energetic and industrious as he was good-natured; work was his recreation, and it was notorious that to his energy it was chiefly due that the firm of which he was a member had attained its eminence. His senior partner characteristically took all the credit to himself, and had gradually brought himself to believe that in establishing the business he had seriously impaired his own health; but everybody else who knew anything about them knew also that the junior partner was the life and soul of the business. Rex was not what would be termed a handsome man by any means, but his frank pleasant good-tempered face proved far more permanently attractive than mere physical beauty without these embellishments could ever hope to be.

Mr Brook differed from both his employers—where indeed will you meet with two men exactly alike? Of the two, however, he most nearly approximated to the senior partner, inasmuch as that, like that gentleman, he entertained a very high opinion of his own abilities, stood greatly upon his dignity, and was childishly jealous of any preference shown for others before himself. Unlike Mr Dale, however, he was a man of limited education; he had read much, but his reading had been almost wholly superficial; he possessed, upon an infinite variety of subjects, that little knowledge which is a dangerous thing. There was consequently no topic of conversation upon which he had not something oracular to say; he was wont to maintain his own opinion with a very considerable amount of heat, and so obstinate was he that it was quite impossible to convince him that he was ever in the wrong. He was essentially a vulgar man; but, as might naturally be supposed from what has already been said, he regarded himself as a polished gentleman, and in his efforts to act up to his ideal of this character he often used words of whose meaning he had but a very imperfect idea, and always in the wrong place. His chief redeeming points were that he was thoroughly master of his business, honest as the day, and did not object to "rough it" when occasion required.

The characteristics of this trio came prominently into view when they, with the rest of the passengers, boarded the ship at Gravesend and proceeded to take possession of their cabins.

The bulk of the passengers' luggage had been shipped in dock, and passed down into the after-hold upon the top of the cargo, in order that it might be out of the way but easily come-at-able if required during the voyage; each one, however, as he or she came up the ship's side and stepped in on deck, bore in his or her hand one or more bundles of wraps, deck-chairs, and other impedimenta.

The first to make his appearance was Mr Forester Dale; he was not ashamed to take precedence even of the ladies. He walked straight aft, glancing neither to the right nor to the left, ascended the half-dozen steps leading up to the top of the monkey-poop, and at once dived down the saloon-companion. Arrived at the bottom of the staircase he stood there, blocking up the way, and began to call discontentedly for the steward to show him his cabin, which that official hastened to do.

Mr Fortescue was among the last to leave the boat which had brought the passengers alongside, and he was closely followed on board by Mr Brook. On reaching the deck they both paused to glance round them and aloft at the towering symmetrical masts and spars, with their mazy network of rigging.

"Jolly craft this, isn't she, Brook?" remarked Rex Fortescue genially; "plenty of room, and clean as a new pin, although they're only just out of dock. I think we shall be comfortable here."

"Oh, yes," assented Brook, "we shall be comfortable enough, I don't misdoubt; and as to 'roomy,' iron ships always is, that's what they builds 'em of iron for."

They then proceeded below, and, like the rest, sought their cabins in order to stow away their luggage.

Rex Fortescue shared a cabin with his senior partner, each cabin containing two sleeping berths. As he entered the one which from the number on its door he knew to be his, he found Mr Forester Dale struggling viciously with a drawer which, in his impatience to open, he had twisted out of position and hopelessly jammed.

"Oh, I say!" exclaimed Rex as he opened the door and noticed how lofty and roomy and how beautifully fitted up was the place, "what jolly cabins!"

"Jolly!" retorted Dale, "I don't see anything jolly about them. I think they're beastly holes; there's not room to swing a cat in 'em."

"Well, you don't want to swing a cat in them, do you?" inquired Rex gravely, firing off the venerable joke at his senior half unconsciously. "I think they are first-rate cabins, considering that they're on board ship; you can't expect to have such rooms here as you have at 'The Blackthorns.' Space is limited afloat, you know."

"Eight you are, Mr Fortescue," shouted Brook through the bulkhead, his cabin adjoining that of the partners, and conversation, unless pitched in a low tone, being quite audible from one to the other; "I call these cabins splendid; moreover than that, look how light and atmospheric they are;

why, you wouldn't find lighter or more luxuriant cabins in the Great Eastern herself."

"I wish, Brook, you'd shut up and mind your own business," snarled Mr Dale as in his irritation he wrenched off a drawer-knob; "you're a good deal too ready with your opinions, and I'll thank you to keep 'em to yourself until you're asked for 'em for the future."

Here Rex Fortescue interposed, pouring by his tact and good-humour oil upon the troubled waters, and bringing harmony out of discord once more; so that, by the time everything had been packed away in its proper place and the dinner-bell had rung out its welcome peal, peace reigned undisturbed in the handsome saloon of the Galatea.

Meanwhile, the passengers having all embarked, the ship at once proceeded down the river in tow, and when the occupants of the saloon rose from the dinner-table and went on deck to enjoy the beauty of the evening they found themselves off Sheerness, in the midst of a fleet of ships and steamers of all builds and all nationalities, some outward-bound like themselves, and others entering the river, either under steam, in tow, or under canvas, as the case might be. Here came a magnificent steamship, towering high out of the water, at the close of her voyage from India, with sallow-complexioned passengers scattered about her decks fore and aft, muffled up in thick overcoats, and pacing briskly to and fro to stimulate the circulation of the thin blood in their veins, and looking the picture of chilly misery, though the evening was almost oppressively warm. There, on the other side, moved sluggishly along under her old, patched, and coal-grimed canvas a collier brig, with bluff bows, long bowsprit, and short stumpy masts and yards, the counterpart of the Betsy Jane of glorious memory. Abreast of her, and sailing two feet to the collier's one, was a river-barge, loaded down to her gunwale with long gaily painted spreet and tanned canvas which gleamed a rich ruddy brown in the rays of the setting sun. Here, again, came a swift excursion steamer, her decks crowded with jovial pleasure-seekers, and a good brass band on the bridge playing "A Life on the Ocean Wave," whilst behind her again appeared a clumsy but picturesque-looking "billy-boy" or galliot from the Humber—the Saucy Sue of Goole—with a big brown dog on board, who, excited by the unwonted animation of the scene, rushed madly fore and aft the deck, rearing up on his hind-legs incessantly to look over the bulwarks and bark at all and sundry. Then came a large full-rigged ship in tow, her hull painted a dead-black down to the gleaming copper, the upper edge of which showed just above the water-line, with the high flaring bow, short counter, and lofty tapering spars, which needed not the "stars and stripes" fluttering far aloft to proclaim her an American. And behind her, again, came a great five-masted ironclad, gliding with slow and stately motion up the river on her way to Chatham.

"Oh, what a monster of a ship!" exclaimed little Blanche Lascelles as the ironclad approached near enough to the Galatea to enable those on board to realise her vast proportions.

"Yes," said Brook, who was standing close by, evidently anxious for an opportunity to ingratiate himself with the ladies. "Yes, that's the Black Prince; I know her well. Fine ship, ain't she?"

"I think you are mistaken, sir, as to the name of that ironclad," remarked Captain Staunton, who was on the poop within ear-shot. "The Black Prince has only three masts, and she has a raking stem, not a ram."

"Oh, no; I'm not mistaken," said the individual addressed. "Wait 'til we see her name; you'll find I'm right."

Another minute or so and the great ship swept close past them, her white ensign drooping from the peak and her pennant streaming out from her main-royal mast-head like a fiery gleam in the sunset glow, the look-out men on her forecastle and the officers on her bridge dwarfed to pigmies by comparison with the huge structure which bore them. As soon as she was fairly past the word Agincourt flashed from her stern in golden letters so large that they could be easily read without the aid of a telescope.

Captain Staunton glanced, with an amused twinkle in his eye, at his over-confident passenger, as much as to say, "What do you think of that?"

Brook looked just a trifle confused for a moment; then his brow cleared, and he replied to the captain's look by remarking in his usual easy confident tone—

"Oh, ah, yes; it's all right. She's been altered, and had her name changed; I remember reading about it somewhere."

"Good heavens!" exclaimed the skipper sotto voce to the chief mate who was standing next him; "why, before the voyage is over the man will be telling us that the Galatea is her own longboat lengthened and raised upon."

At 7:30 p.m. the hands were mustered, when the chief and second officers proceeded to pick the watches. Bob, to his great satisfaction, found himself included in the chief officer's watch, with Ralph Neville for a companion. They were told off, with two able and two ordinary seamen, for duty on the mizzen-mast; the two lads being also required to keep the time and strike the bell, in spells of two hours each.

By seven bells in the first watch (11:30 p.m.) the Galatea was off the North Foreland, with a nice little breeze blowing from E.N.E.

All hands were then called, the canvas was loosed and set, the tow-rope cast off by the tug and hauled inboard, and the voyage, which was to prove of so eventful a character to those entering upon it, may be said to have fairly commenced. The ship was soon under every stitch of sail that would draw, gliding down through the Downs at the rate of about seven knots, and the passengers, most of whom had remained on deck to witness the operation of making sail, then retired to their several berths, where, the night being fine and the water smooth, it is reasonable to suppose they enjoyed a good night's rest.

The Outward Voyage

By eight o'clock next morning—at which hour the passengers sat down to breakfast—the Galatea was off Dungeness, which she rounded with a somewhat freshening breeze, and noon saw her fairly abreast of Beachy Head. The weather was magnificent; the breeze, whilst fresh enough to waft the good ship through the water at the rate of an honest ten knots in the hour, was not sufficiently strong to raise much sea; the only result, therefore, was a slight leisurely roll, which the passengers found agreeable rather than the reverse, and everybody was consequently in the most exuberant spirits, congratulating themselves and each other on so auspicious a commencement to their voyage.

As for Bob, he was in the seventh heaven of delight. The noble proportions of the beautiful craft which bore him so gallantly over the summer sea, her spotless cleanliness, the perfect order and method with which the various duties were performed, and the consideration with which he was treated by his superiors, constituted for him a novel experience, in strong contrast to the wet and dirt, the often severe toil, and the rough-and-ready habits of the collier seamen on board the Betsy Jane. From the moment that Bob had assumed duty on board the Galatea Captain Staunton had taken pains to make matters pleasant for him; he had spoken freely of the heavy obligation under which he considered that Bob had laid him, and had extolled in the most laudatory terms the lad's behaviour during that terrible winter night upon the Gunfleet; Bob, therefore, found himself the possessor of a reputation which commanded universal admiration and respect in the little community of which he was a member, with the result that he was quite unconsciously accorded a distinction which under other circumstances it would have been vain for him to hope. Thus, when our hero found himself, as he frequently did, a guest at the saloon dinner-table (Captain Staunton following the example of the commanders in the navy by occasionally inviting his officers to dine with him), the passengers almost unanimously received him into their midst with a friendly warmth which they accorded to none of the other subordinates on board, agreeing to regard in him as pleasant eccentricities those frequent lapses in grammar and pronunciation which they would have resented in others as the evidences of a decided inferiority, to be kept at a distance by the coldest and most studied disdain.

Captain Staunton took an early opportunity to speak to Bob respecting his unfortunate lack of education and culture. They were alone together in the chart-room at the moment, whither the skipper had called Bob, in order that their conversation might be strictly private.

"Robert," said he—he always addressed Bob as "Robert" when what he had to say was unconnected with duty—"Robert, my boy, I wish to say a word or two to you respecting your education, which, I fear, has been somewhat neglected—as, indeed, might reasonably be expected, seeing how few educational advantages usually fall in the way of a fisher-lad. Now, this must be remedied as speedily as possible. I am anxious that you should become not only a first-rate seaman and thorough navigator, but also a polished gentleman, in order that you may be fitted to fill the highest posts attainable in the profession which you have chosen. When I was your age if a man knew enough to enable him to safely navigate his ship from place to place that was about all that was required of him. But times have changed since then; the English have become a nation of travellers; passenger-ships have enormously increased in number, and the man who now commands one is expected, in addition to his other duties, to play the part of a courteous and intelligent host to those who take passage with him. To enable him to perform this portion of his duties satisfactorily a liberal education and polished manners are necessary, and both of these you must acquire, my boy. There is only one way of attaining the possession of these requisites, and that is—study. The intelligent study of books will give you the education; and the study of your fellow-creatures, their speech, habits, and demeanour, will give you polish, by showing you what things to imitate and what to avoid. Now, you have an excellent opportunity to commence both these branches of study at once. Mr Eastlake, the missionary, takes the greatest interest in you, and has offered not only to lend you the necessary books, but also to give you two hours' tuition daily, an offer which I have ventured to thankfully accept on your behalf. And in addition to this you have sixteen passengers to study. Some of them are perfect gentlemen, others, I am sorry to say, are anything but that. Your own good sense will point out to you what is worthy of imitation and what should be avoided in the manners of those around you, and I think you are sharp and intelligent enough to quickly profit by your observations. Keep your eyes and ears open, and your mouth as much as possible shut, just for the present, and I have no doubt you will soon make headway. In addition to the two hours' tuition which Mr Eastlake has promised you I intend to give you two more; Mr Eastlake's tuition will be in various branches of useful knowledge, and mine will be in navigation. Your studies will be conducted here in the chart-room, and I have very little doubt but that, if you are only half as willing to learn as we are to teach, you will have made a considerable amount of progress by the time that we arrive at Sydney; indeed, as far as navigation is concerned, it is by no means an intricate science, and there is no reason why you should not be a skilled navigator by the time that we reach Australia."

Bob had the good sense to fully appreciate the immense value of the advantages thus proffered to him. He was intelligent enough to at once recognise the vast intellectual distance which intervened between himself, a poor, ignorant fisher-lad, and the highly-educated men and women who were to be found among the saloon passengers, as well as the wide difference between his own awkward, embarrassed manner and the quiet, easy, graceful demeanour which distinguished some of the individuals to be seen daily on the poop of the Galatea. The sense of his inferiority already weighed heavily upon him; the opportunity now offered him of throwing it off was therefore eagerly and gratefully accepted, and he at once plunged con amore into the studies which were marked out for him.

Mr Eastlake—the gentleman who had undertaken to remedy, as far as time permitted, the serious defects in Bob's education—was exceptionally well qualified for the task. Educated at Cambridge, where he had won a double first; naturally studious, a great traveller, endowed with a singularly happy knack of investing the driest subject with quite an absorbing interest, and a perfect master in the art of instructing, he superintended Bob's studies so effectively that the lad's progress was little short of marvellous. Not content with the two hours of daily tuition which had originally been proposed, Mr Eastlake frequently joined the lad on the poop or in the waist for the first two or three hours of the first night-watch, when the weather happened to be fine and Bob's services were not particularly required, and, promenading fore and aft with his pupil by his side, he was wont to launch into long and interesting disquisitions upon such topics as were best calculated to widen Bob's sphere of knowledge and cultivate his intellect.

Nor was Captain Staunton any less successful in that portion of Bob's studies which he had undertaken to direct. Fortunately for our hero his skipper was not one of those men whose acquaintance with navigation consists solely in the blind knowledge that certain calculations if correctly performed will afford certain information; Captain Staunton had studied nautical astronomy intelligently and thoroughly, he knew the raison d'être of every calculation in the various astronomical problems connected with the science of navigation, and was therefore in a position to explain clearly and intelligently to his pupil every step which was necessary, as well in the simple as in the more abstruse and difficult calculations.

Thus admirably circumstanced in the matter of instructors, and aided by his own anxiety to improve, Bob made such steady and rapid progress that by the time the ship rounded the Cape he could "work a lunar," solve a quadratic equation or any problem in the first two books of Euclid, and write an intelligently expressed, correctly spelt, and grammatical letter, in addition to possessing a large store of knowledge on everyday subjects. Nor was this all. The majority of the passengers, moved by Captain Staunton's frequent references to Bob's exploit on the Gunfleet, had taken quite a fancy to the lad, and conversed so frequently and so freely with him that his mauvais honte gradually disappeared, and he found himself able to mingle with them with an ease and absence of self-consciousness which was as pleasing as it was novel to him.

Meanwhile the Galatea sped rapidly and prosperously on her way. The breeze with which she had started lasted long enough to run her fairly into the north-east trades, and once in them the journey to the Line was a short and pleasant one. Here a delay of three days occurred, during which the ship had to contend with light baffling winds and calms, interspersed with violent thunder and rain squalls, the latter of which were taken advantage of to fill up the water-tanks. Then on again to the southward, braced sharp up on the larboard tack, with the south-east trade-wind blowing fresh enough to keep the royals stowed for the greater part of the time; and then, light easterly breezes, just at the time when they fully expected to fall in with strong westerly winds before which to run down their easting.

Here occurred their first check, and instead of being thankful that they had been so greatly favoured thus far, everybody of course began forthwith to grumble. The passengers, perhaps, chafed under the delay quite as much as Captain Staunton, but their outward manifestations of impatience were confined for the most part to dissatisfied glances at the hard cloudless blue sky to windward, as it met their gaze morning after morning when they came on deck, to shrugs of the shoulders whenever the subject happened to be mentioned, and to scornful, sarcastic, or despondent allusions to the proverbial longevity and obstinacy of easterly winds in general. Except Mr Forester Dale, and he, I regret to say, made himself a perfect nuisance to everybody on board by his snappishness and irascibility. The weather was "beastly," the ship was "beastly," and his demeanour was such as to suggest to the other passengers the idea that he considered them also to be "beastly," a suggestion which they very promptly resented by sending him to Coventry. That his metaphorical seclusion in that ancient city was not of the very strictest kind was entirely due to the fact that his partner, Rex Fortescue, and the inimitable Brook wore on board. Rex bore the childish irritability of his senior partner with unparalleled good-humour; his strongest protest being a mere, "Shut up, there's a good fellow, and let a man enjoy his book and his weed in peace for once in a while." Factotum Brook attempted quite a different mode of soothing his superior. He demonstrated—to his own complete satisfaction if not to that of anybody else—that it was a physical impossibility for them to have anything but easterly winds where they were. But, he asserted, there was a good time coming; they had had easterly winds ever since they had started; this, by an unalterable law of nature, had been gradually creating a vacuum away there in the easterly quarter, which vacuum must now necessarily soon become so perfect that, by another unalterable law of nature, the wind would come careering back from the westward with a force sufficient to more than enable them to make up for all lost time.

To do Captain Staunton justice he left no means untried whereby to wile away the time and render less oppressive the monotony of the voyage. He suggested the weekly publication of a newspaper in the saloon, and energetically promoted and encouraged such sports and pastimes as are practicable on board ship; al fresco concerts on the poop, impromptu dances, tableaux-vivants, charades, recitations, etcetera, for the evening; and deck-quoits, follow-my-leader, shooting at bottles, fishing, etcetera, during the day. By these means the murmurings and dissatisfaction were nipped in the bud, harmony and good-humour returning and triumphantly maintaining their position for the remainder of the voyage. The newspaper was a great success, every incident in the least out of the common being duly recorded therein. The editor was one O'Reilly, an Irishman, who enjoyed the reputation of being one of the most successful barristers in New South Wales, to which colony he was returning after a short holiday trip "home." The paper was published in manuscript, and consisted of twenty foolscap pages, which O'Reilly prided himself upon completely filling at every issue. Interesting facts being for the most part very scarce commodities, fiction was freely indulged in, the contributors vieing with each other in the effort to produce humorous advertisements, letters to the editor upon real or imaginary grievances, and startling accounts of purely fictitious occurrences.

In the meantime two of the passengers had discovered a species of amusement quite out of the line of the captain's programme, and which caused that worthy seaman no small amount of anxiety and embarrassment. In a word, Rex Fortescue and Violet Dudley found in each other's society a solace from the ennui of the voyage which onlookers had every reason to believe was of the most perfect kind. Such a condition of things was almost inevitable under the circumstances. There were four ladies on board, and thirteen gentlemen passengers, of whom no less than nine were bachelors. Of the four ladies one, Mrs Staunton, was married and therefore unapproachable. Miss Butler was an old maid, with a subdued expression and manner ill calculated to arouse any feeling warmer than respectful esteem, so that there remained only Blanche and Violet, both young, pretty, and agreeable, to act as recipients of all the ardent emotions of the bachelor mind. Although the art, science, or pastime—whichever you will—of love-making has many difficulties to contend with on board ship, in consequence of the lamentable lack of privacy which prevails there, it is doubtful whether it ever flourishes so vigorously anywhere else. Even so was it on board the Galatea; Violet and Blanche being waited upon hand and foot and followed about the decks from early morn to dewy eve, each by her own phalanx of devoted admirers. These attentions had at first been productive of nothing more serious than amusement to their recipients; but gradually, very gradually, Violet Dudley had manifested a partiality for the quiet unobtrusive courtesies and attentions of Rex Fortescue, which partiality at length became so clearly marked that, one after the other, the rest of her admirers retired discomfited, and sought solace for their disappointment in the exciting sport of rifle shooting at empty bottles dropped overboard and allowed to drift astern, or in such other amusements as their tastes led them to favour. Blanche, however, still kept her division of admirers in a state of feverish suspense, manifesting no partiality whatever for any one of them above another. Indeed she seemed to take greater pleasure in questioning Bob about his former career, and in listening to his quaint but graphic descriptions of the curious incidents of fisher-life, than she did in the compliments or conversation of any of her admirers, a circumstance which caused Bob to be greatly envied.

Whilst this was the state of things aft, matters were not all that they should be in the forecastle. The crew were a good enough set of men, and doubtless would have been all right under proper management, but, thanks to the surly and aggravating behaviour of Mr Carter, the starboard watch, over which he ruled, was in a state of almost open mutiny. And yet so acute was the aggressor that for a long time he gave the men no excuse for legitimate complaint; the utmost that could be said against him being that he was, in the opinion of the men, unduly particular as to the set and trim of the sails, and the superlative cleanliness of everything about the decks. This was all very well during the daytime, but when in the night-watches the men were hustled incessantly about the decks, taking a pull here, there, and everywhere at the halliards, sheets, and braces of the already fully distended and accurately trimmed sails, only to be ordered a few minutes later to ease up the lee braces half an inch and take a pull upon the weather ones; or alternately stowing and setting the "flying kites" or light upper canvas, they could not help seeing that these things were done less from zeal and anxiety to make a quick passage than for the purpose of indulging a spiteful and malicious temper.

At length a crisis arrived. The ship was at the time somewhere about the latitude of the Cape; stretching to the southward and eastward close-hauled, with a fine steady breeze from east-north-east. It was the second mate's eight hours out that night, and although the weather was beautifully fine, with a clear sky, full moon, and steady breeze, he had been indulging in his usual vagaries throughout the last two hours of the first watch (he never attempted anything out of the common when Captain Staunton or any of the passengers were on deck, as some of them generally were until midnight), and he began them again within a quarter of an hour of coming on deck at 4 a.m. The royals were set when he took charge of the deck, and these he had separately clewed up and furled, as well as one or two of the smaller stay-sails. He allowed the men just time enough to settle down comfortably, and then ordered the recently stowed sails to be loosed and set again, which was done. A short interval passed, and then he had the royals stowed once more, and finally he ordered them to be loosed and set again.

Not a man took the slightest notice of the order.

"Do you hear, there? Jump aloft, some of you, and loose the royals," shouted Carter, thinking for a moment that he had failed to make himself heard.

Still there was no response.

"You, Davis, away aloft and loose the fore-royal. Boyd, jump up and loose the main; and you, Nichols, up you go and loose the mizzen. Look lively now, or I'll rope's-end the last man down from aloft," exclaimed the second mate, his passion rapidly rising as he found himself thus tacitly opposed.

As the last words left his lips the watch came aft in a body, pausing just forward of the main-mast.

"Look 'ee here, Mr Carter," said Boyd, a fine active willing young fellow, stepping a pace or two in front of his messmates, "we thinks as them there r'yals 'll do well enough as they am for the rest of the watch. They was set when we come 'pon deck, and that wouldn't do, you had 'em stowed. Then you warn't satisfied with 'em so, and you had 'em set. That wouldn't do, so you had 'em stowed again; and stowed they will be for the rest of the watch, as far as I'm concarned. The night's fine, and the breeze as steady as a breeze can be, and the old barkie 'd carry r'yals and skys'ls too for the matter o' that, but if they was set we should have to stow 'em again five minutes a'terwards; so let 'em be, say I."

A low murmur of assent from the rest of the watch gave the second mate to understand that these were their sentiments also upon the subject.

The foolish fellow at once allowed his temper to get the mastery of him.

"Oh! that's what you say, is it, my fine fellows? Very good; we'll soon see whether, when I give an order, I am to be obeyed or not," he hissed through his clenched teeth.

Saying which he stepped hastily to the door of his cabin, which was situated on deck in the after house, entered, and in a few moments reappeared with a revolver in each hand.

"Now," he exclaimed, planting himself midway between the poop and the main-mast, "let me see the man who will dare to disobey me. I'll shoot him like a dog. Boyd, go aloft and loose the main-royal," pointing one of the revolvers full at him.

"I refuse," exclaimed the seaman. "I demand to be taken before Captain—"

A flash, a sharp report, and the man staggered backwards and fell to the deck, while a crimson stain appeared and rapidly broadened on the breast of his check shirt.

Two of his comrades instantly raised the wounded man and bore him forward; the remainder rushed with a shout upon the second mate and disarmed him, though not before he had fired again and sent a bullet through the left arm of one of his assailants.

The men were still struggling with the second mate when a figure sprang up through the companion, closely followed by a second, and Captain Staunton's voice was heard exclaiming—

"Good heavens! Mr Carter, what is the meaning of this? Back men; back, for your lives. How dare you raise your hands against one of your officers?"

The men had by this time wrenched the pistols out of Carter's hands, and they at once fell back and left him as Captain Staunton and Mr Bowles advanced to his rescue.

The new-comers placed themselves promptly one on each side of the second mate, and then the two parties stood staring somewhat blankly at each other for something like a minute.

"Well, Mr Carter," at last exclaimed Captain Staunton, "have you nothing to say by way of explanation of this extraordinary scene? What does it mean?"

"Mutiny, sir; that and nothing less," gasped Carter, whose passion almost deprived him of speech. "I thank you, sir, and you too, Mr Bowles, for coming to my rescue; but for that I should have been a dead man by this time."

"Oh, no, you wouldn't, Mr Carter," exclaimed one of the men. "We ain't murderers; and we shouldn't ha' touched you if you hadn't touched us first."

"That will do," exclaimed Captain Staunton. "If any of you have anything to say you shall have an opportunity of saying it in due time; at present I wish to hear what Mr Carter has to say," turning inquiringly once more toward that individual.

Thus pressed, Carter related his version of the story, which was to the effect that the men had refused to obey orders, and had come aft in so menacing a manner that in self-defence he had been compelled to arm himself; and further, that hoping to check the mutiny in the bud, he had shot down the "ringleader."

"So that is the explanation of the shots which awoke me," exclaimed Captain Staunton. "And where is the wounded man?"

"In his bunk, sir; bleeding like a stuck pig," replied one of the men, resorting to simile to aid his description, as is the wont of seafaring men generally.

"Phew!" whistled the skipper. "This is serious. Run, Bowles, and rouse out the doctor at once, if you please."

Mr Bowles sped to the doctor's cabin, and found that individual already "roused out," with an open case of surgical instruments on the table, and a drawer open, from which he was hastily selecting lint, bandages, etcetera; the medico having been awakened by the first pistol-shot, and, like a sensible man, bestirring himself at once in preparation for the repair of damages, without waiting to learn first whether there were any damages to repair or not.

"Well, Bowles," he exclaimed, as the worthy "chief" made his appearance, "you want me, eh? What's the nature of the case?"

"A man shot," briefly replied Mr Bowles.

"Just so; heard the shots. Where is the seat of the injury? Don't know? Well, never mind, we'll soon find out. Let me see—tourniquet—probe—splints—lint—bandage—um—um—yes; just carry these for me, Bowles, there's a good fellow, and lead the way."

So saying the worthy man put a quantity of splints, etcetera, into Mr Bowles' hands, and, gathering up the rest of his chattels, followed the mate to the forecastle, where he at once busied himself in ascertaining the extent of and finally dressing poor Boyd's injury.

In the meantime Captain Staunton, assisted by Mr Bowles, who had speedily rejoined him, had been holding a sort of court of inquiry into the case; and after much skilful interrogation, and the giving of a most patient hearing to the statement of each member of the watch, he had succeeded in arriving at a very near approach to the actual truth of the matter.

"This," he said, "is clearly a case wherein both parties have been gravely in fault. I am compelled in justice to admit that you," turning to the members of the watch, "appear to have received great provocation, inasmuch as there can be no doubt that you have been greatly harassed by Mr Carter's habit of unnecessarily interfering with the disposition of the canvas set on the ship. I have, indeed, myself noticed this, my attention often having been arrested by the sounds of making and shortening sail during the night-watches, when you all doubtless thought me fast asleep in my berth; and I have had it on my mind for some time past to speak to Mr Carter on the subject; I should have done so long ago but for my great repugnance to interfere with my officers except upon the most urgent grounds. I confess I had no idea that the provocation had been going on for so long a time; the master of a ship, like other mortals, requires sleep; and doubtless many things are said and done whilst he is taking his rest of which he can know nothing unless they are brought to his notice by others. It was therefore manifestly your duty, in justice to me as well as in obedience to the law, to make complaint to me of any grievances of which you may have considered yourselves the victims; and that, instead of doing so, you took it upon yourselves to resent your grievances by refusing obedience to the orders of your officer, constitutes your offence—an offence which, in my opinion, has been sufficiently punished by the wounds inflicted upon two of your number. You have satisfied me that your lapse of duty was in reality a matter strictly between yourselves and the second officer, and in no wise a defiance of my authority, or I suppose I need scarcely say I should not take this lenient view of your conduct. As for you, Mr Carter," the skipper resumed after a pause, "you have placed me in the very unpleasant position of being compelled to suspend you from duty until the arrival of the ship at Sydney. You have proved yourself incompetent to command a watch with that tact and moderation which is so essential to the safety of a ship and the comfort of those on board; and, led away by your heat of temper, you have hastily and unnecessarily resorted to measures of extreme violence, which might, had the men been of a similar temper, have led to a dreadful disaster. You may retire to your cabin, sir. Mr Bowles, do me the favour to call Mr Dashwood."

Young Dashwood was found sitting on his chest, dressed and ready for any emergency, the entire occupants of the ship being by this time on the qui vive, and he was therefore in the presence of the skipper within a minute of the mention of his name. To him Captain Staunton at once delegated the command of the starboard watch, saying at the same time a few words expressive of confidence in his prudence and seamanship.

"One word more, men," said the skipper, again addressing the watch. "I have suspended Mr Carter not because I regard you as in the right, or as in any way justified in your behaviour, but because he was manifestly wrong. I must therefore very earnestly caution you, one and all, against again refusing obedience to any commands issued by your officers. If those commands are such as to constitute a substantial grievance, or if they should by any chance be such as to manifestly imperil the safety of the ship or the lives of any of those on board, I am always to be found, and the matter must at once be referred to me. I shall always be ready to protect you from tyranny or intemperate treatment; but remember from this time forward there must be nothing even remotely resembling insubordination. Now, go back to your duty."

The men walked quietly away forward, and Captain Staunton, accompanied by Mr Bowles, retired below to make an immediate entry of the occurrence in the official log-book.

The occupants of the saloon were naturally greatly exercised by the event, which formed the staple of conversation next day. It was interesting to observe the way in which the subject was regarded by the various members of the little community. O'Reilly, the editor of the "Galatea Free

Press," was wild with excitement at contemplation of the narrow escape they had had from a mutiny and its attendant fight; and he exhibited a curious study of mingled irritation and satisfaction—of irritation that the fight had not come off, and of satisfaction that he had not been compelled to take up arms against any of the forecastle hands, every one of whom he regarded in his free-hearted way as a personal friend, and with every one of whom he was a prime favourite.

The ladies, who really understood nothing whatever of the merits of the case, with that unerring instinct which invariably leads them to a right conclusion, sided unanimously with the seamen; while a few of the more timid among the male passengers regarded Carter as a sort of hero-martyr, Mr Dale being especially loud and indiscreet in his denunciations of the recklessness manifested in "encouraging the mutinous rascals in their defiance of authority."

"It will end," he dismally prophesied, "in our all being murdered in our beds some night. Oh, dear! I wish I had never come to sea." Brook and one or two more, though they said little, went about the ship for some few days afterwards in evident perturbation of mind, though, to do them justice, had they been obliged they would have doubtless fought and fought well. Rex Fortescue, perhaps, took matters the most coolly of any. He not only went himself forward as usual to hear the yarn-spinning and smoke his cigar on the forecastle during the dog-watches, but he also took Violet with him (he having noticed long before that the presence of a lady was always sufficient to ensure the strictest decorum on the part of the men); thus showing the crew, as clearly as he could, that he at least had no doubt of their loyalty.

Carter's suspension from duty removed the only discordant element which had ever revealed itself on board, as far as the crew of the ship were concerned; and thenceforward matters went smoothly enough on board the Galatea for the remainder of the passage, which proved to be a rapid one, notwithstanding the delay experienced in rounding the Cape. It was also an uneventful one—the foregoing occurrence excepted. Nothing further need therefore be said respecting it, than that in good time the ship safely arrived in Sydney's noble harbour, and, landing her passengers, began forthwith the humdrum operation of discharging cargo.

Homeward Bound

At the date of this story the discharging of a cargo was a much more leisurely operation than it is at the present day; and Bob therefore had several opportunities of taking a run ashore and looking round the town and suburbs of Sydney. The passengers—such of them, that is, as were residents in or near Sydney—had one and all given Bob most pressing invitations to visit them whenever he could obtain leave; and on the day but one following the arrival of the ship, a very prettily-worded and pressing little note had come to him from Blanche Lascelles to say that the friends with whom she and Violet were staying at Cookstown would be delighted to make his acquaintance; so that Bob was never at a loss for a place whither to direct his steps whenever he could get ashore. He consequently managed to see a good deal of the place, and thoroughly enjoyed the seven weeks during which the Galatea lay in Sydney harbour.

The outward cargo discharged, the homeward freight of wool began to come down, and the stevedores were kept busy all day long screwing it into as small a compass as possible in the hold.

Meanwhile Captain Staunton was in great tribulation. The gold-fever was then at its height in Australia. The precious metal had been discovered some years before, but about a month previous to the arrival of the Galatea in Sydney, news had come down the country of the discovery of a new auriferous region, the richness and extent of which was said to be something past belief. The result of this rumour was that every idle loafer who arrived in an Australian port made it his first business to desert from his ship and start hot-foot for the gold-fields. If the matter had ended here the shipmasters would have had cause to congratulate themselves rather than the reverse, but unfortunately for them it was not so. The gold-fever had stricken everybody—merchants even, mechanics, clerks, all in fact but the few cool hands who realised that by remaining in the half-deserted towns they were sure of making that fortune the winning of which at the diggings was problematical; and one consequence of this was that when seamen deserted a ship no one could be found to take their places; and Captain Staunton could stand on his own poop and count at least fifty vessels whose cargoes were on board, hatches battened down, and everything ready for sea; but there they lay, unable to sail for want of a crew to man them.

Now the Galatea was not in quite so bad a plight as this; for when the last bale of wool had been screwed in and the hatches put on, there still remained in her forecastle eight good men and true—six belonging to the port watch and two to the starboard—who had resisted all the alluring dreams of fortunes to be made in a day at the diggings. The other eight had deserted in a body one Sunday, very cleverly eluding the police, whose chief duty it then was to prevent such occurrences. The second mate and the cook were also missing. Hence Captain Staunton's anxiety. On the one hand, he was averse to the extreme step of taking his ship to sea half-manned; and on the other, he was haunted by the constant dread of losing still more of his men if he remained in port until he had made up his complement.

At length, however, to his infinite relief, he chanced upon half a dozen men who, in consideration of the payment of fabulous wages, undertook to ship for the homeward passage. They were as lawless and ruffianly-looking a set of fellows as one need ever care to encounter; but, as Mr Bowles observed, they could at least pull and haul, and once at sea and away from the demoralising influence of the grog-shops, who knew but they might settle down into steady serviceable hands. At all events they would not want for a good example on the part of their shipmates, the remnant of the original crew, for these were without exception thoroughly steady, reliable men, although one of them was Boyd, the man who had been shot by Mr Carter for refusal to obey orders.

These men secured, Captain Staunton resolved to avoid all further risk by sailing at once. It was true that the ship would be still rather short-handed—which was all the more to be regretted inasmuch as she was in light trim and a trifle crank—but he reflected that he might lie in port for the next six months without securing another man; and it therefore seemed to him best under the circumstances to make shift with what he had, and get away to sea forthwith. Hasty summonses were accordingly despatched to the few passengers who had taken berths; and these all coming on board next day, the anchor was hove up, and evening saw the Galatea standing off the land and heading to the eastward, with every sail set and dragging at her like a cart-horse.

The passengers were this time only six in number, namely, Blanche and Violet, Messrs Dale, Fortescue, and Brook, who had lost the contract which they went out in the hope of securing, entirely through the obstinacy of the head of the firm, and a Mr Evelin, formerly a captain in the Royal Engineers, who had thrown up his commission to go gold-digging, and who, thanks to his technical training, supplemented by arduous special study of geology, had been successful to an extraordinary degree, and was now returning home master of a handsome fortune.

Launcelot, or Lance Evelin, was a tall handsome man of about thirty-five, with the physique of a Hercules, the result of some six months' toil and exposure at the diggings, deeply bronzed, clear cut features, half concealed by a heavy moustache and beard of a golden chestnut hue, clear grey eyes, and wavy hair a shade darker than the beard. He proved an immense acquisition to the ladies, who would otherwise have been almost entirely dependent on Rex Fortescue for amusement; Mr Dale being altogether too savage at his recent failure to make an agreeable associate, which indeed he never was, even at the best of times; while Brook, willing though he was to do his best, was too pugnacious, ill-bred, and illiterate to be more than just barely tolerated. Rex Fortescue and Violet, it was perfectly clear, were daily sinking deeper into that condition wherein people are conscious of the existence of two individuals only—their two selves—in the whole world; so that poor little Blanche would soon have found herself quite out in the cold had not Mr Evelin taken compassion upon her and devoted himself to her amusement. He knew London well; and, on comparing notes, it soon transpired that he knew several people with whom Blanche was also acquainted; so they got on capitally together, especially as Lance possessed in an eminent degree the art of making his conversation interesting. Later on, too, when he had thawed a little, he would relate story after story of his adventures at the gold-fields, some of which convulsed his companion with laughter, while others made her shudder and nestle unconsciously a little closer to the narrator.

But notwithstanding this Blanche still found time to chat occasionally with Bob. The lad was very fond of steering, indeed he had won the reputation of being the finest helmsman in the ship, and he was always ready to take a "trick" at the wheel during either of the dog-watches, and so give the rightful helmsman a chance to stay "for'ard" and amuse himself with his shipmates; and when this was the case Blanche generally used to seat herself in a deck-chair near him, and chatter away upon any topic which came uppermost.

She had been thus amusing herself one evening when, as eight bells struck and Bob walked forward on being relieved from the wheel, Lance Evelin, who had been smoking his cigar on the break of the poop, and watching from a distance the "carryings-on" of the men upon the forecastle, sauntered to her side and opened conversation with the remark—

"How singularly exact a repetition of the same features you will observe in some families; doubtless you have often noticed it, Miss Lascelles? Now, there is that fine young fellow Legerton, anyone would recognise him as a connection of yours, and I have often been on the point of asking you in what manner you are related to each, other. Am I unpardonably inquisitive?"

"By no means, Mr Evelin. It is a question easily answered; I am not aware that we are related in the most remote degree."

"You are not?" he exclaimed in a tone of the greatest surprise. "I am sure I most earnestly beg your pardon; how very stupid of me to make such a mistake; but the resemblance between you two is so very striking that, although no one has ever said a word to lead me to such a conclusion, I have never doubted, from the moment I came on board, that you must be closely related. I am sure I am quite at a loss for words wherewith to express my apologies."

"No apology is necessary, I assure you, Mr Evelin," returned Blanche. "On the contrary, I feel rather flattered by your supposition, for I greatly admire Robert's many sterling qualities. And what a bold brave fellow he is too, notwithstanding his quiet unassuming manner. If you feel any curiosity as to his history Captain Staunton will be only too happy to furnish you with full particulars; he can enlighten you far better than I can, and the story is worth listening to; the manner of their first acquaintance especially is a romance in itself."

Lance's curiosity was aroused; but, instead of referring to the skipper, he preferred to hear the story from Blanche's own pretty lips; and sinking down into a deck-chair beside her he listened with interest to all that the fair girl could tell him respecting Bob.

"Poor fellow!" he remarked when Blanche had finished her story, "and he has never been able to find a clue to his parentage! It is very singular; there surely must be relatives of his still in existence somewhere. Did the fishermen who saved his life never make any inquiries?"

"No, it appears not," answered Blanche. "According to Robert's own account, though he always speaks with the greatest respect and affection of the old man who adopted him, the people among whom he was thrown are very simple and ignorant of everything outside the pale of their own calling, and it would seem that they really did not know how to set about instituting an inquiry."

"Well, what you have told me has interested me so much, and the lad himself has made such a favourable impression upon me, that I believe I shall really feel more than half-inclined to undertake the somewhat Quixotic task of seeking his relatives myself when we reach England. Who knows but that it might be my good fortune to gladden the heart of a father or mother whose life has been embittered for years by the loss of perhaps an only son?" half laughingly remarked Lance.

"Ah! do not jest upon such a subject," exclaimed Blanche. "You evidently have not the least idea what a complete blight such a loss may cast upon a parent's life. I have. There is my poor uncle, Sir Richard, who has never held up his head since he lost his wife and child at sea. My mother has told me that before his terrible bereavement there was not a more genial light-hearted happy man living than uncle Dick; but he has never been known to smile since the dreadful news first reached him; and though he has always struggled bravely against his great sorrow, I feel sure he looks forward eagerly to the time when he shall be called away to rejoin his wife and his baby boy."

"How very sad!" remarked Lance in sympathetic tones. "I am slightly acquainted with Sir Richard Lascelles, that is to say, I have met him once or twice, and I have often wondered what great trouble it could be that seemed to be pressing so heavily upon him. If it would not distress you too much I should like to hear how he met with his terrible loss."

"I have no objection to tell you," answered Blanche. "It occurred very shortly after I was born. My uncle was then a younger son, with very little expectation of ever succeeding to the baronetcy, for there were two brothers older than himself, and he had a captain's commission in the army. He had married a lady of whom, because she happened to have no money, his father strongly disapproved, and a serious quarrel between father and son was the consequence.

"Shortly after his marriage my uncle's regiment was ordered off to North America, and uncle Dick naturally took his wife with him. The regiment was moved about from place to place, and finally, when my uncle had been married about three years, was broken up into detachments; that which he commanded being sent, in consequence of some trouble with the Indians, to an important military outpost at a considerable distance up the Ottawa River.

"Of course it was quite impossible for my aunt to accompany her husband into the wilds, especially as she was then the mother of a son some eighteen months old, and the question which arose was, What was she to do?

"It was at first proposed that she should establish herself in Montreal until the return of the expedition; but a letter reaching her just at that time stating that her mother's health was failing, it was hastily decided that my aunt should return to England, taking of course her little son with her.

"Everything had to be done in a great hurry, and my uncle had barely time to pack his wife's boxes and see her safely en route for Montreal before he set out with his detachment for the post to which he had been ordered.

"My aunt arrived safely at Montreal, but failing to find there a ship ready to sail for England, went on to Quebec, which she reached just in time to embark for London. She had written to my uncle from Montreal, and she wrote again from Quebec, the letter reaching her husband's hands as he was on the point of marching out of the fort on a night expedition against a band of hostile Indians who had been discovered in the neighbourhood.

"An engagement took place, in which my uncle was desperately wounded and narrowly escaped falling into the hands of the Indians. His men succeeded, however, in saving him and making good their own retreat into the fort, where poor uncle Dick lay hovering for weeks between life and death. After a long and weary struggle his splendid constitution triumphed; and with the return of consciousness came anxious thoughts respecting his wife and child. He remembered the letter which had been handed to him as he marched out upon that ill-starred expedition, the letter which he had never had an opportunity to read, and he made eager inquiries respecting it. It was found in an inner breast-pocket of his uniform coat, but it had been so thoroughly saturated with his own blood, poor fellow, that it was practically undecipherable; by careful soaking and washing he at last succeeded in ascertaining that my aunt and her baby had actually sailed from Quebec, but on what date or in what ship it was quite impossible to learn. And that was the last news he ever heard of them."

"How very dreadful!" murmured Lance. "Of course he made every possible inquiry respecting their fate?"

"Not immediately," answered Blanche. "He waited patiently for news of my aunt's arrival in England; but as mail after mail came without bringing him any intelligence he grew uneasy, and finally wrote to his mother-in-law asking an explanation of the unaccountable silence. This letter remained unanswered; but just when his uneasiness had increased to such a pitch that he had determined to apply for leave of absence in order to proceed to England, it was returned to him through the dead-letter office. This decided him at once. He applied for leave and it was refused. He then threw up his commission, and at once proceeded to England; the fearful conviction growing upon him that something dreadful had happened. He stopped at Quebec for a fortnight on his way home, making inquiry at all the ship-owners' and brokers' offices in the place, endeavouring to learn the name of the ship in which his wife had been a passenger; but, strange to say, he could gain no trace of them. Whether it was that the people of whom he inquired were careless and indifferent, or whether it was that passenger-lists were not at that time regularly kept as they now are, it is of course impossible to say, but it is a fact that he was compelled to leave America without the smallest scrap of information respecting his dear ones beyond that contained in the blood-stained letter.

"On his arrival in England he proceeded direct to his mother-in-law's former residence, to find it, as he feared, in the possession of strangers. He then, with considerable difficulty, hunted up the lawyer who had managed Mrs Percival's (his mother-in-law's) money matters, and learned from him that the old lady had died some seven months before. And in reply to his further inquiries he was informed that his wife and child had never reached Mrs Percival's home. The old lady had certainly expected them, the lawyer said, but she had never received more than one letter which my uncle had hurriedly written mentioning the fact of their departure for England.

"Poor uncle Dick now found himself completely at a loss; so, as the best plan he could think of, he put the affair into his lawyer's hands, handing him also the blood-stained letter. This letter was soon afterwards intrusted to a chemist, who, in attempting to cleanse it, destroyed it altogether, and thus passed away the only clue which my uncle possessed. It is now rather more than sixteen years since my aunt sailed from Quebec, and poor uncle Dick has never succeeded in gaining a trace of her fate to this day."

"Poor fellow!" ejaculated Lance, in an absent sort of way. "I'm sure I sincerely pity and sympathise with him. What! going below already? Then allow me to conduct you as far as the companion."

Blanche bade Lance good-night at the head of the saloon staircase; he raised his smoking-cap, and then returning sauntered up and down the poop for over an hour, with his hands behind him, and his eyes fixed on the deck, apparently in a brown study.

A few days after the narration of Blanche's story, Lance Evelin, noticing Bob at the wheel, strolled up to him and asked him for his history.

"Miss Lascelles gave me the outlines of it a night or two ago, and it struck me as so peculiar and interesting that I should like to hear full particulars," he explained, puffing lazily at his cigar meanwhile.

"Where would you like me to begin, Mr Evelin?" asked Bob.

"At the beginning of course, my dear fellow," laughingly answered Lance. "I want to know everything. Do you remember being found on board the wreck?"

"Sometimes I think I do; and at other times I think it must be only the recollection of a dream which has produced a more than usually strong impression upon me," answered Bob. "Now and then—perhaps not more than half a dozen times altogether—when I have been lying half asleep and half awake, a confused and indistinct idea presents itself of a ship's cabin seen through a half-opened state-room door, with a lamp swinging violently to and fro; of a woman's face, beautiful as—oh! I cannot describe it; something like Miss Dudley's, only still more beautiful, if you can imagine such a thing. Then the dream, or whatever it is, gets still more confused; I seem to be in cold and wet and darkness, and I fancy I hear a sound like men shouting, mingled with the roar of the wind and the rush of the sea; then—then—I seem to have been kissed—yes—and the beautiful face seems to be bending over me again, but I am in the light and the warmth once more; and—then it all passes away; and if I try to carry my thoughts back to the first circumstance which I can distinctly remember, I see myself again with other boys, paddling about barefoot on the shore at Brightlingsea."

"Ah!" ejaculated Lance, contemplatively. "I have no doubt but that—if the truth could be arrived at, which of course it never can be in this world—this dream, or whatever you like to call it, is the faint recollection which still remains impressed on your memory of some of the incidents connected with the wreck of your ship—what was her name, by the by? The Lightning, of London! Um; that's not a very difficult name to remember, at all events. And the beautiful face of which you spoke—is your impression of it clear enough to enable you to describe it? Or, supposing it possible for you to see a picture of the original, do you think you would recognise it?—Do you mind my asking these questions? No; that's all right; but if it is in the least painful to you, I will not put them. You see, Legerton, I have very little doubt that face was the face of your mother; and I confess I feel a trifle curious to know how far back a man can carry his remembrance of his mother. I cannot remember anything about mine previous to my fourth birthday."

"Well," answered Bob, "I can scarcely remember the face clearly enough to describe it. All I can say about it is that it was very beautiful, with tender loving eyes and dark hair, which I am almost sure must have been worn in curls; but I think that if ever I saw a really good picture of it I should recognise it directly."

"You would, eh?" said Lance. "Very well, now go ahead—if you are not tired of talking—and tell me about the old fellow who found you, and the sort of life you led as a fisherman, and so on; it is all very interesting, I assure you; quite as much so as any of the novels in the saloon book-case."

Bob accordingly went ahead, his companion occasionally interrupting him with a question; and when the story was finished Lance rose and stretched himself, saying as he turned to walk away—

"Thank you very much. Your story is so interesting that I think I shall make a few notes of it for the benefit of a literary friend of mine; so if you meet with it in print some day you must not be very much surprised."

And as Bob saw him shortly afterwards, note-book in hand; and as this story actually is in print, it is to be presumed that Mr Lance Evelin really carried out his expressed intention.

On the day following this conversation the wind, which had been blowing steadily from the westward for some time, suddenly dropped; and by four bells in the afternoon watch it had fallen to a dead calm; the ship rolling like a log on the heavy swell. Not the faintest trace of cloud could be discerned in the stupendous vault which sprang in delicate carnation and primrose tints from the encircling horizon, passing through a multitude of subtle gradations of colour until it became at the zenith a broad expanse of clearest purest deepest blue. The atmosphere was transparent to an almost extraordinary degree, the slow-moving masses of swell rising sharply outlined to the very verge of the horizon, while the mast-heads of a far-distant ship stood out clear and well-defined, like two minute and delicately drawn thin lines on the pale primrose background of the sky.

Suddenly, however, a curious phenomenon occurred. A subtle but distinct and instantaneous change of colour took place, which made it seem as though the spectators were regarding the scene through tinted glass. All the brilliance and purity and beauty of the various hues had died out. The dazzling ultramarine of the zenith became indigo; the clear transparent hues of the horizon thickened and deepened to a leaden-grey; the sun gleamed aloft pallid and rayless, like a ghost of its former self; and the ocean, black and turbid, heaved restlessly, writhing as if in torture. An intense and unnatural silence, too, seemed suddenly to have fallen upon nature, enwrapping the scene as with a mantle, a silence in which the flap of the canvas, the pattering of the reef-points, the cheep of blocks, and the occasional clank of the rudder-chains, fell upon the ear with a sharpness which was positively painful.

The occupants of the Galatea's deck glanced from one to another, dismayed; Violet Dudley's startled whisper to Rex Fortescue of "What dreadful thing is about to happen?" being but the utterance of the thought which flashed through every brain.

Captain Staunton, turning to Mr Bowles, who was standing beside him, in low tones requested that trusty officer to keep a look-out for a minute or two; and then hurried down to the saloon to consult his barometer. He returned to the deck in less than a minute, his face wearing a look of anxiety and concern which was very rarely to be seen there.

"The glass has fallen a full inch within the last half-hour" he muttered, as he rejoined the mate.

Then in a louder tone of voice he added, "Call all hands, Mr Bowles, if you please, and shorten sail at once. Stow everything except the lower fore and main topsails and the fore-topmast stay-sail; I think we are going to have a change of weather."

The seamen were as much startled as the occupants of the poop, by the preternatural change in the aspect of the sky; and they sprang to their posts with all the alacrity of men who anticipate a deadly struggle, and believe they may have none too much time for preparation. The work of shortening sail proceeded rapidly but methodically and in an orderly manner—Captain Staunton had never before in all his experience witnessed anything quite like what was now passing around him, and was oppressed by an undefined foreboding of some terrible catastrophe; but he was too brave a man and too thorough a seaman to allow aught of this to appear in either countenance, voice, or manner; nor would he allow the work to be hurried through with inconsiderate haste; he saw that the men were startled; and it rested with him to steady them, restore their confidence, and so prepare them for the coming struggle, whatever its nature might be.

Meanwhile, the atmospheric phenomena were momentarily assuming a more and more portentous aspect. The sky deepened in tint from indigo to a purple black; the sun lost its pallid sickly gleam and hung in the sable heavens a lurid blood-red ball until it became obscured by heavy masses of dusky vapour which had gathered imperceptibly in the firmament, and now seemed to be settling slowly down upon the ship's mast-heads, rolling and writhing like huge tortured serpents, meanwhile. The silence—broken though it was by the sounds of preparation on board—grew even more oppressively intense and death-like than before; and darkness now came to add new terrors to the scene; not the wholesome solemn darkness of nightfall, but a weird unearthly gloom which was neither night nor day, a gloom which descended and encompassed them stealthily and menacingly, contracting the horizon until nothing could be seen further than half a mile from the ship, and which still seemed to be saturated with a pale spectral shimmering light, in the which men looked in each other's eyes like reanimated corpses. The ocean presented an aspect no less appalling; at one moment black as the waters of the Styx, and indistinguishable beyond the distance of a cable's length, and anon gleaming into view to the very verge of the horizon, a palpitating sheet of greenish ghastly phosphorescent light.

The canvas was stowed, down to the lower fore and main topsail and the fore-topmast stay-sail, and the men were about to hurry down from aloft when Captain Staunton stopped them.

"Clew up and stow the lower topsails as well," he shouted; adding in an undertone to Mr Bowles, "I don't know what to expect; but it threatens to be something terrible; and the less canvas we show to it the better. The stay-sail will be quite as much as we shall want, I expect."

The topsails were stowed, and the men came down on deck again, evidently glad to find themselves there once more, and huddling together on the forecastle like frightened sheep.

The passengers were clustered together on the poop, standing in a group somewhat apart from the skipper and the mate, awaiting pale and silent the dénouement. Bob, who had been aloft helping to stow the mizen canvas, stepped up to them as he swung himself out of the rigging, and, addressing himself more particularly to Violet and Blanche, recommended them to go below at once.

"These warnings," said he, "are not for nothing. The precautions which Captain Staunton has taken show clearly enough that he expects something quite out of the common; and the change is likely enough to come upon us suddenly, bringing perhaps some of our top-hamper about our ears; so, if you ladies will be advised, I would recommend you to go below where you will certainly be in much less danger."

Blanche and Violet looked at each other inquiringly. "I shall remain here," said Violet, unconsciously tightening her hold upon Rex Fortescue's arm as she spoke. "Whatever happens, I would very much rather be here, where I can see the full extent of the danger, than pent up in a cabin picturing to myself I know not what horrors."

Blanche expressed the same determination; but Mr Dale hurried at once to the companion, loudly lamenting that he had ever intrusted his precious self to the 'beastly treacherous sea!'

His remarks attracted Captain Staunton's attention to the party; and he at once stepped hurriedly toward them exclaiming, "Good heavens, ladies and gentlemen! let me beg you to go below at once; I had no idea you were here. The saloon is the safest place for you all at a time like this; you will be out of harm's way there, while here—"

"Look out!" shouted Mr Bowles. "Here it comes with a vengeance. Take care of yourselves, everybody."

The gloom had visibly deepened, until it became difficult for those grouped together on the poop to distinguish each other's features, and a low deep humming sound was now audible, which increased in volume with startling rapidity.

"Go below all of you, I beg," repeated Captain Staunton in anxious tones, "and be as quick as you can about it, please. What is the matter, Mr Dale?" as that individual stood a few steps down the staircase, grasping the handrail on each side, neither descending himself nor allowing anyone else to do so.

"My book," exclaimed Dale; "I left a book on one of the hen-coops, and—"

His further remarks were drowned in the deafening din of the tempest, which at this moment swooped down upon the ship with indescribable fury, striking her full upon her starboard broadside, and hurling her over in an instant on her beam-ends. The group gathered about the companion-way made an instinctive effort to save themselves, Rex Fortescue flinging his arm about Violet Dudley's waist and dragging her with him to the mizen-mast, where he hung on desperately to a belaying-pin. Brook nimbly scrambled upon the upturned weather side of the companion. Evelin, exasperated by Mr Dale's ill-timed anxiety about his book, had stepped inside the companion-way and down a stair or two to summarily remove the obstructor, and the two were flung together to the bottom of the staircase. Blanche, left thus without a protector, clung convulsively for a moment to one of the open doors of the companion; but her strength failing her, she let go and fell backwards with a shriek into the water which foamed hungrily up over the lee rail.

Bob, who had made a spring for the weather mizen rigging, was just passing a turn or two of a rope round his body when, happening to turn his head, he saw Blanche fall. To cast himself adrift and spring headlong after her was the work of an instant, and he succeeded in grasping her dress just in the nick of time, for in another instant the ship would have driven over her, and Blanche's fate would have been sealed. As it was, they both had a very narrow escape, for Bob in his haste had omitted to take a rope's-end with him, and had consequently no means of returning inboard, or rather, for the lee side of the deck was buried in the water, of regaining a place of safety. In this emergency Brook, who was a witness of the scene, acted in a very prompt and creditable manner. The rope, by which Bob had been in the act of securing himself, streamed out in the wind in such a way as to come within Brook's reach, and by its aid he at once drew himself up to windward, and, climbing out on to the weather side of the ship, dexterously dropped from thence a coiled-up rope's-end, which he had taken off a belaying-pin, directly down upon Bob's head. Bob at once grasped the rope with his disengaged hand, and with a rapid twist threw two or three turns round his arm, whereupon Brook, exerting all his strength, drew his prizes steadily up the steeply inclined deck until they were able to scramble into the place he had vacated upon the companion.

Dismasted

As the hurricane swooped down upon the ship, Captain Staunton and Mr Bowles sprang with one accord aft to the helm. It was well that they did so; for when the vessel was thrown upon her beam-ends the wheel flew suddenly and violently round, taking unawares the unfortunate man who was stationed at it and hurling him far over the lee quarter into the sea, where he immediately sank, being probably disabled by a blow from the rapidly revolving spokes. The two officers saw in a moment that the poor fellow was irretrievably lost, so without wasting time in useless efforts to save him they devoted themselves forthwith to the task of preserving the ship. The wheel was put hard up, with the object of getting the craft before the wind; and then the two men stood anxiously watching and awaiting the result. Two or three minutes passed, and there still lay the ship prone on her side, with her lee topsail and lower yard-arms dipping in the water, she would not pay off.

"Bowles," said Captain Staunton, lashing the wheel as he spoke, "make your way forward; muster the carpenter and one or two of the most reliable men you have, and bring them aft with axes to cut away the mizen-mast; we must get her before it somehow; should it come any stronger she will 'turn the turtle' with us. Station your men; but do not cut until I hold up my hand."

Mr Bowles nodded his head; and then set out upon his difficult journey, climbing up to windward by the grating upon which the helmsman usually stood, and then working his way along the deck by grasping the bulwarks, which on the poop were only about a foot above the deck. On reaching the wake of the mizen-mast he was compelled to pause in order to help Rex Fortescue and Violet out of their dangerous position, a position of course altogether untenable now that the order had been given to cut away the mast. This, with Brook's assistance, he with some difficulty accomplished, landing them safely alongside Blanche and Bob upon the companion. The slight delay thus incurred threatened to have the most disastrous consequences; for when the chief mate was once more free to proceed upon his errand he became aware that the ship's inclination had sensibly increased, to such an extent indeed that he momentarily expected to feel her rolling bottom-up. Glancing aft once more, he caught the eye of Captain Staunton, who immediately raised his hand. This the mate took to mean an order to cut away the mast with all possible expedition; and whipping out his keen broad-bladed knife he thrust it into Brook's hand, and tapping the lanyards of the mizen rigging roared in his ear the one word "Cut."

Then without pausing another instant he proceeded as rapidly as he could forward, much impeded by the continuous blinding shower of spindrift which swept across the vessel, and compelled to cling with all his strength to whatever he laid hold of in his progress, in order to escape being literally blown away.

Meanwhile Brook, who now showed that he was made of far better stuff than anyone had hitherto suspected, began without a moment's delay to vigorously attack the rigid and tightly strained lanyards of the weather mizen rigging, being speedily joined by Bob, who turned Blanche over to Rex Fortescue's care the moment he saw that he could be of use. Steadily and rapidly they hacked and notched away at the hard rope, working literally for their lives, for it was now no longer possible to doubt that the Galatea was slowly but surely capsizing. The upturned side which supported them was becoming every moment more nearly horizontal, the lee yard-arms were steadily burying themselves deeper and deeper in the water, and it became apparent that unless relieved, another minute would see the ship bottom-up. Mr Bowles, meanwhile, was out of sight forward, hidden by the gloom and the cloud of spindrift.

At last one of the lanyards was severed by the keen blade in Brook's hand. The others attached to the same shroud immediately began to render through the deadeye, throwing an extra strain upon the lanyards of the other shrouds, one of which immediately parted under Bob's knife; then twang, twang, twang, one after the other, they rapidly yielded, until, as the last lanyard parted, crash went the mizen-mast short off by the deck and away to leeward, carrying away the saloon skylight as it went.

A perceptible shock was felt as the mast went over the side, and every one watched anxiously to see what the effect would be. The disappointment was extreme when it was seen that the relief was not sufficient to enable the ship to recover herself; she still lay down upon her side, and though she now no longer threatened momentarily to capsize, she neither righted nor paid off.

The chief mate now reappeared upon the poop, having by this time mustered a gang of men, whom he had left clinging to the main-rigging, thinking it not unlikely the main-mast would also have to go.

By the time he reached Captain Staunton's side the mind of the latter was made up.

"It is no good, Bowles," he said; "she will do nothing; we must part with the main-mast also. Cut it away at once, and let us get her upon an even keel again if we can."

Mr Bowles hurried forward, and as soon as he became visible to the men clustered about the main-rigging he made a sign to them to cut. The axes gleamed in the darkened air, a few rapid strokes were struck upon the lanyards of the rigging, and the main-mast bowed, crashed off at about ten feet from the deck, and was carried by the wind clear of the lee rail into the sea.

Another shock, almost as if the ship had struck something, accompanied the fall of the main-mast, and then, laboriously at first but finally with an almost sudden jerk, the Galatea swung upright, and, paying off at the same time, began to draw through the water, her speed increasing to some seven knots when she got fairly away before the wind, and was relieved of the wreckage towing alongside.

The well was sounded, and to everybody's intense relief some six inches only of water was found in the hold. The pumps were rigged, manned, and set to work, and the water was so speedily got rid of as to show that it had penetrated only through some portion of the upper works.

The first mad fury of the hurricane was by this time over, but it still blew far too heavily to admit of any other course than running dead before it. The sea, which had hitherto been a level plane of fleecy white foam, now showed symptoms of rising, and the aspect of the sky was still such as to force upon the voyagers the conclusion that they were not yet by any means out of danger. What could be done, however, was done; and the entire crew were set to work, some to get up preventer back-stays and secure the fore-mast, and others to convert the spare spars into jury-masts.

The passengers, meanwhile, had made their way down into the saloon directly the ship recovered herself, where they found Lance Evelin pale, dazed, and barely conscious, bleeding from a very ugly wound in the temple caused by his having fallen heavily against the brass-bound edge of one of the saloon stairs. Mrs Staunton was doing her best single-handed to staunch the blood and bind up the wound, with little May on her knees beside the patient, sobbing as though her tender child's heart would break, for Lance had taken greatly to the sweet little creature, and, grave and quiet though he was in general, was always ready to romp with her or tell her the most marvellous tales. Mr Dale had retired to his cabin and shut himself in. The new arrivals very promptly afforded their assistance, and in a short time Lance was laid carefully in his berth, and packed there with flags, shawls, and other yielding materials in such a way as to prevent the increasing motion of the ship from causing him any avoidable discomfort.

Dinner that day was a very comfortless meal. By the time that it was served the sea had risen so much as to render the "fiddles" necessary on the cabin table, and even with their aid it was difficult to prevent the viands from being scattered upon the floor. The ship, running before the wind, and with only the fore-mast to steady her, rolled like a hogshead, and the act of dining was therefore quite an acrobatic performance, demanding so much activity of eye and hand as to completely mar the enjoyment of the good things which, in spite of the weather, graced the board.

The conversation at table turned naturally upon the disaster which had befallen the ship; the passengers being all curious to know how it would affect them.

"I suppose it means another beastly detention," grumbled Dale. "The ship can't sail all the way to England with only one mast, can she, captain?"

"Well, scarcely," replied Captain Staunton. "The trip home might be made under jury-masts; but it would be a longer and more tedious voyage than any of us would care for, I fancy, and at all events I have no intention of attempting it. Our nearest port is Otago; but as we are pretty certain to get westerly winds again as soon as this breeze has piped itself out, and as the current would also be against us if we attempted to return to the westward, I shall endeavour to reach Valparaiso, where we may hope to restore the poor old barkie's clipped wings."

"Umph! I thought so," snarled Dale. "And how long shall we be detained at that wretched hole?"

"It will depend on circumstances," answered Captain Staunton, "but I think you may reckon on being a month there."

"A month!" ejaculated Dale, too much disgusted to say another word.

"A month!" exclaimed Rex Fortescue, "Jolly! I shall explore the Andes and do a little shooting. I daresay Evelin will join me—or us rather—for I suppose you will go as well, won't you, Brook?"

"Oh yes, I'll go, certainly; 'tain't often as I has a holiday, so I may as well take one when I can get it. But what's them Handles we're to explore, Mr Fortescue? Mr Dale 'll come with us too, I'm sure; he's fond of sleeping in a tent, ain't you, sir?"

"Don't be such a fool, Brook," retorted that worthy. "If ever we get to Valparaiso, which I think is very doubtful, I shall go home overland."

"I am afraid that before you can do that, Mr Dale, you or someone else will have to bridge the Atlantic," remarked Captain Staunton, as he leisurely sipped his wine. "I am extremely sorry for the untoward event which has interrupted our voyage, but it was one of those occurrences which no skill or foresight could have prevented, so I think the best thing you can do is to make as light of it as possible. Worse things than being dismasted have happened at sea before now, and I, for one, am sincerely thankful that we are still above water instead of beneath it, as seemed more than likely at one time."

So saying the skipper rose, and with a bow left the saloon for the deck.

The sky still looked wild, but there were occasional momentary breaks in it, through which the lustrous stars of the southern heavens beamed gloriously down for an instant ere they were shut in again by the scurrying clouds; and the sea, which now ran high, afforded a magnificent spectacle as the huge billows raced after the ship, each with its foaming crest a cataract of liquid fire. And as the ship rolled, and the water washed impetuously across her decks, the dark planking gleamed with millions of tiny fairy-like stars, which waxed and waned with every oscillation of the vessel. The fore-mast had by this time been made secure, and, it being too dark to work any longer to advantage, the men were busy re-lashing the spars which had been cast adrift in the process of overhauling and selecting those most suitable for jury-masts. Mr Bowles, who had hurried up from the saloon after swallowing the merest apology for a dinner, had charge of the deck; and Captain Staunton joining him, the pair began to discuss the future with its plans and probabilities.

Two days later saw the Galatea making her way to the northward and eastward under a very respectable jury barque-rig, which enabled her to show her fore-topmast stay-sail, reefed fore-sail, and double-reefed fore-topsail on the fore-mast; a main topsail with topgallant-sail over it on the spar which did duty for a main-mast; and a reefed mizen set upon the jib-boom, which had been rigged in, passed aft, and set on end, properly stayed, with its heel stepped down through the hole in the poop from which the mizen-mast had erstwhile sprung.

The gale had blown itself out; the sea was rapidly going down; the wind had hauled round from the westward once more; and the ship was slipping along at the rate of some five knots an hour. The minor damages had all been made good, excepting that done to the saloon skylight by the fall of the mizen-mast, and upon this job the carpenter, who was an ambitious man in his own way and not altogether devoid of taste, was taxing his skill to the utmost in an effort to make the new skylight both a stronger and a more handsome piece of work than its predecessor. The barometer was slowly but steadily rising; and everything seemed to point in the direction of fine weather. Lucky was it for our voyagers that such was the case.

The passengers had by this time got over their recent alarm, and were settling back into their old ways. Even the impatient and discontented Dale seemed to have got over to a great extent his annoyance at the delay which the loss of the masts involved; and, catching the contagion of the good spirits which animated the rest of the party, was actually betrayed into an effort or two to make himself agreeable that evening at the dinner-table. So amiable was this generally irritable individual that he positively listened with equanimity to the plans which Fortescue and Evelin—the latter with a broad patch of plaster across his brow—were discussing relative to a properly organised sporting excursion into the Cordilleras—or Andes, as they indifferently termed them, much to the perplexity of Brook—nor did he allow himself to show any signs of annoyance when the last-named individual sought to ruffle his (Dale's) feathers, as he elegantly termed it, by urging him to join the expedition; on the contrary, to the secret but carefully concealed consternation of Rex and Lance, the prime movers in the matter, Mr Dale seemed more than half disposed to yield to Brook's jesting entreaties that he would make one of the party. It almost seemed as though this intensely selfish and egotistical individual were at last becoming ashamed of his own behaviour and had resolved upon an attempt to improve it.

Dinner over, the ladies retired to the poop to witness the sunset, Rex and Lance accompanying them; while Dale and Brook remained below, lingering over their wine.

"Oh, how refreshing this cool evening breeze is, after the closeness and heat of the saloon!" exclaimed Violet as, leaning on Rex Fortescue's arm, she gazed astern where the sun was just sinking out of sight beneath the purple horizon, leaving behind him a cloudless sky which glowed in his track with purest gold and rose tints, merging insensibly into a clear ultramarine, deepening in tone as the eye travelled up to the zenith and thence downward toward the eastern quarter where, almost before the upper rim of the sun's golden disc had sunk out of sight, a great star beamed out from the velvety background, glowing with that soft mellow effulgence which seems peculiar to southern skies.

"Yes," responded Rex, "it is cool and decidedly pleasant. Do you not think it is almost too cool, however, to be braved without a shawl or wrap of some kind after being cooped up for an hour in that roasting saloon. I cannot think why it should have been so warm this evening; to my mind it was hotter even than when we were crossing the line on the outward voyage."

Blanche and Lance, who were standing near enough to overhear these remarks, were also of opinion that it had been quite uncomfortably warm below, and the two gentlemen, who by this time had arrived at that stage of intimacy with the ladies which seemed to justify them in their own eyes for assuming an occasional dictatorial air toward their fair companions, forthwith insisted on returning below to seek for shawls or wraps of some kind.

"Phew! it is like walking into a Turkish bath to come in here," exclaimed Rex, as he passed through the saloon doors; "and what a peculiar smell!"

"Yes," assented Lance. "Smells like oil or grease of some kind. I expect the steward has spilled some lamp-oil down in the lazarette, and the heat is causing the odour to rise. I hope it will pass off before we turn-in to-night, for it is decidedly objectionable."

"Do you know, Miss Lascelles," said Lance, as he settled himself comfortably in a chair by that young lady's side, after carefully enveloping her in a soft fleecy wrap, "I have an idea in connection with that touching story you told me the other night respecting your uncle's loss of his wife and infant son."

"Have you, indeed?" said Blanche. "And pray, what is it, Mr Evelin?"

"Simply this," replied Lance. "I have an impression—almost a conviction—that your cousin is living, and that I can put my hand upon him when required."

"Oh, Mr Evelin! what is this you say?" exclaimed Blanche eagerly. "Have you, indeed, met with anyone in the course of your wanderings, whose history is such that you believe him to be my dear little long-lost cousin, Dick? I do not think you would speak heedlessly or without due consideration upon such a subject; and if your supposition should be correct, and you can furnish a clue to the discovery of my missing relatives, you will give new life to my uncle, and lay us all under such an obligation as we shall never be able to repay."

"Do not place too much confidence in the idea that it would be quite impossible to repay even such an obligation as the one of which you speak," said Lance in a low and meaning tone which somehow caused Blanche's cheek to flush and her heart to flutter a little. "You are right in supposing," he continued, "that I would not make such an assertion without due consideration. I have thought much upon the story you confided to me; and, comparing it with another which I have also heard, I am of opinion that I have discovered a clue which is worth following up, if only for the satisfaction of ascertaining whether it be a true or a false one. If true, your poor aunt is without doubt long since dead; but your cousin is still alive, and—there he stands!" pointing to Bob, who was in the waist leaning musingly over the lee rail.

"Where?" asked Blanche, looking quite bewildered.

"There," replied Evelin, again pointing to Bob. "If my supposition is correct, that lad Bob is your cousin, Miss Lascelles."

"Impossible!" exclaimed Blanche. "Oh, Mr Evelin, tell me:—What has led you to think so?"

"I will," answered Lance. "But I hope the idea is not very distressing to you. It is true that the lad's present position is—well, not perhaps exactly worthy of the cousin of—"

"Oh no; do not say that, Mr Evelin, I beg," interrupted Blanche. "I was not thinking of that in the least. If Bob indeed prove to be my cousin, I shall certainly not be ashamed of him—quite the contrary; but you took me so completely by surprise. I have ever pictured my lost cousin as a chubby little flaxen-haired baby boy, from always having heard him so spoken of, I suppose; and I had forgotten for the moment that, if alive, he must necessarily have grown into a young man. But let me hear why you have come to think that Robert may be my cousin; I am all curiosity and impatience—woman-like, you see—in the presence of a mystery."

"Well," said Lance, "you doubtless remember that on one occasion I remarked upon the striking resemblance he bears to you; and, I might have added, the still more striking resemblance between him and your uncle, Sir Richard. My somewhat bungling remark, as I at the time considered it, led to your relating to me first the history of your friend Bob, and then that of your uncle's loss. As I listened to you, the idea dawned upon me that Bob and your lost cousin might possibly be one and the same individual I got the lad to tell me his story, which was naturally somewhat more full and circumstantial than your own sketch; and comparing dates and so on, I have been led to the conclusion that he may indeed prove to be Sir Richard's son. In the first place, his age, which of course can only be approximately guessed at, is about the same as your cousin's would be, if alive. Next, there is the very extraordinary likeness, almost too striking, I think, to be merely accidental; and lastly, the clothes he wore when found, and which are still in existence, I understand, are marked with the initials R.L., which may stand for Richard Lascelles, the name, as I understood you, which your cousin bore."

At this moment Captain Staunton made his appearance at the head of the saloon staircase, and calling to the chief mate, said—

"Mr Bowles, pass the word for the carpenter to come aft to the saloon at once, if you please. Let him look smart."

The skipper then disappeared below again; but not before the passengers, who were all by this time on the poop, had had time to observe that his features wore a somewhat anxious expression.

The word was passed; and Chips, who was on the forecastle smoking his pipe, at once came shambling aft. At the head of the companion-way he encountered the steward, who went up to Mr Bowles, said a word or two to him in a low tone of voice, and then returned below again.

Mr Bowles nodded; stepped quietly down to the main dock, and put his head inside the door of the deck-house wherein Mr Dashwood was lodged; and in another moment the second mate came out, followed the chief up to the poop, and took charge of the deck; Mr Bowles immediately proceeding below.

No one but Lance appeared to take any particular notice of these movements, so quietly were they executed; and if he suspected that anything was wrong he took care not to show it, but went on chatting with Blanche upon the same subject as before. It may be, however, that his thoughts wandered a little from the matter in hand, for once or twice he halted and hesitated somewhat in his speech, and seemed to forget what he was talking about.

A quarter of an hour passed away; and then Captain Staunton, followed by the chief mate, came on deck. They walked as far as the break of the poop together, and then Mr Bowles gave the word to "pipe all hands aft!"

("There is something amiss," thought Lance.)

In less than a minute the men were all mustered in the waist of the ship, waiting wonderingly to hear what the skipper had to say, for it was perfectly evident that Captain Staunton was about to address them. When the men were all assembled the captain turned to the passengers on the poop, and said—

"Ladies and gentlemen, have the goodness to come a little nearer me, if you please; what I have to say concerns all hands alike—those in the saloon as well as those in the forecastle."

The passengers moved forward as requested, Lance taking Blanche's hand upon his arm and giving it a little reassuring squeeze as he did so.

Captain Staunton then turned himself so that he could be heard by all, and began—

"My friends, I have called you round me in order to communicate to you all a piece of very momentous intelligence. It is of a somewhat trying nature; and therefore, before I go further, I must ask you to listen to me patiently, to obey orders implicitly, and above all, to preserve coolness and presence of mind. With these, I have not a doubt that we can successfully battle with the difficulty; without them it will be impossible for us to work effectively, and the consequences must necessarily be proportionately grave."

He paused a moment; and then, seeing that every one appeared to be perfectly cool and steady, he added—

"I greatly regret to say I have some cause for suspicion that fire has broken out somewhere below—steady, now! steady, lads; wait and hear all I have to say—I repeat I have a suspicion that fire may have broken out on board; the temperature of the saloon is unaccountably hot, and there is a strange smell below which may or may not be caused by fire. It is necessary that the matter should be looked into at once; and I ask every one here to lend me their best assistance. In case of my surmise proving correct keep cool and work your hardest, every man of you, and then there is no reason whatever why we should not come easily out of the scrape. Mr Bowles and Mr Dashwood will each take charge of his own watch. Mr Dashwood, get the fire-engine rigged and under weigh. Mr Bowles, rig the force-pump, get the deck-tubs filled, and arrange your watch in a line along the deck with all the buckets you can muster. Gentlemen," turning to the passengers, "be so good as to keep out of the men's way, and hold yourselves in readiness to assist in whatever manner may be required. Now lads, go quietly to your posts, and do your duty like Englishmen."

A Fiery Ordeal

The chief and second mates had, when named by Captain Staunton, gone down upon the main deck; and upon the conclusion of the skipper's address they at once marshalled their watches and led them to their proper stations. The third mate, boatswain, sailmaker, cook, steward, and apprentices were embodied with the chief mate's gang, part of whom were told off to work the force-pump which was to feed the tank of the fire-engine, while the remainder were formed into line along the deck to pass buckets to the seat of the fire. The fire-engine, which had luckily been frequently in use at fire-drill, was in perfect order, and the men knowing exactly what to do, it was rigged and ready for action, with tank filled, the hose screwed on and laid along the deck, in a remarkably short time.

Captain Staunton, on seeing that the men were cool and thoroughly under control, had immediately gone below again to rejoin the carpenter, whom he had left busily engaged in seeking the locality of the fire, of the actual existence of which he had no manner of doubt; indeed one had need only to go to the companion and breathe the heated and pungent atmosphere which ascended thence to have resolved any doubt he might have entertained upon the subject.

"Oh, how dreadful!" exclaimed Blanche, turning with white quivering lips to Evelin, as the skipper disappeared below; "do you think there really is fire, Mr Evelin?"

"It is quite impossible to say," answered Evelin calmly, keeping to himself his own convictions; "but if there is, it cannot have yet gained much hold, and I daresay a half an hour or so of vigorous work with the fire-engine will effectually drown it out. And if it does not; if, looking at the matter in its worst possible light, the fire should after all get the upper hand and drive us out of the ship, the night is fine, and the water smooth enough to enable us easily and comfortably to take to the boats. Then the boats themselves are amply sufficient to take everybody without crowding; they are in perfect order and the best equipped boats I have ever seen; so that let what will happen, I think we need not alarm ourselves in the least.

"I think, however," he added, the other passengers having gathered round him, "that it could do no possible harm, and might be of advantage, supposing that the worst happens, if you ladies were to go to your berths and make up a package of your warmest clothing, together with any valuables you may have with you, so as to be in perfect readiness to leave the ship, if need be. But take matters quietly, I entreat you; for I sincerely hope it will prove that there is no necessity for any such decided step."

The two girls turned away, and went together to the cabin which they jointly occupied. Mrs Staunton had already followed her husband below; and Dale also hurried away, loudly bewailing his ill-luck in ever having embarked on board such an unfortunate vessel.

"For heaven's sake follow him, Fortescue, and stop his clamour!" exclaimed Lance; "he is enough to demoralise an entire regiment, let alone a small ship's company like this."

Rex nodded, and followed his partner; seizing him by the arm and leading him aft, instead of allowing him to go below as he evidently intended:

Just then the carpenter came on deck, and advancing to the break of the poop, shouted—

"Pass along the hose, boys, and start the engine. There is a spark or two of something smouldering down below, but we'll soon have it out."

The men stationed at the engine gave a ringing cheer and, one of them starting an inspiriting shanty, began at once to work away at the handles.

"Well, this here's a pretty go, ain't it?" observed Brook, addressing himself to Evelin as the two stood together at the break of the poop, watching the men at work.

"A most unfortunate circumstance," replied Lance. "Luckily there are no signs whatever of anything approaching to panic; and if all keep as cool as they are at present, we may hope to get out of this difficulty one way or the other without mishap. You seem tolerably collected, Mr Brook; so perhaps there may be no harm in telling you that I fear matters are much more serious than they at present appear to be. All day to-day the saloon has appeared to me to be extraordinarily hot; and the presence of fire in the ship now sufficiently accounts for it. And if it has been burning for some time, it may prove to have obtained so strong a hold as to defy mastery. In such a case it behoves each one of us to set an example of quiet self-possession to all the rest. You behaved so nobly the other day during the gale that I think we may depend on you not to fail in that respect."

"Oh, I'm all right," returned Brook. "I don't believe in being put out about any think; I'm ready to help anywheres; and I'd begin at once if I knowed where I could do any good. And if the 'governor' (referring presumably to Mr Dale) makes any fuss, I shall roll 'im up in a blanket like a parcel and take care of 'im myself."

A thin vapour of smoke was by this time rising from the companion, accompanied by a strong and quite unmistakable smell of fire; and in a minute or two more Captain Staunton, in his shirt sleeves, appeared on deck and called forward for more water.

"There is rather more of it than we at first thought, lads," he said; "but stick steadily to your work and we'll conquer it yet."

The gang at the fire-engine was rapidly relieved; a fresh shanty was struck up; the chain of men with buckets got to work; and the quickened clank clank of the engine handles showed that the crew were still confident and determined.

"Now is our time," exclaimed Lance to Brook; "cut in here," as a rather wide gap in the chain of bucket-men revealed itself just at the head of the saloon staircase; and in another moment both were hard at work, with their coats off, passing buckets.

Another twenty minutes might have elapsed when Captain Staunton and the carpenter staggered together up the saloon staircase to the deck, gasping for breath, their clothes and skin grimy with smoke, and the perspiration streaming down their faces.

"Send two fresh hands below, if you please, Mr Bowles," shouted the skipper; "and you, lads, drop your buckets, and lend a hand here to cut some holes in the deck; the fire is spreading forward, and we must keep it to this end of the ship if possible."

Two of the most determined of the crew at once stepped forward and volunteered to go below; Captain Staunton nodded his permission, and led them to the scene of their labours; while the chain of men who had been passing buckets along the deck dropped them, and, under the carpenter's supervision, at once commenced the task of cutting through the deck. The smoke was by this time pouring in volumes up the companion and through the skylight. Lance had been too busy to take much notice of this whilst engaged in passing the buckets; but now that a respite came he had time to look about him. He saw the great dun cloud of smoke surging out of the companion and streaming away to leeward; and he saw indistinctly through it at intervals a small group gathered together aft by the weather taffrail. He thought he would join this group for a moment, if only to ascertain whether the girls had succeeded in securing such things as they were most anxious to save; and he sauntered toward them in his usual easy and deliberate manner. As he drew near Violet rose and said—

"Oh, Mr Evelin! I am so glad you are come; I was beginning to feel quite anxious about Blanche—but where is she; I do not see her with you?"

"She is not with me, Miss Dudley," answered Lance; "what led you to suppose she would be?"

"Not with you! Oh, Mr Evelin, where is she, then? If she is not with you she must still be in her cabin. I stayed there until the smoke was too thick to see or breathe any longer, and then I came on deck. I spoke to her, urging her to come also, and receiving no reply thought she had left without my noticing it; but she is not here anywhere."

The latter part of this speech never reached Lance's ears, for, upon fully realising that Blanche—"his own sweet darling," as he had called her in his inmost thoughts a thousand times—was missing, he darted to the companion-way and plunged down the stairs, three or four at a time, into the blinding pungent suffocating smoke which rushed momentarily in more and more dense volumes up through the opening.

On reaching the foot of the staircase, he found that several of the planks had been pulled up to allow the men tending the hose to get below the saloon floor and approach as near as possible to the seat of the fire. So dense was the smoke just here that it was only by the merest chance he escaped falling headlong into the abyss. Catching sight, however, of the aperture just in time to spring across it, he did so; and glancing back for an instant on reaching the other side, he saw a broad expanse of glowing white-hot bales of wool, and, dimly through the acrid smoke and steam, the forms of the men who were plying the engine hose.

Groping his way into the saloon, which was by this time so full of smoke that he could barely distinguish through it a feeble glimmer from the cabin lamp, he made his way in the direction of the state-room appropriated to Blanche and Violet. The smoke got into his eyes and made them water; into his throat and made him cough violently; into his lungs, producing an overpowering sense of suffocation, and impressing unmistakably upon him the necessity for rapidity and decision of movement. Blind, giddy, breathless, he staggered onward, groping for the handle of the state-room door. At length he found it, wrenched the door open, and rapidly felt with hands and feet about the floor and in each berth. No one there. Where then could Blanche be? She was not on deck, and it was hardly probable she could have fallen overboard. Then as he hastily began the search anew his foot kicked against something on the floor, which he at once picked up. It was a boot—a man's boot unmistakably, from its size and weight. This at once satisfied him that in the obscurity he had groped his way into the wrong state-room; and he must prosecute his search further.

But he was suffocating. Already his brain began to reel; there was a loud humming in his ears; his eyes ached and felt as though they would burst out of their sockets; and he found his strength ebbing away like water. Should he at once prosecute his search further? That seemed physically impossible. But if Blanche were in that fatal atmosphere she must soon die, if not dead already. And if he left the cabin to obtain a breath of fresh air was he not likely to go astray again, and lose still more precious time? No; the search must be proceeded with at once; and, reeling like a drunken man, Lance felt for the state-room door, staggered into the saloon, and felt along the bulkhead for the handle of the next door. Oh, heavens! what a search that was. His head felt as though it would burst; he gasped for breath, and inhaled nothing but hot pungent smoke; the saloon seemed to be miles instead of yards in length. Thank God! at last; the handle is found and turned, and the door flung open. Lance, with the conviction that unless he can escape in a very few seconds he will die, gropes wildly round and into the berths. Ah! what is this? Something coiled-up at the foot of the bottom berth. A human body! A woman! Lance grasps it tightly in his arms; stumbles out through the door with it, along the saloon, through the passage. A roaring as of a thousand thunders is in his ears; stars innumerable dance before his eyes; he sees as in a dream the yawning gulf in the floor; a broad glare of fierce white light reels madly to and fro before him; a confused sound of hoarse voices strikes upon his ear; he feels that the end is come—that he is dying; but with a last supreme effort he staggers up the saloon staircase to the deck, turns instinctively to windward out of the smoke, and with his precious burden still tightly clasped in his arms, falls prostrate and senseless to the deck.

Rex Fortescue, who had been present when Violet spoke to Lance of Blanche's absence, and who had witnessed the hasty departure of his friend upon his perilous search, was at the head of the companion, on his way below, having grown anxious at Lance's prolonged absence, when the latter reappeared on deck; and assistance having been hastily summoned, the pair who had so nearly met their deaths from suffocation were, with some little difficulty, at length restored to consciousness.

Meanwhile, it had become apparent to Captain Staunton that the fire was of a much more serious character than he had anticipated, and that it was every minute assuming more formidable proportions. He therefore at length decided, as a precautionary measure, to get the boats into the water without further delay. He was anxious more particularly about the launch and pinnace, as these boats were stowed over the main hatch and would have to be hoisted out by means of yard-tackles. This would be a long and difficult operation, the ship being under jury-rig; and should the fire attack the heel of the main-mast before these craft were in the water, the two largest and safest boats in the ship might be seriously damaged, if not destroyed, in the process of launching, or perhaps might defy the unaided efforts of the crew to launch them at all. There would be no difficulty about the other boats, as they could be lowered from the davits.

The mates were busy superintending and directing the efforts of their respective gangs towards the extinguishing of the fire; Captain Staunton, therefore, after a moment or two of anxious deliberation, confided to Bob the important duty of provisioning and launching the boats, giving him as assistants the cook, steward, and two able seamen, and soliciting also the aid of the male passengers.

Now it happened that the Galatea's boats were somewhat different in character from the boats usually to be found on board ship. Captain Staunton had, when quite a lad, been compelled, with the rest of the ship's company of which he was then a junior and very unimportant member, to abandon the ship and take to the boats in mid-ocean; and he then learnt a lesson which he never forgot, and formed ideas with respect to the fitting of boats which his nautical friends had been wont to rather sneer at and stigmatise as "queer." But when the Galatea was in process of fitting out he had, with some difficulty, succeeded in persuading his owners to allow him to carry out these ideas, and the boats were fitted up almost under his own eye.

The chief peculiarity of the boats lay in their keels. These were made a trifle stouter than usual, and of ordinary depth. But they were so shaped and finished that a false keel some eight or nine inches deep could be securely fastened on below in a very few minutes. This was managed by having the true keel bored in some half a dozen places along its length, and the holes "bushed" with copper. The copper bushes projected a quarter of an inch above the upper edge of the keel, and were so finished as to allow of copper caps screwing on over them, thus effectually preventing the flow of water up through the bolt-holes into the interior of the boat. The false keel was made to accurately fit the true keel, and was provided with stout copper bolts coinciding in number and position with the bolt-holes in the true keel. To fix the false keel all that was necessary was to unscrew the caps from the top of the "bushes," apply the false to the true keel, pushing the bolts up through their respective holes, and set them up tight by means of thumb-screws. The whole operation could be performed in a couple of minutes, and the boats were then fit to beat to windward to any extent.

As far as the gigs were concerned (with the exception of the whaleboat gig, which was an exquisitely modelled boat, fitted with air-chambers so as to render her self-righting and unsinkable), beyond greater attention than usual to the model of the craft, this was the only difference which Captain Staunton had thought it necessary to make between the boats of the Galatea and those of other ships; but in the cases of the launch and pinnace he had gone a step further, by fitting them with movable decks in sections, which covered in the boats forward and aft and for about a foot wide right along each side. These decks were bolted down and secured with thumb-screws to beams which fitted into sockets under the gunwale; and when the whole was once fixed each section contributed to keep all immovably in place. The decking being but light it was not difficult to fix, and in an hour after the order was given to launch the boats, the launch and pinnace were in the water alongside, and the gigs hanging at the davits ready to lower away at a moment's notice.

Thanks also to Captain Staunton's never-ceasing care with regard to the boats, they were all in perfect condition, and not leaky as baskets, as are too many boats when required to be lowered upon an unexpected emergency. The gigs and the launch were regularly half-filled with water every morning before the decks were washed down, and emptied at the conclusion of that ceremony; while the pinnace, which was stowed bottom-up in the launch, was liberally soused with water at the same time. In addition to this the proper complement of oars and rowlocks, the stretchers, boat-hook, mop, baler, anchor, rudder, yoke, and tiller, together with the compass, masts, and sails, were always stowed in the boat to which they belonged, and were carefully overhauled once every week under the skipper's own eye.

Thus, on the present occasion, there was none of that bewildered running about and searching high and low for the boats' gear; it was all at hand and ready for use whenever it might be wanted; there was nothing therefore to do but to make sure that each boat was amply provisioned. This, the launch and pinnace being safely in the water, was Bob's next task, to which he devoted himself coolly but with all alacrity.

The boats' water-breakers, which were slung, ready filled, between the fore and after gallows, under two of the gigs (each breaker bearing painted upon it the name of the boat to which it belonged), were cast adrift and passed into their proper boats as they were lowered, and then followed as large a quantity of provisions as could possibly be stowed away without too much encumbering the movements of the occupants.

Meanwhile the scuppers had all been carefully plugged up, the decks pierced, and all hands set to work with buckets, etcetera, to flood them, and still the fire increased in volume. It was 11:30 p.m. by the time that the boats were veered astern, fully equipped, and ready to receive their human freight; and at midnight the main-mast fell, flames at the same time bursting up through the saloon-companion and skylight. Upon perceiving this it became evident to Captain Staunton that it was quite hopeless to further prolong the fight; the crew had been for four hours exerting themselves to their utmost capacity, with the fire gaining steadily upon them the whole time; they were now completely exhausted, and the fire was blazing furiously almost throughout the devoted ship; he therefore considered he had done his full duty and was now quite justified in abandoning the unfortunate Galatea to her fiery doom. He accordingly gave orders for the crew to desist from their efforts, to collect their effects, and to muster again upon the quarter-deck with all possible expedition.

The men needed no second bidding, they saw that the moments of the good ship were numbered; and, throwing down whatever they happened to have in their hands, they made a rush for the forecastle, and there, in the midst of the already blinding and stifling smoke, proceeded hurriedly to gather together their few belongings.

In less than five minutes all hands were collected in the waist, waiting the order to pass over the side.

The boats had meanwhile been hauled alongside, and the ladies, with little May, carefully handed into the launch. This, when the attempt came to be made, proved a task of no little difficulty, for the ship's sides were found to be so hot that it was impossible to touch them. However, by the exercise of great caution it was accomplished without mishap; and then the male passengers were ordered down over the side, Rex and Lance going into the launch with the ladies, while Dale and Brook were told off to the pinnace. The crew were then sent down; each man as he passed over the rail being told what boat he was to go into. Mr Bowles was appointed to the command of the pinnace, and Mr Dashwood was ordered to take charge of the whaleboat gig, with six hands as his crew.

The passengers and crew of the Galatea were distributed thus:—

The launch, under the command of Captain Staunton, carried Mrs Staunton, her little daughter May, Violet Dudley, Blanche Lascelles, the bosom friends Rex and Lance, Bob and his three fellow apprentices, and the steward—twelve in all.

The pinnace, commanded by Mr Bowles, had on board Mr Forester Dale, Brook, the carpenter, the sailmaker, and two of the seamen, numbering seven all told.

The whaleboat gig, the smartest boat of the fleet, was manned, as already stated, by Mr Dashwood and six picked hands; she was to act as tender to the launch.

The second gig, of which the boatswain was given charge, carried the remainder of the crew, five in number, or six including the boatswain.

Captain Staunton was of course the last man to leave the ship, and it was not until the moment had actually arrived for him to do so that the full force of the calamity appeared to burst upon him. Up to that moment he had been working harder than any other man on board; and whilst his body had been actively engaged, his mind was no less busy devising expedients for the preservation of the noble ship with the lives and cargo which she carried, and for the safety of all of which he was responsible. But now all that was done with; the ship and cargo were hopelessly lost, and the time had come when they must be abandoned to their fate. It was true that many precious lives were still, as it were, held in his hands; that upon his skill and courage depended to a very large extent their preservation; but that was a matter for the future—the immediate future, no doubt, but at that supreme moment Captain Staunton seemed unable to think of anything but the present—that terrible present in which he must abandon to the devouring flames the beautiful fabric which had borne them all so gallantly over so many thousand leagues of the pathless ocean, through light and darkness, through sunshine and tempest, battling successfully with the wind and the wave in their most unbridled fury, to succumb helplessly at last under the insidious attack of that terrible enemy fire.

The last of the crew had passed down over the side and had been received into the boat to which he was appointed; the boats had all (excepting the launch) shoved off from the ship's side and retired to a distance at which the fierce heat of the victorious flames were no longer a discomfort, and it was now high time that the skipper himself should also leave. The flames were roaring and leaping below, above, and around him; the scorching air was surging about him, torrents of sparks were whirling around him, yet he seemed unable to tear himself away. There he stood in the gangway, his head bare, with his cap in his hand, and his eyes roving lingeringly and lovingly fore and aft, and then aloft to the blazing spars and sails. At length the fore-mast was seen to tremble and totter, it wavered for a moment, and then with a crash and in a cloud of fiery sparks plunged hissing over the side, the opposite side, fortunately, to that on which the launch lay. This aroused Captain Staunton; he gazed about him a single moment longer in a dazed bewildered way, and then, as the ship rolled and the launch rose upon a sea, sprang lightly down into the boat, and in a voice stern with emotion, gave the order to shove off.

"Oh, papa," cried little May, "I's so glad you's come; I sought you weren't coming;" and the sweet little creature threw her arms lovingly about her father's neck.

Do not deem him unmanly that he hid his eyes for a moment on his child's shoulder, perchance to pray for her safety in the trials, the troubles, and the dangers which now lay before them. Then handing the little one back to her mother, he hailed in a cheery voice the rest of the boats to close round the launch as soon as she had withdrawn to a safe distance.

In a few minutes the little fleet lay on their oars close together, at a distance of about a hundred yards from the blazing ship. Captain Staunton then in a few well-chosen words first thanked all hands for the strenuous efforts they had made to save the ship; and then explained to them his plans for the future. He proposed in the first place, he said, to remain near the Galatea as long as she floated; because if any other craft happened to be in their neighbourhood, her crew would be certain to notice the light of the fire and bear down to see what it meant, in which case they would be spared the necessity for a long voyage in the boats. But if no friendly sail appeared within an hour or two of the destruction of their own ship, it was his intention to continue in the boats the course to Valparaiso which they had been steering when the fire broke out. By his reckoning they were a trifle over eighteen hundred miles from this port—a long distance, no doubt; but he reminded them that they were in the Pacific, and might reasonably hope for moderately fine weather; their boats were all in perfect order, well supplied, and in good sailing trim, instead of being loaded down to the gunwale, as was too often the case when a crew were compelled to abandon their ship; and he believed that, unless some unforeseen circumstance occurred to delay them, they could make the passage in a fortnight. And finally he expressed a hope that all hands would maintain strict discipline and cheerfully obey the orders of their officers, as upon this would to a very great extent depend their ultimate safety.

His address was responded to with a ringing cheer; after which the occupants of the various boats subsided into silence and sat watching the burning ship.

The Galatea was by this time a mass of flame fore and aft. Her masts were gone, her decks had fallen in, and her hull above water was in several places red-hot; while as she rolled heavily on the long swell, burying her heated sides gunwale-deep in the water, great clouds of steam rose up like the smoke of a broadside, and hid her momentarily from view.

The fire continued to blaze more and more fiercely as it spread among the cargo, until about a couple of hours after the boats had left the ship, when the intense and long-continued heat appeared to cause some rivets to give way, or to destroy some of the iron plates; for a great gap suddenly appeared in the Galatea's side, a long strip of plating curling up and shrivelling away like a sheet of paper, and momentarily revealing the white-hot contents of the glowing told; then the water poured in through the orifice; there was a sudden upbursting of a vast cloud of steam accompanied by a mighty hissing sound; the hull appeared to writhe like a living thing in mortal agony; and then—darkness upon the face of the waters. The scorched and distorted shell of iron which had once been as gallant a ship as ever rode the foam was gone from sight for ever.

At the Mercy of Wind and Wave

The silence which followed the disappearance of the Galatea was broken by a plaintive wail from little May, who sobbed out that she was "Oh! so sorry that poor papa's beautiful ship was all burned up."

Her sorrows, however, were speedily charmed away by the representation made to her by her mother that if the ship had not been burnt they would probably never have thought of going for a delightful sail in the boats, as they now were; and soon afterwards the poor overtired child fell into a deep dreamless sleep in her mother's arms.

As everything had been made ready in the launch before she left the ship's side, the ladies had now nothing to do but make themselves thoroughly comfortable for the night on and among the blankets and skin rugs which had been arranged for them in the stern-sheets.

A cosy enough little cabin, of necessarily very limited dimensions, was also arranged in the bows of the boat for the gentlemen; and to this, upon Captain Staunton's assurance that their services would certainly not be needed for at least some hours, Rex and Lance betook themselves, accompanied by Bob and young Neville, the former of whom was to keep watch alternately with the skipper.

The night now being so far advanced, Captain Staunton announced to the occupants of the other boats his intention to wait for daylight before making sail; and, the tired crews at once composing themselves to slumber, silence soon fell upon the little fleet of boats which lay there riding lightly over the majestic slowly-heaving swell of the Pacific under the solemn starlight.

The hours of night passed peacefully away; and the watchers on board the several boats at length saw the velvety darkness in the eastern quarter paling before the approaching day. The stars, which but a short time before had risen into view over the dark rim of the horizon, dwindled into lustreless insignificance and finally disappeared; the sky grew momentarily paler and bluer in tint, the light sweeping imperceptibly higher and wider over the ethereal vault; then suddenly above the eastern horizon appeared a faint delicate rosy flush, followed by a brilliant golden pencilling of the lower edges of a few flecks of cloud invisible before: long shafts of golden light sprang radiating upward from a point below the horizon; and in another moment the upper edge of a great golden disc rose into view, flooding the laughing waves with shimmering radiance, and transforming in a moment the hitherto silent and sombre scene into one of joyousness and life. Sea birds hovered screaming high in the air, on the look-out for breakfast; flying-fish sparkled like glittering gems out of the bosom of the heaving deep; dolphins leaped and darted here and there; a school of porpoises rotated lazily past, heading to the westward; and away upon the very verge of the horizon a large school of whales appeared spouting and playing.

It was day again.

Bob at once, in accordance with his instructions, called Captain Staunton, who had lain down an hour or two before to snatch a little rest. The skipper, who had turned-in "all standing," that is to say, without undressing, soon made his appearance; and, first glancing keenly all round the horizon in the vain hope of discovering a sail, at once hailed the other boats, ordering them to make sail and to proceed upon a north-easterly course, extending themselves in line to the right and left, and to maintain as great a distance apart during the day as would be compatible with an easy interchange of communication by signal; to keep a sharp look-out all day; and to close in again upon the launch at nightfall.

The order was promptly obeyed, and in five minutes afterwards the little fleet were dancing gaily along over the low liquid hills of the Pacific swell, tossing tiny showers of spray out on each side from their bows, and leaving a long glistening wake of miniature whirlpools behind them.

The slight bustle of making sail on the boats, combined with the novelty of their situation, was sufficient to rouse all hands; and a few minutes after the boats were fairly under weigh, the ladies and little May emerged from their quarters in the stern-sheets of the launch. The excitement of the previous night had been completely overcome by the fatigue of preparation to desert the ship, and the lateness of the hour of retirement had secured for these, our heroines, a few hours of sound repose, so that when they made their appearance aft, refreshed by sleep and exhilarated by the pure bracing morning breeze, they looked and felt as little like castaways as one can well imagine. Indeed, they appeared more disposed to regard the adventure as a pleasantly exciting escapade than anything else—a state of feeling which the gentlemen of the party were careful to foster and encourage by every means in their power, judging it highly probable that there would be enough and more than enough to damp their high spirits before this singular boat-voyage, just commenced, should be over.

On board the launch, the fortunes of which we propose to follow for the present, all was pleasant activity. Even the skipper, whose reflections must necessarily have been of a somewhat sombre character, glad to observe such a prevalence of good spirits among his fellow voyagers, resolutely put all disagreeable thoughts behind him, and chimed in with the others, feeling the importance of prolonging to its utmost extent so favourable and pleasant a state of affairs.

Lance, whose experiences in the Australian bush had evidently made him fertile of resource, now rummaged out from among his baggage a diminutive but effective cooking apparatus, the fuel for which was supplied from a goodly jar of spirit stowed away in the eyes of the boat; and, initiating the steward into the peculiarities of its management and explaining to him its capabilities, an appetising breakfast of coffee and fried chops, cut from the carcass of a sheep hastily slaughtered the previous night, was soon served out to the occupants of the boat. Fishing-lines were afterwards produced, and, if the sport was meagre and the amount of fish captured but small, the expedient had at least the good effect of providing occupation and amusement for the ladies during the greater part of the day. As the weather continued fine, and there was absolutely nothing to do but to steer the boat upon a given course and keep a bright look-out, Captain Staunton seized the opportunity to take a good long spell of sleep, not only to make up for that lost on the previous night, but also to lay in a stock, as it were, against the time when probably many long and weary hours would have to be passed without it. Lance and Rex took the helm in turns throughout the day, while the ladies tended the fishing-lines, chatted with their male companions, or played with little May, as the humour took them. About an hour before sunset a small red flag was hoisted on board the launch as a signal for the other boats to close, the signal being repeated by each boat as soon as it was observed and kept flying until the most distant craft had answered it by bearing up or hauling to the wind as the case might be; and by the time that the stars were fairly out the little fleet was once more sailing along in a close and compact body.

So ended the first day in the boats.

This pleasant and satisfactory state of affairs lasted for five days, and then came a change. On the afternoon of the fifth day light fleecy vapours began to gather in the sky, growing thicker as the afternoon waned, until by sunset the entire canopy of heaven was veiled by huge masses of dense slate-coloured cloud, which swept heavily across the firmament from the eastward. The aneroid which Captain Staunton had ordered to be put oh board the launch indicated a considerable decrease of atmospheric pressure, which, coupled with the appearance of the sky, led the skipper to believe that bad weather was at hand; accordingly, when the other boats closed in upon the launch at sundown, word was passed along the line to keep a sharp look-out and to be prepared for any change which might occur.

About nine p.m. the wind died almost completely away; and shortly afterwards a few heavy drops of rain fell, speedily followed by a drenching shower. This killed the remaining light air of wind, and the boats lay idly upon the water, their saturated canvas flapping heavily against the masts. But not for long; the sails were speedily lowered down and spread across from gunwale to gunwale to catch the precious moisture, and so heavy was the downpour that in the quarter of an hour during which the shower lasted the voyagers were enabled to almost entirely refill their breakers, the contents of which had by this time very materially diminished.

The rain ceased suddenly, and a few minutes afterwards a puff of wind, hot as the breath of a furnace, swept over the boats from the north-east, and passed away, leaving a breathless calm as before. This was repeated twice or thrice; and then with a heavier puff than before a stiff breeze set in from the north-east, breaking off the boats from their course, and necessitating their hauling close upon a wind on the port tack.

By midnight the wind had increased so much that it became necessary to reef; the launch and pinnace double-reefing their canvas in order that they might not run away from the other boats. The sea now began to rise rapidly, and when day at length broke it revealed a dismal picture of dark tempestuous sky, leaden-grey ocean, its surface broken up into high, racing, foam-capped seas, and the little fleet of boats tossing wildly upon the angry surges, the launch leading, the pinnace next, and the others so far astern that it took Captain Staunton quite ten minutes to satisfy himself that they were all still in sight.

It was by this time blowing a moderate gale, and appearances seemed to indicate that downright bad weather was not far off; the captain decided, therefore, to heave-to at once, as it would be quite impossible in any other way to keep the little fleet together. The canvas on board the launch was accordingly still further reduced, the jib-sheet hauled over to windward, and the boat left to fight it out as best she could. The pinnace soon afterwards joined company and followed suit, the remainder of the boats doing the same as they came up.

As the day wore on the gale increased in strength, the sea rising proportionally and flinging the boats about like corks upon its angry surface. So violent was the motion that it was only with the utmost difficulty the steward succeeded in preparing a hot meal at mid-day, and when evening came our adventurers were obliged to content themselves with what Lance laughingly called "a cold collation." The day was indeed a wretched one; there was no temptation whatever to leave such slight shelter as the tiny cabins afforded, for the launch, and indeed all the other boats as well, were constantly enveloped in spray blown from the caps of the seas by the wind, while, cooped up below, it was unpleasantly warm, and the motion of the boat was so violent that her occupants were compelled to wedge themselves firmly in one position to avoid being dashed against their companions.

If the day was one of discomfort, the night which followed was infinitely worse. The gale continued steadily to increase; the sea rose to a tremendous height, breaking heavily; the spray flew continuously over the launch in drenching showers; the little craft, under the merest shred of canvas, was careened gunwale-to by the force of the wind every time she rose upon the crest of a sea, and the most watchful care of the skipper, who had stationed himself at the helm, was sometimes insufficient to prevent a more than ordinarily heavy sea from breaking on board. The increasing frequency of these occurrences at length necessitated the maintenance of one hand continually at the baler in order to keep the boat free of water, and in spite of all the ladies were unable to escape a thorough wetting. Nor was this the worst mishap. The water rose so high in the interior of the boat on one or two occasions that it got at the provisions, so seriously damaging some of them that there was little hope of their being rendered again fit for consumption. It was a most fortunate circumstance for those in the launch that, thanks to the captain's foresight, she had been fitted with a partial deck, otherwise she must inevitably have been swamped. How it fared with the other boats it was impossible to say; the darkness was too profound to permit of their being seen, if they still remained afloat; but the manner in which the launch suffered caused the skipper to entertain the gravest apprehensions for the rest of the fleet, and he almost dreaded the return of daylight lest it should reveal to him the realisation of his worst fears.

It seemed to the occupants of the launch as though that miserable night would never end. The tardy dawn, however, made its appearance at last, reluctantly, as it seemed to those drenched and weary watchers, and the moment that there was light enough to enable him to see distinctly Captain Staunton staggered to his feet, and steadying himself by grasping the boat's main-mast, took a long anxious look all round the horizon. At first he could distinguish nothing save the wildly rushing foam-capped seas, and the scurrying shreds of cloud which swept rapidly athwart the black and stormy sky; but after some minutes of painfully anxious scrutiny he descried, about three miles away to leeward, a tiny dark object, appearing at intervals against the leaden-grey of the horizon, which his seaman's eye told him was the pinnace.

The remainder of the fleet had disappeared.

It was no more than a realisation of his forebodings; but Captain Staunton possessed far too feeling a heart not to be powerfully affected by the loss of the two boats and the thirteen brave fellows who manned them. He ran over their names mentally, and recalled that no less than nine of the thirteen had arranged for half their pay to be handed over to their families at home; and he pictured to himself the bitter grief and distress there would be in those nine families when it came to be known that the husband, the father, the bread-winner was gone, overwhelmed and swallowed up by the remorseless ocean which knows no pity, not even for the wife and the helpless children.

With a powerful effort the captain dismissed these painful reflections from his mind, and turned his attention to matters nearer home. He had already searchingly scrutinised the aspect of the weather with most unsatisfactory results. As far as his experience went there was every prospect of a continuance—nay more, an increase—of the gale. The sky to windward looked wilder and more threatening than ever; while that the sea was still rising was a fact about which there could be no mistake. He dived into the little cabin or shelter aft, and took a long look at the aneroid, to find that it still manifested a downward tendency. It was evidently hopeless to expect a favourable change in the weather for some hours at least, and to attempt any longer to maintain the boat's position, in the face of an increasing gale, was to expose her and those in her to imminent risk of destruction; he therefore decided to watch his opportunity and seize the first favourable moment for bearing up and running before it.

Bob and his fellow apprentices, together with Lance and Rex, were soon summoned, and preparations made for bearing up. It was an anxious moment, for should the boat be caught broadside-on by a breaking sea she would to a dead certainty be turned bottom-up, when nothing could save her occupants.

Captain Staunton stood at the tiller, intently watching the onward rush of the mountainous seas as they came swooping down with upreared threatening crests upon the launch. Presently, as the boat fell off a trifle from the wind and the main-sail filled, he gave the order to "let draw the jib-sheet." The weather sheet was let go and the lee one hauled in like lightning, and the boat began to forge ahead. A sea came swooping down upon the little craft, but it was not a dangerous one; the skipper sent the boat manfully at it, and with a wild bound she rose over the crest and plunged into the liquid valley beyond. The next sea was a much more formidable one, but by luffing the boat just in the nick of time she went through and over it, with no worse consequences than the shipping of a dozen or so buckets of water, a mishap to which they were by this time growing quite accustomed, and then there occurred a very decided "smooth."

"Brail up the main-sail, boys," shouted the skipper cheerily, and in a second it was done; the helm was put up, the boat's head fell off, and away she went with a rush, broadside-on to the sea. With a sickening heave she rose into the air as the next sea lifted her, and this time too a little water came on board, but nothing to speak of; and by the time the next wave caught her, her quarter was fairly turned to it, and she was rushing away before the wind. The fore-sail was then set and the main-sail stowed, and everybody sat down to watch the result.

The change was certainly for the better; for though a sea still occasionally broke on board it did so with less violence than before, and most of it now flowed off the deck and overboard again, instead of falling into the body of the boat as before.

As soon as the fore-sail was set, Captain Staunton steered for the pinnace, with the intention of ordering her also to bear up, as well as to inquire whether they had seen either of the other boats.

Suddenly, Bob, who was watching the little speck in the distance which showed against the horizon when both launch and pinnace happened to be on the summit of a wave together, caught sight for a single instant of what appeared to him to be an attempt at a signal made on board the latter.

"Hillo!" he exclaimed, "What's wrong with the pinnace? They're waving to us, sir."

"Indeed!" said the skipper in a tone of concern. "Are you sure, Bob? Here, take the tiller for a moment and let me have a look. Keep her dead before it."

"Ay, ay, sir," responded Bob, as he changed places with his superior; the latter going forward and steadying himself by the fore-mast as he watched for the reappearance of the pinnace.

Presently he caught sight of her, and caught sight too, most unmistakably, of a flag—or something doing duty therefor—being very energetically waved on board.

"You are right, Bob," he sharply exclaimed, "they are signalling us. I fervently hope there is nothing wrong with them. Starboard a little; there, steady so. Keep her at that as long as you can, and only run her off when it is absolutely necessary in order to avoid a breaking sea."

In about twenty minutes the launch had reached the pinnace. As the two boats closed, it was seen that all hands on board her were busy baling; and she appeared to be low in the water. When the launch was near enough for a hail to be heard, Mr Bowles stood up and, placing his two hands together at his mouth, so as to form an impromptu speaking trumpet, shouted—

"Can you make room for us on board the launch, Captain Staunton? We are stove and sinking."

"Ay, ay," responded the skipper. "We'll round-to and come alongside."

He then sprang aft to the tiller, which he seized, shouting at the same time, "To your stations, lads! In with the fore-sail, smartly now."

The sail was speedily taken in; the close-reefed main-sail was set; and the moment that the sheet was hauled aft the helm was jammed hard down and the boat brought to the wind, without wasting a moment to watch for a favourable opportunity. The launch was flying swiftly away from the pinnace, and the latter was sinking; there was therefore no time for watching for opportunities; by the frantic way in which Mr Bowles resumed his task of baling the instant that he had communicated his momentous tidings Captain Staunton saw that the danger on board the pinnace was imminent; and the boat was at once rounded-to, shipping in the operation a sea which half-filled her.

"Man the buckets, every man of you," shouted the skipper as the launch, now close-hauled, began slowly to forge ahead in the direction of the devoted pinnace. The seas broke heavily against the bows of the boat as they swept furiously down upon her; but Bob and his comrades baled like madmen, while the skipper handled the little craft like the consummate seaman he was; and between them all, they managed to keep her above water.

"Drop your bucket, Bob, and stand by to heave them a line," presently shouted the captain. Bob sprang forward, and seized the end of the long painter which was neatly coiled-up and stopped with a ropeyarn or two.

Whipping open his knife he quickly severed the stops, and was just arranging the coil in his hand when Captain Staunton cried sharply—

"Heave with a will, Bob. There she goes!"

Bob glanced at the pinnace, now some twenty feet distant, just in time to see a heavy sea break fairly on board the water-logged boat and literally bury her. There was a wild cry from her occupants, as they felt the boat sinking under them, and in another instant they were left struggling for their lives in the furious sea.

Bob hove the line with all his strength, and with unerring aim into the midst of the little crowd of drowning human beings, and then called for assistance. Some of them he saw had seized it; and he at once began to haul in. The other apprentices with Lance and Rex sprang to his aid, and presently hauled on board Brook and one of the seamen.

By this time the launch had crept up to the spot where the pinnace had disappeared; and by reaching out their hands those on board were able to seize and drag inboard three more of the drowning men.

Mr Bowles' body, however, was seen floating face downwards some five-and-twenty feet away; and, close to it, Mr Forester Dale struggling desperately, and uttering wild screams which were every moment changed to choking sobs as the pitiless sea broke relentlessly over his head.

It was Bob who first caught sight of these two; and without an instant's pause or hesitation he sprang headlong from the launch's gunwale, and with a few powerful strokes reached the struggler. Mr Dale promptly flung both arms and legs round his would-be deliverer, clasping Bob like a vice, and pinioning him so completely that he was unable to move hand or foot. The result was that both instantly sank beneath the surface. Poor Bob thought for a second or two that his last hour was come; and there, in the depths of that wildly-raging sea, he lifted up his whole heart to God in a momentary but earnest prayer for mercy and forgiveness. Doubtless that swift prayer was heard, for as it flashed from his heart he felt his companion's grip relaxing, and in another instant he had wrenched himself free and was striking strongly upward, with one hand firmly grasping Mr Forester Dale by the collar of his coat.

Bob rose to the surface within a few feet of Mr Bowles' still floating body; and with a violent effort he soon succeeded in reaching it, knowing that, encumbered as he was, he would have to trust the launch to come to him, he could never reach her. As he seized his staunch friend and superior officer by the hair and twisted him over on his back he heard a wild cheer, instantly followed by a cheery shout of "Look out for the line, Bob!"

As the sound reached him the rope came flying over him, striking him sharply in the face. He seized it with his teeth; and then heard the skipper's voice say—

"Haul in handsomely now, and take care you don't jerk; he has gripped it with his teeth."

A very few seconds afterwards, which, however appeared an age to Bob, and he found himself floating alongside the launch, where he was speedily relieved of his two inanimate charges, and finally dragged on board himself, half-drowned, with about ten feet of water in his hold as he expressed it, but full of pluck as ever.

The first business claiming attention was of course that of endeavouring to restore consciousness to the inanimate bodies of Mr Dale and the chief mate; and this was at length achieved. Mr Dale was the first to come round; and as soon as he was so far recovered as to be able to speak he was stowed away in the men's sleeping berth forward, and made as comfortable as circumstances would permit. He lay there, warmly wrapped up, bemoaning for a time his hard fate in ever having come to sea, but at length the spirits which had been liberally poured down his throat took effect, and he dropped off to sleep.

Mr Bowles' case was somewhat more serious, he having received a violent blow on the head from some of the floating wreckage, just after the foundering of the pinnace. The blow had inflicted a long scalp-wound from which the blood flowed freely; and when he at length revived he seemed quite dazed and light-headed, so that it was impossible to get a coherent reply to any of the questions put to him. He too was at last stowed away forward; and Bob, who was somewhat exhausted by his exertions in the water, and scarcely fit for other work, was detailed to watch by and attend to the two invalids.

The launch had in the meantime been once more got before the wind, and was again flying to leeward under jib and fore-sail, the mountain-seas pursuing her and necessitating the utmost watchfulness on the part of the helmsman to prevent her from being broached-to.

As soon as the two invalids had been satisfactorily disposed of, the order for breakfast was given; and after a vast amount of trouble the meal, consisting of biscuits, fried rashers of bacon, and hot coffee, was served. The company were indebted to the efforts of Rex and Lance for the cooking; they having taken counsel together and come to the conclusion that after a night of such great discomfort it was absolutely necessary that the females at least should be served with a good substantial hot meal; and they had accordingly joined forces in the preparation of the same, Lance seating himself coolly in the bottom of the boat, with the water washing all round him, and balancing the cooking apparatus carefully on his knees while Rex knelt before him enacting the part of chief cook.

This meal, unromantic as it may sound to say so, was inexpressibly comforting to those weak women and poor little May, all of them having passed a wretched sleepless night, cooped up in the close confined covered-in space in the stern of the launch, which, for want of a more appropriate name has been termed a cabin, with the water in the bottom of the boat surging up round them and wetting them to the skin as the boat tossed on the angry surges, while the continuous breaking of the seas on board filled their souls with dread that the boat could not possibly outlive the gale much longer.

When all hands were fairly settled down to the discussion of breakfast, Captain Staunton turned to the carpenter, who had established himself close beside the skipper, and said—

"Now, Chips, let us hear how the mishap came about whereby you lost the pinnace this morning;—but, before you answer me that question, tell me do you know anything about the other boats?"

"Well, sir," responded Chips, "I can't say as I do, rightly. But when day broke this mornin' an' we first missed 'em, Mister Bowles, he jumped up and took a good look round, and the first thing he made out were the launch away to wind'ard, hove-to. Then he had another good look all round, and presently I see him put his hand up to his eyes and stand looking away down to leeward. 'Do you see anythink, sir?' says I. And he says—still with his hand up shadin' his eyes—'I don't know, Chips,' says he, 'but I'm most certain,' says he, 'that one of them boats is thereaway,' pointin' with his finger away down to leeward. 'It's too dark and thick down there to see werry distinctly,' he says, 'but every now and then I keeps fancyin' I can see a small dark spot like a boat's sail showin' up in the middle of the haze,' says he. And I don't doubt, sir," continued Chips, "but what he did see one of them boats; Mr Bowles has a eye, as we all knows, sir, what ain't very often deceived."

"In which case," remarks the skipper, thinking aloud rather than addressing the carpenter, "there can be no doubt that the officer in charge, finding it impossible to face the gale any longer in safety, bore up like ourselves, only a little earlier. And if one of the boats did so, why not the other? And why should they not both be safely scudding before it at this moment, some ten miles or so ahead of us?"

"Very true, sir; I don't doubt but it's just as you say, sir," responded the carpenter, who was in some uncertainty as to whether he was expected to reply to the skipper's remark or not.

"We will hope so at all events, Chips," cheerily returned the skipper. "And now tell me how you managed to get the pinnace stove?"

"Well, sir, the fact is, it were just the doin' of that miserable creatur, Mister Dale. Our water were gettin' low; and yesterday Mr Bowles ups and puts us on 'lowance—a pint a day for each man. Well, I s'pose it weren't enough for this here Mister Dale; he got thirsty durin' the night, and made his way to the water-breakers to get a drink on the quiet. And he was that sly over it that nobody noticed him. Hows'ever, like the lubber he is—axing your pardon humbly, sir, for speakin' disrespectable of one of your passengers, sir—he lets the dipper slip in between the breakers; and in tryin' to get it out again he managed to cast off the lashin's; two of the breakers struck adrift; and before we could do anything with 'em they had started three of the planks, makin' the boat leak that bad that, as you saw yourself, sir, it were all we could do to keep her above water until you reached us."

Captain Staunton made no comment upon this communication, though it is probable that he thought all the more. The loss of the pinnace was, particularly at this juncture, a most serious misfortune. For at the very time when, in consequence of the bad weather with which she had to contend, it was of the utmost importance that the launch should be in the best possible trim, she was suddenly encumbered with the additional weight of seven extra men, which, with the twelve persons previously on board, raised her complement to nineteen, and caused her to be inconveniently crowded. Then these additional seven men had to be fed out of the rapidly diminishing stores belonging to the launch, for not an ounce of anything had been saved from the pinnace. This rendered it imperatively necessary that all hands should at once be put upon a very short allowance of food and water; a hardship trying enough to the men of the party, but doubly so to the women and poor little May. However, no one murmured or offered the slightest objection to the arrangement, when at mid-day Captain Staunton explained the state of affairs and laid before the party his proposal. Except Mr Dale. That individual, on hearing the proposition, promptly crawled out of his snug shelter, and hastened to remind the skipper that he, the speaker, was an invalid; that his health, already undermined by the privations and exposure which he had been lately called upon to suffer, had been completely broken up, and his nervous system shattered by his recent immersion; that what might be perfectly right and proper treatment for people in a state of robust health—as everybody in the boat, excepting himself, appeared to be—would be followed by the most disastrous consequences if applied to himself; and that, finally, he begged to remind Captain Staunton that he had duly paid his passage-money, and, ill or well, should expect to be fully supplied with everything necessary for his comfort. Captain Staunton looked at the objector for some moments in dead silence, being positively stricken dumb with amazement. Then in accents of the bitterest scorn he burst out with—

"You despicable wretch! Is it actually possible, sir, that you have no sense whatever of shame?—that you are so full of selfishness that there is no room in you for any other feeling? Are you forgetful of the fact, Mr Dale, that it is to your greed and clumsiness we are indebted for the greatly increased hardships of our situation? But for you, sir, the pinnace would probably have been still afloat; yet you are the one who presumes to murmur at the privations of which you are the direct cause. I wish to Heaven I had never seen your face; you positively make me feel ashamed of my sex and of my species."

"That's all very well," sneeringly retorted this contemptible creature, "but I didn't come to sea to be bullied by you, so I shall withdraw from your exceedingly objectionable neighbourhood; and if ever we reach England I'll make you smart for your barbarous treatment of me, my good fellow."

Saying which, he slunk away back in no very dignified fashion to the most comfortable spot he could find in the bows of the boat, and rolled himself snugly up once more in the shawls and blankets which the women had eagerly given up for his benefit when he was first fished out of the water.

THE ALBATROSS

All that day the launch continued to scud before the gale; getting pooped so often that it was the work of two men to keep her free of water.

Toward evening Mr Bowles came aft, reporting himself "all ataunto" once more, and ready to resume duty. He still looked pale and haggard, but was as keen and determined as ever; and he demurred so vehemently to Captain Staunton's suggestion that he would be all the better for a whole night between the blankets that the skipper was at last compelled to give in, which he did with—it must be confessed—a feeling of the greatest relief that he now had so trusty a coadjutor to share the watches with him; for since the springing up of the gale the poor fellow had scarcely closed his eyes.

The night shut down "as dark as a wolf's mouth,"—to use the skipper's own metaphor; and the chief mate took the first watch, with Bob on the look-out.

It must have been somewhere about six bells, or 11 p.m., when the latter was startled by seeing the crest of the sea ahead of him breaking in a cloud of phosphoric foam over some object directly in line with the launch's bow.

"Keep her away, sir!" he yelled. "Starboard, for your life, starboard hard!"

Up went the boat's helm in an instant; and as she dragged heavily on the steep incline of the wave which had just swept under her, Bob saw floating close past a large mass of tangled wreckage, consisting of a ship's lower-mast with the heel of the topmast still in its place, and yards, stays, shrouds, braces, etcetera, attached. Dark as was the night there was no difficulty whatever in identifying the character of the wreckage, for it floated in a regular swirl of lambent greenish phosphorescent light.

"Stand by with the boat-hook, there forward," shouted Mr Bowles, "and see if you can get hold of a rope's-end. If you can, we will anchor to the wreck; and we shall ride to leeward of it as snug as if we were in the London Dock—almost."

As he spoke, he skilfully luffed the boat up under the lee of the mass; and Bob, with a vigorous sweep or two of the boat-hook, managed to fish up the standing part of the main brace with the block still attached. Through this block he rove the end of the launch's painter, and belayed it on board, thus causing her to ride to the wreckage by a sort of slip-line. The other apprentices meanwhile lost no time in taking in and stowing the canvas; and in a few minutes the launch was riding at her floating anchor in perfect safety and in comparative comfort; still tossing wildly, it is true, but no longer shipping a drop of water excepting the spray which blew over her from the seas as they broke on the wreckage.

Toward noon on the following day the gale broke; and by sunset it had moderated to a strong breeze. On that evening they were blessed with a glimpse of the sun once more, for just before the moment of his setting the canopy of cloud which had hung overhead for so long broke up, leaving great gaps through which the blue sky could be seen, and revealing the glorious luminary upon the verge of the western horizon, surrounded by a magnificent framework of jagged and tattered clouds, the larger masses of which were of a dull purplish hue, with blotches of crimson here and there, and with edges of the purest gold; while the smaller fragments streamed athwart the sky, lavishly painted with the richest tints of the rainbow.

They hung on to the wreckage all that night, the wind being still against them; and the next morning Lance, suspecting that there might be a few fish congregated about the mass of broken spars, as is frequently the case, roused out the lines and managed to hook over a dozen gaudily marked and curiously shaped fish of decent size, the whole of which were devoured with the greatest gusto that day at dinner, notwithstanding the rather repulsive aspect which some of them presented.

That night the wind, which had dwindled away to a gentle breeze, changed, and blew once more from the westward; and the sea having also gone down to a great extent, our adventurers cast off from the wreckage which had so opportunely provided them with a shelter from the fury of the gale, and with whole canvas and flowing sheets stood away once more on a north-easterly course.

In addition to the delay which the gale had occasioned them, Captain Staunton estimated that they had been driven fully five hundred miles directly out of their course; after a very careful inspection therefore of their stock of provisions the skipper was reluctantly compelled to order a further reduction in the daily allowance of food and water served out.

And now the sufferings of those on board the launch commenced in grim earnest. The women, especially, as might be expected, soon began to feel their privations acutely. Buffeted as they had been by the gale, they were completely exhausted, and needed rest and an abundance of nourishing food rather than to be placed on short commons. They bore their privations, however, with a quiet fortitude which ought to have silenced in shame the querulous complaints and murmurings of Mr Dale; though it did not. The most distressing part of it all was to hear poor little May Staunton piteously crying for water, "'cause I'm so veddy thirsty mama," as the dear child explained. She was not old enough to understand the possibility of a state of things wherein food and drink were scarcities; and her reproachful looks at her father when he was obliged to refuse her request almost broke his heart. Not, it must be understood, that she was limited to the same quantity of water as the others. The men—always excepting Mr Dale—preferred to suffer in a heightened degree the fiery torture of thirst themselves, rather than to see the child suffer; and they quietly arranged among themselves to contribute each as much as he felt he could possibly spare of the now precious liquid, as it was daily served out to them, and to store it up in a bottle which was to be May's exclusive property. And the same in the matter of food. It was wholly in vain that the child's father protested against this sacrifice; they were one and all firm as adamant upon this point; and he, poor man, notwithstanding his anxiety that all should be treated with equal fairness, could not contest their determination with any great strength of will. Was she not his own and only child, for whom he would cheerfully have laid down his life; and how could he urge with any strength a point which would have resulted in a dreadful deprivation and a terrible increase of suffering to the winning and helpless little creature? Therefore he at last contented himself with pouring the whole of his daily allowance of water into May's bottle, and cheerfully submitted for her innocent sake to endure the tortures of the damned.

Reader, have you ever experienced the torment of thirst while exposed in an open boat to the blazing rays of the pitiless sun? You have not? Then thank God for it, and earnestly pray that you never may; for none can realise or even faintly imagine the intensity of the suffering but those who have borne it.

The women, from whom it was of course impossible to conceal the circumstance that May was receiving more than her own share of food and water, were anxious to follow the example of their male companions by also setting apart a portion of their own allowance for the use of the child, but this was at once decidedly vetoed; yet they were not so easily to be deterred from their generous disposition, and many a sip and many a morsel which could ill be spared did the poor little child receive from their sympathetic and loving hands.

"After the storm comes the calm," says the proverb, and its truth was fully borne out in the present instance.

On the fourth day after casting off from the wreckage the wind began to drop, and by sunset it had fallen so light that the launch had barely steerage-way. This was still another misfortune, for if the calm continued it would seriously delay their progress and thereby protract their sufferings. Next to a gale of wind, indeed, a calm and its consequent delay was what they had most to dread, for they were in a part of the ocean little frequented by craft of any description, except a stray whaler now and then, and their only reasonable hope of salvation rested upon the possibility of their being able to reach land before starvation and thirst overcame them.

Mr Bowles had the first watch, and Bob was posted at the now all but useless helm. The wind had subsided until it was faint as the breath of a sleeping infant, and the boat's sails flapped gently against the masts as she rode with a scarcely perceptible swinging motion over the long stately slow-moving swell which followed her. The vast blue-black dome of the heavens above was devoid of the faintest trace of cloud, and the countless stars which spangled the immeasurable vault beamed down upon the tiny waif with a soft and mellow splendour which was repeated in the dark bosom of the scarcely ruffled ocean, where the reflected starbeams mingled, far down in its mysterious depths, with occasional faint gleams and flashes of pale greenish phosphorescent light. The thin golden crescent of the young moon hung low down in the velvety darkness of the western sky, and a long thin thread of amber radiance streamed from the horizon beneath her toward the boat, becoming more and more wavering and broken up as it neared her, until within some twenty fathoms of the launch it dwindled away to a mere occasional fluttering gleam. A great and solemn silence prevailed, upon which such slight sounds as the flap of the sails, the pattering of the reef-points, the creak of the rudder, or the stir of some uneasy sleeper broke with almost painful distinctness.

Mr Bowles drew out his watch, and holding it close to his face, discovered that it was a few minutes past midnight. For the previous half-hour he had been sitting on the deck near Bob, with his legs dangling into the little cockpit abaft the stern-sheets, and staring in an abstracted fashion astern. As he replaced the watch in his pocket he glanced once more in that direction, but now his look suddenly grew intense and eager. For a full minute he remained thus, then he withdrew from its beckets beneath the seat a long and powerful telescope, which he adjusted and levelled. For another full minute he gazed anxiously through the tube, and then, handing it to Bob to hold, he crept silently forward, so as not to disturb the sleeping women, and quietly called the relief watch.

"Well, Mr Bowles," said the captain, as he rose to his feet, "what weather have you had? Is there any wind at all?"

"Very little, sir," answered the chief mate, replying to the last question first; "just a cat's-paw from the west'ard bow and then, but nothing worth speaking about; and it's been the same all through the watch. I want you to take a squint through the glass before I turn-in, sir, and to tell me whether I've been dreaming with my eyes open or no."

"Why, what is it, Bowles? Do you think you've seen anything?"

"Well, yes, I do, sir," answered the mate, "but it's so very indistinct in this starlight that I don't care to trust to my own eyes alone."

Without another word the pair moved aft, and when they were fairly settled in the cockpit Mr Bowles took the glass from Bob and put it into the skipper's hand. He then looked intently astern for perhaps half a minute, when he laid his hand on the skipper's arm and said—

"D'ye see them two stars, sir, about a couple of hand's breadths to the south'ard of the moon? They're about six degrees above the horizon, and the lower one is the southernmost of the two; it has a reddish gleam almost like a ship's port light."

"Yes," replied the skipper, "I see them. You mean those, do you not?" pointing to them.

"Ay, ay, sir; them's the two. Now look at the horizon, just half-way between 'em, and tell me if you can see anything."

The skipper looked long and steadfastly in the desired direction, and at length raised the telescope to his eye.

"By Jove, Bowles, I believe you are right," he at length exclaimed eagerly. "There certainly is a something away there on the horizon, but it is so small and indistinct that I cannot clearly make it out. Do you think it is either of the other boats?"

"No, sir, I don't," answered Bowles. "If it's anything it's a ship's royals. If 'twas one of the boats, she'd be within some five miles of us for us to be able to see her at all, and at that distance her sail would show out sharp and distinct through the glass. This shows, as you say, so indistinctly that it must be much more than that distance away, and therefore I say that if it's anything it's a ship's royals."

The skipper took another long steady look through the telescope, and then closing it sharply, said—

"There is undoubtedly something astern of us, Bowles, and under the circumstances I think we shall be fully justified in hauling our wind for an hour or two in order to satisfy ourselves as to what it really is."

Mr Bowles fully concurred in this opinion, and the boat was accordingly at once brought to the wind, what little there was of it, on the starboard tack, which brought the object about two points on her weather bow.

"If it is indeed a ship, Bowles," observed Captain Staunton when the boat's course had been changed and the mate was preparing to "go below," as he phrased it, "we have dropped in for a rare piece of luck, for, to tell you the plain truth, I had no hope whatever of falling in with a craft of any description about here. She will be a whaler, of course, but she is a long way north of the usual fishing-grounds, isn't she?"

"Well," returned Bowles meditatively, "you can never tell where you may fall in with one of them chaps. They follows the fish, you see; sometimes here, sometimes there; just where they think they'll have the best chance. Then, I have heard say that sometimes, if they happen to hit upon a particularly likely spot, such as a small uninhabited island, where there's a chance of good sport, they'll put a boat's crew ashore there with boat, harpoons, lines, a stock of provisions, and two or three hundred empty barrels, just to try their luck, like, for a month or so, and go away on a cruise, coming back for 'em in due time, and often finding 'em with every barrel full. Perhaps yon craft is up to something of that sort."

"It may be so," returned Captain Staunton. "Indeed in all probability it is so if our eyes have not deceived us. At all events, whatever she is, we are pretty sure of a hearty welcome, and even a not over clean whaler will be a welcome change for all hands, and especially for the ladies, from this boat, particularly now that the provisions are getting low. And I have no doubt I shall be able to make arrangements with the captain to carry us to Valparaiso with as little delay as possible."

"Ay, ay," returned Bowles, "I don't expect there'll be much trouble about that. I only hope we shall be able to get alongside her. I wouldn't stand on too long on this tack if I was you, sir. My opinion is that she's coming this way, and if so we ought to tack in good time so as not to let her slip past us to windward or across our bows. Good-night, sir!"

The night being so fine, and with so little wind, Captain Staunton took the tiller himself, and ordered the rest of the watch to lie down again; there was nothing to do, he said, and if he required their assistance he would call them. Accordingly, in a very short time, he was the only waking individual in the launch, the others were only too glad of the opportunity to forget, as far as possible, their miseries in sleep.

It is, of course, scarcely necessary to say that the skipper, as he sat there keeping his lonely watch, fixed his gaze, with scarcely a moment's intermission, on that part of the horizon where the mysterious object had been seen. He allowed a full hour to pass, and then drawing out the glass, applied it to his eye, sweeping the horizon carefully from dead ahead round to windward. He had not to seek far, for when the tube of the telescope pointed to within about three points of the starboard bow a small dark blot swept into the field of view. Yes, there it was, quite unmistakably this time, and a single moment's observation of it satisfied the anxious watcher that he saw before him the royals and topgallant-sails of a vessel apparently of no very great size.

The fact that the stranger's topgallant-sails had risen above the horizon within the hour since he had last looked at her was conclusive proof to his mind that the craft was standing toward them; that, in fact, they were approaching each other, though at a very low rate of speed, in consequence of the exceedingly light air of wind that was blowing. Fully satisfied upon this point he at once put the boat's helm down, and she came slowly and heavily about, the captain easily working the sheets himself.

By four bells Captain Staunton was able to discern with the naked eye the shadowy patch of darkness which the stranger's canvas made on the dusky line of the horizon, and when he called Mr Bowles at eight bells, or four o'clock in the morning, the patch had become darker, larger, and more clearly defined, and it lay about one point before the weather beam of the launch. The telescope was once more called into requisition, and it now showed not only the royals and topgallant-sails, but also the topsails of the stranger fairly above the horizon.

"Thank God for that welcome sight!" exclaimed the chief mate, laying down the telescope and reverently lifting his hat from his head. He remained silent a minute or two, and then raising his eyes, allowed his glance to travel all round the horizon and overhead until he had swept the entire expanse of the star-spangled heavens. Then, with a sigh of intense relief, he said—

"We're all right, I do verily believe, sir. There's the craft, plain as mud in a wine-glass, bearing right down upon us, or very nearly so. We've only to stand on as we're going and we shall cross her track. There's very little wind, it's true, but the trifle that there is is drawing us together; we're nearing each other every minute, and there's no sign of any change of weather, unless it may happen to be that the present light air will die away altogether with sunrise. I fancy I know what you're thinking of sir; you're half inclined to say, 'Out oars, and let's get alongside her as soon as possible.' And that's just what I should say if there was any sign of a breeze springing up, but there ain't; she can't run away from us, and therefore what I say is this: the launch is a heavy boat, and we're all hands of us as weak as cats; she's about six miles off now, and it would knock us all up to pull even that short distance, whereas if we go on as we are we shall drop alongside without any trouble by eight bells, or maybe a trifle earlier; and if the wind should die away altogether, it'll be time enough then to see what we can do with the oars."

"That's exactly the way I have been arguing with myself ever since you called me, Bowles," returned the skipper. "It is true that we are all suffering horribly from thirst, and in that way every moment is of value to us; but on the other hand, everybody except our two selves is now asleep and oblivious, for the time being, of their sufferings: let them sleep on, say I; the toil of tugging at heavy oars, and the excitement of knowing that a sail is at hand would only increase tenfold their sufferings, without helping us forward a very great deal; so I think, with you, that we had better let things remain as they are for another hour or two; we can rouse all hands at any moment, should it seem desirable to do so. Now, if you will take the tiller, I will just stretch myself out on the planks here, close at hand; I could not sleep now if the whole world were offered me to do so."

Saying which, the skipper suited the action to the word; he and the mate continuing their chat, but carefully pitching their voices in so low a tone that the ladies, close at hand, should not be disturbed in their slumbers.

By and by the sky began to pale in the eastern quarter; the stars quietly twinkled out, one by one; a bright rosy flush appeared, and then up rolled the glorious sun above the horizon.

The wind, light all night, had been imperceptibly dying away; and when the sun rose his bright beams flashed upon a sea whose surface was smooth as oil. The launch lost way altogether, and refused any longer to answer her helm.

As for the stranger, there she was, just hull-down; her snowy canvas gleaming in the brilliant morning sunshine, and so clearly defined that every rippling fold in the sails was distinctly visible as they flapped against the mast to the lazy roll of the vessel over the long sleepy swell.

"Now," said Captain Staunton, "we'll rouse the steward, make him prepare and serve out a first-rate breakfast to all hands; and then 'Hey! for a pull to the ship.'"

This was accordingly done. The breakfast was prepared, no great matter of a meal was it after all, though the last scrap of provisions and the last drop of water went in its composition; and when it was ready the cramped and hungry voyagers were roused with the good news that a sail was in sight, and the meal placed before them.

Frugal as it was, it was a sumptuous banquet compared with their late fare; and the poor famished creatures devoured it ravenously, feeling, when it was finished, that they could have disposed of thrice as much. Perhaps it was just as well that there was no more; in their condition a moderately full meal even would have proved injurious to them if administered without great caution; but while there was not sufficient to provoke hurtful results there was just enough to put new life into them, and to temporarily endow them with vigour and strength enough for an hour or two's toil at the oars.

The meal over, the oars were eagerly manned; and the men dividing themselves into two gangs, and working in short spells of a quarter of an hour each, the launch was headed straight for the stranger, which having now lost steerage-way had swung broadside-on, and showed herself to be a small brig.

"I tell you what it is, Bowles," said the captain as he sat at the tiller steering during one of his spells of rest from the oars, "we are a great deal further to the westward than I imagined we were. We must be not very far from the outlying islands of that vast archipelago which spreads itself over so many hundreds of leagues of the South Pacific. That fellow is no whaler; look at his canvas, no smoke stains from the try-works there: he is a sandal-wood trader, or is after bêche-de-mer. I am very glad it is so; it will be much more pleasant for the ladies; and if she is a Yankee, as a good many of these little traders are, the skipper will probably be glad enough to earn a few dollars by running us all across to the mainland."

"To my mind," remarked Bowles, "the craft looks rather too trim and neat aloft for a trader. And look at the hoist of her topsails; don't you think there is a man-o'-war-ish appearance about the cut and set of them sails, sir?"

"She certainly does look rather taunt in her spars for a merchantman," returned Captain Staunton. "We shall soon see what she really is, however; for she will be hull-up in another five minutes; and in another half-hour we shall be on board her. Ah! they have made us out; there go her colours. Take the glass, and see what you can make of them, Bowles."

The chief mate took the telescope and levelled it at the brig, taking a long and steady look at her.

"A ten-gun brig, by the look of her," he presently remarked, with the telescope still at his eye. "Anyhow, her bulwarks are pierced; and I can see the muzzles of five bull-dogs grinning through her starboard port-holes.

That's the stars and stripes hanging at her peak, as far as I can make out; but it's drooping so dead that I can see nothing but a mingling of red and white, with a small patch of blue next the halliard-block. She's a pretty-looking little thing enough, and her skipper's a thorough seaman, whoever he is. Ay, she's a man-o'-war sure enough—Up go the courses and down comes the jib, all at once, man-o'-war fashion. And there's clue up royals and t'gallan's'ls—to prevent 'em from beating themselves to pieces against the spars and rigging, that is, for all the canvas she could set wouldn't give her steerage-way, much less cause her to run away from us. She hasn't a pennant aloft, though—wonder how that is? And the hands on board seem to be a rum-looking lot of chaps as ever I set eyes on; no more like man-o'-war's men than we are—not a single jersey or man-o'-war collar among 'em; nor nothing like a uniform aft there. I s'pose they're economical, and want to save their regular rig for harbour service."

"Well, thank God for His mercy in directing us to her," exclaimed the skipper fervently, as he lifted his cap from his head. "Our troubles are all over now, ladies," he continued, turning to the women, who were now eagerly watching the brig. "The craft is small; but she is plenty big enough to carry us all to Valparaiso; and, once there, I think we shall have very little difficulty in getting a passage home."

Half an hour more of toilsome tugging at the oars, and the heavy launch ranged up alongside the brig.

"Look out for a rope," shouted one of the crew, as he sprang upon the rail with a coil of line in his hand.

"Heave," shouted Bob.

The rope was dexterously thrown and caught; the heavy oars were laid in; and as the boat touched the brig's side a man dressed in a suit of white nankeen, his head sheltered by a broad-brimmed Panama hat, and his rather handsome sun-browned face half hidden by a thick black beard and moustache, sauntered to the gangway from the position he had occupied abaft the main-rigging, and leaning over the bulwarks remarked—

"Morning, straangers. I guess you found it hot work pullin' down to us in that heavy boat. Looks to me as though you had had rayther bad times lately."

"Yes," answered the skipper. "We were burned out of our ship—the Galatea of London. We have been in the boat a fortnight to-day; and for the last five days—until this morning, when we consumed the last of our provisions—some of us have never tasted water."

"Waal, stranger, that's bad news to tell. But I calculate we can soon put you all right. Here," he continued, addressing himself to the men who were peering curiously over the bulwarks at the occupants of the boat, "jump down, some of you, and help 'em up over the side."

There was a hearty laugh at this order, to the intense surprise of our adventurers; but the skipper of the brig was evidently a man who was not to be trifled with; with two strides he was among the jeering crowd of men with a revolver in each hand.

"Now, git," he exclaimed, levelling the pistols; and the men waited for no second bidding. In an instant some half a dozen of them sprang into the boat; the brig's gangway was opened, and the boat's crew were somewhat sullenly assisted up the side of the brig and on to her deck.

The black-bearded man met them as they came up the side, and held out his hand to Captain Staunton.

"Morning, straanger," he repeated. "I'm powerful glad to see you all."

"Thank you," returned the skipper. "I can assure you we are all at least equally glad to see you, and to find ourselves once more with a deck beneath our feet. What ship is this, may I ask, and by what name shall we call the gentleman who has given us so kind a reception?"

"The brig's called the Albatross; and my name is Johnson—at your service."

"You are an American cruiser, I presume?" continued Captain Staunton, looking first at the beautifully kept decks, and then more doubtfully at the gang of desperadoes who crowded round.

"Sorter," briefly replied the man who had called himself Johnson; and the reply seemed for some reason to mightily tickle his crew, most of whom burst into a hearty guffaw.

Captain Staunton glanced round upon them with such stern surprise that the fellows fell back a pace or two; and the skipper of the brig, first darting a furious glance upon his followers, led the way aft to the cabin, saying—

"I sorter waited breakfast when I made out through the glass that you were a shipwrecked crew, calculatin' that prob'ly you'd be glad to find yourselves in front of a good square meal. Your crew will have to make themselves at home in the fo'ks'le; and if my lads don't treat 'em properly, why they must just knock 'em down. My people are a trifle orkard to deal with at first, but I guess they'll all pull together first-rate arter a while."

Captain Johnson Explains Himself

The cabin of the Albatross was a much larger apartment than one would have expected to find in a craft of her size. It was about twenty feet long and eighteen feet broad, occupying the entire width of the ship; the state-rooms—of which there were two only—being outside the cabin, at the foot of the companion staircase. The apartment was well lighted and very airy, light and air being admitted not only through the skylight, but also through the stern-ports and dead-lights fitted into the sides of the ship. The fittings were extremely rich, though somewhat out of harmony with each other, conveying to Captain Staunton's educated eye the idea that they had been collected at odd times from a number of other ships. The rudder-case, for example, was inclosed in a piece of elaborate carved and gilded work representing the trunk and branches of a palm-tree; but it had apparently been found too large, and the sections had accordingly been cut down to make them fit, the result being that the carving did not match at the junctions. The trunk of the tree had also been cut off rather clumsily at the base and fitted badly to the cabin floor, while the branches had been cut through in places where the beams crossed the ceiling, and had been nailed on again in such a way as to make them look as though they had grown through the beams. Then again the cushions to the lockers were of different sizes, colours, and materials, some being of velvet and others of horsehair, and every one of them from one to three sizes too large. The sides of the cabin were divided into panels by carved and gilded pilasters, which exhibited in a very marked degree the same incongruity, the eight pilasters in the cabin exhibiting no less than three different patterns. Some half a dozen pictures, one or two of which were really valuable paintings, were securely hung in the panels; and the stern-windows were fitted with handsome lace curtains, much too large for the position which they occupied. Two very handsome swinging lamps, of different designs, were suspended from the beams; a tell-tale compass and a ship's barometer occupied respectively the fore and after ends of the skylight; and the bulkhead which formed the fore end of the cabin was fitted above the sideboard with racks in which reposed six repeating rifles; the panels which were unoccupied by pictures being filled in with trophies of stars and other fanciful devices formed with pistols, daggers, and cutlasses.

Such was the apartment to which our adventurers found themselves welcomed; but if the truth must be told, their eyes—notwithstanding their recent meal on board the launch—were chiefly attracted to the cabin table whereon was spread—on a not over clean table-cloth—an abundant display of plate and a substantial yet appetising meal to which their host urged them to do full justice, himself setting a good example.

For a short time, and while host and guests were taking the keen edge off their appetites, very little was said. At length, however, Captain Johnson looked up, and addressing Captain Staunton, said—

"Waal, stranger, as I said before, I'm real glad to see you all; yours are the first friendly faces I've looked upon for many a long day; but I guess I'm considerable troubled what to do with you all. You see our accommodation is sorter limited. There's plenty of room for your men in the fo'ks'le; but here's no less than ten of you, reckonin' the piccaninny—bless her dear purty little face! I wish she'd give me a kiss. Four years ago I left just such another on the wharf at New York, kissin' her hand to me and wavin' me good-bye as we cast off our moorin's, and I guess I'll never see her sweet face ag'in."

At her mother's suggestion, little May slid down off the locker on which she was perched, and, somewhat reluctantly, went to the man's chair and held up her little mouth for a kiss.

Johnson at once bent down, and taking her on his knee, gazed long and eagerly into the bright young face uplifted to his own in childish curiosity. Then he kissed her eagerly three or four times, stroked her curly head tenderly with his great brown hand, and finally burst out—

"See here, my purty little dearie—If e'er a one of them great rough men on deck there says a bad word to you, or dares to as much as look unkind at you, you tell me, and curse me if—I beg your pardon, strangers, I guess I didn't know just then what I was talking about. Run along, little 'un, and get your breakfast."

The child at once slid down from his knee, and with some little haste returned to her former place by her mother's side, Johnson's gaze following her abstractedly.

"You were speaking about the inconvenience to which our appearance seems likely to put you," at length suggested Captain Staunton.

"I guess not, stranger," he retorted, pulling himself together as it were with a jerk. "I was simply p'inting out that our accommodation for passengers is kinder limited; and I'm puzzled to know where I can stow you all away. The inconvenience 'll be yourn, stranger, not mine. There's reasons, you see, why I should keep possession of my own cabin; and there's reasons, too, why the mate should keep possession of his'n. I reckon the best plan 'll be to clear away a place for you down in the after-hold, where you must try and make yourselves as comfortable as you can for the few days you'll be on board. And as for you ladies, I'd sorter advise you to stay below all you can. If you must go on deck at all let it be at night-time, when there ain't so much chance of your bein' seen."

"Where are you bound, captain?" inquired the skipper.

"Waal, we are bound now to an island which, as it's not shown on the chart, I've christened 'Albatross Island,' arter the brig. We're goin' there to refit," was the reply.

"Then I presume you have established a sort of depôt there?" interrogated Captain Staunton.

"That's just it; you've hit it exactly, stranger," answered the Yankee.

"And how long will it take you to refit?" was the next question.

"Maybe a week; maybe a month. It just depends upon whether the hands are in a working humour or no."

Captain Staunton raised his eyebrows somewhat at this singular answer. After a moment or two of silence he said—

"I presume you would find no difficulty in running us across to—say—Valparaiso, if you were well paid for the service?"

"Cash down?"

Captain Staunton was about to say "Yes," having saved from the burning ship a bag of specie sufficient in amount to convey the entire party home in perfect comfort; but an idea struck him that it would perhaps be better to promise payment after rather than before the performance of the service, so he said—

"Well, no, I could not promise that. But I would draw on my owners for the amount of our passage-money, and pay you immediately on our arrival at Valparaiso."

"Waal, I guess I'll have to think it over," remarked Johnson. "I must go on deck now, but you kin remain here as long as you like; in fact I reckon you'd better stay here altogether until I can get a place arranged for you below." Saying which, he abruptly rose from the table and went on deck.

"Rather an unique specimen of the genus Yankee," observed Rex, as soon as their host had fairly disappeared. "I hope, captain, you will succeed in persuading him to take us over to the mainland."

The skipper was apparently plunged deep in thought, for he made no reply.

"Does it not strike you, Bowles, that there is something rather peculiar about the craft, and her crew?" remarked Lance.

"These Yankees are generally a queer lot," answered the mate nonchalantly; but immediately afterwards he made a sudden and stealthy movement of his fingers to his lips, while the ladies were looking in another direction, throwing at the same time an expression of so much caution and mystery into his glance that Lance made no attempt to continue the conversation.

Shortly afterwards Captain Staunton rose from his seat at the table, and, touching his chief mate lightly on the shoulder, said—

"Come, Bowles, let us go on deck and see if we can make terms with this Captain Johnson. The rest of you had perhaps better follow that gentleman's advice in the meantime and remain here, since he evidently has some motive for expressing the wish."

As the two were ascending the companion-ladder the skipper turned and whispered hurriedly to his mate—

"What is your opinion of things in general Bowles?"

"Can't say yet," answered that individual. "Looks mighty queer though. She ain't a man-o'-war, that's certain."

On reaching the deck they found the after-hatch off, and their host in somewhat hot discussion with the ship's carpenter.

"That is quite sufficient," they heard him say, without a trace of the Yankee twang in his speech, "you have your orders, and see that they are executed forthwith. In this matter I intend to have my own way."

The man muttered something in a sullen undertone, and then turned to go forward, saying he would get his tools and set about the job at once.

Johnson turned impatiently away from him with an ugly frown upon his brow, which however vanished in an instant upon his finding our two friends at his elbow.

"See here, stranger," he said, passing his arm within that of Captain Staunton, and drawing him toward the hatchway, "I want to show you what I'm going to do. See them beams? Waal, I'm going to send some hands down below to trim a few of them bales you see there up level with the tops of the beams; then we'll lay a couple of thicknesses of planking over all, which 'll make a tol'able floor; and then I'm going to have a sail nailed fore and aft to the deck-beams, dividing the space into two, one for the women-folks and one for the men; and another sail hung athwart-ships 'll make all sorter snug and private; and I guess you'll have to make yourselves as comfortable as you can down there. You see the brig's small, and your party's a large one, and—I guess that's the best I can do for you."

"Thank you," said Captain Staunton. "As far as we men are concerned, we can manage perfectly well down there; but I'm afraid it will be rather a comfortless berth for the ladies. And yet I do not see very well what else can be done—unless indeed we could come to some arrangement by which you and your chief mate could be induced to surrender the cabin altogether for their use—"

"Which we can't," Johnson broke in sharply. "I tell you, stranger, it ain't to be done. I reckon I was a fool to let you come aboard here at all. It was seein' that little girl of yours that did it," he added, his voice at once softening again, "but I guess there's going to be trouble about it yet, before all's done."

"Oh, no, I hope not," returned the skipper. "Why should there be trouble, or with whom? Certainly not with us."

"Waal, I hope not," said Johnson. "But I reckon you'll have to do just exactly as I say, strangers, or I tell you I'll not answer for the consequences."

"Assuredly we will," observed Captain Staunton. "And as for the inconvenience, we must put up with it as best we can, and I only hope we shall not be compelled to intrude upon your hospitality for any great length of time. Indeed you might rid yourself of our presence in a fortnight by running us across to Valparaiso; and I think I could make it worth your while to do so."

Johnson turned away and walked thoughtfully fore and aft, with his chin sunk upon his breast, evidently in painful thought, for some ten minutes; then he rejoined the pair he had left standing at the hatchway, and said—

"See here, strangers; I reckon it's no use to mince matters and go beating about the bush; the thing's got to come out sooner or later, so you may as well know the worst at once. You must give up all notion of going to Valparaiso, because the thing ain't to be done. We're a crew of free-traders, rovers—pirates, if that term 'll serve to make matters more clear to you; and although we've only been cruising in these waters about six months, I guess we've made things too hot here for us to venture into any port but the one we're bound to. There you'll be put ashore, and I calculate you'll have to make yourselves useful at the depôt. There's plenty of work to be done there, and not too many to do it, so you'll be valuable there. I won't keep you on board here, because I can see you'd never work with me or be anything else but an anxiety to me; but there you can't do me any harm.

And, take my advice, stranger, don't cut up rough—go slow and sing small when you get there, because my chief mate—who is a Greek, and is in charge there—is a powerful short-tempered man, and apt to make things downright uncomfortable for them that don't please him."

Captain Staunton and Bowles looked each other in the face for a full minute, too much overcome by consternation and dismay to utter a single word. Then the skipper, recovering himself, turned to Johnson, who stood by intently watching them, and said:

"I thank you, sir, for having come to the point and put our position thus explicitly before us with so little waste of time. Happily the evil is not yet irreparable. We can never be anything but a source of anxiety and disquietude to you, as you have already admitted; therefore I trust you will allow us to return to our boat as we came; by which act we shall relieve you of a very great embarrassment, and at the same time give ourselves a chance—a very slight one, it is true—of arriving at the place we are so anxious to reach."

"Too late, stranger," replied Johnson. "Here you are, and here you must now stay. Look over the side and you will see that your boat is no longer there. She was stove and cast adrift half an hour ago. And even if she had still been alongside, do you think my men would let you go now that you have been aboard of us and seen our strength? I tell you, stranger, that before you could get ten yards from the brig they would bring her broadside to bear upon you and send you all to the bottom, riddled with grape, and I couldn't stop 'em. No; you're here, and I reckon you'll have to stay and make the best of it. You'll find your traps down below there; the lads wanted to overhaul them, but I guess I shamed them out of that," drawing half out of his pockets a pair of revolvers as he spoke.

"Are we to consider ourselves as prisoners then, and to look upon the hold there as our jail?" inquired Captain Staunton.

"That's as you please," retorted Johnson. "So long as you keep quiet and don't attempt any tricks you can come on deck as often as you like—only don't let the women-folks show themselves, or they'll get into trouble, and I—nor you—won't be able to help 'em. Tell 'em to stay in the cabin until it's dark to-night, and then when all's quiet, the watch below in their hammocks and the watch on deck 'caulking' between the guns, just you muffle 'em up and get 'em down there as quick as ever you can."

"And what about the rest of my people—those of them who were sent forward to the forecastle?" inquired Captain Staunton.

"Waal," replied Johnson, "I felt myself sorter obliged to clap 'em in irons down in the fore-hold. You see you muster a pretty strong party, and though you could never take the brig from us, I didn't know what you might be tempted to try, when you found out the truth; and so, just to prevent accidents, I had the irons slipped on to 'em. They'll be well treated, though; and if any of 'em likes to jine us, so much the better—we're uncommon short-handed, one way and another. If they don't like to jine, they'll just be put ashore with you to work at the depôt. And, see here, stranger, don't you go for to try on any tricks, either here or ashore, or it'll be awful bad for you. This is a friendly warning, mind; I'd like to make friends with you folks, for, to tell you the solid petrified truth, I ain't got one single friend among all hands. The mate hates me, and would be glad to put me out of the way and step into my shoes, and he's made the men distrust me."

"Why not retire from them altogether, then?" inquired Captain Staunton.

"Because I can't," answered Johnson. "I'm an outlaw, and dare not show my face anywhere in the whole civilised world for fear of being recognised and hanged as a pirate."

"A decidedly unpleasant position to be in," remarked the skipper. "However, if there is any way in which we can lawfully help you, we will do so; in return for which we shall of course expect to be treated well by you. Now, Bowles," he continued, turning to his chief mate, "let us talk this matter over, and discuss the manner in which this bad news can best be broken to the others."

Saying which, with a somewhat cold and formal bow to the pirate, Captain Staunton linked his arm in that of his chief mate, and walked away.

The two promenaded the deck for nearly an hour, "overhauling the concern in all its bearings," as Bowles afterwards described it, and they finally came to the conclusion that it would be only fair to let their companions in misfortune know the worst at once, then all could take counsel together, and as "in a multitude of counsellors there is wisdom," some one might possibly hit upon a happy idea whereby they might be enabled to escape from this new strait.

They accordingly descended to the cabin, where their reappearance had been anxiously looked for.

"Well, captain," exclaimed Dale upon their entrance, "what news have you for us? Have you made arrangements for our conveyance to Valparaiso?

I hope we are not going to be kept cooped up very long in this wretched little vessel."

"We are to leave her sooner than I anticipated," replied Captain Staunton, "but I regret to say that I have been quite unable to make any arrangements of a satisfactory character. And, as to news, I must ask you to prepare yourselves for the worst—or almost the worst—that you could possibly hear. We are on board a pirate, and in the hands of as unscrupulous a set of rascals as one could well encounter."

The skipper then proceeded to describe in extenso his interview with the pirate captain, throwing out such ideas as presented themselves to him in the course of his narrative, and winding up by pointing out to them that though the situation was serious enough it was not altogether desperate, the pirate leader being evidently anxious to escape from his present position, and as evidently disposed to look with friendly eyes upon all who might seem to have it in their power to assist him, either directly or indirectly, in the attainment of his purpose.

"Our first endeavour," he said in conclusion, "must be to impress upon this man that, though we are his prisoners, we are still a power, by reason of our numbers as well as of our superior intelligence and knowledge of the world, and that we can certainly help him if we have the opportunity; and this idea once firmly established in his mind, he will listen to and very possibly fall in with some of our suggestions, all of which, I suppose I need hardly say, must be made with a single eye to our own ultimate escape. Our future is beset by difficulties, very few of which we can even anticipate as yet; but I think if each one will only take a hopeful view of the situation, it will be singular indeed if one or another of us does not hit upon a means of escape."

By the time that he had finished speaking the brains of his hearers were literally teeming with ideas, all, that is to say, except Mr Dale, who, with elbows on the table, his head buried in his hands, and his hair all rumpled, abandoned himself to despair and to loud bewailings of the unfortunate combination of circumstances which led to his venturing upon the treacherous ocean. The others, however, knew him thoroughly by this time; and none troubled themselves to take the slightest notice of him except Rex Fortescue, who exclaimed—

"Do shut up, Dale, and cease making a fool of yourself. I wonder that you are not ashamed to behave in this unmanly way, especially before ladies, too. If you can't keep quiet, you know, we shall have to put you on deck, where I fancy you would get something worth howling about."

This threat had the desired effect; Mr Dale subsided into silence, and the rest of the party at once, in low cautious tones, began an interchange of ideas which lasted a long time but brought forth no very satisfactory result; the council finding itself at the close of the discussion pretty much where it was at the commencement.

At one o'clock a thoroughly substantial dinner was served to them, followed by tea at six in the evening, at both of which meals the pirate captain did the honours with a manifest desire to evince a friendly disposition toward his guests, and about nine p.m. a quiet and unobtrusive removal from the cabin to their new quarters in the after-hold was effected; after which most of the party disposed themselves comfortably upon the bedding which they found had been provided for them, and enjoyed a night of thoroughly sound repose, such as they had been strangers to ever since the destruction of the Galatea.

When our friends awoke on the following morning they became aware, by the motion of the ship and the sound of the water gurgling along her sides, that a breeze had sprung up. Most of the gentlemen—all of them, in fact, except Dale—went on deck, and, finding the watch busy washing decks, borrowed of them a few buckets with which they gave each other a most hearty and refreshing salt water douche, much to the amusement of the crew.

As soon as breakfast was over, Lance, with that cool insouciance characteristic of the man who has so often found himself environed by perils that he ceases to think of them, went again on deck, with the intention of mingling freely with the pirate crew, and, if possible, placing himself upon such easy terms with them as would give him an opportunity of acquiring whatever information it might be in their power to give. The first individual he saw on emerging from the hatchway was Johnson, the pirate captain, who was leaning moodily over the lee rail abaft the main-rigging, smoking a well-seasoned pipe.

"Good morning, captain," exclaimed Lance genially, as he sauntered up to the man. "What a delightful morning—and how good your tobacco smells! I have not enjoyed the luxury of a pipe for the last fortnight; have you any tobacco to spare?"

"Help yourself, stranger," answered Johnson rather surlily, as he tendered his tobacco-pouch.

"Thanks," said Lance, returning the pouch after he had filled and lighted his pipe. "Ah! how good this is," as he took the first whiff or two. "You have a fine breeze after yesterday's calm; and the brig seems quite a traveller in her small way."

"In her small way!" exclaimed Johnson indignantly; "why, she's a flyer, stranger, that's what she is. I reckon you don't know much about ships, or you wouldn't talk like that. I guess you ain't a sailor, are you?"

"I am a soldier by profession," answered Lance, "but for all that I am not exactly an unmitigated land-lubber; on the contrary I am quite an enthusiastic yachtsman, and I flatter myself that I know a good model when I see one."

"And yet you don't take much account of the brig, stranger?"

"She seems a good enough little craft of her kind," admitted Lance, "and as a mere trader I have no doubt she would answer well enough. But it strikes me that, to gentlemen of your profession, a really fast and powerful vessel is an absolute necessity if you would insure your own safety. In weather like this I daresay you would manage tolerably well; but if a frigate were by any chance to fall in with you in a fresh breeze, or, worse still, in heavy weather, I fear you would find yourselves in a 'tight place;' she would have you under her guns in less than an hour."

"That's so, stranger; yes, I reckon that's so," conceded Johnson with evident reluctance. "There are ships as can outsail us, I know, for we've fallen in with some half a dozen clippers, and we couldn't do nothing with 'em; they just walked away from us. And though I don't calculate that there's ever a frigate afloat as could get alongside them tea-ships if the tea-ships didn't want 'em to, yet I guess there's frigates as could overhaul us in heavy weather. And so you're a yachtsman, eh? Then I reckon you know something about quick sailing. How fast, now, do you calculate a yacht would sail in this breeze?"

"That depends entirely upon the build and model of the craft. If she were a racing schooner of, say the tonnage of this brig, I daresay her speed under such circumstances as these would be thirteen or perhaps fourteen knots; if, however, she were merely a cruising yacht, such as my own, I do not imagine she would average more than eleven."

"Eleven knots! Jeosh—I say, stranger, how many knots do you reckon we are making just now?" exclaimed Johnson.

Lance looked over the side for a moment, marked a piece of weed floating past, and then answered—

"About eight, I should think; certainly not more."

"I guess you're wrong, stranger," returned the pirate skipper with animation, "she's going ten if she's going an inch."

"You can easily test it by heaving the log," suggested Lance.

"Aft here, two of you, and heave the log," shouted Johnson.

Two men came sauntering aft, at the call; the line and glass were prepared; and Johnson himself made ready to test the speed of the brig.

"Turn!" he cried to the man who held the glass, as the last of the "stray" passed out over the taffrail.

The glass was smartly turned; the reel spun rapidly round; the marks flew through Johnson's fingers, and his countenance brightened with exultation.

"Stop!"

The sand had all run out; and Johnson grasped the line just before the eighth knot reached his hand.

"Tarnation! you're right, stranger," he angrily exclaimed. "Waal, I swan I made sure she was going ten at the very least."

"You skippers very often make that kind of mistake," remarked Lance. "Or rather, it is not so much a mistake as a self-deception; you would like your ship to have a speed of ten knots in such weather as this, and 'the wish is father to the thought.' Besides which, having formed an attachment for your ship, you are naturally anxious to give strangers also a favourable impression of her."

"That's so, stranger, sure as you're standin' there; you've exactly hit it I knew the craft wan't doin' over eight at the outside; but the way you talked about that yacht of yours sorter put my back up, and I 'lowed I wan't goin' to let you have all the big talk to yourself. About this yacht of yours, colonel; where is she now?"

"Where I left her, no doubt," answered Lance with a smile; "safe and sound on the mud of Haslar creek, inside Portsmouth harbour."

"I suppose, as she's such a flyer, that one of the crack English builders put her together?" inquired Johnson.

"No, indeed," said Lance. "She was built at Weymouth by an ordinary shipbuilder, who, for aught I know, had never in his life built a yacht before. I was stationed there at the time, and I designed her myself, and of course superintended her construction."

"You don't say. Waal, I knew that the soldiers did most everything; but I didn't 'low that they designed yachts!" exclaimed Johnson.

"Neither do we, professionally," admitted Lance; "but some of us, of whom I happen to be one, take up the study of naval architecture as an amusement; and those who, like myself, belong to the Engineer corps, are to some extent qualified by our technical education to achieve excellence in the art. I can assure you that some of the officers in my corps have turned out exceedingly creditable craft."

"Waal now, that beats ah," exclaimed Johnson. "So you're an Engineer, and can design yachts into the bargain! Stranger,"—laying his hand impressively on Lance's arm—"I'm real glad I took you all aboard. About this schooner of yours—she is a schooner, I reckon!"

Lance nodded an affirmative.

"Waal, about this schooner of yours, is she a pretty sea-boat?"

"She is as comfortable a vessel as I would ever wish to have under my feet," answered Lance with just a slight touch of enthusiasm. "She will face any weather a frigate would dare to look at; and in a gale of wind, such as once caught us in the Bay of Biscay, is a great deal drier and more comfortable than many frigates would be."

"Waal now, I call this real interesting," exclaimed Johnson with sparkling eyes. "And I s'pose she was tol'able weatherly?"

"About the same as other vessels of her class. All yachts, you know, if they are the least worthy the name, go to windward well; it is one of their strong points."

"Do you think now, colonel, you could recollect enough to design another yacht just like your own schooner?" asked Johnson eagerly.

"Well," said Lance, slowly, as he first began to perceive the direction in which Johnson's thoughts were tending. "I am by no means sure that I could. However," as a brilliant idea dawned upon him, "I am certain that, with the experience I have gained since I designed the Fleetwing, I could build one which should excel her in all respects."

"Waal now, this is what I call a real pleasant conversation," exclaimed Johnson, with enthusiasm. "Now, see here, colonel, I guess I'll get you to draw out that design right away."

"I am sure I shall be very pleased," said Lance. "But why do you wish for such a thing? You will surely not venture, after what you have already told us, to visit a civilised port and order a vessel to be built?"

"I guess not, stranger. I've three prizes lyin' in harbour not far off, which I kept, thinkin' they might come in useful some day; and we'll break 'em up to build this new craft. You shall superintend the work; and, as you're an engineer, I reckon I'll get you to fortify the harbour also, so's to make things secure in case one of them frigates you was talking about should come along and take a fancy to look inside."

"Very well," said Lance; "I will do what I can, both in the matter of fortifying the harbour and building the new craft, upon the express condition, however, you must understand, that we are all treated well as long as we remain with you; and that you will make an early opportunity to free us as soon as the work is done."

"Don't you be afraid, stranger," returned Johnson. "You do the best you can for me, and I guess I'll do the right thing by you. That's a bargain."

"There is just one point which occurs to me," remarked Lance. "It is this. To do what you propose we shall require a great deal of assistance. Now where are we to find it?"

"If it's men you mean, I reckon you'll find plenty of 'em at Albatross Island. Men ain't always to be picked up at sea just when they're wanted," said Johnson, "so I've took to keepin' my prisoners alive and landing 'em there, so's I can draw upon 'em when I want to; and I've found that if they won't cut in and take a hand with us exactly to oncet they gen'lly will a little later on, just to escape bein' worked to death ashore."

"And what about materials?" persisted Lance. "To construct a battery, and to make it serviceable, you know, stone, lime, iron and wood in considerable quantities are required; to say nothing of guns, powder and shot with which to arm the battery when it is finished."

"We've got it all," exclaimed Johnson; "all, that is, exceptin' iron, and that we're very short of. There's stone in the island, and I guess you can make lime from the coral, can't you? And as to the guns and ammunition, why it's only three months ago that we helped ourselves to a whole battery-full belonging to the Spaniards away there on the mainland."

"Well," said Lance, "I cannot of course decide exactly how to use your resources to the best advantage until I have seen them and the place. As far, however, as the design of the new ship is concerned, I can set about it at once. I must ask you, however, to release the carpenter and Bob, the apprentice, and to allow them to join us aft. The carpenter is a practical man, whose advice and assistance will be most valuable to me; and as for Bob, he has been brought up in a district famous for yacht-building, and will be sure to prove helpful to us."

"Very well, colonel, I reckon you can have 'em," said Johnson. "Only don't you be persuaded to try any tricks on account of having two extra hands, because if you do, I calculate you'll find us always ready."

"All right," laughed Lance, "I'll keep your warning and advice in mind. By the by, before I go below, let me suggest that as a few of us are, like myself, smokers, a pound or so of tobacco now and then would be regarded as a delicate attention on your part."

"Right you are, colonel," answered Johnson cordially, "you shall have the terbacker and some cigars too if you like 'em; I guess we've got plenty of both on board."

So saying Johnson turned upon his heel and dived below for his sextant.

Johnson Hoodwinks a Frigate

Left to himself Lance sauntered aft, glanced first at the binnacle, then at the sails, and finally essayed a conversation with the helmsman. The man proved at first to be exceedingly surly, suspicious, and taciturn, but Lance Evelin was a man of consummate tact, and his manner was at once so refined and so genial that there were very few who could for any length of time withstand its fascinating influence. In less than half an hour he had so won upon the man, who was by no means all bad, that everything approaching to reserve had completely vanished, and when Johnson came on deck after working out his sights he found the strangely assorted pair conversing as freely together as though they had been old shipmates. Lance was very careful to confine his conversation to generalities, and religiously abstained from asking any questions whatever; he quite realised that the party to which he belonged were in a position of great difficulty and danger, their escape from which, if indeed they should ever escape at all, would certainly be a work of time, demanding the utmost caution and patience; and his first endeavour, therefore, was to create a favourable impression rather than to risk suspicion by a too early attempt to acquire information. When Johnson saw the two in conversation he at once edged his way aft with the evident intention of ascertaining what they were talking about; but although Lance at once noted the movement and made a mental memorandum to the effect that the pirate skipper was clearly a man of suspicious temperament, he gave no outward sign of having observed any such thing, but simply continued the conversation as unrestrainedly as though Johnson had not been there.

Lance remained on deck until dinner-time, which was 1 p.m. on board the Albatross, when he rejoined his friends below.

"Well," said he, as he seated himself at the rough deal table which had been knocked together for their accommodation, "I have spent a very pleasant, and, I hope, a very profitable morning on deck."

"Have you?" remarked Captain Staunton, "I am glad to hear that. We were beginning to wonder what had become of you. What have you been doing?"

"Merely ingratiating myself with the skipper and the man whose trick it happened to be at the wheel," answered Lance. "And I flatter myself that, for a first attempt, I have managed pretty well. I have been obliged to blow my own trumpet a little, it is true; but by a judicious performance upon that instrument I have succeeded in showing our friend Johnson very clearly that it is in our power to be of the greatest possible service to him, and I have secured an order to build a new ship for him, and to fortify the harbour in which she is to be built."

"To build a new ship for him!" exclaimed Captain Staunton.

"To fortify his harbour!" ejaculated Rex and Brook together.

"Precisely that, gentlemen," continued Lance. "I happened accidentally to touch upon rather a sore point with him by disparaging the speed of the brig, which he evidently wished to persuade himself was almost matchless; then I gently insinuated to him that he would be very awkwardly situated if he happened to find himself in the presence of a frigate in heavy weather; and finally I mentioned to him in a casual way the fact that I had designed and built a yacht of my own which could sail round his brig in any weather, and also that I happened to be by profession a military engineer. The results of which are as I have already stated. There is one other result, by the bye, I have secured the release of our friend Robert, and also the carpenter. I daresay they will be allowed to join us some time to-day."

"Well," remarked Captain Staunton, "that is an advantage certainly; every man we can secure makes us so much the stronger, and perhaps, if we could get one or two more, something might be done in the second night-watch. We might possibly be able to—"

"Take the brig?" interrupted Lance with a laugh. "Not to be thought of for a single moment, my dear sir. Our friend Johnson is far too suspicious a man, and has too much at stake to give us any such opportunity, if watchfulness on his part can prevent it. Why, he has already anticipated the possibility of such an attempt on our part, and was good enough to caution me that we should always find him ready."

"Um!" ejaculated the skipper, meditatively, "that is bad news. We have evidently a difficult man to deal with. I have heard it said, more than once, that the man who can circumvent a Yankee can circumvent the Father of Mischief himself. But about this ship-building and fortification business, do I understand that you regard Johnson's plans in that respect as favourable to us? Because, if so, I should be very glad if you would explain; I must admit that at present I can scarcely see how we are likely to derive any advantage from it."

"Well," remarked Lance, "you must understand that at present my plans are of the crudest description, they will require a great deal of maturing before they can be put into successful operation, and in this I anticipate that you will all be able to afford me the greatest assistance. Roughly, however, my idea is this. We must choose, if possible, for the ship-building-yard a spot which is not only suitable for the purpose, but which will also admit of being effectually defended by the battery which is to be built. We must secure as assistants as many as possible of our own men, and when the ship is built and launched we must contrive somehow to seize and make our escape in her. This plan will, I admit, involve many months' detention here, but it is the only feasible way of escape which has, so far, presented itself to my mind; and my conversation with Johnson this morning has convinced me that we have nothing to hope for from him. He is glad to have us, and will possibly be civil to us because of our ability to be of service to him, but I can see that he is an unscrupulous rascal who will freely make promises in order to secure our aid and co-operation, and unhesitatingly break them the moment that his ends are served."

They were all busily engaged in the discussion of Lance's projects when a hail was heard from aloft. They did not quite catch the words, but the gruff voice of the brig's chief mate ordering the crew to make sail caused them to surmise that a ship had just been sighted. The first impulse of the males in the party was to rush on deck, but Captain Staunton immediately resumed his seat again and requested the others to do so likewise, pointing out that too eager a curiosity on their parts respecting the movements of the brig would possibly only provoke suspicion and resentment against them in the breasts of the pirates, and that there would be ample opportunity later on for them to see how matters stood. They accordingly resumed the discussion upon which they had been engaged, but were shortly afterwards interrupted by the appearance of Johnson's steward, who descended the hatchway-ladder bearing a couple of boxes of cigars and a dozen sticks of excellent tobacco "with the cap'ns compliments."

This afforded them an excellent opportunity for going on deck in a thoroughly natural way; those who smoked accordingly cut up a quantity of the tobacco, and, filling their pipes, adjourned to the deck in a body for the purpose of enjoying their post-prandial smoke Johnson was standing aft near the man at the wheel, "with one eye aloft and the other in the binnacle." He looked fierce and excited; he took no notice whatever of the party who had just made their appearance on deck, and his features wore so forbidding an expression that it was at once patent to everybody that the best plan just then would be to leave him entirely alone.

The first thing which they noticed was that the brig had been kept away off her former course, and was now running to leeward, with the wind on her quarter. The canvas had been rapidly packed upon her, and she was now slipping very fast through the water, with topgallant, topmast, and lower studding-sails set to windward, and all the rest of her canvas, fore and aft as well as square, tugging at her like cart-horses. This, as it afterwards appeared, was her favourite point of sailing.

That a sail was in sight was perfectly evident, but nothing could be seen of her from the deck, though the horizon was perfectly clear all round; it was therefore rather difficult at first to ascertain her whereabouts. But it did not long remain so, for in about five minutes the mate came on deck with his sextant in his hand, and suspending the instrument very carefully from his neck by a piece of stout marline, he at once made his way up the main-rigging, and finally settled himself comfortably in the cross-trees, facing aft, and bringing the telescope of the sextant at once to bear upon an object which seemed to lie about a couple of points on the lee quarter. The craft in sight must therefore be astern of the brig, and the mate's movements clearly indicated that she was in chase, and that he was very anxious to ascertain which ship gained upon the other.

The instrument, apparently after being carefully adjusted, was removed from the mate's eye and suspended from the cross-trees in such a manner that it should not strike against the mast or any of the rigging with the roll of the ship, and then the observer drew forth a pipe, which he filled and proceeded to smoke with the greatest apparent calmness and contentment.

The pipe was at length finished, and then the smoker, with the same deliberation which had characterised his former movements, once more applied the sextant to his eye.

"Well," shouted Johnson, "what news of the stranger aloft there?"

"Gaining on us, hand over fist," was the reply.

"That'll do then; you may as well come down," snarled the pirate skipper. "Your staying perched up there, like an owl in an ivy bush, won't help us any; come down and make yourself useful, d'ye hear?"

"Ay, ay," answered the mate, "I'm coming, boss." And he forthwith proceeded to descend the rigging in a careless nonchalant manner which evidently drove his superior almost to the verge of frenzy.

Half an hour passed, and then there appeared far away on the horizon, on the brig's lee quarter, a tiny white speck, which steadily though imperceptibly increased in size until the snowy royals of a large ship stood fully revealed.

This was about half-past three in the afternoon, at which time the wind showed signs of failing.

By half-past four o'clock the stranger had risen her topgallant-sails above the horizon, and it could clearly be seen, even with the unaided eye, that she had royal as well as topgallant studding-sails set, and there could not be a shadow of doubt that she was after the brig.

The spirits of our friends rose to such a high pitch of exultation at this agreeable sight that they found it difficult to conceal their delight when Johnson, abandoning his post near the helmsman, joined them.

"Well, strangers," he remarked with a grim smile, "there's a chance for you yet, you see. That's one of them cursed frigates you was talking about this morning, colonel, but she's a tarnation sight smarter'n I gave any of 'em credit for being. I tell you, cap'n, if this had been the forenoon-watch instead of the first dog-watch it would have been all up with this brig. But now I don't feel quite so sorter anxious as I did. I reckon that unless the breeze freshens, which it ain't going to do, it will take that craft till midnight to get alongside of us; and if she can do it then, why she's welcome to the brig and all aboard of her, curse me if she ain't. See them clouds gathering, away there to the nor'ard? That's a thunder-storm working up, but it won't break for some hours yet, I calculate, and them clouds is going to do me a good turn before that. I reckon you'll have to make up your minds to go to Albatross Island yet, strangers."

And he dived below to his cabin, evidently in an easier state of mind than he had enjoyed an hour before.

By six o'clock the frigate's topsails had risen more than half their height above the horizon, and when Lance, Captain Staunton, and Bowles returned to the deck after the evening meal, the waning light just enabled them to see the stranger's lower yards fairly clear of the water. Before they lost sight of her altogether half her courses had risen into view.

The night closed down very dark, there being no moon, and the sky was entirely overspread with heavy black murky-looking thunder-clouds which completely hid the stars. The wind, too, had dropped to such an extent that an occasional ominous flap was heard from the canvas aloft, though the brig still slid through the water at the rate of about four knots in the hour.

Johnson was in high spirits again. He sat aft near the taffrail, attentively watching the frigate through his night-glass long after she had disappeared from the naked eye; and when it at last became difficult to make her out even with the aid of the glass, he would lay it down, rub his eyes, take half a dozen turns along the deck, then pick up the glass again and have another spell at it. Finally he turned to the mate, who was standing near him, and tendering the glass, said—

"There, take a look, Ben, and tell me if you can pick her out."

The mate peered long and attentively through the telescope, moving it very slowly about that part of the horizon where he knew the frigate to be, but without success.

"It's no go, boss," he said, "my eyes are pretty good, but they're not good enough to see through such darkness as this."

Johnson chuckled. "Do you think," said he, "it looks any lighter ahead? Would our sails show against that cloud-bank in the wake of the fore-mast?"

"Not they," answered the mate confidently. "Why, it's darker, if anything, ahead than it is astern."

"That's so," agreed Johnson with another chuckle. "Now, what," he continued, "what do you think was the last thing the skipper of that frigate did before the darkness closed down?"

"Well," said the mate, "if he knew his business, I should say he would take our bearings."

"And you may take your oath that's exactly what he did," returned Johnson. "Now, take a look round and tell me what you think of the weather."

"The weather?" repeated the mate; "why, a child almost could tell what the weather's going to be. We're going to have thunder, which will bring a northerly breeze along with it while it lasts."

"Capital!" exclaimed Johnson. "Do you think, now, that the captain of that man-o'-war astern is of the same opinion as you and I are about the weather?"

"He's certain to be if he's a seaman," was the reply.

"Now, once more," proceeded Johnson, "supposing you thought of giving the frigate the slip, as we might very easily do this dark night, what course would you steer?"

"I should steer to the nor'ard," answered the mate, "so as to be to wind'ard when the change comes."

"I knew it," exclaimed Johnson delightedly; "I was dead certain of it. Now, we're going to give that frigate the slip by steering to the south'ard; because her skipper will argue as you do, and when he finds he's lost the run of us, he'll haul up to the nor'ard directly. Now, just pass the word for the carpenter to bring along that water-cask I ordered him to rig up this afternoon."

The word was passed, and in a minute or two three men came aft bearing what appeared to be a water-cask with a pole passed down through the bung-hole, and right out through the other side, about six feet of the pole projecting on each side of the cask. To one end of this pole was lashed a short light batten, and to the other end the men now proceeded to secure a small pig of iron ballast. This done, the whole was launched overboard from the taffrail, the cask floating bung up, with half the pole and the light batten standing perpendicularly above it like a mast. To the upper end of this batten was lashed an old horn lantern with a lighted candle in it, after which the whole apparatus was suffered to go adrift.

"Now, in stunsails, and brace sharp up on the port tack," ordered Johnson.

This was soon done; and the brig now feeling the full strength of what little wind there was, seemed to slip along through the water quite as fast as before.

Johnson looked away out over the weather quarter to where the beacon-lantern glimmered in the intense darkness.

"There," said he; "that'll perhaps help to mislead 'em a bit. They'll take it for our binnacle-light, and'll keep straight on till they run over it. Then, finding we've played 'em a trick, they'll haul straight up to the nor'ard, thinking we've gone that way too, and we shall soon be out of sight of one another."

Johnson kept his gaze intently fixed upon the tiny light as long as it remained visible to the naked eye, and when it could no longer be seen in that fashion he deliberately set himself to watch it through his night-glass. More than an hour had elapsed since the cask had been sent adrift before he manifested any signs of emotion, but at length he began to chuckle audibly—

"Now they're nearing it," he murmured, with his eye glued to the tube. "I can see the craft clearly now; they've cast loose the guns and opened the ports; I can see the light of the lanterns shining through 'em. She's creeping up to it pretty fast; but I guess we've walked away from it quite a considerable distance too. There! Now they've run aboard of that tarnation old water-barrel; they know what 'tis by this time, and I reckon the skipper of that frigate is ripping and tearing and cussing and going on till the air smells of brimstone for a quarter of a mile all round. Ah! just as I expected. They've hauled up to the nor'ard; her stern's towards us, for I can see the lights shining out of her cabin-windows; and now every minute 'll take us further apart. Waal, I'm glad I thought of laying for 'em with that old lantern; it'll sorter tell 'em that we're having a good laugh at 'em; won't it, colonel?" turning to our friends and addressing Lance in high good-humour.

"Doubtless you have succeeded in greatly provoking them, if that was your object," replied Lance; "but if I were in your place I don't think I should feel quite easy in my mind yet. If that thunder-storm which has been brewing for so long were to break, as it may do at any moment, the flash of the lightning would be certain to reveal your whereabouts to them."

"I reckon we'll have to take our chance of that," remarked Johnson in a more sober tone; "but let it keep dark half an hour longer, and I don't care how much it lightens after that. Ah, tarnation! look at that."

This last ejaculation was provoked by the sudden illumination of the northern heavens by a brilliant flash of sheet lightning, which revealed not only every detail of the vast bank of murky clouds which lay heaped up, as it were, upon the horizon, but also distinctly showed the frigate on its very verge, still holding steadily northward, her hull and sails standing out sharply like a block of ebony against the faint bluish gleam of the electric light.

Another flash soon followed, then another, and another, the flashes following each other with increasing rapidity, to Johnson's manifest discomfiture; but, though he was evidently unaware of it, the brig was so far perfectly safe from discovery; for the lightning continued to flash up only in the northern quarter, leaving the remainder of the horizon veiled in impenetrable darkness; so that, though the frigate was distinctly revealed to the brig, the brig was completely hidden from the frigate.

The lightning, however, though it had not yet shown the brig's whereabouts, had enabled those on board the frigate to ascertain that she was not ahead of them, as they had supposed, for when the next flash came the man-o'-war was seen nearly broadside-on to the brig, and heading about south-west, her captain having evidently come to the conclusion that the Albatross, after setting her lure, had doubled back like a hare upon her former course.

Johnson waited until another flash came, revealing the frigate still upon the same course, and then he gave orders for his vessel to be kept away, steering this time to the southward and eastward, or about at right angles to the course of the frigate. Ten minutes later the latter was hull-down.

"Now we're safe!" ejaculated the pirate skipper delightedly. "Clew up and furl everything, lads, and be smart about it, for in another five minutes we'll have the lightning flashing all round us; but under bare poles I guess it'll take sharp eyes to pick us out."

"Waal, colonel," he remarked to Lance, shortly afterwards, "I reckon that was a narrer squeak for us, that was. If I'd been fool enough to go to the nor'ard, they'd have had us for sure. That's a right smart frigate, that is; and I guess she's a Yankee. You Britishers don't build such smart boats as that. After this I'm bound more'n ever to have that schooner you promised to build for me, for I don't mind owning up that I began to feel skeered a bit when I saw how we was bein' catched up. Do you think, now, colonel, you could build a schooner that would have walked away from that frigate?"

"Oh dear, yes!" answered Lance, "I am quite sure I could; only, remember, I must not be interfered with in any way. I cannot have people troubling me with suggestions, or, worse still, insisting upon my grafting their ideas on to my own. The ship must be exclusively my own design, and then I can promise you we will turn out a craft capable, if need be, of running away from the fastest frigate that ever was launched."

"All right, colonel; don't you trouble about that," was the reply. "Only say what you want, and it shall be done; and if anybody tries to interfere with you, just point 'em out to me, that's all."

"Very well," returned Lance. "Then I shall consider that a bargain; and now I will wish you good-night, as I think there will be rain shortly, and I've no particular fancy for a drenching unless it comes in the way of duty."

The following morning dawned bright and fair, the thunder-storm of the preceding night having broken and raged furiously for a couple of hours soon after our friends left the deck, and then cleared completely away. When Captain Staunton went on deck he found a fine breeze blowing once more from the westward, and the brig dashing along at a slashing pace under topgallant-sails, with her nose pointing to the northward. The air was clear and transparent; not a cloud flecked the deep blue of the sky overhead; and a man, who had shinned aloft at Johnson's orders as far as the main truck, was just in the act of reporting that there was nothing anywhere in sight. So that any lingering hopes which Captain Staunton may have entertained as to the possibility of the frigate rediscovering them were speedily dashed to the ground.

The fine weather lasted; and three days afterwards, about two o'clock in the afternoon, the look-out aloft reported, "Land ho! right ahead!"

"What is it like?" hailed Johnson from his seat on the skylight.

"It's Look-out Peak, sir; I can make out the shape of it quite well."

"That's all right," returned Johnson. "Stay where you are, and let me know if you see anything like a signal."

In a couple of hours more the land was distinctly visible from the deck, the peak spoken of as "Look-out Peak" appearing first, and then the land on each side of it, rising gradually above the ocean's brim until it lay stretched along the horizon for a length of some half a dozen miles. As they drew in towards the island, our friends (all of whom, excepting the ladies, were on deck) half expected to be sent below in order that they might not become acquainted with the navigation of the harbour-entrance; but this idea did not appear to have presented itself to Johnson, who, on the contrary, joined the group, and began chatting with them in what was evidently meant to be understood as an affable manner.

When they had approached within a mile of the place, the pirate skipper turned to Lance and asked him what he thought of the harbour, and whether he believed he could make it tolerably safe with a dozen guns or so.

"Harbour!" answered Lance, "I see no harbour,—no sign even of one on that part of the coast which we are now approaching. I can distinguish nothing but a rocky shore, against which the surf is breaking heavily enough to dash to pieces the strongest ship that was ever built. Perhaps the harbour lies somewhere beyond that low rocky point which forms the western extremity of the island? But if so, why not steer directly for it?"

"The entrance to the harbour is exactly in line with our jib-boom-end just now," explained Johnson in high good-humour; "but I guess you would never know it unless you was told; would you, colonel?"

"That indeed I should not," answered Lance; "and even now I scarcely know how to believe you."

Lance might well say so, for the whole coast-line in front of them presented an apparently unbroken face of rocky cliffs of various heights, from about thirty to two hundred feet, backed by grassy slopes thickly dotted with dense clumps of trees of various kinds, many of which glowed with the most brilliant tints from the flowers with which they were loaded. Immediately ahead, where Johnson had said the entrance to the harbour lay, a great irregular mass of low jagged rocks projected slightly beyond the general face-line of the cliffs, and behind it was a gap which had the appearance of being caused by the projecting mass of rock having at some remote period broken away and slipped into the sea. The brig, however, continued to stand on boldly, and when she had arrived within about three cables'-lengths of the shore, it became apparent that the large mass of rock ahead, or rather on the lee bow by this time, the brig having luffed a trifle, was entirely detached from the island, leaving a narrow channel of water between it and the cliffs behind it. But it was not until the brig had actually borne away to enter this channel that the entrance to the harbour revealed itself. Then indeed it was seen that the cliff behind, instead of preserving an unbroken face, curved inwards in the form of a cove, the eastern and western arms of which consisted of two projecting reefs jutting out toward the mass of rock in front of them, which in its turn now revealed its true shape, which was that of a crescent, the horns of which overlapped the two projecting reefs forming the eastern and western sides of the harbour-entrance, and acted as a perfect natural breakwater, effectually protecting the harbour itself in all weathers.

Winding her way through the short narrow channel between the rock and the cliffs, the brig hauled sharply round the western point and shot into the cove or harbour itself, which consisted of an irregularly-shaped expanse of water some two hundred acres in extent. At the entrance the rocks on both sides sloped steeply down into the deep blue water; but further in they were fringed along their bases by a beautiful white sandy beach which widened as it approached the bottom of the bay, the land on each side sloping more gradually down to the water, and finally spreading out, where the water ceased, into a broad and lovely valley which stretched inland some three miles, rising gradually as it receded until it became lost among a group of hills which formed the background of the picture.

At anchor in the bay were three hulks, no doubt the three prizes spoken of by Johnson as destined to be broken up for the building of the new craft; and on the grassy plateau at the bottom of the bay and close to the beach stood two large buildings and some half a dozen smaller ones, all constructed of wood. Behind these, a plot of ground, some two acres in extent, was fenced in to form a garden, and a very fruitful one it proved too, if one might judge by the luxuriant growth apparent in its various products. Corn of two or three kinds waved on the eastern slopes, half a dozen head of cattle and perhaps a couple of dozen sheep grazed on the opposite side of the valley; cocoa-nuts reared their tall slender stems and waved their feathery branches by hundreds, and behind them again as the ground sloped gently upward it became more and more densely covered with palm, banana, and plantain groves thickly interspersed with various trees, some of considerable size and dense foliage, among which brilliant orchids and gaudy parasites of the gayest hues entwined themselves to the very summits.

A light gig shot alongside the brig as her anchor was let go, and a tall swarthy man with the unmistakable classic features of a Greek stepped on board. He would have been a strikingly handsome man but for the expression of cunning and cruelty which glittered in his keen black eyes.

"Well, capitan," said he to Johnson as he joined the pirate skipper, "so you have returned once more, and with a full hold, I hope. The people began to think you were gone for good, you have been away so long time."

"Yes," returned Johnson, "back again, Alec, like a bad penny; and we've not brought so very much with us, either; but the little we have 'll be useful, I daresay. The brig don't seem to sail so well as she used to, and we fell in with over half a dozen fine craft that we couldn't get near. They just walked away from us like we was at anchor. We've come in now to give the old hooker an overhaul—she wants it badly enough—and then I think I shall try my luck further to the east'ard, away on t'other side of the Cape altogether. But if we haven't brought a whole ship-load of plunder, I guess we've brought what's most as good. We picked up boat-load of shipwrecked people, and among 'em there's one—that tall soldier-looking chap over there on the larboard side of the skylight—who says he can fortify the place for us, and build us out of these old hulks a craft that 'll beat anything we're likely to meet, 'cepting perhaps steamers."

"Says!" ejaculated the Greek contemptuously.

"Ay, and he can do it too," remarked Johnson. "He's one of them English soldiers who does all the battery-building and fortifying business, and he has a yacht which he designed himself, and which sails so fast that he didn't think the brig's sailing amounted to shucks. I tell you, Alec, the way he talked about that yacht jest set me a longing, it did, sure as you're there. Now, I'm going to leave 'em here with you when I sail next time. They'll fortify the harbour so's it'll be safe if any of them sneakin' men-o'-war comes pryin' about—and we was as near took by one of 'em a few nights ago—as near as near—and they'll build us a regular flyer of a schooner, on condition that they're properly treated; so as long as the work's about I want you to act amiable to 'em, and after we've got all the help out of 'em that we want, I don't care what comes to 'em. They've got some women with 'em—worst luck—and they seem mighty particular about 'em, so I hope you'll see that the gals don't come to any harm. You see, Alec, my boy, we must be civil to 'em if we want 'em to do their best for us; but after they've done their work you can have your own way with the whole lot."

The Greek (whose name, by the way, was Alessandro Ralli) listened to his chief in sullen silence, and when Johnson had finished speaking beckoned him to follow him down into the cabin.

These worthies had been standing during this short conversation just at the foot of the main-mast, and seemed to be either oblivious of or indifferent to the fact that a seaman was just over their heads stowing the driver, and near enough to hear every word that passed. The individual referred to had been taking his time—a good deal of it too—over his task, but no sooner were the skipper and the Greek fairly out of sight down the companion than, with a few dexterous movements, he rapidly passed the last turns of the lashing and slid down on deck.

It was our old friend Bob.

ON ALBATROSS ISLAND

On the following morning all hands on board the brig were stirring early, and, assisted by a strong party from the shore, first moved the vessel down to the bottom of the bay until she took the ground on a beautiful level sandy bottom, and then began to discharge her.

Her cargo comprised a most extraordinary collection of heterogeneous articles, including three pianofortes (two of which were in packing-cases, whilst the other had evidently been taken from a ship's cabin), several cases of arms, a large quantity of powder and lead, bales of silk, a few kegs of Spanish dollars, fifty ingots of gold and as many of silver; several cases of machinery, a large boiler in sections, an immense quantity of provisions of various kinds, ten brass nine-pounder guns taken out of a Spanish ship, several boxes of clothing, and a large quantity of new rope, bolts of canvas, sails—which from their size had evidently never been made for the brig—cases of furniture, etcetera, etcetera.

These articles were all landed in boats, and conveyed with more or less difficulty up to one of the large buildings before-mentioned, and there housed.

There was great jubilation among the men at the sight of so rich a cargo; Ralli, the Greek, quite laying aside his former moroseness of manner and exhibiting an almost childish delight at the sight of the bullion and the kegs of dollars. The men worked hard all day, and by sunset more than half the brig's cargo was on shore. It was not difficult, however, to detect that among these men there were a few—perhaps a dozen—who took no interest in their labour, manifesting very little curiosity as to the nature of the articles which they were handling, and working solely because they had no other choice. These our friends rightly conjectured to be prisoners who had not chosen to cast in their lot with the pirates.

Early in the day that portion of the party from the Galatea in which we are more immediately interested had been conveyed on shore under Johnson's own protection, and taken up to one of the smaller buildings which stood on the beach, with the intimation that they were at liberty to occupy it. It was a small two-story building, constructed of wood; the upper floor being reached through a trap-door which was led up to by a wooden step-ladder. This floor, like the one below, consisted of a single room, and was lighted by two windows, one at each end, the two longer walls of the room being fitted with three tiers of bunks similar to those found on board ship. The ground floor was fitted up with a fire-place, shelves all round the room, a rough deal table and two long benches, and had evidently been used as a general living-room.

The place was wretchedly dirty, and on being inducted into it the first act of the men was to procure an abundance of soap and water, and set vigorously to work to give it a thorough cleansing. This occupied them all the morning.

At noon a bell rang, which was the signal for all hands to knock off work and get their dinner, the messman of each gang going to the galley, a small building near the store, and drawing from the cook a sufficient quantity of food for the party to which he belonged.

Bob, who with the carpenter had been duly liberated according to promise, cheerfully took upon himself the duties of messman for the party to which he belonged, and presenting himself with the others, he obtained without difficulty the wherewithal to set before our friends a very respectable meal.

While they were at dinner, Lance tore a leaf out of his pocket-book and jotted down the various articles, such as bedding, crockery, and utensils of various kinds which they required, and on the completion of the list he hurried away with it to Johnson, who at once wrote at its foot an order to the storekeeper for the issue of the articles named. These were soon conveyed to the hut, and by sunset they had the place in very tolerable order.

Now that they were on shore, however, they felt that the time had arrived when a little more privacy could be enjoyed by the ladies of the party; so a few boards were obtained and with them a partition knocked up, dividing the upper room into two equal parts, the half which was approached through the trap-door being devoted to the ladies, while the men obtained access to their sleeping apartment by means of a ladder and the open window, the ladder being drawn up into the room at night.

At six o'clock the bell rang again, upon which all hands knocked off work for the day, and after half an hour devoted to cleaning up, etcetera, tea, or supper as most of the men termed it, was served.

On this particular evening, however, there was a slight deviation from the usual order of procedure; the messmen being detained at the galley until all were present (instead of being served and despatched in the order of their arrival), when Johnson made his appearance on the scene and announced that the kegs of dollars landed that day from the brig would be distributed in the capstan-house that evening at eight o'clock, and that any of the prisoners not yet belonging to the "brotherhood" who chose to present themselves there at that hour, and would sign the "bond of brotherhood," would be entitled to an equal share of the spoil. Bob duly mentioned this item of information on his arrival with the viands; and it was at once decided that, as all the pirates would thus be engaged for some time, advantage should be taken of so favourable an opportunity to give the ladies a little fresh air and exercise.

They waited until all the pirates appeared to have betaken themselves to the capstan-house, and then sallied out in a body upon an exploring expedition up the valley. It was a lovely night, as light as day, the full moon riding high overhead in an unclouded sky, and so flooding the heavens with her silvery light that only a few stars of the first magnitude were visible. There was very little wind, and a heavy dew was falling; but that, after the hardship of exposure in an open boat, was a trifle so insignificant that it attracted no one's attention.

The walk was a most enjoyable one to all, but it was especially delightful to three couples who early paired off together, and in a quiet unostentatious fashion dropped into the rear. Captain and Mrs Staunton had naturally much to say to each other upon matters interesting only to themselves; while as for Violet and Rex, Blanche and Lance, this was their first opportunity for an exchange of these sweet nothings in which lovers delight since the eventful evening on which they had been driven out by the flames from the unfortunate Galatea. Tempted by the beauty of the night they strayed a long distance; and when at length they returned to the hut, weary with the unaccustomed exercise, but happier than they had been for a long time, the settlement was wrapped in the silence of repose.

On the following morning, immediately after breakfast, Johnson presented himself, with the request that Lance, Captain Staunton, and the carpenter would accompany him on a visit to the prizes, for the purpose of deciding which of them should be broken up to build the new schooner. Two of these vessels were barques, and one a full-rigged ship. The ship was teak-built, and an unmistakable East-Indiaman; while of the barques, one was oak-built and copper-fastened, and the other a soft-wood vessel put together with iron. The oak-built ship was nearly new, the copper which covered her bottom up to the bends had not a wrinkle on its entire surface, and her deck-planking showed no signs of wear; but she was modelled for carrying, rather than for speed; it was therefore decided without much hesitation that she should be the one to be broken up.

The next point to be settled was the position of the building-yard.

Lance had given this matter a great deal of quiet consideration, and had come to the conclusion that for many reasons it would be better to have the yard as far away as possible from the rest of the settlement, one consideration which greatly weighed with him being the possibility that their best chance of escape might be in launching the schooner on the quiet during the night and taking her from the stocks direct to sea.

Johnson had already made up his mind that the best site for the stocks would be on the sandy beach immediately in front of the capstan-house; and there was a great deal to be said in favour of this, a carpenter's shop being already in existence close to the spot, and all the cordage and tackle of every description being stored in the capstan-house. But this did not at all chime in with Lance's plans, so he merely remarked that it would do well enough if no better place could be found, but that the flatness of the ground and the consequent shoal water at that spot would prove serious difficulties in the way of launching; and that it would be advisable before deciding to give the entire shore of the bay a very careful examination.

Some hours were accordingly spent in this work; and a site was at last fixed upon in a locality thoroughly favourable to Lance's secret wishes. This was a small indentation in the harbour-face of the breakwater rock which marked the entrance to the bay.

This indentation was about an acre and a half in extent, with a smooth rocky floor sloping down into the water at an inclination of just the right gradient for the launching-ways. It is true it was a long way away from the settlement; but Lance's arguments in favour of adopting it were so convincing that Johnson was fain to give way, which, he at last did with a very good grace.

This matter settled, Lance intimated that he should like to devote a little more time to the examination of the rock; as it appeared to him that here was the proper place to construct the battery which was to defend the harbour. They accordingly climbed with great difficulty to the highest point of the rock, which was immediately behind or to seaward of the future shipyard, and which had an elevation of nearly a hundred feet above the sea-level.

The top of the rock was very irregular in shape; but Lance soon saw that a few charges of powder judiciously placed would give them a nearly circular platform of about sixty feet diameter, which would be ample space for such a battery as he proposed to construct. His first idea had been to evade the construction of this battery altogether if possible; but a little reflection had shown him that a time might come when its existence would be of the utmost importance to themselves, and he therefore decided to go on with the work. He accordingly pointed out to Johnson the strength of the position they occupied, the complete command over the harbour-entrance which a battery would have at that point, and the effective defence it would constitute to the new shipyard; and the pirate was speedily convinced of the soundness of Lance's views.

These points settled, the party returned to the bottom of the bay; and Johnson then invited Lance to present himself at eight o'clock that evening in the capstan-house, there to submit his plans for the new schooner to a committee of the pirates for approval.

The drawings were in fact scarcely ready; but by working hard for the remainder of the day not only were they completed, but the carpenter had also prepared a half-model of the hull by the hour at which the committee was to meet; and, armed with these, Lance, Captain Staunton, and the carpenter duly presented themselves at the capstan-house at eight o'clock.

They were met at the door by Johnson, who conducted them up a step-ladder into an apartment in the first floor of the building. It was a room about sixty feet long by forty feet broad, and was apparently used as a sort of general assembly-room, being fitted up with rows of benches from the door right up to a platform at the further end. On this platform there stood, upon the present occasion, a large table lighted by a pair of handsome lamps, and surrounded by a dozen chairs, some of which were already occupied when Lance and his companions entered.

Our friends quietly seated themselves, Lance on one side of Johnson, Captain Staunton on the other, with the trusty carpenter next him. Johnson then ordered the bell to be rung to summon the laggards; and in a few minutes afterwards the entire committee, some eight men in all, had assembled.

Johnson then rose to address the party. He remarked that they were already aware of the purpose for which they had been summoned, namely to inspect the plans of a new schooner which he proposed to have built; but he had been led to understand that doubts had been expressed in certain quarters (here he glanced at Ralli) as to the necessity for such a proceeding; and he had therefore invited them there to meet him in order that he might lay before them his views upon the matter and answer such questions as any of them might wish to put to him. He then cited several unsuccessful chases in which he had engaged, as well as his recent narrow escape from the frigate, as evidence in support of his assertion that not only their profit but their actual safety depended upon their becoming possessed of a much faster vessel than the Albatross as speedily as might be; winding up his speech by requesting that each man present would give the committee the benefit of his views on the matter in hand.

A somewhat excited debate then ensued, Ralli making himself especially conspicuous by his opposition to Johnson; but in the end the latter succeeded in carrying his point, and the construction of the vessel was definitely decided upon.

Lance was then called upon to submit his drawings for inspection; which he forthwith did, explaining at the same time the peculiarities of the design. The vessel he proposed to build was to have a broad shallow hull, with a very deep keel; and her water-lines were simply faultless. There was a considerable difference of opinion as to the desirability of having a vessel of that type; but Lance, who was anxious above all things to build a craft which would carry his party safely, comfortably, and speedily home, provided they should be so fortunate as to obtain possession of her, ably combated all adverse criticism, in which he was ably seconded by Johnson, who seemed greatly taken with the design, and in the end they had their own way.

This important point being settled, the meeting broke up; and on the following morning the first step was taken toward carrying the work into execution. The vessel which had been selected for breaking up was unmoored and brought close in to the shore abreast the capstan-house, where she was anchored. A strong party was then told off for the purpose of loading her, under the joint-superintendence of Lance, Johnson, Captain Staunton, and the carpenter of the Galatea, who went by the name of "Kit," short for Christopher. Lance requisitioned the stores of the pirates with the utmost freedom, taking everything he thought likely to be in the least degree useful; and in this way three days were consumed. On the fourth day the hulk was once more unmoored, and, with three boats ahead, towed to the rock at the mouth of the harbour and grounded upon it. The work of landing the stores and materials then commenced; and when these had all been conveyed safely ashore, the erection of workshops, etcetera, was begun. And it was at this period that Johnson began to realise for the first time how valuable an acquisition to his band he had gained in the persons of Lance, Rex, Brooke, and Kit. The three first were quite in their element when it came to the designing and erecting of the various buildings and of the battery, which was at the same time commenced, whilst Kit displayed an amount of intelligence in the carrying out of their instructions which was beyond all praise. Johnson chuckled with inward satisfaction and made certain secret resolves; but he said nothing.

Meanwhile the Albatross had been careened, her copper stripped off where necessary, and replaced after caulking the planking underneath; the copper had been scoured all over, down to the very keel, until it shone like gold; the top-sides had been caulked; then the deck; the hull repainted inside and out; and when the buildings at the new dockyard were about being begun, the spars, sails, and rigging of the brig were in process of undergoing a thorough overhaul. It looked very much as though the Albatross would be ready for sea in another fortnight at the outside; while Lance estimated that, with the strength then at his command, it would be at least a month before the keel of the schooner could possibly be laid. Now Johnson had set his heart upon seeing this done before he sailed; when therefore he found that it would be impossible unless he strongly augmented Lance's working party, he took half the men working upon the brig and turned them over to the dockyard gang, with the result that the work on the brig was retarded while that at the shipyard was expedited so greatly as to ensure the gratification of his wish. So eager was he to hasten on the building of the schooner that he even proposed the abandonment of the old settlement at the bottom of the bay, and the establishment of a new one on the rock itself. This, however, by no means suited Lance's views. It would be manifestly impossible to launch and make off with the schooner if they were to be environed by a gang of men every one of whom would be sure to regard the new-comers with more or less of suspicion and distrust; so Lance threw out a few mysterious hints about secret passages and hidden chambers beneath the battery and in the heart of the rocks, which for Johnson's own individual sake it would be wise to keep from the knowledge of all but those actually engaged in constructing them; and by this means he managed to avert the threatened transfer. The thought occurred to him that possibly the Galatea party might be more safe if quartered upon the rock, and thus entirely separated from the pirates; but on reconsidering the question and talking it over with the others the conclusion arrived at was that the rock was an exposed and sterile spot for a habitation, in addition to which it possessed other disadvantages; and that perhaps, for the present, it would be better not to propose it.

At length the eventful day arrived on which the ceremony of laying the keel of the new schooner was to be performed. The pieces of timber of which it was to be composed—some of which had already formed part of the keel of the old ship—had all been shaped, the blocks laid in position, and every other preparation fully made; and nothing remained but to lay down the keel-pieces on the blocks placed ready for their reception, and to bolt them together.

In the fulness of his delight Johnson resolved that the day should be a regular fête day; and accordingly on the morning in question the shipyard was gaily dressed with flags—of more than one nationality—which were hoisted upon poles hastily set up for the purpose; and all hands, clean shaven, and dressed in their best, prepared to assist in the ceremony.

The proceedings were inaugurated by Johnson, who, attired in the full uniform of a captain of the American navy, took up a position on one of the keel-blocks, and from thence made an animated address to his followers, in which he rapidly sketched the history of the band from the day on which they had entered upon their present career by taking from their officers the Amazon tea clipper, in which they had sailed from China for England, down to the present time. He reminded them of the difficulties and misfortunes with which they had been obliged to contend; how they had unfortunately lost the Amazon upon an island some hundreds of miles to the westward of their present position; how they had been compelled to leave the island in open boats; of the sufferings which they subsequently endured; and how by a lucky accident they were finally enabled to obtain possession of the Albatross. He next dwelt upon the good fortune which had since attended them; the many valuable prizes they had taken; the rich store of booty they had accumulated; and the steady augmentation of the numbers of the brotherhood. Then, giving free rein to his fancy, he enlarged upon his plans for the future. What had already been done was, he said, nothing—a simple preliminary effort, a mere trial of strength—compared with what he would do. He would never be satisfied, he informed them, until he could finally lead them all out of that harbour on board a fleet of at least ten well armed, swift, and fully manned ships, in which it would be possible for them to ravage the entire coast of Spanish South America, despoiling the rich towns and laughing at all opposition. In this way, he promised them, he would place them in possession of such an unheard-of amount of treasure that every man among them should be worth his millions; after which, by following a plan which he would unfold to them at the proper time, they could quietly disband and settle down for the remainder of their lives, each man on that particular spot of earth which pleased him best, in the peaceful enjoyment of his well-earned gold. And they were assembled there that day, he added in conclusion, to lay the keel of the first of the ten clippers by which this glorious result was to be accomplished.

It was an eloquent and masterly speech. Johnson was most accurately acquainted with the characters of those who surrounded him; he was making a great bid for the recovery of that popularity which in some unexplained way—but largely through the machinations of Alec Ralli, he shrewdly suspected—had been steadily slipping away from him; and he believed that the making of such dazzling promises as he had just indulged in was the surest way of winning it back. And if vociferous and tumultuous cheering was to be taken as an indication of success the pirate chief had every cause to be gratified. The enthusiasm was intense. Cheer after cheer rent the air; the men shook hands all round and then pressed forward, hustling each other, eager to perform the same ceremony with Johnson, vowing as they did so the blindest and most unswerving fidelity to him, and calling down the most frightful imprecations upon all traitors.

Ralli stood at some little distance in the background, his arms folded across his chest, and a cynical smile wreathing his lips.

"Ah right," he muttered; "go on and shout yourselves hoarse, you swine! Yell, cheer, and swear fidelity until you are out of breath if it pleases you so to do; I like to see and hear it, for what is it after all but froth; you are all in a ferment just now, and it is best that this noisy gas should have its vent; you will soon sober down again, and then—we shall see. As for you," he continued, with a furtive scowl at Johnson, whose face beamed with gratification, "you have had your day, and, blind bat as you are, you were beginning to see it just for a moment, but this fine speech of yours has thrown you off your guard again. You doubtless think that with a few empty boastful words you have recovered your lost position, but you are mistaken, my good friend, as you will find out when you return from your next cruise—if indeed you ever return at all. Well, enjoy your own opinion while you can; rejoice in the ease with which you have re-established yourself; I shall not attempt to undeceive you—at least just now, so I will go and add my plaudits to those of the herd—pah!" and he spat contemptuously on the ground as he moved forward to shake Johnson cordially by the hand.

Order being at length restored, the ceremony of laying the keel was proceeded with. The several pieces were already on the ground, properly shaped, with bolt-holes bored, the bolts fitted, and in short every preparation made for fastening them together; and now, at a word from Johnson, a hundred eager hands seized the heavy timbers, and, under Lance's superintendence, placed them upon the blocks. The joints were next brought closely together, the bolts inserted, the perfect straightness of the entire length of keel accurately tested, and finally the bolts were all simultaneously driven home and the keel "laid," amidst the deafening cheers of the pirates and the roar of a battery of guns which had been placed temporarily in position to do due honour to the ceremony.

The men were then served with an extra allowance of grog, after which they were dismissed to amuse themselves in any way they pleased for the remainder of the day.

Johnson saw fit to leave the shipyard in the boat which conveyed Lance, Captain Staunton, and the rest of the Galatea party back to the settlement at the bottom of the bay, and it was evident during the passage that he was most anxious to make himself agreeable and to leave behind him a favourable impression. At last, when the boat was nearing the beach at which the party intended to land, he said to Lance—

"Look here, colonel, I've been thinking about them women-folk of yourn; they must find it mighty lonesome here, with nothing much to do; do you think it'd please 'em if I was to send one of them planners to your diggin's? 'Cause, if you do, they shall have one. The cussed things ain't no use to us, and I don't hardly know what I fetched 'em along for."

"Thank you very much," said Lance. "I have no doubt a little music now and then would prove a solace to them; indeed, it would make the evenings much more pleasant for us all, and if you feel disposed to spare us an instrument we shall remember you all the more gratefully."

"Then you may consider it done," Johnson replied, as the boat's keel grated on the beach and the party stepped ashore. "Come up to the capstan-house with me, and you can choose which you will have, and I will send it along at once."

Lance accordingly proceeded to the capstan-house with Johnson, while the remainder of the party wended their way straight to the hut, well pleased at what they considered a mark of great consideration on the part of the pirate chief.

When Lance found himself alone with his companion he thought it would be a favourable opportunity to prefer a request which had been in his mind for several days, but which he had had no previous chance of mentioning.

"I am glad," he said, "to have this opportunity of thanking you, captain, in the name of our party, for all you have done for our comfort, under circumstances which I could not fail to perceive have been somewhat trying to you. I now want to ask you to add one favour more, and that is, to supply us with a sufficiency of arms and ammunition to enable us to defend ourselves, if need be, in your absence. Whilst you are on the island we feel ourselves to be safe, but I confess I am not altogether without doubts as to the treatment which we may receive at the hands of your Greek friend Ralli after your departure. And it would add very greatly to our feeling of security in your absence if we were provided with the means of resisting any attempt at unfair dealing on his part. I presume it is unnecessary for me to say that we should only use the weapons in a case of absolute necessity?"

"Waal now, colonel," said Johnson, "what you ask is fair enough, and for my own part I'd be willing enough to let you have all you want, but I vow I don't just see exactly how I'm to do it. The key of the arm-chest is in the armourer's pocket, and I can't issue anything out of that chest without his knowledge. Now, I know that cuss, he's no friend of mine, and he'd just go straight away and tell Ralli what I'd done, and that'd set the Greek dead agin you all for a certainty and make things just as uncomfortable for you as could be. Besides which, Ralli 'd just take 'em all away from you again as soon as my back was turned, and then you'd be worse off 'n ever. No, that won't do, we'll have to go some other way about it; but you leave it to me, general; you may bet your pile I'll find out a way to do it before I sail. Now, which of these boxes of music will you have?"

They had arrived by this time at the capstan-house, and were standing near the pianofortes, all of which had been placed together on the floor of the sail-loft, the packing-cases having been ripped off and probably used for firewood. Lance ran his fingers over the key-board of each instrument in turn, striking a few chords and harmonies to test the quality of the tone and touch, and finally selected a superb "grand" by Broadwood.

"All right, general, I'll have the durned thing taken down to your quarters to oncet. But do you mean to say that you know how to thump music out of them things as well as how to build batteries and ships and so forth?" ejaculated Johnson.

"Well, yes," said Lance, laughingly, "I believe I must plead guilty to being somewhat of a musician, though I have not touched an instrument for many a day until now."

"Then sit right down there, colonel, and play me something good," said Johnson, rolling a nail-keg as a seat up to one of the instruments.

Lance, thoroughly amused at the comical incongruity of the situation, sat down and rattled off "Yankee Doodle," an air which he judged would be likely to find appreciation with his queer companion.

Johnson stood for a moment spell-bound as the well remembered strains fell upon his ear, then a broad grin of delight overspread his features, and finally he began to caper about the sail-loft in the most extraordinary manner, and to utter certain unearthly sounds which Lance fancied was Johnson's idea of singing.

"Something else! gimme some more," the pirate captain exclaimed rapturously, when his entertainer at length raised his fingers from the key-board. Whereupon Lance began to play and sing "Hail, Columbia." Johnson stood still and silent as a statue now, the stirring strains touched an altogether different chord of his memory, and for an instant something suspiciously like a tear glistened in his eye.

"Thank you," he said very quietly, when Lance had finished, "that will do now; I would rather not hear any more at present. Let me keep the sound of that song in my mind as long as I can; my little maid at home used to sing that to me. But, look here," he added, as Lance closed the instrument, "if you wish to be on good terms with the men after I am gone, have them all up in the meeting-room sometimes of an evening, and treat them to a little music; they will appreciate that, and you could do nothing more likely to win their regard. Why shouldn't you give 'em—give us all—a concert to-night, to-day being a holiday?"

Lance hesitated for a moment before making answer to this strange and unexpected proposal.

"To tell you the truth," he said at last, "I am afraid your people will be hardly in a mood to-night to appreciate such music as I could give them; the grog will have got into their heads, and they will be more inclined to sing among themselves than to sit quietly to listen to me."

"Not at all," answered Johnson, who, now that a serious mood was upon him, had entirely dropped his Americanism of speech, "not at all; I have taken care to give orders that they shall not have sufficient to make them noisy. You will find them perfectly quiet and orderly, and I confess I should like to see the effect of a little genuine good music upon them."

"Very well," answered Lance nonchalantly, "I am sure I have no objection; and, now that you have mentioned it, I confess I feel curious to see the result of so novel an experiment."

"Then it is settled," said Johnson; and he forthwith summoned a party of men, to some of whom he gave orders to remove to the hut the pianoforte Lance had chosen, while to others was deputed the task of taking one of the other instruments into the large room used for purposes of general assembly, and placing the room in proper order for the evening's entertainment, which was fixed to commence at the orthodox hour of eight o'clock.

When Lance Evelin sauntered into the hut he was assailed by a general chorus of questions.

"What ridiculous story is this which my husband has been telling us, Mr Evelin?" inquired Mrs Staunton.

"About the piano, you know," added Violet.

"Is it actually true, Lance, that that absurd creature is really going to let us have one?" chimed in Blanche.

"It would be a good deal more sensible of him if he would provide us with more comfortable quarters," grumbled Dale.

"I agree with you there, Dale, it certainly would," said Rex Fortescue. "Of course I am speaking now of the matter as it affects the ladies; for ourselves, we can rough it well enough, but I certainly wish they could be made more comfortable. However, the fellow seems to have done his best for us; I have seen no better building than this in the whole settlement, so I suppose we must endeavour to be content as long as we are obliged to remain here; and as for the piano, why it will enable the ladies to beguile an hour or two; but it is a queer present to make under the circumstances, and the man who made it is certainly a bit of an eccentric."

"You are right," replied Evelin; "and this gift is by no means his only eccentricity. Guess what is his latest request, or command, I scarcely know which to call it?"

They all decided that it would be utterly impossible for them to guess, there was no saying what absurd whim might seize upon such a man; they would be surprised at nothing which he might ask, and so on.

"Well, then, I will tell you," said Lance. "He wishes me to give the men a concert to-night at eight o'clock in the assembly-room."

"Oh, Lance, what an extraordinary request!" exclaimed Blanche. "You will of course refuse; you will never trust yourself alone among all those men?"

"Certainly I shall," answered her lover, "why not? There will not be the slightest danger. The men are not in an excited state by any means, and I have an idea that a little music now and then may increase our popularity among them and place us on a more secure footing, if indeed it does not enable us to reach and awaken whatever of good may still exist in their breasts. Besides," he added with a gay laugh, "I feel curious to see what effect I can produce upon them."

"If you go, Lance, I shall go with you," said Rex.

Violet Dudley glanced quickly and somewhat appealingly at the last speaker, but she had too much spirit to say a word which would keep her lover away from the side of his friend when there was a possibility that that friend might stand in need of help.

"I think I may as well go also," remarked Captain Staunton. "It seems hardly fair to leave you all the work to do, Evelin, when any of the rest of us can help you. I can sing a fairly good song, I flatter myself, if I am not much of a hand at the piano, and so when you feel tired I'll give you a spell."

"All right," said Lance. "The more the merrier; we shall at least show them that we are no churls. Are there any more volunteers?"

"Certainly," said Bob, "I'm one, Mr Evelin, if you will have me. I am something like Captain Staunton; I'm no hand at a piano, but I can sing, and I know a recitation or two which I think may serve to raise a good-humoured laugh."

"I'm no singer," said Brook, "but I know a few rather taking conjuring tricks, and I should like to go with you; but perhaps it would be hardly prudent to leave the ladies without any protection, would it? Therefore I think I'll remain to-night, and go some other evening if there's going to be any repetition of this sort of thing."

Mr Dale said nothing; he simply sat moodily plucking at his beard and muttering to himself; by the look of his countenance he was utterly disgusted with the whole proceeding.

Thus, then, it was finally arranged, and at a few minutes before eight o'clock, Lance and his party issued from the hut on their way to the assembly-room, which they could see was already brilliantly lighted up.

Ralli Explains Himself;
So Does Lance

On entering the assembly-room, our friends found that it was not only, as they had seen from the outside, well lighted, but that a very successful attempt had been made to decorate it by the draping of flags all round the walls, and the arrangement of an elaborate and well-designed flag-trophy on the wall at the back of the elevated platform, or stage, as it may be called. The long table, with its accompaniment of chairs, had been pushed back against the wall, and the pianoforte stood in the centre of the platform. The room was quite full, and the men appeared, for the most part, disposed to behave quietly and decorously. There were only some half a dozen young fellows who seemed at all inclined to be noisy or boisterous, and they occupied seats in the centre of the room. Johnson occupied a chair on one side of the platform, and Ralli balanced him on the opposite side. Johnson appeared rather surprised to see four of the Galatea party put in an appearance instead of one only; but he made no remark, merely waving them to accommodate themselves with chairs from those placed against the wall.

"I am rather better than my word, you see," observed Lance to him as the four friends stepped upon the platform.

"I promised to do what I could in the way of furnishing your people with a little entertainment to-night, and I have brought three volunteers with me, which will enable us to infuse into the proceedings a little more variety than I could hope to impart to them alone."

"So much the better, colonel," returned Johnson. "It's real kind of you, I call it; and if the lads don't appreciate it, they ought to; that's all I can say. I've told 'em what you're going to do for 'em and all that; so, as soon as you're ready, I guess you can fire away."

Lance turned and opened the piano, looking quietly over the audience as he did so. His eye fell upon the half-dozen who seemed disposed to interrupt the proceedings, and stepping forward to the edge of the platform, he waved his hand for silence and said—

"Your captain informs me that he has already explained to you the reason for his invitation to you to be present here this evening. To-day has been a somewhat notable day in the annals of the settlement. You have this morning laid the keel of a new ship, and commenced an undertaking which will tax your utmost skill, energy, and resource to carry through to a successful issue; and Captain Johnson has thought it an event of sufficient importance to be specially marked. Hence he has made it a holiday for all hands; and, finding that I possessed some little skill as a musician, he invited me to help in the celebration of the day by closing it with a musical performance. This I willingly consented to do, in the belief that it might afford you a little pleasure and recreation; and I may as well take advantage of the present opportunity to tell you all that my friends and myself will always be found ready to do everything in our power to promote your comfort and welfare. But I must remind you that we are here to-night for your pleasure rather than our own. We will do our best to amuse you, and I hope that you in your turn will individually do what you can to maintain quiet and order. We may not perhaps succeed in pleasing you all; if such should be the case, let those who are dissatisfied rise and quietly leave, and not disturb others, or interfere with their enjoyment by giving noisy expression to their dissatisfaction, I notice one or two who seem inclined to be a little unruly, but I hope they have sense enough to see that such conduct on their part would be in the worst possible taste, and that they will think better of it."

Loud exclamations of approval greeted this speech, mingled with shouts of "If they don't behave themselves we'll turn 'em out, guv'nor," and such like. There was a good deal of noise and confusion for about five minutes, during which Lance calmly seated himself and waited patiently for silence; and, when this was at length restored, he went to the piano and sang to his own accompaniment Dibdin's "Tom Bowline." Lance possessed a full deep rich bass voice of exceptionally fine quality; and as the words of the song pealed through the room, a breathless silence was maintained by his strange audience,—the silence of surprise and delight. Many of the men knew the song; had sung it or heard it sung hundreds of times on a ship's forecastle during the dog-watch; but not one of them had probably ever heard it sung before by a man of refined feeling, capable of expressing the full sentiment of the words, and it now came upon them almost like a revelation. Sailors as a class are proverbially fond of music, but very few of them ever have—or, perhaps it would be more true to say, give themselves—the opportunity to hear anything of better quality than the trash sung in music-halls; and most, if not all, of Lance's audience now therefore experienced for the first time the refining power of really good music. Their enthusiastic applause at the conclusion of the song was perfectly deafening.

Captain Staunton then stepped forward and sang in true seamanlike style "The Bay of Biscay," the chorus of which was given with great unction and enjoyment by the whole audience.

Rex Fortescue followed with "The Death of Nelson;" and then Bob gave in excellent style a laughable recitation, which convulsed his audience, even to the tickling of the sullen Ralli into a grim smile. Then Lance sang again; and so the entertainment proceeded for a couple of hours, to the unbounded gratification of all hands, when the pirates dispersed in a perfectly quiet and orderly manner, after giving, at Johnson's call, three cheers for their entertainers.

"Thank you, colonel! thank you heartily all of you!" said that individual as our friends parted from him outside the capstan-house. "You've given us a real treat to-night, and I guess all hands 'll feel ever so much more friendly to you for it. Give 'em another dose or two of the same sort of thing now and again, and I reckon they'll take care you don't get ill-treated while I'm away."

"What about the arms and ammunition which I asked for to-day?" said Lance.

"You leave that to me, general," replied Johnson. "I guess I'll find a way to let you have 'em before I sail; I won't forget it; you trust me. Good-night."

"Good-night," was the reply; and our friends turned away in the direction of the hut.

"Would you mind walking a little way up the valley, gentlemen, before we go inside?" said Bob. "I want to tell you something I ought perhaps to have told you long ago; but we have been so busy, I could never find an opportunity without speaking before the ladies, who, I think, ought not to know anything about it."

"Certainly, Robert," said Captain Staunton; "let us hear what it is by all means. It is doubtless something of importance, or you would not speak so earnestly."

"Well, sir," said Bob, "I wanted chiefly to warn you all not to trust Johnson too much. He seems friendly enough, but I doubt very much whether he is sincere. The day that we arrived in port, when the hands went aloft to stow the canvas, I jumped aloft with them, just to keep my hand in, as it were, and stowed the driver. While I was passing the gaskets, that fellow Ralli came on board and entered into conversation with Johnson, who spoke to him about us, and more particularly about you, Mr Evelin. He said that you were going to design a very fast vessel for him, and that we were to assist in the building of her, and in the fortification of the harbour; and that as long as we could be of use we were to be treated civilly; but that when we had done everything required of us, he wouldn't care how we were treated, or what became of us."

"The false, treacherous scoundrel!" exclaimed Captain Staunton indignantly. "Was that all he said, Robert?"

"All that I heard," said Bob. "After that they both went into the cabin. I wasn't eaves-dropping, you know, sir; but I was just overhead, so that I couldn't help hearing every word they said; and as they were talking about us, I thought I was justified in keeping my ears open."

"Quite right, Robert, so you were," answered the skipper. "We are surrounded by and at the mercy of a band of men who have outraged every law, both divine and human; it therefore behoves us, for our own sakes, and even more for the sake of the helpless women dependent upon us, to take every possible precaution, and to ascertain by every possible means, what are their actual intentions regarding us. They are detaining us here against our will; they have imposed upon us tasks which they have not a shadow of right to lay upon us; and if they meditate treachery—which, from what you say, seems only too probable—we are justified in resorting to craft, if necessary, to protect ourselves. Is not that your opinion, gentlemen?" turning to Lance and Rex.

"Unquestionably," answered Lance promptly; "the men are, one and all—excepting, of course, the few who have refused to join the 'brotherhood,' as they call it—outlaws; and, as such, they have no claim whatever to be treated in the straightforward fashion with which one deals with a lawful enemy, such as one meets with in ordinary warfare. Your information, Robert, is valuable, not altogether on account of its novelty, but rather as being confirmatory of what has hitherto amounted merely to conjecture on our part. I have long suspected that our friend Johnson is not quite so straightforward as he would have us believe. Well, 'forewarned is forearmed;' we are evidently in a very critical position here, a position demanding all the coolness, self-possession, and foresight we have at our command to enable us to successfully extricate ourselves; and I think we should give the matter our immediate consideration—now—to-night, I mean—we shall perhaps never have a better opportunity—and endeavour to decide upon some definite plan of future action."

"Very well," said Captain Staunton, "let us continue our walk, and talk matters over. It is perfectly evident, as you say, Mr Evelin, that we are in a very critical and difficult position, and the question is, What steps ought we to take in order to extricate ourselves? I think it is pretty clear that this man Johnson has no intention of releasing us of his own free-will; we can be much too useful to him for him ever to do that; if, therefore, we are ever to get away from this place, it will have to be done in spite of him. And as we are too weak to escape by force, we must do so by craft; I can see no other way for it, can you?"

"Well," said Lance slowly, blowing a long thin cloud of cigar-smoke meditatively up into the warm still night air, "I fancy we shall have to try a combination of both. I cannot conceive any practicable course which will allow of our escaping without coming to blows with the pirates; I wish I could. Of course I do not care on my own account, although—notwithstanding my former profession—I am not particularly fond of fighting if it can be done without. But there are the ladies and poor little May; it is of them I always think when the idea of strife and bloodshed suggests itself. Then there is their comfort as well as their safety to be thought of; were it not for them I believe there would not be very much difficulty in seizing a stock of provisions and water, together with a boat, and slipping quietly out to sea some dark night, trusting to good fortune—or Providence rather—to be eventually picked up by a passing ship. But I should certainly be slow to recommend so desperate a course under present circumstances, save in the very last extremity. The hardships those poor creatures passed through in their last boat-voyage I have not yet forgotten."

It is not necessary to repeat every word of the discussion which followed; suffice it to say that it was of so protracted a character that the three individuals engaged in it did not enter their hut until the first faint flush of dawn was brightening the eastern sky. Bob had been dismissed within an hour of the termination of the concert with a message to the effect that Captain Staunton and his two companions felt more disposed for a walk than for sleep, and that the rest of the party had therefore better retire when they felt so inclined, as the hour at which the three gentlemen would return was quite uncertain. The time thus spent had not, however, been thrown away; for, after a very earnest discussion of the situation, the conclusion arrived at was that they could not do better than adhere to their original plan of endeavouring to make off with the new schooner, and that her construction should therefore be pushed forward with all possible expedition; but that, as there was only too much reason to dread a change from the present pacific and friendly disposition manifested toward them by the pirates, an attempt should also be made to win over as many as possible of the prisoners, not only with the object of effecting these poor creatures' deliverance from a cruel bondage, but also in order that the fighting strength of the Galatea party (as they came to term themselves) might be so far increased as to give them a slightly better chance of success than they now had in the by no means improbable event of a brush with the enemy.

Now that the keel of the new schooner was actually laid, operations were resumed with even more than their former alacrity on board the Albatross, and on the evening of the fourth day after the events related in the last chapter she was reported as once more ready for sea.

During these four days Captain Staunton and the rest of his party—excepting Dale, who positively refused to do any work whatever—had, in accordance with their resolution, been extremely busy at the new shipyard, getting out and fixing in position the stem and stern posts; and it was only by the merest accident that they heard, on the evening in question, that the brig was to sail on the following day.

As Lance had heard no more about the promised arms and ammunition, he at once determined to see Johnson once more respecting them. He accordingly set out in search of the pirate captain, but, to his chagrin, was quite unable to find him or to learn his whereabouts. He searched for him in vain the whole evening, venturing even on board the brig; and it was not until after eleven o'clock that night that he gave up the search in disgust with a strong impression that Johnson had been purposely avoiding him.

On the following morning, however, he was more successful, having risen before daylight in order that he might catch his bird on his first appearance in the open air. At six o'clock the bell rang as usual for the hands to turn to, and a few minutes afterwards the whole place was astir. Lance walked down to the landing-place with Captain Staunton and the others, and saw them embark in the boats detailed to convey the working party to the new shipyard. He then whispered a word or two of explanation to his friends and allowed the boats to go away without him. They had been gone about ten minutes or a quarter of an hour when Lance saw the man he sought emerge from the capstan-house and walk hurriedly down toward the beach, where a boat, fully manned, appeared to be awaiting him. A few steps, and Lance was by his side.

"Good morning, Captain Johnson," he said with inward amusement as he noted the confusion of the pirate at the unexpected and evidently unwished-for meeting.

"Good mornin', general," was Johnson's response, given with a heartiness which was visibly assumed. "This is a real fine morning, I call it. Nice little breeze, too, off the land; I guess we shall make short miles of it to-day. I am downright glad you missed the boats this morning; overslept yourself, I s'pose; I wanted to say 'good-bye' to you and your chums, and I declare to goodness I was only just thinkin' when you come up to me that I'd be obliged to heave the brig to off the rock and run ashore in a boat just to shake nippers with you. Well, I guess I must be off; there's the foretop-sail just let fall, and I'm bound they've passed the messenger already. I'm real sorry I can't take you all with me and shove you ashore somewhere on the quiet; but you see how 'tis; that feller Ralli—but I ain't got time to talk any more, I swow. Good-bye. By the time I get back I reckon you'll have the schooner pretty nigh ready for launching, eh?"

"I hope so," said Lance. "By the bye, have you made any arrangements for letting us have the arms you promised? That fellow Ralli, as you have remarked—"

"The arms? Well, now, only to think of that!" exclaimed Johnson with well-feigned annoyance. "What a dog-goned forgetful cuss I am; blamed if I ain't forgot all about 'em. I've been that busy, if you'll believe me, general, I ain't had time to swaller a mouthful of grub this four days; half-starved to death I am; just look at my waistcoat—fits me like a sack. But about them arms—I declare I am real sorry I forgot 'em, general; but never mind, I guess you won't want 'em. If you do"—he button-holed Lance and whispered him confidentially—"just you take 'em—help yourself to 'em; I give you my permission, I swow. And now I really must say 'good-bye.' Take care of yourself, general, and go ahead with that schooner as fast as ever you can. Get her finished by the time I come back, and the battery too, and I promise you shall leave the island as soon as you like arterwards."

They were by this time at the water's edge; and as Johnson uttered the last words of his farewell he sprang into the boat which was waiting for him, and flinging himself into the stern-sheets, gave the order to "shove off."

Ten minutes later the same boat was swinging at the brig's quarter-davits, and the brig herself, with her anchor-stock just showing above water, was moving slowly away towards the harbour-entrance under topsails and jib.

At a little distance from Lance stood Ralli, watching the departure of the brig.

"Ah!" he muttered, "there you go, you vile American dog, you cowardly mean-spirited cur; take my parting curses with you; may you meet with nothing but ill-luck and perplexity; may misfortune follow you; may the very wind and the sea war against you; may the treachery which I have planned prevail over you; and may you die at last with the jeers of your enemies ringing in your ears. Good-bye! good-bye!" he shouted, bringing the tips of his fingers together at his lips and wafting with them an ironical salute after Johnson, who at that moment glanced shoreward and waved his cap. "Good-bye, and the devil himself go with you. Aha! my Yankee friend, you little know that you are taking your last look at this scene; you little dream that the brig carries a dagger whose blade is thirsty for your heart's blood, and whose point I have directed at your breast. Adieu, miserable coward, for ever. I hope Antonio will not forget to tell you, as he drives home his blade, that it was I who ordered the blow; my revenge will else be robbed of half its sweetness. You thought, doubtless, that because it suited me to receive your insults in silence that I should soon forget them. Bah! you should have known better; my very quietness—the repression of my resentment—should have warned you; but you are a poor blind fool without any discernment, or you would have known that a Greek never forgives a wrong. Good-bye once more, and for the last time—good-bye; I wish you all speed on your road to perdition."

And he waved his hat smilingly at the fast receding brig as he saw Johnson raise a telescope to his eye and level it in his direction.

When the Albatross had at length finally disappeared beyond the harbour's mouth Ralli turned for the first time and caught sight of Lance. Stalking up to him he said scoffingly—

"So, Mister Soldier, you have lost your friend at last."

"Yes," said Lance very quietly, "if, as I imagine, you refer to your captain. But I must protest against your styling him my friend; he is nothing of the kind."

"Ah, yes," sneered Ralli. "Now that he is gone, and can no longer protect you, you disown him. But that will not do. You and he were friends, whatever you may say. He is my enemy, and his friends are therefore my enemies also; and they will be treated as such; do you understand me?"

"Not in the least," said Lance, "I have not the faintest notion of your meaning."

"Then listen to me and I will explain," said Ralli, his eyes gleaming vindictively. "Do you know that your friend yonder is fated never to return?"

"What is the meaning of this?" thought Lance. "Some treachery or other on the part of this rascally Greek, I'll wager. But it will never do to allow him to suppose that he is master of the situation so—"

"I believe," he said carelessly, "there is some sort of arrangement to that effect, is there not?"

The Greek gazed at him in unaffected alarm.

"Aha!" he ejaculated, "how came you to know that?"

Lance smiled at him compassionately. "Did you really flatter yourself," he said, "that your plans were so astutely devised—so cunningly concealed that none but you and your partisans could possibly know anything about them! Really, Mr Ralli, I fear you are greatly overrating your own sagacity. But we appear to be wandering away from the point. You were about to explain the meaning of an obscure remark you made a minute or two ago?"

Lance had never removed his glance for a single instant from Ralli's face since the commencement of the conversation; and he was physiognomist enough to detect the signs of a fear almost approaching to panic in the countenance of the Greek; he knew therefore that his bold guess had not been very far from the truth; and he continued to puff his cigar with all his wonted insouciance as he waited calmly for the reply to his interrogation.

"Yes," said Ralli, recovering his self-possession with evident effort. "I was about to explain two things—First, I wish you to understand that Johnson is not my captain, nor is he the captain of anyone now on this island. We have thrown off our—what do you term it? our—"

"Allegiance?" blandly suggested Lance.

"Our allegiance—yes, that word will do; it explains my meaning, though it is not the word I intended to use," answered Ralli. "We have thrown off our allegiance. We are tired of him—this man Johnson—and we will have no more of him; he will never return here; and now I am capitan. You understand!"

Lance nodded.

"Good. The next thing I was about to explain is, that his friends are our enemies; you and your people especially. Is that plain?"

"Perfectly," answered Lance, still outwardly calm and unconcerned as ever, though inwardly much perturbed. "And I presume you intend us to accept these remarks of yours in the light of a threat of some kind?"

Ralli looked hard at his interrogator before replying. He could not in the least understand this man who received with such perfect sang-froid the intelligence that he and his friends were to be regarded and treated as the enemies of a company of ruthless outlaws such as he must know Ralli and his associates to be.

"Yes," he said at last, slowly and almost doubtingly, "you may take what I say as a threat. I mean to pay to you and your friends all the great debt of vengeance which that other friend of yours, Johnson, has allowed to accumulate against him. I will be doubly avenged; I will be avenged upon him, and upon you as well."

Lance laughed gaily as he lightly knocked off with his little finger the ash from his cigar-end. This was a serious, a direful business; but he had no intention to let the Greek see that his words had any alarming or disturbing effect upon him, so he said with a smile—

"Excuse me for laughing at you, but, under the circumstances I really could not help it. Your ignorance of the true state of affairs strikes me as so positively ludicrous. You forget, my good sir, that I am behind the scenes—in your secret, you know," he added, seeing a look of bewilderment at the other expression. "Why, man, you and all your people are absolutely at our mercy. You look surprised, but I assure you such is the fact. I really do not know whether I ought to explain myself to you; I scarcely think you deserve it after your recent threats—no; I will keep my own counsel; you shall remain in your ignorance."

And he turned to walk away.

"Stop," gasped Ralli, "what is it you mean? I must know."

Lance paused for a full minute as though irresolute; at last he said—

"Well, perhaps it would be better for all parties that there should be after all a clear understanding. You and your people outnumber our party many times, and it is indisputable that you have it in your power in consequence to make us very uncomfortable; but, for all that, you are absolutely at our mercy; and therefore it will be greatly to your advantage to treat us well. You will perhaps understand this better if I inform you that your plot against Johnson has been betrayed" (he did not think it necessary to explain that, as far as he knew, the only betrayal of it had been in the incautious words uttered by the Greek himself at the opening of their present conversation); "and that if he does not return neither will the brig; and then how will you be situated! You could possibly contrive to exist for a year upon the provisions left on the island; you might even, aided by the productions of the island itself, find sustenance for many years. But would the spending of the rest of your lives on this island be in accordance with your plans and wishes? And do you not think it possible that Johnson, in revenge for your plot against him, may find means to direct some cruiser to your hiding-place? Your imagination, I take it, is vivid enough to picture the consequences of any such step on his part."

"We shall have the battery and the schooner," muttered Ralli.

"Yes," said Lance, "if we build them for you; not otherwise. There is not a man on this island, outside our own party, who could complete the schooner, much less build the battery. Now, do you begin to understand that I was only speaking the truth when I spoke of your being at our mercy."

Ralli was silent. He stood with knitted brows intently cogitating for some minutes; then suddenly looking up into Lance's face with a smile he said—

"Ah, bah! what obtuse people you English are; how impossible for you to understand a little joke! Well, I will joke no more since you cannot understand it. We will be good friends all round; the best of friends; you shall have no cause to complain of bad treatment; and you will work hard to finish the schooner and the battery early, please. I like not what you said just now about Johnson and the frigate. But that too was all a joke I know."

"You are mistaken," said Lance. "I confess I was dense enough not to understand that you were joking, so I spoke in earnest. But I think we clearly understand each other now; so I hope we shall hear no more about threats, revenge, and nonsense of that kind."

And flinging his cigar-end into the water, Lance turned on his heel and walked away.

Knowing, or at least shrewdly guessing that Ralli was watching him, he sauntered away in his usual careless and easy fashion toward the hut, which they had laughingly dubbed "Staunton Cottage," and entered it.

The ladies were busying themselves about various domestic tasks, and little May was amusing herself with an uncouth wooden doll which Bob had constructed for her. Lance was a prime favourite with May, so the moment that he entered the doll was flung into a corner, and the child came bounding up to him joyously exclaiming—

"Oh, you funny Mr Evelin, how is it that you have not gone with my papa? Did you stay at home on purpose to play with me?"

"Well, not exactly, little one," answered Lance, catching her in his arms and tossing her high in the air, to her infinite delight. "Not exactly; although a man might be worse employed than in amusing you, you mischievous little fairy. No; I am going to papa presently—and would you like to come with me, May, in a nice little boat?"

"I don't know," answered the child doubtfully. "How far is it? I don't think I like boats."

"No, you poor little mite, I expect not; it would be wonderful if you did after what you have suffered in them," remarked Lance, holding the child now in his arms, while she played with his long beard. "But we shall not have very far to go, pet; only over to that big rock," pointing out of the window, "and I will take great care of you."

"And shall I see my papa?" inquired May.

"Oh, yes," was the reply; "you will be with him all day. And Robert is over there too, you know; and I daresay he will play with you if you ask him prettily."

"Then I'll go," she decided promptly; and forthwith went away to her mother with the request that her hat and jacket might be put on, "'cause I's going with Mr Evelin to see papa," as she explained.

"I daresay you are somewhat surprised to see me here," remarked Lance, as he replaced his tiny playfellow on the floor. "The fact is that I have been watching the departure of the brig; and the idea has occurred to me that now she is gone, and so many of the remaining men are away at the shipyard all day, you ladies may with, I believe, perfect safety indulge in the unwonted luxury of a daylight walk. You all stand greatly in need of fresh air and exercise; and I really think there is now no cause to fear any molestation, otherwise I should not of course suggest such a thing. It will never do, you know, for you to remain cooped up here day after day—you will get low-spirited and out of health; and I am inclined to believe it will be rather a good idea than otherwise to accustom these fellows to the sight of you moving freely and fearlessly about."

The ladies were quite unanimous in their cordial welcome to this suggestion, Blanche only venturing to add in a whisper, and with a pleading look—

"Can you not come with us, Lance? We should feel quite safe then."

"I really could not, darling," he answered gently. "It would not be fair to the others, you know. Beside which, I am urgently wanted at the yard to-day, and we must not let pleasure, however tempting, interfere with the progress of the schooner. I should like it immensely, of course, and if I thought there was the least particle of danger in your expedition I would go; but I believe there is none. At the same time, you will of course keep your eyes open, dear, and be on the watch for any suspicious circumstance; and if you really must have an escort, there is Dale; shall I ask him?"

"Oh, Dale!" ejaculated Blanche with such a contemptuous toss of her pretty little head that Lance said no more; it was sufficiently evident that the ladies would be badly in want of an escort indeed before they would accept Dale.

The three ladies were soon ready; and as they took their way up the valley Lance stood at the door with May on his shoulder, watching them; and when at last they passed out of sight he made his way down to the landing-place, seated the child carefully in the stern of a small dingy which he found moored there, cast off the painter, stepped in himself, and, shipping the short paddles, drove the tiny boat with long easy leisurely strokes down toward the rock, chatting gaily with his tiny companion the while, and causing her childish laughter to peal musically and incessantly across the placid surface of the land-locked water.

The Ladies Make a Discovery; and Bob Distinguishes Himself

It was a most delightful day for a walk, the ladies averred enthusiastically; and their enthusiasm was quite justified. The azure of the sky overhead was relieved by a bank of soft dappled fleecy clouds, which served in some measure as a screen against the ardent rays of the sun; and a gentle breeze from the westward imparted a feeling of freshness to the air, whilst it wafted to the pedestrians the subtly mingled perfumes of the thousand varied plants and flowers which flourished in the deep rich soil of the island. As the ladies walked quietly on up the gently sloping valley toward the hills their enjoyment increased with every step. Hitherto they had only ventured abroad at night; and lovely as the landscape had appeared in the clear mellow radiance of the moon—the soft silvery light boldly contrasted with broad masses of rich grey-brown shadow—they agreed that it was incomparably more beautiful when viewed by the full light of day and in all the glory of brilliant sunshine. A thousand gorgeous colours on leaf and blossom, on gaily-plumaged bird and bright-winged insect, charmed their eyes and enriched the foreground of the picture; while the dense masses of foliage, with their subtle gradations of colour, light, and shade, as they gradually receded into the background, and finally melted into the rich purply grey of the extreme distance, balanced and harmonised the whole, completing one of the most beautiful prospects perhaps upon which the human eye had ever gazed.

Their spirits rose as they walked steadily onward and upward, breathing with intense enjoyment the strong pure perfume-laden air, exhilarating in its effect as a draught of rich wine; and temporarily forgetting, in the pleasure of the moment, not only their past sufferings but their present and future perils, they chatted merrily and arranged a hundred plans, many of which, could they but have known it, were destined never to attain fruition.

Hitherto they had been following a faintly defined track in the luxuriant grass, a track which had always up to the present determined the direction of their longer walks; but arriving at last at a point where this trail turned abruptly off, and passed down a gentle declivity apparently toward the sea on the eastern side of the island, they determined to abandon it, and, tempted by the shade, to plunge boldly into a broad expanse of park-like timber which spread before them. The welcome shade was soon reached; and, somewhat fatigued with their ramble, they seated themselves at the foot of a gigantic cork-tree, and in the rich green twilight shadow of its luxuriant foliage discussed the luncheon with which they had had the forethought to provide themselves.

The luxuriant grass which had hitherto carpeted the earth here gave place to graceful ferns in rich variety, interspersed with delicate mosses of velvety texture, and here and there, in the more open spaces, small patches of a heath-like plant with tiny waxen blossoms of a tint varying from the purest white to a dainty purple. The silence of the forest was broken only by the gentle murmur of the wind in the tree-tops and the soft rustle of the foliage overhead, save when now and then a twittering bird flashed like a living gem from bough to bough; but there was a low, deep sound vibrating on the air, which told of the never-ceasing beat of the surf on the island's rock-girt shore.

Rested and refreshed, the ladies at length rose to their feet once more and continued their way through the wood. The ground soon began to rise steeply; and after nearly an hour's steady climbing they emerged once more into the full and dazzling sunlight to find themselves standing on the edge of a steep rocky ravine, through which, some fifty feet below, there flowed a tiny stream of crystal purity.

The rocks were of a character quite new to them, and, ignorant of geology as they were, they would doubtless have passed them by without a second glance, had they not been attracted by a peculiar glitter here and there upon their surface, which proceeded, as they discovered upon a closer inspection, from the presence of minute particles of a dull yellow substance embedded in the stone. But what chiefly riveted their attention was a small basin-like pool with a smooth level sandy bottom, as they could clearly see from their elevated stand-point. The water appeared to be about two feet deep, and the basin itself was roughly of a circular form, about ten yards in diameter. That it was obviously intended by nature to be used as a bath was the thought which flashed simultaneously through the minds of the three fair gazers; and as each one glanced half-timidly around, only to feel reassured by the utter absence of any indication of probable unwelcome intrusion, the thought speedily found vent in words.

"Just look at that pool," exclaimed Mrs Staunton; "what a delightful bath it would make!"

"Oh, Mrs Staunton!" said Blanche, "do you know that is exactly the thought which occurred to me. I feel tired, and I should so enjoy a plunge into the beautiful clear, cool water. Do you think we might venture?"

"I do not see why we should not," was the reply. "What do you think, Violet?"

"I think it would be nothing short of a luxury," answered Violet. "I too feel tired, and I am sure it would refresh us. I am not afraid, if you are not."

"Then let us risk it," said Mrs Staunton with a sudden show of intrepidity, which was, however, only half genuine; and, each borrowing courage from the companionship of the others, they hurriedly scrambled down the rocky slope, and in a few minutes more were flashing the bright water over each other like naiads at play, their clear laughter echoing strangely among the mighty rocks of the ravine.

The water proved to be much deeper than they had supposed, being quite four feet deep in the centre of the pool, which rendered their bath all the more enjoyable. The sand was, on the whole, beautifully fine, white, and firm beneath their feet, but occasionally they experienced the sensation of treading upon small, hard, roughly-rounded objects among the finer particles; and finally Blanche encountered a lump so large and hard that, curious to see what it could be, she, with a motion of her foot, swept away the sand until the object was exposed to view. It seemed to be a rough, irregularly-shaped pebble somewhat larger than a hen's egg, of a dull yellow colour; and, reaching down her arm, she plunged beneath the water and brought the odd-looking object up in her hand.

"What a curious stone; and how heavy it is!" she remarked, holding it up to view.

Her companions came to inspect it, and Mrs Staunton took it in her hand to make a close examination.

"Stone!" she exclaimed excitedly. "Why, my dear girl, this is gold—a genuine nugget, unless I am greatly mistaken. Mr Thomson, a friend of my husband's in Sydney, showed us several gold nuggets, and they were exactly like this, only they were none of them nearly so large."

"Do you really think it is gold?" asked Blanche. "My dear Mrs Staunton, my dear Violet, only fancy what a delightful thing it will be if we have actually discovered a gold mine; why, we shall be able to present our husbands with a magnificent fortune each."

A charming blush mantled the speaker's cheek as she said this, notwithstanding the fact that by this time the three women had no secrets from each other.

"I wonder if there are any more," remarked Mrs Staunton; "surely that cannot be the only one here. I fancy I stepped on something hard just now."

The three women at once went groping along the sand with their feet, and not in vain. First one, and then another encountered a hard object which proved to be similar in substance to the one found by Blanche; and in a quarter of an hour they had between them collected upwards of a dozen of them, though one only—found by Mrs Staunton—exceeded in size that of the first discovery.

Then, feeling somewhat chilled by their long immersion, they returned to terra firma, and were soon once more wending their way homeward. In passing through the wood they contrived to lose their way; but, as it happened, this proved of but slight consequence, as though they eventually came out at a point nearly a mile distant from the pathway which they had followed in the morning, they were quite as near the settlement as they would have been had they faithfully retraced their original footsteps; and by four o'clock in the afternoon they found themselves once more within the shelter of the walls of Staunton Cottage, greatly fatigued, it is true, by their long ramble, but with an elasticity of spirits and a sense of renewed life to which they had long been strangers.

Meanwhile the party at the shipyard had been thrown into a state of unwonted excitement by an incident which at one moment threatened to have a tragic termination.

A strong gang of men were at work upon the rock—all, indeed, who were left upon the island, excepting some dozen or fourteen, most of whom were employed in providing for the daily wants of the others, such as in baking bread, cleaning out the huts, airing bedding, and so on—and the scene at the mouth of the harbour was therefore a tolerably busy one.

Captain Staunton was in charge of the ship-building operations, with Kit as foreman-in-chief, while Rex and Brook were superintending operations at the battery; the former, with a roll of rough-and-ready drawings in his hand, "setting out" the work, while the latter overlooked the construction of a lime-kiln. Bob was making himself generally useful.

It was while all hands were at their busiest that Lance put in an appearance, leading little May by the hand. She of course at once made a dash at her father, flinging her tiny arms round his neck, kissing and hugging him vigorously, and showing in a hundred childish ways her delight at being with him; and the unwonted sight of the pretty little creature created quite a temporary sensation. A large majority of the men there were steeped to the lips in crime, yet there were very few among them who had not still left in them—hidden far down in the innermost recesses of their nature, and crushed almost out of existence by a load of vice and evil-doing, it may be—some remnant of the better feelings of humanity; and their features brightened and softened visibly as they witnessed the delight of this baby girl at finding herself with her father, and looked at her happy innocent face. Her visit was like a ray of sunshine falling upon them from out the bosom of a murky and storm-laden sky; and as she flitted fearlessly to and fro among them, they felt for the moment as though a part of their load of guilt had been taken from them; that in some subtle way her proximity had exercised a purifying and refining influence upon them, and that they were no longer the utterly vile, God-forsaken wretches they had been. Fierce, crime-scarred faces lighted up with unwonted smiles as she approached them; and hands that had been again and again soaked in human blood were outstretched to warn or remove her from the vicinity of possible danger. For the first few minutes Captain Staunton had been anxious and apprehensive at her unexpected presence among the ruffianly band; but his face cleared, and his knitted brow relaxed as he saw the effect which the sight of her produced, and when Lance joined him he said—

"Let her alone; she is doing more in a few minutes to humanise these men than you or I could achieve in a year."

The child was naturally interested in everything she saw, and with tireless feet she passed to and fro, pausing now and then to gravely watch the operations of some stalwart fellow hewing out a timber with his adze, driving home a bolt with his heavy maul, or digging into the stubborn rock with his pickaxe, and not infrequently asking questions which the puzzled seamen strove in vain to answer.

At length, having satisfied her curiosity by a thorough inspection of all that was going forward, she wandered down to the spot where the hulk had been broken up. This was a tiny sheltered bay or indentation in the rocks; and a large raft had here been constructed out of the dismembered timbers and planking, which were kept afloat in order that the powerful rays of the sun might not split and rend the wood. Two or three detached planks formed a gangway between the raft and the rocks, and along these planks May passed on to the raft, without attracting the attention of anyone, it happening that just at that moment most of the hands were summoned to tail on to the fall of a tackle which was being used to raise one of the timbers into its place. Gradually she strayed from one end of the raft to the other; and presently her attention was attracted by a curious triangular-shaped object which she saw projecting out of the water and moving slowly along. She wondered what it could possibly be, and, in order the better to see it, ran nimbly out upon the end of a long plank which projected considerably beyond the rest. So eager was she to watch the movements of the strange object that she overshot her mark and with a splash and a cry of alarm fell into the water.

The triangular object immediately disappeared.

Luckily at this instant Bob glanced round, just in time to see the splash caused by May's involuntary plunge and to note the simultaneous disappearance of a dark object in the water close at hand. Divining in a moment what had happened, he set off with a bound down the sloping rocky way toward the raft, shouting as he went—

"A shark! A shark! And May has fallen overboard."

For a single instant there was a horror-stricken pause; then tools were flung recklessly aside, the tackle-fall was let go and the timber suffered to fall unheeded to the ground again, and the entire gang with one accord followed in Bob's wake, hastily snatching up ropes, boat-hooks, poles, oars, anything likely to be useful, as they ran.

Meanwhile Bob, running with the speed of a hunted deer, had passed—as it seemed to the spectators—with a single bound down the rocks and along the entire length of the raft, from the extreme end of which he plunged without pause or hesitation into the sea. A bright momentary flash as he vanished beneath the surface of the water, seemed to indicate that he carried a drawn knife or some such weapon in his hand.

Simultaneously with the disappearance of Bob, May's golden curls reappeared above the surface; and the child's aimless struggles and her choking bubbling cries lent wings to the rescuing feet of those who had listened again and again unmoved to the death-screams of their fellow men. Another moment, and there was a tremendous commotion in the water close to the child; first a sort of seething whirl, then a dark object flashed for a moment into view, there was a furious splashing, a darting hither and thither of some creature indistinctly seen amid the snowy foam; and then that foam took on a rosy hue which deepened into crimson; the commotion subsided, and Bob appeared once more on the surface, breathless and gasping. With a couple of strokes he reached May's side, and half a dozen more took him alongside the raft in time to deliver her into Captain Staunton's outstretched arms.

"Unhurt, sir, I believe, thank God!" Bob gasped, as he delivered up his charge; and then, when the little one had been raised out of the water and clasped with inarticulate thanksgivings to her father's breast, he added—

"Give us a hand, some of you fellows, will you? And heave handsomely, for I believe my leg's broke."

"Lay hold, boy;" and a dozen eager hands were outstretched to Bob's assistance—foremost among them being that of a great black-bearded fellow named Dickinson, who had formerly been boatswain's mate on board a man-o'-war, but who had deserted in order to escape the consequences of a sudden violent outburst of temper—"Lay hold."

Bob grasped the proffered hand and was brought gently alongside the raft.

"Now then," exclaimed Dickinson, assuming the direction of affairs, "kneel down on the edge of the raft, one of you—you, 'Frenchy,' you're pretty handy with your flippers—kneel down and pass your arm under his legs, as high up as you can. Say 'when.' Are you ready? Then lift, gently now, and take care you don't strike him against the edge of the raft. So! That's well. Now, lift him inboard; that's your sort. Now, off jackets, some of us, and let's sling him; he'll ride easier that way. Are we hurting you, my lad?"

"Not much, thank'ee," answered Bob cheerfully. "There," he added, as they once more reached the rocks, "that'll do, mates; lay me down here in the shade, and tell Mr Evelin I'm hurt—presently, you know; after he's brought the little girl round."

In the meantime Lance, almost as much concerned as Captain Staunton, had hurried after the latter, and offered his assistance, which was thankfully accepted. But there was very little that needed doing. So prompt had been Bob in his movements that the poor child had never actually lost consciousness; and after a great deal of coughing up of salt water and a little crying, May was so far herself again as to be able to call up a rather wan smile, and, throwing her arms round her father's neck, to say—

"Don't be frightened any more, papa dear; May's better now."

Great seemed to be the satisfaction of the crowd of men who had clustered round the group as they heard this welcome assurance; and then in twos and threes they slunk away back to their work, seemingly more than half ashamed that they had been betrayed into the exhibition of so human a feeling as interest in a mere child's safety.

"If the little un's all right, mister, you'd better have a look at the chap that pulled her out. His leg's broke, I think," remarked Dickinson's gruff voice at this juncture.

"His leg broken? Good heavens! I never dreamed of this," exclaimed Captain Staunton. "Poor fellow! poor Robert; let us go at once and see what can be done for him, Evelin."

"You'll find him there, under that rock," remarked the ex-boatswain's mate in a tone of indifference, indicating Bob's resting-place by a careless jerk of the thumb over his left shoulder as he walked away.

Captain Staunton and Lance rose to their feet, and, the former carrying his restored darling in his arms, went toward the spot indicated. They had gone but a few paces when they were overtaken by Dickinson, who, with a half-sulky, half-defiant look on his face said—

"I s'pose I can't be any use, can I? If I can, you know, you'd better say so, and I'll lend you a hand—and let me see the man that'll laugh at me. I ain't quite a brute, though I daresay you think me one. I like pluck when I see it, and the way that boy jumped in on the shark was plucky enough for anything. If it hadn't been for him, skipper, that little gal of yourn 'd have been a goner and no mistake."

"You are right, Dickinson, she would indeed. Thank God she is spared to me, though. You can no doubt be of the greatest use to us; and as to thinking you a brute—I do nothing of the kind, nor does Mr Evelin, I am sure. I believe you make yourself out to be a great deal worse than you really are. Well, Robert, what is this, my boy? Is it true that your leg is broken?"

"I am afraid it is, sir," answered Bob, who looked very pale, and was evidently suffering great pain. "But I don't care about that, so long as May is all right."

"She is, Robert, thanks to God and to your courage. But we will all thank you by and by more adequately than we can do now. Let us look at your leg, that is the first thing to be attended to."

"Will you allow me, Captain Staunton?" interposed Lance. "I have some knowledge of surgery, and I think my hand will be more steady than yours after your late excitement."

The skipper willingly gave place to Lance; and the latter, kneeling down by Bob's side, drew out a knife with which he slit up the left leg of the lad's trousers.

A painful sight at once revealed itself. The leg was broken half-way between the ankle and the knee, and the splintered shin-bone protruded through the lacerated and bleeding flesh. Captain Staunton felt quite sick for a moment as he saw the terrible nature of the injury; and even Lance turned a trifle pale.

"A compound fracture, and a very bad one," pronounced Evelin. "Now, Dickinson, if you wish to be of use, find Kit, the carpenter, and bring him to me."

The man vanished with alacrity, and in another minute or two returned with Kit.

Lance explained what he wanted—a few splints of a certain length and shape, and a supply of good stout spun-yarn.

"Do you think Ralli would give us a bandage or two and a little lint from one of his medicine-chests?" asked Lance of Dickinson.

"If he won't I'll pound him to a jelly," was the reckless answer; and without waiting for further instructions the man ran down to the water, jumped into the dingy, and, casting off the painter, began to ply his oars with a strength and energy which sent the small boat darting across the bay with a foaming wave at her bows and a long swirling wake behind her.

In less than half an hour he was back again with the medicine-chest and all its contents; which he had brought away bodily without going through the formality of asking permission.

The splints were by this time ready; and then began the long, tedious, and painful operation of setting and dressing the limb, in the performance of which Dickinson rendered valuable and efficient service. The long agony proved almost too much for Bob; he went ghastly pale and the cold perspiration broke out in great beads all over his forehead; seeing which the boatswain's mate beckoned with his hand to one of the men standing near, and whispered him to fetch his (Dickinson's) allowance of grog.

The man went away, and soon returned with not a single allowance but a pannikin-full of rum, the result of a spontaneous contribution among the men as soon as they were informed that it was wanted for Bob. With the aid of an occasional sip from this pannikin the poor lad was able to bear up without fainting until Lance had done all that was possible for him; and then Dickinson and three other men, lifting him upon a strip of tarpaulin lashed to a couple of oars, carried him down to one of the boats, and jumping in, with Lance and Captain Staunton—who could not be persuaded to trust May out of his arms—pushed off and rowed him down to the bottom of the bay.

About a couple of hundred yards from the rocks they passed the body of a great dead shark floating belly upwards upon the surface of the water. The creature appeared to be nearly twenty feet long; and the blood was still slowly oozing from three or four stabs and a couple of long deep gashes near the throat. The mouth was open; and as the boat swept past its occupants had an opportunity to count no less than five rows of formidable teeth still erect in its horrid jaws. Captain Staunton pressed his child convulsively to his breast as he gazed at the hideous sight; and Dickinson, who pulled the stroke-oar, averred with an oath his belief that there was not another man on the island with pluck enough to "tackle" such a monster.

"By the bye, Robert," said Captain Staunton, "you have not yet told us how you came to break your leg. Did you strike it against the timber when you jumped overboard, or how was it?"

"No, sir," said Bob. "It was this way. Just as I reached the end of the plank I caught sight of the brute rushing straight at May. I could see him distinctly against the clean sandy bottom, and he was not above six feet off. So I took a header right for him, whipping out my sheath-knife as I jumped; and luckily he turned upon me sharp enough to give little May a chance, but not sharp enough to prevent my driving my knife into him up to the hilt. Then I got hold of him somewhere—I think it was one of his fins—and dug and slashed at him until I was out of breath, when I was obliged to let go and come to the surface. The shark sheered off, seeming to have had enough of it, but in going he gave me a blow with his tail across the leg and I felt it snap like a pipe-stem."

"And, instead of making for the raft, you swam at once to May, thinking of her safety rather than of the pain you were suffering," said the skipper. "Bob, you are a hero, if ever there was one. This is the second time you have saved my child from certain death; and I shall never forget my obligations to you, though God alone knows whether I shall ever have an opportunity to repay them."

"I say, mister, I wish you wouldn't have quite so much to say about God; it makes a chap feel uncomfortable," growled Dickinson.

"Does it?" said Captain Staunton. "How is that? I thought none of you people believed in the existence of such a Being."

"I can't answer for others," sullenly returned Dickinson, "but I know I believe; I wish I didn't. I've tried my hardest to forget all about God, and to persuade myself that there ain't no such Person, but I can't manage it. The remembrance of my poor old mother's teaching sticks to me in spite of all I can do. I've tried," he continued with growing passion, "to drive it all out of my head by sheer deviltry and wickedness; I've done worse things than e'er another man on this here island, hain't I, mates?"—to his fellow-oarsmen.

"Ay ay, Bill, you have."

"You're a reg'lar devil sometimes."

"A real out-and-outer, and no mistake," were the confirmatory replies.

"Yes," Dickinson continued, "and yet I can't forget it; I can't persuade myself; and the more I try the worse I feel about it, and I don't care who hears me say so."

"Well, you seem to be in earnest in what you say, Dickinson; but I really cannot believe you are. No man who really believed in the existence of a God of Justice would continue to live a life of sin and defiance," said the skipper.

"Wouldn't he?" fiercely retorted the boatswain's mate. "Supposin' he'd done what I've done and lived the life I've lived, what would he do? Answer me that."

"Come up to our hut next Sunday morning at eleven o'clock, and I will answer you."

"What! do you mean to say that you'll let me in, and them women-folks there too?"

"Certainly we will," said Captain Staunton heartily. "We are all mortal, like yourself; and the ladies will not refuse, I am sure, to meet a man who feels as you do."

"Then I'll come," exclaimed the man with a frightful oath, intended to add emphasis to his declaration, and then, as the boat's keel grated on the beach, he and his mates sprang into the shallow water, and, lifting Bob in his impromptu stretcher carefully upon their shoulders, they proceeded with heedful steps to bear him toward the hut.

"Now, there," remarked Captain Staunton in a low voice as they hurried on ahead to get Bob's bunk ready for him, "there is an example of a human soul steeped in sin, yet revolting from it; struggling desperately to escape; and in its despair only dyeing itself with a deeper stain. It is a noble nature in revolt against a state of hideous ignoble slavery; and I pray God that I may find words wherewith to suitably answer his momentous question."

"Amen," said Lance fervently, raising his hat reverently from his head as the word passed his lips.

In another ten minutes they had poor Bob safely in the house and comfortably bestowed in his berth. The medicine-chest had been brought back in the boat and was soon conveyed to the hut; and while Lance busied himself in mixing a cooling draught for his patient, Dale, to the intense astonishment of everybody, voluntarily undertook to prepare some strengthening broth for him. The man's supreme selfishness gave way, for the moment, to admiration of Bob's gallant deed—so immeasurably beyond anything of which he felt himself capable—and, genuinely ashamed of himself, for perhaps the first time in his life, he suddenly resolved to do what little in him lay to be useful.

When Lance came down-stairs for a moment after administering the saline draught, he found Dickinson and his three companions still hanging about outside the door in an irresolute manner, as though undecided whether to go or stay. He accordingly went out to them and, with an earnestness quite foreign to his usual manner, thanked them warmly yet courteously for their valuable assistance (Lance never forgot that he was a gentleman, and was therefore uniformly courteous to everybody), and then dismissed them, adding at the last moment a word or two of reminder to Dickinson as to his promise for the following Sunday, which he emphasised with a hearty shake of the hand.

The boatswain's mate walked away down to the boat silently and in a seemingly dazed condition, holding up his right hand before him, turning it over, and looking at it as though he had never seen it before. He never opened his lips until the boat was in mid-channel, when, resting on his oar for a moment, he said—

"Well, shipmates, you've heard me say to-day words that I wouldn't have believed this morning I could find courage to say to any human being. Now, I'm not ashamed of 'em—I won't go back from a single word—but you know as well as I do what a rumpus there'd be if it got to be known that there'd been said what's been said this arternoon. I don't care about myself, not a single curse; you and as many more fools as choose can laugh at me until you're all tired; but mind—I won't have a word said about them; if this gets abroad they'll be made uncomfortable, and I won't have it—D'ye hear, mates, I won't have it. The first man that says a word about it—well"—with a powerful effort to curb his passion—"the best thing he can do is to take to the water and swim right out to sea; for the sharks 'll be more marciful to him than I will."

"All right, matey, all right," good-humouredly answered one of the men, "you needn't threaten us—no occasion for that; we're not going to split on yer, old man; perhaps, if the truth was knowed, there's others besides yourself as don't feel pertickler comfortable about this here piratin' business—I won't mention no names—and anyhow you may trust me not to say a word about what we've heard to-day upon it; and there's my hand upon it."

"And mine."

"And mine."

The proffered hands were silently grasped with fervour; and then the oars were resumed and the boat sped on her way to the shipyard.

Lost!

When the three ladies entered Staunton Cottage they were greatly surprised to find Captain Staunton and Lance there, both busy scraping lint; and still more surprised to see Dale bending over a fire with his coat off, diligently stirring the contents of a small tin saucepan.

May was the first to throw any light upon the situation, which she did, directly the door opened, by rushing up to her mother and exclaiming excitedly—

"Oh, mama! what do you think? I fell into the water, and Bobbie jumped in too; and a naughty shark hurt poor Bobbie and made his leg bleed; so papa and Mr Evelin and some sailors brought him home and put him to bed; and he's up there now, mama, so poorly."

Mrs Staunton turned mutely to her husband for an explanation. For a single moment she felt quite incapable of speaking intelligibly. Her mental vision conjured up a picture of her child in some terrible danger, and, in her anxiety, her mind refused to take in more than that one awful fact, overlooking for the time the circumstance of Bob having received an injury. The danger to which May had been exposed; that was all she thought about—all she could think about just then; and, until she had heard the story, she had not attention for anything or anyone else.

So Captain Staunton bade them all sit down, and then he related the full details of May's adventure, with Bob's gallant rescue of her, and the unfortunate accident which accompanied it. It is not necessary to repeat the frequent exclamations of horror and admiration which were elicited from the fair auditors as the various details of the occurrence were related; nor to describe the convulsive way in which May was clasped to her mother's breast, and fondled and cried over by all three of the sensitive loving women together as they listened to the story of her terrible peril. Suffice it say that, when the narrative was over, the womenkind went with one accord up to Bob's bedside, and there so overwhelmed him with thanks and praises that the poor fellow was quite overcome, so that Lance had finally to interfere, and with mock severity order their immediate withdrawal.

Later on, when the excitement had somewhat subsided, and while they were all sitting down quietly to tea, the ladies produced their nuggets, passing them round for inspection, and relating the manner in which they had been found. Lance's experience as a gold-digger now served the party in good stead, for he had no sooner taken the dull yellow lumps into his hand than he pronounced them to be veritable nuggets of pure gold; and after extracting from the fair finders as accurate a description as they could give him of the locality in which the discovery had been made, he declared his belief that one or more "pockets" of gold existed in the immediate vicinity of the pool, and said he would take an early opportunity of personally inspecting the spot.

The somewhat exciting events of the day caused the party to sit up chatting rather late that evening, and about midnight they were startled by the sound of knocking at the door. Captain Staunton opened it, and there stood Dickinson, who explained with some hesitation that, "Bein' as he couldn't sleep very well, he'd made so bold as to come up, seein' a light in the winder, to ask how the little missie was a'ter her ducking, likewise the youngster as had got his leg hurt."

The skipper was able to give satisfactory answers to both inquiries, and Mrs Staunton, hearing that someone was asking after May, came out herself and thanked the ex-boatswain's-mate so sweetly for his interest in her child that the poor fellow went away more dazed than ever, but with a heart so light that he felt as if walking upon air; and during the short journey between the hut and his quarters he solemnly and silently registered sundry fearful vows as to what he would do to anyone who dared so much as to think any harm of the inhabitants of Staunton Cottage.

For the next two days everybody was exceedingly busy; the men being hard at work at the shipyard, while the women felt as though they could not do enough for Bob, or make enough of him; indeed, in their anxiety to show their gratitude and admiration, they—Violet and Blanche, at least—let enthusiasm outrun discretion so far that they bid fair to do the patient more harm than good, so that Mrs Staunton was fain at last to take him under her own exclusive charge, forbidding the younger ladies to enter the room more than twice a day,—once in the morning and again in the evening,—and then rigorously limiting their visits to five minutes on each occasion.

The third day following Bob's accident was Sunday. This day was always observed as a holiday by the pirates; not, it need scarcely be said, in deference to the Fourth Commandment, but simply because the men insisted upon having one day of rest from work—a day on which the more sober and steady members of the band were wont to devote some little attention to the toilet and to the repairs of their clothing; while the remainder—by far the greater number—gave themselves up to unrestrained riot and drunkenness, a circumstance which, as may easily be understood, always caused a considerable amount of anxiety to the inmates of Staunton Cottage.

But however anxious they may have been—however fearful that, in their unbridled licence, the pirates might at any moment break in upon the privacy of the cottage and attempt some outrage—divine service was invariably performed twice each Sunday in the lower apartment of the cottage.

The day in question was no exception to the rule; and when the party began to assemble for the morning service, they saw that Dickinson had posted himself at a little distance from, but within easy hail of, the door. He was accordingly invited in; and when he made his appearance, with his hair freshly cut, his long bushy beard and moustache carefully trimmed, and his person decently arrayed in a nearly new suit of blue pilot-cloth, he looked not only every inch a sailor, but also a very fine specimen of manhood. He entered with some show of diffidence, and seemed half-inclined to beat a hasty retreat again, when Mrs Staunton invited him to occupy a seat next her. However, he remained, conducting himself with the greatest propriety during the service, and evidently still having in remembrance the forms of the Episcopal ceremonial. When prayers were over Captain Staunton delivered, according to his usual custom, a short address, in which he strove earnestly to give a plain and comprehensive answer to the question which Dickinson had propounded to him in the boat. It is not within the province of such a book as this to repeat what was said on the occasion; suffice it to say that the skipper so far succeeded in his object that, when the service was over, the strange guest went away a happier and a more hopeful man than he had been for years. He presented himself again at the evening service, remaining, at Mrs Staunton's invitation, to listen to the sacred music in which the party generally indulged for an hour at the close of the day. Thenceforth he was a changed man.

On the following morning Lance announced that he proposed to make, in Blanche's company, a visit to the "gold mine," as they laughingly called it. Blanche's presence was required ostensibly in order that she might act in the capacity of pilot; but no one attempted to pretend that he or she was blinded by so exceedingly transparent an excuse. Everybody knew how eagerly the occasion was welcomed by the pair as affording an opportunity

for a long day's uninterrupted enjoyment of each other's society, and
everybody had accordingly something jocular to say about it.

But what cared they, these two, happy in the first rosy flush of mutually
acknowledged love. They laughingly returned jest for jest, and set off in
high glee directly after breakfast, saying they were not to be expected back
at any definite time, as they should stay until Lance had made a thorough
examination of the entire locality. Deeply in love, however, as they both
were, they had the forethought to provide themselves with a good
substantial luncheon, and Evelin also slipped a tolerably heavy hammer and
a cold chisel into his pocket.

Blithely the pair stepped out,—for is not happiness always light of
foot?—and in due time, a much shorter time, by the way than was occupied
in the previous journey, they arrived at the brink of the ravine, and looked
down upon the tiny crystal stream and the pool wherein the nuggets had
been found.

Lance took in the geological characteristics of the place at a glance. He
recognised the rocks as genuine out-crops of gold-bearing quartz, and the
minute yellow specks therein as the precious metal itself, their visible
presence being an indication of the extraordinary richness of the reef.

"Why, Blanche darling!" he exclaimed, all his miner's instincts fully
aroused as he chipped and broke off "specimens" here and there, to find
tiny pellets and nodules of gold thickly clustering in each, "this mine of
yours is worth a nation's ransom; I do not believe there is such another reef
as this in the whole world. With proper crushing machinery we might all
make our fortunes in a month. But let us take a look at the pool; unless I
am greatly mistaken there is a princely fortune lying about here, and to be
had for the mere picking up, without the need of machinery at all."

They scrambled down the side of the ravine and stood by the margin of
the pool. Then Lance looked upward in the direction of the flow of the
rivulet, attentively noting the "run" of the strata. Glancing about him, he
saw a small broken branch lying on the ground at no great distance; and
securing it he cut away with his knife the sides of the larger end so as to
produce a flat surface, making of the branch a very narrow-bladed wooden
spade, in fact. Reaching as far forward as he could, he plunged the blade of
his extemporised spade into the sandy bottom of the pool, pressing it gently
down into the sand until he could get it no deeper, when he "prized" it
upward, so as to bring to the surface a specimen of the subsoil. Raising it
very carefully, the end of the branch at length came into view, bringing
with it a small quantity of yellow glittering sand. Some of this, by care and

patience, he managed to get out of the water before it was quite washed away; and, placing it in the palm of his hand, he gently agitated it to and fro beneath the surface of the water until all the lighter particles were washed away, when there remained in his hand a minute quantity of fine yellow dust.

"There," he said, "what do you think of that, Blanche? It is gold-dust, my dear girl; and if we could drain off the water from this pool—and it might be done without much trouble—we should find plenty of it underneath that fine white sand. Now, let us inspect a little further."

They accordingly began to walk slowly up the border of the stream, which descended the ravine by a series of miniature cataracts a foot or so in height, usually with small sandy-bottomed basins beyond. One of these basins proved to be so small and so shallow that, standing on a projecting ledge of rock, Lance was able to make a tolerably thorough examination of its bed with the aid of the before-mentioned branch, and he had not been very long stirring up the sand with it when he turned up four very fine nuggets, varying in size from a hen's egg to a six-pound shot.

"Just as I expected," he exclaimed. "Now, the spot from which this gold originally came is at the head of this ravine. These nuggets have all been brought down here by the water; and the higher we go the larger will the nuggets be, because of course, the heaviest of them will have travelled the shortest distance. But before pushing our investigations further, I propose that we sit down here and have luncheon; this is a picturesque spot; and, what is perhaps more to the purpose, I am frightfully hungry."

They accordingly seated themselves upon a great moss-grown rock, and partook of the contents of the basket with all the appetite of healthy people who had passed a long morning in the fresh pure air.

Luncheon over, and Lance having, at Blanche's request—or perhaps the word command would be nearer the truth—lighted a cigar, the pair proceeded with their investigations.

The characteristics of the stream continued to be the same; short lengths of sparkling water flowing over a boulder-strewn bed; diminutive rapids; tiny cataracts; and occasional quiet pools between. One or two of the smallest and least difficult of these pools Lance cursorily examined, finding in each case one or more nuggets, the sizes increasing as the searchers made their way upward, and thus confirming Lance's theory. He did not, however, devote much time to the actual search for gold; his object was just then to trace the gold to its source, and, at the same time, to note what capabilities existed for damming off the most promising spots, with a view to future operations.

A happy idea, as Blanche thought it, suddenly occurred to that young lady.

"Oh, Lance!" she exclaimed, "what geese we are?"

"Are we, darling?" said her companion. "Probably if anyone happened to see us just now," sliding his arm round her waist and kissing her, "they would be inclined to think so. Nay, you need not pout, it is entirely your own fault; the fact is, that you looked so pretty the temptation was simply irresistible."

"Was it?" she retorted. "Well, I think it very rude of you to interrupt me like that, just at the moment I was about to give utterance to a brilliant idea; but seriously, Lance dear, do you not think we could collect a sufficiency of this gold to purchase our freedom from these horrid men."

Evelin thought the matter over for a minute or two.

"I am afraid not," he said at last. "I have not the slightest doubt about our being able to collect a sufficient quantity of gold; the ground seems to be absolutely gorged with it; but the difficulty would be in the effecting of an arrangement by which these fellows would be persuaded to release us after the payment of the ransom. They would take the gold and afterwards simply break faith with us. No; our services are of too much value to them, unluckily, for them ever to voluntarily permit our departure; and we shall therefore have to follow out our original plan of escape, if possible—unless a better offers. But we will endeavour to possess ourselves of some of this enormous wealth; and we must trust to chance for the opportunity to convey it away with us."

They were now near the head of the ravine, which seemed to terminate in a sort of cul-de-sac, a huge reef of auriferous rock jutting out of the ground and forming an almost perpendicular wall across the end of the ravine. On reaching the base of this wall, the tiny stream they had been following was found to have its source a yard or two from the face of the rock, bubbling up out of the ground in the midst of a little pool some three yards across. It was near this spot, therefore, in all probability, that the precious metal would be found in richest abundance. Lance accordingly began to look around him for indications of the direction in which he ought to search.

About ten feet up the face of the rock-wall he saw what appeared to be a fissure in the stone; and, thinking it possible that an examination of this fissure might aid him, he, with some difficulty managed to scramble up to it. When he reached the spot he found, however, instead of a mere fissure or crack in the rock, as he had imagined, a wide projecting shoulder of the reef which artfully masked a low narrow recess. Penetrating into this recess, Lance found that, after he had proceeded two or three yards, the walls widened out, and the whole place had the appearance of being the entrance to a subterranean cavern.

Thinking that, if such were indeed the case, the discovery might prove of great value, as affording the party a perfectly secure place of refuge in case of necessity, he emerged once more, and, discovering from his more elevated stand-point an easy means of descent, hastened down to Blanche, and, informing her of his discovery, requested her to sit down and rest whilst he completed his explorations. He then looked about him for something to serve the purpose of a torch, and at length found a fragment of dry wood, which on being ignited promised to burn steadily enough for his purpose. Armed with this he was about to reascend the face of the rock when Blanche begged that she might be allowed to accompany him, as she was sure she would feel lonely sitting out there by herself. Lance accordingly gave her his hand, and without any very great difficulty managed to get her safely up on the narrow platform in front of the opening.

Relighting his torch, which he had extinguished after satisfying himself that it would burn properly, Lance led the way into the cleft; holding his brand well before him and as high as possible, and giving his disengaged hand to Blanche, who suffered from the disadvantage of being in total darkness, her lover's bulky form almost entirely filling up the narrow passage they were traversing, and completely eclipsing the light. Soon, however, they found the walls receding from them on either side, the roof rising at the same time; and when they had penetrated some fifty or sixty yards they were able to walk side by side. It was a curious place in which they found themselves. The rocky walls, which met overhead like an arch, were composed entirely of auriferous quartz, the gold gleaming in it here and there in long thin flakes. The passage sloped gently upward, whilst it at the same time swept gradually round toward the right hand; and though the air was somewhat close, there was an almost utter absence of that damp earthy smell which is commonly met with in subterranean chambers.

As they continued on their way the rocks about them gradually underwent a change, the gold no longer showing in thin detached thread-like layers, but glittering in innumerable specks and tiny nodules all over the surface, so that, as the flickering uncertain light of the torch fell upon the walls, they glistened as though covered with an unbroken coating of gold-leaf.

But this novel appearance, attractive as it was, was nothing to the surprise which awaited them further on. They had penetrated some eight or nine hundred yards, perhaps, into the bowels of the earth, and were thinking of returning, when they suddenly emerged from the passage into a vast cavern, so spacious in all its dimensions that their tiny light quite failed to reveal the farther side or the roof. But what little they did see was sufficient to root them to the ground, speechless for the moment with wonder and admiration.

The rocky floor upon which they stood was smooth as a marble pavement, apparently from attrition by the action of water through countless centuries, though the place was now perfectly dry. What chiefly excited their admiration, however, was the circumstance that the floor was not only smooth, it was as polished as glass, and in places quite transparent, while it glowed and sparkled with all the colours of the rainbow. They seemed to be standing on a surface of purest crystalline ice, seamed, streaked, veined, and clouded in the most marvellous and fantastic manner with every conceivable hue, through and into which the faint light of their torch gleamed, flashed, and sparkled with an effect of indescribable splendour.

"Oh, Lance!" whispered Blanche at last, "was ever anything so lovely seen before?"

"A perfect palace of the gnomes, darling, is it not?" returned Lance in his usual tone of voice; and then they stood awe-struck and enthralled, as his words were caught up by countless echoes and flung backward and forward, round and round, and in the air above them, in as many different tones, from a faint whisper far overhead to deep sonorous musical bell-like notes reverberating round the walls and echoing away and away, farther and farther, fainter and fainter, until at last, after an interminable time, as it seemed to them, the sounds died completely away and silence reigned once more.

"It is marvellous! superb!" whispered Evelin, not caring to again arouse the echoes of the place. "Come, Blanche, sweetheart, let us explore a little further while our torch still holds out."

Hand in hand, and with cautious steps—for the floor was almost as slippery as ice—they began to make the tour of this fairy-like cavern; but they had not proceeded a dozen steps before they were again arrested, spell-bound. The walls, as far as the feeble light of the torch would reveal them, were of rock of the same character as the floor; only that instead of being smooth and even they were broken up into fantastic projections of every imaginable form, while here and there huge masses started boldly out from the face, forming flying buttresses with projecting pinnacles and elaborate carved-work, all executed by Nature's own hand; while elsewhere there clustered columns, so regular and perfect in their shape that they might have been transferred with scarcely a finishing touch of the chisel to the aisles of a cathedral. Where the light happened to fall upon these the effect was bewilderingly beautiful, the rays being reflected and refracted from and through the crystals of which they were composed until they shone and sparkled like columns of prismatic fire.

Then a new wonder revealed itself; for, on approaching more closely to the glittering walls, it became apparent that they were seamed with wide cracks here and there, the cracks being filled with a cement-like substance, so thickly studded with nuggets of gold of all sizes, that in less than five minutes a man might have gathered more than he could carry away. Passing along the walls, Lance found that it was everywhere the same, and that in stumbling upon this subterranean palace of the fairies they had also discovered a mine of incalculable wealth.

Hastily gathering a few of the finest nuggets within reach, they set out to return.

They had apparently made the entire circuit of the cavern, for there close to them yawned the black mouth of a passage. This was fortunate; as the torch had now burned so low that Lance saw with consternation it would be necessary for them to make the greater part of their return journey in darkness.

"But never mind, Blanche darling," he said cheerfully, remarking upon this unpleasant circumstance. "It is all plain sailing; there are no obstacles in our way; and if we have to grope slowly along, still the marvellous sight we have seen is well worth so trifling a penalty. Give me your hand, sweetheart, and let us get into the passage, for I shall have to abandon the light, it is scorching my fingers as it is."

Blanche silently gave her hand to her lover, a trifle nervous at having to traverse so long a distance in impenetrable darkness, and buried—who knew how deep—beneath the surface. Buried! The idea was a most unpleasant one just then; and she shuddered as they plunged hand in hand into the passage, Lance at the same moment flinging the charred stump of the burnt-out torch back into the great cavern behind them.

Cautiously they groped their way onward, Lance feeling his way along the wall of the passage, and making sure of his footing at every step by passing his foot lightly forward over the ground before advancing.

In this manner the pair proceeded for what seemed to them a considerable length of time—at least Blanche thought it so, for at last she said with a slight tremor in her voice—

"How much longer do you think we shall be, Lance! Surely we cannot be very far from the entrance now."

"No, we must be getting pretty close to it," said Lance; "but surely you are not feeling frightened, little woman?"

"Not exactly frightened," answered Blanche; "but this terrible darkness and this awful silence makes me nervous. It seems so dreadful to be groping one's way like this, without being able to see where one is going; and then I have a stupid feeling that the rocks above us may give way at any moment and bury us."

"Not much fear of that," said Lance with a laugh, which went echoing and reverberating along the passage in such a weird unearthly manner that Blanche clung to her companion in terror. "These rocks," he continued, "have supported for years—probably centuries—the weight above them, and it is not at all likely they will give way just now without any cause. I daresay the time does seem long to you, darling, but you must remember we are walking at a much slower pace now than we were when we passed over the ground before. Of course we might walk faster, since we know the ground to be tolerably even and regular; still it is best to be cautious; if either of us happens to stumble here in the dark we might receive a rather severe blow. However, keep up your courage, we cannot be very much longer now."

Once more they continued their way in silence, the ground sloping gently downwards all the while, as they could tell notwithstanding the darkness; and still no welcome ray of daylight appeared in the distance to tell them that they were approaching their journey's end.

At length a vague and terrible fear began to make itself felt in Lance's own mind. Recalling the incidents of their inward journey, he tried to reckon the time which they had occupied in passing from the open air along the gallery into the great cavern, and he considered that they could not possibly have been longer than twenty minutes, probably not as long as that. But it seemed to him that they had been groping there in the intense darkness for two hours at least! No, surely it could not be so long as that; the darkness made the time lag heavily. But if they had been there only one hour, they ought by this time to have reached daylight once more, slowly as they had been moving. Surely they had not—oh, no, it was not possible—it could not be possible—and yet—merciful God! what if they had by some dreadful mischance lost their way.

The strong man felt the beads of cold perspiration start out upon his forehead as the dreadful indefinable haunting fear at length took shape and presented itself before his mind in all its grisly horror. He had faced Death often enough to look him in the face now or at any time without fear; but to meet him thus—to wander on and on in the thick darkness, to grope blindly along the walls of this huge grave until exhaustion came and compelled them to lie down and die—never to look again upon the sweet face of nature—never again to have their eyes gladdened by the blessed light of the sun or the soft glimmer of the star-lit heavens—to vanish from off the face of the earth, and to pass away from the ken of their friends, leaving no sign, no clue of their whereabouts or of their fate—oh, God! it was too horrible.

Not for himself; no, if it were God's will that thus he must die he had courage enough to meet his fate calmly and as a brave man should. Thank God, he had so lived that, let death come upon him never so suddenly, he could not be taken unawares. Lance Evelin was by no means a saint; he knew it and acknowledged it in this dread hour; but he had always striven honestly and honourably to do his duty, whatever it might be, with all his strength; and then, too, like the apostle, he knew in Whom he trusted.

No, Lance was not afraid of death on his own account; it was for the weak timorous girl by his side that all his sympathies were aroused. Doubtless she too possessed a faith firm enough to enable her to meet her fate undismayed—he believed she did; but what terrible bodily suffering must she pass through before the end came.

But perhaps, after all, he was alarming himself unnecessarily; even now they might be within a few yards of the outlet and yet not be able to see it, because, as he suddenly remembered, the passage was curved from its very commencement.

But then, he also remembered, the passage at its outer end was so narrow that Blanche had to walk behind him, and here they were, walking hand in hand and side by side, as they had been ever since they had entered this interminable passage.

"Blanche," said he, steadying his voice as well as he could, "put out your hand, dear, and see whether you can reach the right-hand wall."

He felt her lean away from him, and then came her reply in a broken voice—

"No, Lance, I cannot."

"Why, pet," he exclaimed, "I really believe you are crying."

"Yes, I am," she acknowledged. "Forgive me, Lance dear, I really cannot help it; I shall be better by and by, perhaps, but—oh! it is so dreadful. You are very brave, and very good to me, but I know you must have realised it before now—the dreadful truth that we are lost here."

"Tut, tut; nonsense, child," Lance answered cheerily; "why, Blanche, you will get quite unnerved if you suffer such thoughts to take possession of you. There, lay your head on my shoulder, darling, and have your cry comfortably out; you will feel better and braver afterwards."

He put his arm round her as he spoke; and the poor frightened girl laid her head upon his breast, trustfully as a child, and sobbed as though her heart would break.

Her companion let her sob on unchecked; he did not even say a word to comfort her—what could he say, with that frightful suspicion every moment gathering force and strengthening itself into certainty? No; better not to say anything; better not to buoy her up with delusive hopes; and, oh! how thankful he felt that the terrible task of breaking to her the news of their awful position had been spared him.

The sobs gradually grew less violent, and at length ceased altogether. Then Blanche raised her head and said quietly—

"Now, Lance, I am better, and feel able to listen to the worst you can tell me. I will not ask you to give me your candid opinion of our position, because I know it is—it must be the same as my own. But what do you propose that we should do?"

"Well," said Lance, as cheerily as he could, "the first thing I intend to do is to light a match and take a glance at our surroundings. It was stupid of me that I did not think of doing so before."

He drew a box of matches from his pocket—being a smoker he was never by any chance without them—and the next moment a sharp rasping noise was heard, and a tiny flame appeared. The light, however, was too feeble to penetrate that Egyptian darkness; they saw nothing but each other's faces; hers pale, with wide-open, horror-stricken eyes; and his, with contracted brow and firmly compressed lips, indicative of an unconquerable determination to struggle to the last against this dreadful fate which menaced them.

"This will not do," said he; "we must improvise a better torch than this."

He fumbled once more in his pockets, and presently found a sheet or two of paper on which he remembered jotting down some notes relative to matters connected with the construction of the battery. These he folded very carefully; so loosely as to burn well, yet tightly enough to burn slowly and so give them an opportunity for at least a momentary glance round them. Then he struck another match, applied it to one of the tiny torches, and raised the light aloft.

As he did so, Blanche uttered a piercing shriek, and seizing him by the arm, dragged him back against the rocky wall of the passage. Then, pointing before her, she gasped—

"Look, Lance; look!"

Lance looked in the direction toward which she pointed, and grew faint and sick as he saw that they had been standing on the very verge of a precipice. A stone, dislodged by Blanche's hasty movement had rolled over the edge, and they now heard it bounding with a loud echoing clang down the face of the rock, down, down, down, the sound, loud at first, growing fainter and fainter, until at last a dull muffled splash told that it had reached water more than a hundred fathoms below.

Blanche and Her Lover Have to Swim for It

"Stand close against the wall, Blanche, and do not move," commanded Evelin, as the paper torch burnt down and went out. "Now," he continued, "I am about to light up another of these papers; and we must utilise the light to get past this gulf, if possible; it will never do for us to remain where we are. The question is—In which direction will it be most advisable for us to proceed? We must devote a moment or two to a hasty survey of the place, as far our light will allow us, before we move. Neither the time nor the light will be wasted. And it will be better that you should turn your glance upward and away from the edge of the chasm; your nerves will then be all the steadier when we have to make a move. Now, I am going to light up once more."

Another paper was lighted; and, placing himself in front of his companion, or between her and the edge of the chasm, in order to guard against the possibility of her turning faint or giddy and falling over, Lance raised the light at arm's-length above his head to glance round. As he did so, the tiny flame wavered, as if fanned by a faint draught. He looked at it intently for a moment, and noticed that the wavering motion was continuous, and such as would be produced by a steady current of air flowing in the direction in which they had been proceeding. Then he knelt down and held the lighted paper close against the surface of the ground. The flame burnt steadily for an instant and then betrayed a very slight draught in an opposite direction. Then it went out, the paper being all consumed.

He thought intently for a moment; then turned to his companion and said—

"Blanche, dearest, we are saved. Pluck up your courage, my own love, and thank God with me for showing us a way out of this terrible labyrinth."

"I don't understand you, Lance," answered the girl, trembling with agitation; "are you only saying this to sustain my courage a little while longer, or do you really mean that you believe there is still a chance of our emerging once more into the blessed light of day?"

"I mean, dear, that I hope and believe we shall escape. Listen. That bit of lighted paper has revealed the presence of two distinct currents of air flowing along this passage. That means that an outlet to the open air exists somewhere. The upper current, which is the warmer of the two, is flowing in the direction of that outlet; and all we have to do is to follow in the same direction, if we can, and we shall eventually reach the opening."

"Then let us proceed at once, Lance dear, please," pleaded poor terrified Blanche. "I feel as though I should go mad if we remain here much longer. I have a frightful feeling urging me—almost beyond my powers of resistance—to fling myself forward over the edge of that dreadful chasm which is yawning to receive me. Oh! save me, Lance darling, save me for pity's sake."

"I will save you, dear, if it is in man's power to do so," answered Lance, "but you must help me by keeping up your courage; you know I cannot possibly think and reason calmly whilst you continue in this deplorable state of nervousness. Now, I will light another paper—our last—and we will move forward at once. Keep close to the wall, and be ready to give me your right hand as soon as the light shines out."

Another moment, and a feeble glimmer once more illumined the Cimmerian darkness.

Holding the light in his right hand, Lance gave his left to Blanche, and they cautiously resumed their way. The ledge along which they were passing was about six feet wide; but a yard or two further on it narrowed abruptly, leaving a path barely twelve inches in breadth. It continued thus for a length of some twenty feet, and then widened out abruptly again, apparently to the full width of the passage. It seemed, in short, as though the terrible chasm terminated at this point.

Luckily, Lance was the first to see it, and his resolution was at once taken. He dropped the lighted paper as if by accident, and extinguished it by setting his foot upon it. He knew that if his companion caught so much as a single momentary glimpse of the short but frightfully perilous passage she would have to make, her nerve would utterly fail her, and too probably a dreadful catastrophe would happen. So he resolved upon the hazardous attempt to get her past the danger blindfold.

"Tut! what a clumsy fellow I am!" he exclaimed pettishly, as though in reference to his having dropped the lighted paper. "Now I shall have to expend another match. But, Blanche, your nerves are still unsteady; the sight of this threatening gulf is too much for you. I think you would do better blindfold. Give me your handkerchief, dear, and let me tie it over your eyes. I will remove it again as soon as we are past the chasm."

"Thank you," said Blanche. "I really believe I should feel better if the sight of that dreadful place were shut out. I can trust to your care and courage; but I confess with shame that, as far as I am concerned, I am thoroughly unnerved."

Lance took the handkerchief which Blanche put into his hand, and bound it gently but firmly over her eyes, arranging it as well as he could in the darkness in such a manner as to make the blinding perfectly effectual.

He then led her cautiously forward a step or two until he felt with his outstretched foot the edge of the precipice, when, bidding her stand perfectly still and to cling firmly to the irregular surface of the rock, he once more lighted the short remaining end of paper, utilising its brief existence to note well the perilous path they had to tread.

"Now, sweetheart," he said briskly, "do you feel better, and fit to go on?"

"Oh, yes," was the reply, in a tone so bright and cheerful that Lance felt intensely relieved; and he forthwith set about the difficult task of getting his companion past the narrow ledge without further delay.

By the last expiring gleam of his short-lived taper, Lance took one more rapid glance at the terrible pass, and then, as the thick darkness once more closed round them, he said—

"Now, dear, you must be very cautious how you move. Keep close against the rock, and take a firm hold of any projections you can find. Do not move until you have a firm hold with both hands, nor without telling me of your intention, as I shall keep close to you and give you the support of my arm. And do not loose your hold of the rock with one hand until you have secured a firm grip with the other. Now, have you a tight hold? Then move gently along, side wise; and keep close to the rock."

The dreadful journey was begun. Slowly and cautiously the pair groped their uncertain way along that narrow ledge, each pausing until the other was ready to proceed; and Lance with difficulty restrained a shudder as once during the passage he felt that the heel of his boot actually projected over the awful ledge. A dozen times he felt outwards with his foot to ascertain whether the chasm was passed or not, and at last, with an involuntary sigh of ineffable relief he found that there was solid ground beyond him as far as his foot could reach.

"Now stand quite still for a moment, Blanche," he said. "I am about to light another match."

He did so, and found that they had indeed achieved the awful passage—with some six inches to spare. At his very feet still yawned the hungry gulf, but they were beyond it, thank God, and once more in comparative safety. Hastily seizing his companion's hand, he hurried her far enough away from the spot to prevent her seeing the deadly nature of the peril to which they had been exposed, and then removed the bandage from her eyes.

"There," he said cheerfully, "we are past the chasm at last, and now you may have the use of your eyes once more."

Lighting another match, the imprisoned pair now pressed forward as rapidly as circumstances would permit, taking care to keep a match always alight in order that they might not stumble unawares upon a possible second chasm or other danger. They pressed forward in silence, except for an occasional word of caution or encouragement from Lance, both being far too anxious to admit of anything like a connected conversation.

Suddenly Lance stopped short. To his sense of hearing, acutely sharpened by the long-continued death-like silence of the place, there had come a sound, fainter than the breathing of a sleeping infant, a mere vibration of the air, in fact, but still—a sound.

What was it? He knelt down and placed his ear close to the ground. Yes; now he caught it a trifle more distinctly; the faintest murmur still, but with something of individuality appertaining to it. It rose and fell rhythmically, swelling gradually in volume, and then subsiding again into silence.

"Hurrah!" he shouted joyously. "The sea! the sea! I can hear it. Courage, Blanche darling, our journey is nearly at an end. One short half-hour at most, and, with God's help, we shall be free."

Again they pushed eagerly forward; with high hopes and grateful hearts now, and with every yard of progress the gladdening sound rose clearer and clearer still until there could no longer be any possible mistake about it; it was indeed the regular beat of surf upon the shore.

At length a faint gleam of light became perceptible upon the rocky walls in front; gradually it strengthened, until the more prominent projections of the rock began to stand out bold and black against the lighter portions beyond; and at last, as the path curved gently round, their eager eyes were gladdened by the sight of an opening into which the sea was sweeping with a long lazy undulating motion until it curled over and plashed musically upon a narrow strip of sandy beach.

They both paused for a moment, with one consent, to feast their eyes upon the gladsome sight, and to restore their disordered faculties. Then they saw that the long passage or gallery within which they stood terminated at its outer end in a cavernous recess, opening apparently on a precipitous part of the shore. The floor of the passage sloped gradually down until it met the short strip of sand upon which the mimic waves were lazily beating; and a yard or two from the water's edge the sand was marked with a well-defined line of stranded weed and drift-wood, which indicated the inner limit of the wash of the sea. A single glance was sufficient to show that the auriferous rock had been left behind; that which now surrounded them being a coarse kind of granite. Pursuing their way the pair soon stood upon the strip of beach. Then came the question, How were they to get out of the cavern, now that they had reached its mouth? The sides rose perpendicularly, and the top arched over in such a manner that escape seemed impossible. Lance made several attempts on each side of the entrance to work his way out, but the face of the rock was worn so smooth with the constant wash of the water that the nearer he approached the entrance the more difficult did he find it to proceed, and at last, failing to find any further foot-hold, he was compelled to abandon his efforts and return to Blanche, who meanwhile had been resting her tired limbs on the soft grey sand.

"Well, Blanche," he said, "I thought our troubles were over when I first caught sight of that opening, but it appears they are not. There seems to be only one possible mode of escape from this place and that is by swimming. Now, I can manage the matter easily enough if you will only trust me; the distance is the merest trifle, the water is smooth, and if you think you have nerve enough to rest your hands on my shoulders and to refrain from struggling when we get into deep water, I can support your weight perfectly well, I know, and carry you safely round to the beach, which I have no doubt we shall find at a short distance on one side or the other of the opening. It will involve a ducking, certainly, but we cannot help that; and if we walk briskly afterwards we shall take no harm."

Blanche laughed—she could afford to do that now. "If that is our only difficulty, it is but a trifling one," she said. "I can trust you implicitly, Lance; and, what is perhaps almost as important, I can also trust myself. I can swim a little; and if I should tire I shall not be frightened, having you to help me."

"Very well," was the reply; "that is better than I dared hope. Would you like to rest a little longer, or shall we make the attempt at once?"

Blanche announced her perfect readiness to make the attempt forthwith; and without further ado the pair straightway entered the water, hand in hand, Lance first taking the precaution to place his watch in his hat and ram the latter well down upon his head. They waded steadily in until Blanche felt the water lifting her off her feet, when they struck out, Lance regulating his stroke so as to keep close beside his companion. The water was delightfully warm, the sun having been beating down upon it all day, and the immersion proved refreshing rather than otherwise. It took them only about a couple of minutes to reach the mouth of the cave; and then Lance began to look about him for a suitable landing-place. He had expected to find a beach on one side or the other of the opening; but there was nothing of the kind as far as he could see. Perpendicular cliffs rose sheer out of the water on both sides of the opening for a distance of perhaps a hundred yards; and where the cliff terminated the ground sloped steeply down, with huge masses of rock projecting here and there, the foot of the slope being encumbered with other rocks which at some distant period had become detached and rolled down into the water. In bad weather it would have been death to attempt landing upon any part of the shore within Lance's range of vision; but fortunately the weather was fine and the water smooth; so they made for a spot which Lance thought would serve their purpose, and in another ten minutes succeeded in effecting a landing among the rocks. The scramble up the steep face of the slope before them was not without its perils, but this also was happily accomplished; and at last they found themselves standing safe and sound on tolerably level ground, just as the last rays of the setting sun were gilding the summits of the hills before them.

Lance found that they had come out on the eastern side of the island; and as the harbour lay on the south side he knew pretty well in which direction they ought to walk; they therefore at once set out at a brisk pace toward a large patch of forest fringing a hill at some distance in front of but a little to the south of them.

They had not gone very far before Lance, who was keeping a keen look-out for some familiar landmark, recognised a dip between the hills as the ravine up which they had passed in the morning; and altering their course a little they came in about half an hour to the stream, which they crossed without difficulty, and then followed it down until they reached the pool in which the first discovery of gold had been made. Thence their way was tolerably easy—though, in the darkness which had by this time closed down upon them, they went somewhat astray while passing through the wood—and in another hour they found themselves once more safely within the shelter of Staunton Cottage, thoroughly tired-out with their long and adventurous day's ramble.

Their entrance was greeted with exclamations of mock horror at the length to which they had spun out the day's ramble; but Blanche's pale cheeks, draggled dress, and general "done-up" appearance speedily apprised her friends that a contre-temps of some kind had occurred; and their jesting remarks were quickly exchanged for earnest and sympathetic inquiries as to what had gone wrong. Whereupon Lance—having first suggested to his late companion the advisability of immediate retirement to her couch, and bespoken Mrs Staunton's kind services in the preparation of a cup of tea for each of the tired-out wanderers—proceeded to give a succinct account of their day's adventure, the recital of which elicited frequent exclamations of wonder, alarm, and admiration, the latter being vastly increased when he produced his valuable specimens, to which he had resolutely "stuck" through it all notwithstanding that their weight had proved a serious encumbrance to him during his swim.

"Now," he said in conclusion, "the net result of the day's exploration amounts to this. We have discovered a mine of incalculable wealth. What are we to do in the matter? There is so much gold there—in the cave, I mean—that a short period of resolute and well-directed labour will enable us to collect sufficient not only to fully recoup the underwriters for their loss through the burning of the Galatea, but also to make every individual among us enormously rich. Are we to let it lie there, and trust to the future for an opportunity to come back and fetch it, or shall we make an effort now to collect what will suffice us, and trust to chance for the opportunity to carry it off with us when we go?"

In answer to this, everybody declared at once without hesitation their opinion that an attempt ought to be made to collect and carry off the gold with them; Captain Staunton very sensibly remarking that if anything occurred to prevent the safe transport of their prize home they could then organise an expedition for a second attempt; but that it would be folly to make a necessity of this if by some extra effort on their part the business could be managed without it.

This point being settled, the next question to be decided was—how they were to set about the collection of the precious metal; for it was obvious that any attempt to absent themselves from their daily attendance at the shipyard would not only excite suspicion, but it might also provoke a very unpleasant manifestation of active hostility on Ralli's part.

Here Violet Dudley came to the rescue with a very practical suggestion.

"If you, Lance," said she, "can contrive to mark the two passages out of the great central cavern in such a manner that we women cannot possibly mistake one for the other, and so go astray, we might perhaps be able to collect the gold and convey it to a suitable spot for removal; and when enough has been gathered we can take our time about transporting it down here."

"An admirable suggestion, Miss Dudley!" said Captain Staunton. "That effectually disposes of one part of the difficulty. But it will never do to bring the gold here; we could not possibly convey it on board the schooner without detection, even if we were quite sure of the success of our plan for making our escape in her. Do you think, Evelin, the pirates have any knowledge of the existence of this cave of yours?"

"I am pretty certain they have not," was the reply. "There is no sign of any human foot having ever passed over the ground before our own; and it is so eminently well adapted for a place of concealment for their booty—and, indeed, for themselves as well—in the event of the island ever being attacked, that I feel sure they would, had they known of it, have stocked it with provisions and in other ways have prepared it as a place of refuge. It was only by the merest accident that I discovered the spot to-day; and but for the fact that our search not only led us up to the head of the ravine but also actually caused me to scale the face of the rock, it would have remained undiscovered still. A man might stand within twenty feet of the entrance without suspecting its existence; and, unless he had occasion to scramble up the rock as I did, and in exactly the same place, he would never find it."

"Very well, then," said Captain Staunton, "what I propose is this. Since the ladies are kindly disposed to give them we will thankfully accept their services to this extent. Let them collect the gold and convey it to the edge of the gulf or chasm which you so providentially escaped tumbling into to-day. Then we men must undertake the task of conveying it to the other side and stacking it up in a position from which we can easily remove it with the aid of a boat. If we succeed in securing the schooner, we shall simply have to call off the mouth of the cave and remove our booty in that way. Can anyone suggest anything better?"

No one could; it was therefore decided that the skipper's proposal should be adopted, especially as it left them free to alter their plans at any time, should circumstances seem to require it. This decision arrived at, the party retired for the night, most of them, it must be confessed, to dream of the wonderful cave and the equally wonderful wealth of which they had been talking.

The next day was spent by all hands, Dale included, at the shipyard. This individual had, ever since poor Bob's accident, manifested a growing dissatisfaction with himself, and an increasing amount of shame at the selfishness which caused him to live a life of idleness and comparative ease, while every one of his companions, the ladies included, were doing all they could to aid in maturing the great plan of escape; and now at last shame at his unmanly conduct fairly overcame him, and on this particular morning he startled everybody by putting in an appearance at the same time as the rest of the male portion of the party, saying in explanation that henceforward he too should go daily to work, as he was quite sure he could be of assistance. He was, of course, assured that he undoubtedly could be of very great use if he chose; and there the matter ended. But a rather unpleasant feeling was excited when Ralli, who was always promptly down at the beach to watch the departure of the working party, noticed and commented upon Dale's presence.

"Aha! my fine fellow," he remarked sneeringly, "so you have made up your mind to go to work at last, have you? That is very well, sare. You must surely have dream last night that I had my eye on you. You think, perhaps, I have not take notice; but I have; and if you had not gone to work to-day, I should have said to you, 'Look here, my good man, suppose you not work you not eat;' and I should have stopped your 'lowance. But you are going to work; so now that is all right."

It certainly served Dale right; but, all the same, it was a disagreeable sensation to the rest to feel that this sly Greek had been in all probability keeping a stealthy watch upon them and their movements. They inwardly resolved to be very much more circumspect in their goings-out and in their comings-in for the future; and they lost no time either in communicating this resolve to each other.

All day long their thoughts were busy upon the subject of the gold mine; and by the time that they got back to the cottage that evening each man had an idea in connection with it to communicate to the others. They were unanimous upon one point, which was that—after Ralli's remark to Dale in the morning, and the espionage which it seemed to suggest—it would be most unwise for any of the male portion of the party to visit the cave during the day. Henceforward their visits there would have to be as few and far between as possible, and such visits as were unavoidable must be made during the night. With the women it would, of course, be different. They could now safely venture out every day, it was believed; and as the walk up the valley was the one which involved the least exertion, it would only appear natural that they should almost invariably take it. But, in order to disarm suspicion, in case anything of the kind happened to exist, it was deemed best that an occasional walk should be taken in some other direction until they could resume the road toward the ravine with the certainty that they had not been watched and followed.

It was further agreed all round that the task of carrying the gold, when collected, over the most dangerous part of the path along the edge of the ravine was not to be thought of, especially as Captain Staunton had thought out a plan by which all danger might be completely avoided. His idea was exceedingly simple, and consisted merely in the erection on each side of the chasm of a short stout pair of sheers connected together at their heads by a good strong sound piece of rope, having rove upon it a thimble with a pair of clip-hooks attached. The gold could then be put into a canvas bag suspended from the clip-hooks, and, with the aid of a hauling-line, hauled easily enough across the chasm to the other side.

These details agreed upon, they determined to proceed with their arrangements that same night. Accordingly, as soon as the evening meal was over, the men retired to their bunks for a few hours' sleep—all, that is to say, except Dale, who, quite unaccustomed to bodily labour, felt thoroughly exhausted with his day's work, and was therefore readily excused. He volunteered, however, to remain up on watch until all the lights in the pirates' quarter were extinguished, and then to take a good look round the settlement, and call the others when all was quiet; a raid upon the capstan-house being the first thing necessary to enable them to carry out their plans successfully.

The pirates, working hard all day in the open air, were, as a rule, tolerably early birds; and by eleven o'clock that night the place was wrapped in darkness and repose. Having thoroughly satisfied himself that this was the case, and that the coast was quite clear for his comrades, Dale roused the latter and then tumbled into his own berth with the comforting reflection that he had at last taken the right course, and done something to regain that respect from his companions which he was beginning to be acutely conscious of having forfeited.

Five minutes later four forms might have been seen—had anyone been on the look-out—stealing quietly across the open space between Staunton Cottage and the capstan-house. Fortunately no one was on the look-out, and they reached the building undiscovered, ascended the ladder, and found themselves standing in the thick darkness which enshrouded the long loft-like apartment.

Here Lance promptly produced his box of matches, and, on striking a light, they were fortunate enough to discover hanging to a nail near the door a lantern ready trimmed. This they at once lighted, and, carefully masking it, proceeded to rummage the place for such things as would be likely to prove useful to them. The place was almost like a museum in the variety of its contents; and they were not long in confiscating a dozen fathoms of three-inch rope, the remains of a coil of ratline, a small ball of spun-yarn for seizings, a sledge-hammer, an axe apiece, a marline-spike, a few long spike-nails, which Lance decided would be capital tools for the ladies to use in picking out the nuggets, and a few other trifling matters. Then, hanging the lantern upon its nail once more, they extinguished it, and made the best of their way down the ladder again.

A pause of a minute or so to look round and assure themselves that no midnight prowler was in their vicinity, and they set off at a brisk pace up the valley, lighted on their way by the clear soft effulgence of the star-studded sky.

They were not long in reaching the shelter of the dense wood at the head of the valley; and once fairly through it, they laid down the bulk of their booty where they could easily find it again, and, returning to the wood, selected a couple of young pines, which they quickly felled. The branches were soon lopped off, after which they cut from the tall slender trunks four spars about ten feet in length to serve for sheers.

Shouldering these, they sought out the remainder of their belongings, and—by this time pretty heavily loaded—continued their way into and up the ravine, arriving at last, under Lance's guidance, at the great rock which veiled the entrance to the cavern.

Lance and Brook at once scrambled up to the narrow ledge before the entrance, taking with them the ratline and such other small matters as they could carry, while Captain Staunton and Rex remained below to "bend on" and send up the remainder. Many hands—especially if they be willing—make light work, and a quarter of an hour sufficed to transfer everything, themselves included, to the ledge. Torches, chopped out of the remainder of the pines, were then lighted, and, once more loading up their possessions, they plunged boldly into the cavern, Lance as pilot leading the way.

In about half an hour they found themselves standing in the great central hall or cavern, which, lighted up as it now was by the glare of four flaming torches, looked more bewilderingly beautiful than ever. A hurried glance round was, however, all that they would now spare themselves time to take, and then they at once set vigorously to work. The first thing necessary was to mark in a legible manner—and in such a way that the mark could be identified in the darkness if need be—the inner extremity of the passage through which they had just passed. Rex and Brook undertook to do this; and as they had already agreed what the mark should be, these two began, with the aid of the sledge-hammer and a spike, to chip in the face of the rock a circular depression on the right-hand side of the passage, at a height of about three feet from the ground, so that it could easily be found and identified in the dark by a mere touch of the hand. Leaving these two busily employed, Lance and Captain Staunton hurried away in search of the other passage. They soon found an opening which proved to be the right one, though a third was afterwards found to exist further along the circular wall of the cavern. The second, however, was the passage they wanted; for, on going a short distance into it, Lance's and Blanche's footprints were distinctly traceable in a thin coating of fine dust which was met with. The identity of the passage being thus established, it was marked in a similar way to the other, but with a cross instead of a circle. The marking of the two passages proved to be a long and tedious job, owing to the hardness of the rock and the imperfect character of the tools, but it was done at last; and then they set out to execute the real task of their journey, namely, the erection of the sheers.

Now that they had lights the journey along the second passage to the spot where the sheers were to be erected was accomplished in a trifle less than an hour; but a shudder ran through them all as, following the footprints, they saw that Blanche had twice or thrice walked for several yards on the extreme verge of the yawning chasm without being aware of it. And when at last they came to the narrowest part of the path—that which Blanche had traversed blindfold—they felt their very hair rising as they craned over the edge and heard the pebbles they threw in go bounding down until the sound of their ultimate splash in the water was so faint as to be hardly distinguishable. It was nervous work, the passage along that narrow ledge, but it had to be done and they did it, hauling the poles across afterwards with the aid of the rope; and this part of the work successfully accomplished, the rest was not long in the doing; another hour saw both pairs of sheers erect, properly stayed, and the three-inch-rope bridge strained across, with the clip-hooks and hauling-line attached, and, in short, everything ready for the commencement of operations. The axes and other matters were then taken back to the great central chamber, where they were left for future use, and the party made the best of their way into the open air, and thence homeward, arriving finally at Staunton Cottage about an hour before the great bell rang the summons for all hands to come forth to another day's labour.

Bob Wants to Be Rich

The problem as to the working of the gold mine being so far satisfactorily solved, it only remained to ascertain how the arrangements would answer when put into practice, and this the ladies did without loss of time. Their plan was that one of them should remain at home to look after Bob and little May, while the other two devoted a few hours of the day to the cave. As they took it in turns to remain at home in the capacity of nurse, each of them had two days in the cave to one at the cottage.

In the meantime, thanks to Lance's skill and the careful nursing of the ladies, Bob was making steady progress toward recovery, and within a month of the occurrence of his accident was beginning to ask how much longer he was going to be kept a prisoner.

He had been made aware of the gold discovery, by occasional references to it on the part of the others in his presence, but he had never heard the complete story; so one day, when it was Blanche's turn to remain at home, he asked her to give him the entire history; which she did.

He listened most attentively; and when the story was over remained silent, apparently wrapped in profound thought, for several minutes.

Looking up at last, with a flush of excitement on his face, he exclaimed—

"Why, there must be gold enough there to make millionaires of every one of us!"

"Yes," said Blanche, "I believe there is; at least Lan— Mr Evelin says so, and I have no doubt he knows."

"Oh yes," exclaimed Bob enthusiastically, "he knows. I believe he knows everything. And what a splendid fellow he is, isn't he, Miss Lascelles?"

This last with a sly twinkle in his roguish eye.

Blanche appeared to think it unnecessary to comment upon or reply to this remark; at all events she remained silent. But the window-curtain somehow needed adjustment just at that moment, and the haste with which she rose to attend to this little matter—or something else—caused a most lovely pink flush to overspread her cheeks. Bob saw it; perhaps he knew exactly what caused it; but if he did he was too much of a gentleman to show that he had noticed it. So when Blanche had adjusted the curtain to her satisfaction he remarked with a heavy sigh—

"Oh dear! I wish I was well enough to be out and at work again. I long to have the handling of some of that gold."

"You must have patience, Robert," said Blanche. "The worst part of your illness is now over, and in due time you will no doubt be able to take your share of the work once more. But whether such is the case or not, you may rest satisfied that you will have your share of the gold. Whatever there may be, whether it be much or little, I know the gentlemen have decided that it shall be divided equally among us, even to little May."

"I am sure it's very kind of them," said Bob with a touch of impatience in his tone; "but I want to be up and able to work at it—to gather it in and see it accumulate. I want to be a really rich man."

"For shame, Robert," said Blanche, with just the faintest feeling of disgust—the first she had ever experienced toward Bob. "If you talk like that I shall leave you. I am disappointed in you; I should never have suspected you of being mercenary."

"Well, I am then," returned Bob, quite unabashed. "I am mercenary, if that means being anxious to be rich. And so would you be, Miss Lascelles, if you had seen as much misery as I have; misery, too, which could be cured by the judicious expenditure of comparatively trifling sums of money. Only think how jolly it would be to go up to every poor hungry man, woman, and child you met, clap a sovereign in their hands, and say, 'There, go and enjoy the luxury of a good unstinted meal for once in your life.' But a rich man's power goes a great deal further than that. If ever I am rich I shall not be satisfied with the bestowal of relief of such a very temporary kind as a solitary meal amounts to; I shall hunt up some really deserving cases and put them in the way of earning their own livings. Real relief consists, to my mind, of nothing short of the stretching out of a helping hand and lifting some poor soul clean out of that miserable state where one's very existence depends upon the fluctuating charity of one's fellow-creatures. I've seen it, and I know what it means. There's any amount of real misery to be met with in the neighbourhood of the Docks, ay, and all over London, for that matter, if one only chooses to keep one's eyes open. Of course I know that many of the beggars and match-sellers, and people of that kind are rank loafers, too idle to work even when they have the chance—people who spend in drink every penny that's given them—and in my opinion they richly deserve all the misery they suffer. But there are plenty of others who would be only too happy to work if they could; and they are the people I should seek out and help, the poor women and children, you know. It makes me fairly sick, I give you my word, Miss Lascelles, when I think of the vast sums of money that are squandered every year in ways which leave nothing to show for the expenditure. Take gambling for instance. I've heard that thousands of pounds are lost every year at card-playing and horse-racing. The money only changes hands, I know; but what good does it do? If a man can afford to part with a thousand pounds in such a way, how much better it would be for him and everybody else if he would expend it in furnishing a certain number of persons with the means to earn their own living. I don't believe it's right for people to squander and waste their money; I believe that money is given to people in trust, and that everybody will have to answer for the way in which they discharge that trust; don't you, Miss Lascelles?"

"Certainly I do, Robert," answered Blanche, very gravely. "But I must admit that I have never until now viewed the matter in the serious light in which you put it. I must beg your pardon, and I do most sincerely, for the way in which I spoke to you just now. I had no idea that you had any such good reasons as you have given for desiring to be rich. But what would you be able to do single-handed, no matter how rich you might be?"

"Ah!" ejaculated Bob with a gesture of impatience, "that's just what everybody says, and that's exactly where the mischief lies; they don't do anything because they can't do everything, and because they can't get others to join them. But I shouldn't look at it like that; I should just do my duty, whether other people did theirs or not; if others choose to shirk their duty it is their own look-out, it affords no excuse for me to shirk mine. But there—it's no use for me to talk like this; perhaps I never shall be rich; the gold is there, you say; but that is a very different thing from having it banked in England. How do they think we are going to get it away from the island without discovery? You may depend upon it that, whenever we go, it will be all in a hurry."

Blanche explained Captain Staunton's plan as to the carrying off of the gold; but Bob shook his head dubiously.

"It is a capital plan, I admit," he said, "but its success depends upon everything turning out exactly as arranged, and—you mark my words—things won't turn out that way at all; they never do. Will you do me a favour, Miss Lascelles?"

"Certainly I will, Robert, provided of course that it is in my power," answered Blanche.

"Thank you," said Bob. "You can do it easily enough. Bring home here—and get the other ladies to do the same—every day when you return from the cavern, as many nuggets as you can conveniently carry—say two or three pounds' weight each of you, you know—and hand them over to me. I'll contrive to find a safe hiding-place for them, and when the moment comes for us to be off I'll see that they go with us if such a thing is at all possible; then we shall not be quite destitute if after all we have to leave the heap in the cave behind us. But don't say anything about this to the gentlemen; Captain Staunton might not like it if he heard that I doubted the practicability of his plan."

Blanche readily gave the desired promise, and there the matter ended for the time.

Meanwhile the work went steadily forward at the shipyard, and by the time that Bob was once more able to go on duty the framework of the schooner was complete, and the planking had been begun, whilst the battery was in so forward a state that another fortnight would see it ready to receive the guns. Ralli was in a high state of delight; but Bob had not been at work many days before he discovered that things were no longer as they had been when he received his hurt. The Greek had never been courteous in his behaviour to the Galatea party, but now he was downright insolent, and his insolence seemed to increase every day. At the outset of the work the gentlemen of the party, that is to say, Captain Staunton, Lance, and Rex, had been required to look on and direct the progress of the work only, but now Lance was the only one to whom this privilege was granted, a privilege which he scorned to accept unshared by the others, and accordingly when Bob once more joined the working party he found his friends with their coats off and sleeves rolled up to the shoulders performing the same manual labour as the rest. Seeing this, he of course did the same, and thus they all continued to work until—the end came.

Bob was greatly surprised at this state of things; so much so that he sought an early opportunity to inquire of Lance the meaning of it. Neither Lance nor anyone else in the party were, however, able to give any explanation of it; all they could say with regard to the affair was that Ralli had been gradually growing more insolent and tyrannical in his treatment of them until matters had reached the then existing unpleasant stage. But he was earnestly cautioned by Captain Staunton not to mention a word respecting it to the ladies, as it was extremely desirable that they should be kept for as long a time as possible quite free from all anxiety of every kind.

"But can nothing be done to make this fellow mend his behaviour?" inquired Bob of the skipper as they separated from the rest of the working party and walked toward the cottage on landing from the boats that night.

"I fear not," was the reply. "While the schooner and the battery were still to be built we had the man to some extent in our power; but now that the battery is so near completion, and the hull of the schooner fully modelled, he is independent of us, and he has sense enough to know it. His own people are quite capable of finishing off the schooner now that her framework is complete, so that threats on our part would be useless—nay, worse than useless—since they would only irritate him and lead to increasing severity toward us."

Bob lay awake a long time that night, quite satisfied that the time had arrived when something ought to be done, but what that something should be he puzzled his brain in vain to discover.

About a fortnight after this a serious accident occurred at the shipyard, or rather at the battery. This structure was now so far advanced that it was ready to receive the guns which were intended to be mounted in it. The armament was to consist of six 24-pounder iron muzzle-loaders of the ordinary old-fashioned type, to which Johnson had helped himself in some raid on the Spanish-American coast; and on the morning in question a gang of men was told off to hoist these guns up the cliff into the battery.

Lance had, as a matter of course, undertaken the supervision of this operation; but the work had hardly commenced when Ralli made his appearance on the scene, announcing his intention to himself direct operations at the battery, and roughly ordering Lance to return at once to his work on the schooner, "and to be quick about it too, or he (Ralli) would freshen his way."

Evelin of course returned at once to the shipyard without condescending to bandy words with the Greek, and the work went forward as usual.

Ralli soon had a pair of sheers rigged, and in due time one of the guns was slung ready for hoisting.

Lance had been watching Ralli's operations, first with curiosity and afterwards with anxiety, for he soon saw that the man knew nothing whatever about handling heavy guns. He now saw that the gun which was about to be hoisted was wrongly slung, and that an accident was likely enough to result. So, forgetting his former rebuff, he threw down his tools and hurried to the place where the men were working about the gun and told them to cast off the slings.

"You have slung it wrong, lads," said he, "and unless you are very careful some of you will be hurt. Cast off the slings, and I will show you the proper way to do it."

The men, accustomed to working under his directions, were about to do as he bade them, when Ralli looked over the parapet and angrily ordered them to leave the lashings as they were and to sway away the gun.

"As for you, mister soldier," he said, shaking his fist at Lance, "you have left your work contrary to my orders, and I will seize you up to a grating and give you five dozen to-night as a lesson to you. Now go."

Lance turned on his heel and walked away. Things had come to a crisis at last, he thought; and he began to wonder how the crisis was to be met; upon one thing he was quite resolved, and that was that he would never submit to the indignity of the lash; Ralli might kill him if he chose, but flog him—never.

His sombre meditations were brought to an abrupt ending by a sudden crash accompanied by a shout of consternation in the direction of the battery. Looking that way he saw the tackle dangling empty from the sheers, with the lower block about half-way up the cliff face, and at the base of the cliff were the men grouped closely together about some object which was hidden by their bodies. Suddenly one of the men left the rest and ran toward the shipyard, shouting for help.

"There has been an accident," thought Lance. "The gun has slipped from the slings, and likely enough somebody is killed."

"Muster all the crowbars and handspikes you can, lads," said he, "and take them over to the battery; there has been an accident, I fear."

A strong relief gang was soon on the spot, only to find Lance's fears confirmed. The gun had been hoisted nearly half-way up the cliff when the guide-rope had fouled a rock. The armourer had stepped forward to clear it, and in doing so had given it a jerk which had canted the gun in its slings, and before the unfortunate man had realised his danger the gun had slipped and fallen upon him, crushing both his legs to a jelly.

There was an immediate outcry among the men for Lance, an outcry which Ralli would have checked if he could; but his first attempt to do so showed him that the men were now in a temper which would render it highly dangerous for him to persist, so he gave in with the best grace he could muster and ordered one of the men to fetch Evelin to the spot. On receiving the message Lance of course at once flung down his tools and hastened to the assistance of the injured man. When he reached the scene of the catastrophe he found all hands, Ralli included, crowded round the prostrate gun, and everybody giving orders at the same time, everybody excited, and everything in a state of the direst confusion.

As he joined the group Ralli stepped forward with a smile on his lips, which in nowise cloaked his chagrin at being obliged to yield to the demands of the men, and began—

"You see, mister soldier, we cannot do without you it seems, after all. Just lend the men a hand to—"

But Lance brushed past him without deigning the slightest notice; and, pushing his way through the crowd, called upon a few of the men by name to assist him in relieving the unfortunate armourer from the ponderous weight of the gun, which still lay upon the poor fellow's mangled limbs. Such implicit confidence had these men in him, prisoner among them though he was, that his mere presence sufficed to restore them to order; and in a few minutes the armourer, ghastly pale, and with every nerve quivering from the excruciating pain of his terrible injuries, was safely withdrawn from beneath the gun.

"Now, make a stretcher, some of you—ah, Dickinson, you are the man for this job; just make a stretcher, my good fellow—the same sort of thing that you made for the lad Bob, you know—and let's get our patient into a boat as quickly as possible; I can do nothing with him here," said Lance.

"Ay, ay, sir," answered Dickinson promptly; and away he went with two or three more men to set about the work, Lance plying the injured man frequently with small doses of rum meanwhile.

Ralli stood upon the outskirts of the crowd angrily watching the proceedings. He could not shut his eyes to the fact of Lance's popularity with the men, and he vowed within himself that he would make him pay dearly for it before the day was done, even if he were compelled to seize him up and flog him himself.

The stretcher was soon ready, and the armourer having been placed upon it, was carried as carefully as possible down to the boat. As the procession passed the shipyard Lance beckoned to Captain Staunton, saying—

"I shall need your assistance in this case. It will be a case of amputation unless I am greatly mistaken, and if so, I shall require the help of someone upon whose nerve I can depend."

Captain Staunton, upon this, hurried back for his coat, and rejoined Lance just as the party was on the point of embarking in the boat. As the men propelled the craft swiftly across the bay Lance related in a loud tone to the skipper Ralli's behaviour during the morning, and his threat. They were still discussing the matter anxiously together when Dickinson, who was pulling stroke-oar, and who doubtless guessed from catching a stray word or two what was the subject of their conversation, broke in upon their conference by inquiring of Lance whether he thought the armourer would recover.

"It is impossible to say yet," answered Lance cautiously. "Of course we shall do our best for him, poor fellow, but he will require more attention than I fear Ralli will allow me to give him."

"If that's all," remarked Dickinson, "I think you needn't trouble yourself, sir; the Greek knows too well what he's about to interfere with you when it comes to doctoring a hinjured man—a man as was hurt too all along of his own pride and obstinacy. And as to that other matter—the flogging, you know, sir—axing your pardon for speaking about it so plain, sir—don't you trouble yourself about that. He sha'n't lay a hand upon you while me and my mates can pervent it—shall he, mates?"

"No, that he sha'n't, bo'," was the eager answer.

"No, he sha'n't," coincided Dickinson. "We can't do much to help you, you see, sir," he added, "'cause, worse luck, we don't all think alike upon some things; but we've only got to say the word to the rest of the hands, and I knows as they won't hear of you bein' flogged. There isn't one of us but what respects you, sir, but what respects you gentlemen both, for that matter; you've always had a good word for everybody, and that goes a long way with sailors sometimes—further than a glass o' grog—and you may make your mind easy that the Greek won't be let to—to—you know what, sir."

"Thank you, Dickinson," said Lance with outstretched hand, "thank you with all my heart. You have relieved me of a heavy load of anxiety; for, to tell you the truth, I had quite made up my mind not to submit to the indignity; and if Ralli attempts to carry out his threat it will probably lead to precipitate action on our part, which at the present time would be simply disastrous."

"So 'twould, sir; so 'twould," agreed Dickinson. "You needn't say another word, sir; we understands. Only we'd like you to know sir—and this here's a very good opportunity for us to say it—that whenever the time comes you may reckon upon all hands of us in this here boat."

"How do you mean?" ejaculated Lance, considerably startled. "I really do not understand you."

"Oh, it's all right, sir," returned Dickinson cheerfully. "We warn't born yesterday, ne'er a one of us, and you don't suppose as we believes you've all settled down to stay here for the rest of your nateral lives, do you? Lord bless you, sir, we knows you must have got some plan in your heads for getting away out of this here hole; and the long and the short of it is this:—When you're ready to go, we're ready to lend you a hand, perviding you'll take us with you. We're sick and tired of this here cursed pirating business; we wants to get away out of it; and we've been talking it over—me and my mates—and we've made up our minds that you're sartain to be off one of these fine days, and we'd like to go with you, if you'll have us. We want to give the world another trial, and see if we can't end our days as honest men; ain't that it, mates?"

"Ay, ay, Bill; that's it and no mistake; you've put it to the gentlemen just exactly as we wanted it; what you says, we'll say, and whatever promises you makes we'll keep 'em; we wants another chance, and we hopes that if so be as these here gen'lemen are thinking of topping their booms out of this they'll just take us along with 'em," replied the man who was pulling the bow-oar, the others also murmuring an assent.

"But what makes you think we have an idea of effecting our escape? And how many others of you have the same opinion?" inquired Captain Staunton.

"Well, I don't know as I can rightly say what makes us think so; but we do," answered Dickinson. "P'raps it's because you've took things so quiet and cheerful like. As to how many more of us thinks the same as we do—why, I can't say, I'm sure. I've only spoke about it to some half a dozen or so that I knowed would be glad of a chance to leave, like myself."

"Well," said Captain Staunton after a pause, "I really do not think we can say anything to you, either one way or another, just now. What you have just said has been so utterly unexpected that we must have time to think and talk the matter over among ourselves; but I think we may perhaps be able to say something definite to you to-morrow in answer to your proposition. Don't you think so, Evelin?"

"I think so," answered Lance.

"Very well, then," said the skipper. "Let the matter rest until to-morrow, and we will then tell you our decision. In the meantime it must be understood that none of you say a word to anyone else upon the subject until you have our permission."

A promise to this effect was readily given by each of the men, and then the matter dropped, the boat shortly afterwards reaching the landing-place at the bottom of the bay.

The armourer was at once taken out of the boat and carried by Lance's directions up to the building in which he slept. The miserable man was by this time in a dreadfully exhausted condition; but on the arrival of the medicine-chest Lance mixed him a powerful stimulating draught, under the influence of which he revived so much that Evelin felt himself justified in attempting the operation of amputation. This, with Captain Staunton's assistance, was speedily and successfully performed; after which the patient was placed in his hammock, and Lance sat himself down near at hand, announcing his intention of watching by the poor fellow until next morning.

The operation successfully performed, Dickinson and his three companions returned to the shipyard, maintaining an animated and anxious consultation on the way. The result of this consultation was that when the four men resumed work they had a great deal to say—after answering numberless anxious inquiries as to the state of the wounded man—upon the subject of Ralli's treatment of Lance and his threat to flog him. They denounced this conduct as not only unjust but also impolitic to the last degree, dwelling strongly upon the unadvisability of offending a man so skilled as Lance in medicine and surgery, and impressing their audience with the necessity for discouraging—and, if necessary, interfering to prevent—the carrying out of the threat.

And as sailors are very much like sheep—where one jumps the rest jump also—they had not much difficulty in arranging for a general demonstration of popular disapproval in the event of Ralli's attempting the threatened indignity. Fortunately for himself—fortunately also in all probability for those in whom we are chiefly interested—he allowed the affair to pass over; in going about among the workers that day he overheard enough to feel assured that, for the moment at all events, he was an unpopular man, and as among such turbulent spirits as those with whom he had to deal, unpopularity means loss of power, his own common sense suggested to him the extreme impolicy of pitting himself against them while they continued in so antagonistic a mood. But he was quite resolved that if he could not have in one way what he called his "revenge," he would have it in another; and from that day forward his insolence and tyranny of demeanour toward Lance and his friends grew more and more marked, until at length it became so unbearable that they were driven to the very verge of desperation.

Meanwhile Lance, sitting there watching his patient, soon saw that he was about to have his hands full. The hectic flush of fever began to chase away the deadly pallor from the sufferer's cheek; his eyes glittered and sparkled like coals of fire; and as feeling began to return to his hitherto benumbed limbs, and the smart of his recent operation made itself felt, he tossed restlessly in his hammock, tormented with an unquenchable thirst.

"Water! water!" he muttered. "For the love of God give me water!"

Lance gave him some in a tin pannikin. In an instant the vessel was glued to the unfortunate man's lips, and in another instant it was drained to the last drop.

"More—give me more," he gasped, as soon as he had recovered his breath.

But this Lance declined to do. Bidding the poor fellow be patient for a few minutes, he went to the medicine-chest and mixed him a cooling draught. This also was swallowed with avidity; and then the armourer lay quiet for a few minutes. Not for long, however; he soon began to toss restlessly about once more; and by the time that the hands returned from their day's work at the shipyard he was in a raging fever—raving mad in fact; and Lance was at last compelled to have him laced up in his hammock to prevent him from doing himself a serious injury.

Lance Evelin will probably remember that night as long as he lives. In the delirium of the fierce fever which consumed him the unhappy armourer was visited by visions of all the evil deeds of his past life; and Lance's blood curdled in his veins as he listened to his patient's disjointed ravings of murder, rapine, and cold-blooded cruelty of so revolting a character that he wondered how any human mind could conceive it in the first instance, and how, after it had been conceived, human hands could bring themselves to perpetrate it. And then the man's guilty conscience awakened from its long torpor, and, acting upon his excited imagination, conjured up a thousand frightful punishments awaiting him. He writhed, he groaned, he uttered the most frightful curses, and then, in the same breath shrieked for forgiveness and mercy. It was perfectly appalling; even his comrades—those who had shared with him in the dreadful deeds about which he raved—found the scene too trying for their hardened and blunted feelings; and such of them as had their hammocks slung in the same dormitory abandoned them and slept in the open air rather than remain to have their souls harrowed by his dreadful utterances.

This terrible state of things existed until the afternoon of the following day—rather more than twenty-four hours after he had received his injuries—and then the fever subsided, but only to leave the once powerful man in the last stage of exhaustion. So completely prostrate was he that he had no power to so much as lift his hand, and he was only able to speak in the merest whisper. Now was the time when all Lance's skill was most urgently required. Fagged as he was by his long night of watching, he tended his patient with the most unremitting assiduity, administering tonics and stimulants every few minutes; and racking his brain for devices by which he might help the man to tide over this period of extreme prostration. But it was all of no avail; the poor fellow gradually sank into a state of stupor from which all Evelin's skill was unable to arouse him; and at length, about eight o'clock in the evening, after a temporary revival during which all the terrors of death once more assailed him, his guilty soul passed away without opportunity for repentance; prayers and curses issuing from his lips in horrible confusion up to the last moment of his existence. His death was witnessed by several of his companions in crime; and, while some tried to laugh and scoff away the unwelcome impression which the scene produced upon their minds, there were others who went into the open air and wandered away by themselves to ponder upon this miserable ending of a crime-stained life.

ALARM AND DISASTER

Lance's long and fatiguing watch beside the death-bed of the unfortunate armourer of course delayed to some extent Captain Staunton's reply to the suggestion which Dickinson had made on behalf of himself and certain of his comrades. But the skipper had, to save time, discussed the matter with the rest of the party, coming to the conclusion that they would be quite justified, under the circumstances, in accepting the services of these men; and on the morning following the armourer's death—Lance having enjoyed a good night's rest—his opinion was taken upon the question, with the view of giving the men an answer forthwith.

Evelin listened attentively to everything that was said; and then remarked—

"Well, gentlemen, I quite agree with you that the assistance which the men have it in their power to afford us would be most valuable; it would clear away a good many of our difficulties and would go a long way toward ensuring success in our endeavour to escape—an endeavour which I must confess I have always secretly regarded with a considerable amount of doubt and misgiving. It has always presented itself to me as an undertaking of a decidedly desperate character; and now it appears more so than ever, having regard to the very disagreeable change in Ralli's treatment of us. The only question in my mind is one of duty—duty to our country and to the world at large. We must not forget that the men who now come to us with offers of assistance are men who have, in the past, outraged every law, human and divine; and justice demands that they shall be delivered up to punishment. Now, if we accept their services we certainly cannot afterwards denounce them; it would be rank treachery on our part. How do you propose to overcome this difficulty?"

"We have thought of that," replied Captain Staunton; "it is the only question which has bothered us; and, for my own part, I can only see one solution of it. No word has, it is true, been said by them as to our keeping their secret, but I think there can be no doubt that such a stipulation was intended to be understood; and in any case I fully agree with you that we cannot justly avail ourselves of their assistance and afterwards hand them over to the authorities. My view of the case is this. Here we are, in what is beyond all doubt a most desperate scrape. A chance—and a very slight chance it is—offers for our escape, and most opportunely these men come forward with an offer of assistance. If we let slip this slight chance it is extremely doubtful whether we shall ever have another; and that, I imagine—taking into account the future possibilities of evil in store for the helpless women dependent upon us—counts for something, and justifies us is accepting help from almost any source. Then, as regards the men themselves. It is undoubtedly true that they have committed crimes which place them quite outside the pale of human mercy, if justice alone is to be considered. But for my own part I believe that they have repented of their past misdeeds—at any rate they say so, and we have no reason to doubt the truth of their assertion. They ask for an opportunity to reform; they desire a chance of making amends, as far as possible, for the past evil of their lives; and I have an idea, gentlemen, that though, in giving them such a chance, we might not be acting in accordance with man's idea of strict justice, we should be following pretty closely upon God's idea of it. He breaks not the bruised reed nor quenches the smoking flax; and if He thus declares his readiness to give even the most doubtful and unpromising of His creatures another trial, I really do not see that we are called upon to be more strict than He is. My proposal, therefore, is that we should accept these men's proffered assistance; that we should do what we may be able to do for them in the way of giving them the opportunity they desire; and if justice is to overtake them—if punishment is to follow their past misdeeds, let it be due to some other agencies than ours. If God intends them to suffer punishment at the hands of their fellow-creatures, He will provide the instruments, never fear. But I think it far more likely He will give them another chance."

"I, too, believe He will," said Lance. "You take a view of the matter which I confess with shame had not presented itself to me, and I am convinced. These men have committed crimes of exceptional enormity, it is true; but it is not for us to draw the line—to say to whom mercy shall be granted and from whom it shall be withheld; therefore let us accept their offer, and leave the matter of their punishment in God's hands."

Thus, then, it was decided; and Bob—as the least likely to excite suspicion if seen in conversation with any of the pirates—was deputed to inform Dickinson that his offer and that of his mates' had been accepted, and to request him to call—without exciting observation, if possible—at the cottage that evening.

When the gentlemen returned home at the close of the day's work, they found Blanche and Violet in a state of considerable nervous excitement, owing, they asserted, to their having been frightened that day while at their work of gold-collecting in the cavern. On being asked for a detailed account of the circumstance which had alarmed them, Violet said—

"We had been at work about two hours, and had just reached the edge of the gulf with our second load, when we were startled by hearing somewhere near us a sound like a deep long-drawn sigh, followed almost immediately afterwards by a loud moan. I have no doubt you will think us dreadful cowards, but it is no use concealing the truth—we simply dropped the gold and flew back along the passage to the great cavern at our utmost speed. Arrived there, we sat down to recover ourselves, and at length succeeded so far that we were both inclined to believe we had been victimised by our own imaginations—you know what an eerie place it is, and how likely to excite weird fancies in the minds of nervous timid women like ourselves. So we summoned up all our courage and went to work once more. We naturally felt somewhat reluctant to visit the scene of our fright again; but we overcame the feeling and made our third journey to the chasm without experiencing any further shock to our nerves. On our fourth journey, however, we had reached the place, deposited our load, and had just set out to return when the same sounds were repeated, much more loudly than at first, and accompanied this time by a loud prolonged hiss such as I should imagine could proceed only from some gigantic serpent. We were thoroughly terrified this time, and fled once more, not only to the cavern but thence into the open air, and home. I do not know how we may regard the matter in the morning; but at present I really do not feel as though I could ever venture into the place again until the mystery has been solved and the cause of those terrifying sounds discovered."

"Of course not," said Captain Staunton. "None of you must attempt to visit the cavern again until we have had an opportunity of investigating the matter. It is possible—though, mind you, I don't think it at all probable—that a serpent or large reptile of some kind may have made its way into the gallery. And, at all events, it will never do for you ladies to run the slightest risk. What do you think, Evelin?" he added, turning to Lance. "Is it likely that there may be a snake or something of the sort there?"

"Not likely, I should say," responded Lance; "we have never encountered a reptile of any description, large or small, in the course of our rambles about the island. But of course there is just the bare possibility—I cannot put it any stronger than that—of a snake drifting here on an uprooted tree or large branch. I have heard of snakes being seen in the branches of trees drifting down rivers in flood-time, and there is no reason why, under such circumstances, they should not be carried clear out to sea. Whether, however, a serpent could exist long enough to make the voyage from the mainland to this island is, in my opinion, exceedingly doubtful. Still, I quite agree with you that the ladies ought not to make any further visits to the cavern until we have discovered the source of their alarm."

This singular circumstance gave rise to a considerable amount of speculation among the members of the party; and they were still discussing the matter when a knocking was heard at the door, and, in obedience to Captain Staunton's stentorian "Come in," Dickinson entered.

"Sarvent, ladies," exclaimed the new-comer with an elaborate sea-scrape. Then, seating himself in the chair which Captain Staunton indicated, he continued, "Well, cap'n, and gentlemen all, I've just comed up, you see, in obedience to your commands of the forenoon sent through the young gentleman there"—pointing to Bob—"and to talk matters over as it were."

"That's all right, Dickinson," answered Captain Staunton; "we are very glad to see you. Robert of course told you that we have decided to accept the assistance of yourself and such of your shipmates as are to be thoroughly relied upon?"

"He did, sir; and right glad and thankful I was to hear it," replied Dickinson. "Of course we knowed right well, sir, how much we was axing of you when we offered to chime in on your side. We was just axing that you'd take us upon trust as it were, and believe in the honesty and straight-for'ard-ness of men as had proved theirselves to be rogues and worse. But you've took us, sir, and you sha'n't have no cause to repent it; we're yours, heart and soul; hence-for'ard we takes our orders from you, and we're ready to take any oath you like upon it."

"No oath is necessary, my good fellow," said Captain Staunton; "your bare word is quite sufficient, for if you intend to be faithful to us you will be so without swearing fidelity; and if you mean to betray us an oath would hardly stop you, I am afraid. But we do not doubt your fidelity in the least; the only thing we have any fear about is your prudence."

"Ah, yes; there sir, we may fail," said Dickinson with a mournful shake of the head. "But you give your orders, sir, and we'll do our best to obey 'em. But afore you lays your plans I think you ought to know how things is standing among us just now. I'm greatly afeared you're like so many young bears—with all your troubles afore you. That Greek rascal, Ralli, has been doin' his best to stir up all hands of us against you—and particler against you, Mr Evelin—by saying as it was all along of you as the poor armourer lost his life. He holds as how you killed him by taking off his legs, and that you desarves to be severely punished for doing of it; and there's some of the chaps as is fools enough to listen to what he says and to believe it too. But there's me and Tom Poole and two or three more—we're going to hold out to it that you did the best you could for the poor chap; and that if it hadn't ha' been for Ralli's own obstinacy the man wouldn't never have been hurt at all. And, however the thing goes, you may depend upon me to give you timely warning."

"Thank you, Dickinson," said Captain Staunton. "This information which you have just given us is most valuable, and renders it all the more necessary that we should promptly mature our plans. Now, to show you how thoroughly we trust you, I will explain those plans as far as we have yet arranged them; you can then tell us what you think of them; and you will also be better able to understand in what way you and your shipmates can prove of most use to us."

"Well, if that don't beat all!" exclaimed Dickinson, after Captain Staunton had stated their plans. "To think as you should go for to arrange to run away with the schooner herself! Why, I thought the most you'd do would be to provision and seize the launch, and go off to sea in her, taking your chance of being picked up some time or another. Well, there ain't a soul amongst us, I knows, as has so much as the ghost of a hidee about your taking the schooner. Some of the hands seems to have a kind of notion—I've found out since I spoke to you t'other day—that you may try to slip off some day if you gets the chance; but they just laughs at it you know, and asks how you're to manage, and how far you'd get in a boat afore the schooner'd be alongside of you, and that-like. But your plan's the right one, cap'n—no mistake about that. And now, just say what you want us chaps to do, and we'll do it if it's any way possible."

"How many of you are there?" asked the skipper. "How many, I mean, upon whom we can absolutely depend. Bear in mind that no one who is not thoroughly trustworthy is to be let into the secret."

"All right, sir; you trust me for that," answered Dickinson. "For my own sake—letting alone yours and the ladies'—you may depend on't I won't let out the secret to the wrong people. Well; let me just reckon up how many of us there'll be in all. Firstly there's eight of you, counting in Mr Bowles and Kit, and leaving out the ladies. Then there's the three other lads and the four men as was brought in with you, that's seven—seven and eight's—"

"Fifteen," interjected the skipper.

"Thank'ee, sir, I ain't much of a hand at figgers myself, but in course you're right—fifteen it is," said Dickinson. "Then there's me and Tom

Poole—that's my pertickler mate—promoted he is to the armourer's berth—and Dick Sullivan and Ned Masters—that's four more, making fifteen, sixteen, seventeen, eighteen, nineteen—nineteen, ain't it, sir?"

"Quite right," answered Captain Staunton.

"Then there's the prisoners, as we calls 'em—men, you know, sir, as has been took out of ships and wouldn't jine the 'Brotherhood'—I won't say much about them just yet, but there's about half a dozen very likely hands among 'em that I think'll just jump at the chance of getting out of this. Tom and me'll sound 'em cautious like, and hear what they've got to say for theirselves."

"Very well," said Captain Staunton. "And in the meantime it seems that there are nineteen of us, all told, who are to be absolutely relied upon—quite enough to handle the schooner if we can only manage to get away with her. Now, what we have to do is this. The ballast and the water-tanks are already fixed in their places, so that need not trouble us; but we must contrive to get the tanks filled as early as possible. Then, as soon as the decks are laid we must get conveyed on board all the provisions we can possibly manage. Then we shall want arms and ammunition; the guns too must be hoisted in, under the pretence of fitting the slides properly. The spars are already commenced. They, or at least the lower-masts and bowsprit, must be stepped before the craft is launched; that can easily be managed, I think; the other spars also should be finished and got on board as early as possible, and likewise the sails. There are the stores of every kind also to be got on board—in short, I should like to have the craft in a state of readiness to go to sea directly she leaves the stocks. But I really don't see how it is to be managed; we shall never be able to do a quarter of what we want without arousing Ralli's suspicions."

"Oh, bless you, sir! yes, you will," said Dickinson confidently. "Ralli's taken a mortal dislike to you all, and 'specially to Mr Evelin,—sorry I am to say so,—and he just hates to be dictated to. Now, whatever you want, just let Mr Evelin tell him he ought to do the opposite of it, and, take my word for it, he'll just go and do exactly what he thinks you don't want him to; he'll do it out of sheer contrariness. But, whether or no, now that we knows what's wanted, we—that's me and my mates—we'll do as much of it as we can, and you'll have to manage Ralli so's to get the rest."

"Very well, Dickinson," said the skipper, "we understand each other fully now, so I will not detain you any longer. Do what you can to forward the plan, and let us know from time to time what success you are meeting with."

"All right, sir, I will; thank'ee, sir. Good-night, ladies and gentlemen all."

And Dickinson, taking the hint, retired.

The gentlemen sat for an hour or two after that, talking over matters as they smoked their pipes, and then Captain Staunton, Lance, and Bowles rose and left the cottage to pay a visit to the cavern.

In due time they reached the place, proceeding at once to the chasm, where they forthwith commenced a vigorous but unsuccessful search for the origin of the mysterious sounds which had disturbed the ladies. Finding nothing, they began their task of conveying the gold collected that day across to the heap on the other side of the gulf. This heap was now assuming goodly proportions. There was more of it than an ordinary ship's boat could take at a single trip, even in the calmest of weather; and Lance was in the act of remarking to Captain Staunton that he thought enough had now been collected to satisfy their every want, when a weird, unearthly moan smote upon their ears from the depths of the abyss. The sound, though not particularly loud, was so startling, echoing and reverberating, as it did, among the cavernous recesses far below, that the work was brought to a sudden standstill, and the three bewildered men felt their hair bristling as they listened.

"What, in Heaven's name, can it be?" ejaculated the skipper as he turned his startled gaze upon Lance.

"Impossible to say," answered the latter. "One thing, however, is certain; no human lungs could possibly give utterance to such a sound. And yet I don't know; the echoes of the place may have the property of magnifying and prolonging it. Hillo, there! is there anyone below?" he continued, raising his torch aloft and peering with craned neck down into the black depths of the chasm.

There was no response. And the light of the torch was quite inadequate to the illumination of more than a few feet from the surface.

"It is possible that, if there is anyone down there, he may be unable to hear me. Sound rises, you know. Here, Bowles, come across to this side. We will unite our voices and see if that will evoke any response," said Lance.

Bowles scrambled nimbly along the narrow and dangerous pathway, which, having traversed it so often, now had no terrors for any of them, and speedily joined the others.

"Now," said Lance, "I will count three, and then we will all shout together, 'Hillo!' One, two, three—Hillo!"

The cry went pealing away right and left of them along the dark gallery, the echoes taking it up and tossing it wildly from side to side, up and down, until it seemed as though every rock in the vast cavern had found a voice with which to mock them; but no answering cry came from below.

"There is no one there," said Lance. "Indeed there can be no one there; nobody has been missed, and—"

"Hark! what was that?"

A long-drawn sobbing sigh, such as a child will utter after it has cried itself to sleep, but very much louder; and immediately afterwards a gust of hot air, which brought with it a distinct odour of sulphur, swept past them down the gallery.

"God of mercy! can it be possible?" ejaculated Lance. "Yes, it must be. Fly for your lives; we may not have a moment to lose."

"What is it?" gasped Captain Staunton, as the three started at a run up the gallery in the direction of the great cavern.

"A volcano," answered Lance. "There are subterranean fires in activity at no great depth beneath our feet, and they may break into open eruption at any moment."

This was enough; his companions wanted to hear no more. The few words they had already heard lent wings to their feet, and in an incredibly short time they found themselves, panting and exhausted with their unwonted exertions, once more in the open air.

"Now we are comparatively safe," said Lance as they walked rapidly down the ravine. "What I chiefly feared was one of those earthquake shocks such as sometimes precede a volcanic eruption. A comparatively insignificant one might have proved sufficient to cause the walls of the cavern to collapse and bury us. Of course the ladies must be cautioned not to venture near the place again; but I think perhaps it will be better not to tell them why. It will only alarm them—perhaps unnecessarily—and keep them on the tiptoe of nervous anxious expectancy. The better plan will be to say that we consider we have now as much gold as we think it probable we shall be able to take away. Don't you think so, Staunton?"

"Assuredly I do," answered the skipper emphatically. "Why, I would not allow my wife to enter that cavern again for all the gold it contains."

They reached the cottage without further adventure; and on the following morning the ladies were told by Captain Staunton that, sufficient gold having now been collected, there would be no further necessity for them to continue their visits to the cavern, which, moreover, Mr Evelin considered unsafe, the peculiar noises which had startled them all being in his opinion an indication of its liability to collapse at any moment.

After this a month passed away unmarked by anything worthy of record, except the ever-increasing insolence and tyranny of Ralli toward our unfortunate friends.

The battery was by this time complete, the guns mounted, and the ammunition stored in its magazine; whilst the schooner was also in a very forward state. She was fully planked, decks laid, the ballast stowed, bulwarks and hatchways completed, her bottom coppered up to the load water-line, her hull outside painted with a coat of priming, and the carpenters, assisted by the handiest men they could pick out, were busy finishing off the fittings of the cabin and forecastle. Lance had been anxiously watching for a favourable opportunity to put into operation Dickinson's suggestion as to the mode in which Ralli should be approached in order to secure the completion of the work in the manner most favourable to their own plans, but hitherto no such opportunity had presented itself. This was peculiarly unfortunate, as the work was now in so forward a state that, whenever Ralli opened his mouth, he expected to hear the dreaded order given for the preparation of the ways and the construction of the cradle for launching.

But at length the coveted opportunity came. It was about nine o'clock in the morning when Lance saw Ralli step out of his gig on to the rocky platform at the lower end of the shipyard and walk straight toward the schooner. The Greek paused at a little distance from where Lance was at work, taking up a position from which he could obtain a favourable view of the vessel's beautifully modelled hull and gracefully sweeping lines; and then, with one eye shut, he began a critical scrutiny of her, shifting his position a few inches occasionally in order to test the perfection of the various curves.

"Now," Lance thought, "is my time. I must tackle him at once, whatever comes of it; it will never do to defer the matter any further. Another hour's delay may upset all our plans."

So, throwing down his tools, he stepped up to Ralli and said—

"I want to speak to you about the launch. We have now done nearly all that we can do to the schooner whilst she remains on the stocks, and our next job will be to lay down the ways and—"

Ralli turned suddenly upon him with an evil gleam and glitter in his eyes which spoke volumes as to the envy and hatred he bore to this man, who, though a prisoner and practically a slave, still revealed in every word and gesture his vast and unmistakable superiority to every other man on the island, its ruler included.

"Aha! mister soldier," he said—using the mode of address which, for some reason known only to himself, he deemed most offensive to Lance—his lips curling into a sneering smile as he spoke, "what are you doing away from your work? Go back to it at once, unless you wish me to start you with a rope's-end as I would an unruly boy."

"I have no work to go back to," said Lance; "I am simply wasting my time at present, and I wanted to learn your wishes as to what is to be done next I presume you will have the craft launched forthwith, as she is now ready to take to the water; and I should be glad to know what timber we are to use for the ways."

"You presume I will have the craft launched at once," repeated Ralli, the spirit of opposition rising strong within him, and the sneer upon his lips growing more bitter with every word he uttered. "Why should you presume any such thing, eh, you sare?"

"Because it is the right and proper thing to do," answered Lance. "Every lubber knows that a ship is launched before she is rigged. Besides, if you were to decide upon having the spars stepped and rigged, the stores stowed, and the guns hoisted in before she leaves the stocks, I should have a lot of extra trouble in calculating the proper distribution of the weights so as to ensure her being in proper trim when she takes to the water, and I want to avoid all that if possible."

The Greek grinned with vindictive delight as he listened to this apparently inadvertent admission on Lance's part. It revealed to him, as he thought, a new and unexpected method of inflicting annoyance upon this man whom he hated so thoroughly, and his eyes fairly sparkled with malice as he answered—

"What do you suppose I care about your extra trouble, you lazy skulking hound? I tell you this: I will have every spar stepped, rigged, and put in its place; the running rigging all rove; every sail bent; every gun mounted; the magazine stowed; the stores and water all put on board; and everything ready for the schooner to go straight out to sea from the stocks, before she leaves them. Poole! Dickinson!"—to the two chums who were working at no great distance—"come here and listen to what I say. This stupid fellow—this soldier who thinks himself a sailor—says that the schooner ought to be launched at once. I say that she shall be finished ready for sea before she leaves the stocks; and I place you, Dickinson, in charge of the work to see that my orders are obeyed. This fellow will no longer give any orders; he will be only a common workman; he will obey you in future, or you will freshen his way with a rope's-end. You understand?"

"Ay, ay," answered Dickinson, "I understands yer, Ralli, and I'll do it too, never fear,"—with a scowl at Lance for Ralli's benefit. "Why, the man must be a fool—a perfect fool—not to see as it'd be ever so much easier to get things aboard now than when she's afloat. Now, you"—turning to Lance—"you just top your boom and git away back to your work at once, and don't let me see no more skulking or you'd better look out."

Lance simply shrugged his shoulders, as was his habit whenever he received any insolence from the members of the "Brotherhood," and, turning on his heel, walked back to his work, secretly exulting in the complete success of his manoeuvre.

Dickinson looked after him contemptuously for a moment or two, and then, his face clouding, he remarked—

"Arter all, I wish I hadn't spoke quite so rough to him; the chap's got his head screwed on the right way; he knows a mortal sight of things as I don't understand, and I'd ha' been glad to ha' had his help and adwice like in many a little job, as I'm afeared we'll make a bit of a bungle of without him."

"That is all right," said Ralli. "You shall be able to talk him over, Dickinson. Be a bit civil to him and he will tell you all that you will want to know. Leave the—what you call?—the bullying to me; I shall take the care that he enough has of that."

And now—on that same morning, and only an hour or two after the conversation just recorded—there occurred an unfortunate incident which completely dissipated Lance's exultation, filling him with the direst and most anxious forebodings, and threatening to utterly upset the success of all their carefully arranged plans.

It happened thus. Some timber was required by the carpenters on board the schooner; and Dickinson, eager to properly play his part in the presence of the Greek—who was standing close by—ordered Lance and Captain Staunton to bring up a large and heavy plank which he pointed out. They accordingly shouldered it, and, staggering under the load, proceeded upon their way, which led them close past the spot where Ralli stood. As they were passing him it unfortunately happened that Lance stepped upon a small spar, which, rolling under his feet, caused him to stagger in such a way that the plank struck Ralli full in the mouth, knocking away three or four teeth and cutting open both lips. The fellow reeled backwards with the severity of the blow, but, recovering himself, whipped out his long knife, and, pale as death with passion, rushed upon Lance. Captain Staunton saw what was about to happen, and shouted in warning, "Look out, Evelin!" flinging the plank to the ground at the same instant in such a way as to momentarily check the rush of the Greek. Lance at the call turned round, and was just in time to save himself from an ugly blow by catching Ralli's uplifted arm in his left hand. The pirate, lithe and supple as a serpent, writhed and twisted in Lance's grasp in his efforts to get free, but it was all in vain; he was helpless as a child in the iron grasp of the stalwart soldier, and he was at length compelled to fling his knife to the ground and own himself vanquished.

But no sooner was he once more free than, calling to his aid a dozen of the most ruffianly of his band, he ordered them to seize Lance and the skipper, and to lash them hand and foot until the irons could be brought and riveted on.

This was done; and an hour afterwards, to the grief and consternation of all concerned in the plan of escape, the two to whom they chiefly looked for its success were marched off to the "Black Hole," each man's ankles being connected together by a couple of close-fitting iron bands and two long fetter-links.

Bob Gives Way to Violence

Great was the consternation and distress at Staunton Cottage that night when the workers returned from the shipyard and reported the arrest and imprisonment of Captain Staunton and Lance Evelin. That these two should be placed in durance at all was regarded as a serious misfortune; but, coming as it did at so critical a time, just as the work on the schooner was drawing near its completion and when the long-looked-for opportunity to escape might present itself at almost any moment, it was justly regarded as a disaster of the gravest character. The imprisoned men were the two who had most completely retained their coolness and self-possession throughout the whole of the reverses which had befallen the party; it was their fertile brains which had devised the audaciously daring plan of escape, and without them the rest of the party felt that they dare not do anything for fear of marring the whole scheme. And there was still another misfortune attending this arrest: supposing a favourable opportunity presented itself for the carrying out of the plan, it could not be seized so long as these two men were prisoners; all, even to Dale, were fully agreed that escape without them was not to be thought of for a moment. For two of the party—poor Mrs Staunton and Blanche—there was still another source of anxiety. Now that Ralli had at last completely laid aside the mask of friendliness which had at first concealed his feeling of ill-will—now that he had cast off the last remains of a semblance of forbearance—to what terrible lengths might he not allow his vindictiveness to carry him? Would he stop short at the humiliation of imprisonment and fetters? Or was it not too greatly to be dreaded that he would now proceed also to active violence! This fear was fully shared by the rest of the party, but they were careful to hide it from the two poor heart-broken women who were chiefly interested in the prisoners, striving rather to inspire them with hopes which they themselves did not entertain. A long and most anxious discussion of the situation that night, Rex and Bowles taking the lead by virtue of their superior resolution and experience, was productive of absolutely no result except to place an additional damper upon their already sufficiently depressed spirits. Bob said nothing, but, like the queen's parrot, he thought the more. Brook frankly acknowledged himself quite unequal to the emergency, as did Dale, but both cheerfully stated their readiness to do anything they might be directed to do. And here it may be stated that misfortune had been gradually doing for the latter—as it does for so many people—what prosperity had utterly failed to do, it had been driving out of him that peevishness of temper and that utter selfishness of character which had been his most disagreeable characteristics, and it had developed in their place an almost cheerful resignation to circumstances and a readiness to think and act for others which promised to make of him eventually a man whom it would be possible to both respect and esteem.

The following day brought with it a full revelation of the state of things which our friends would have to expect in the future; Captain Staunton and Lance being taken out of their confinement only to be employed all day in fetters upon work of the most laborious description, and locked up again at night in the loathsome Black Hole; while for the benefit of the whole party—and for the rest of the prisoners also, for that matter—Ralli had provided himself with a "colt," which he applied with merciless severity to their shoulders whenever the humour seized him. This last indignity was almost greater than they could bear; but Lance saw that the time was not yet ripe for action, and that there was really nothing for it but to bear everything in dignified silence at present and with as much fortitude as they could summon to their aid, and he managed to whisper as much to Bob, and to request him to "pass the word" to the others, which at intervals during the day Bob did. Before the day was over most of the prisoners, excepting those belonging to the Galatea party, had had enough of Ralli's colt, and signified their readiness to join the "Brotherhood;" they were accordingly sworn in at nightfall on their return from work.

This most unfortunate state of affairs had prevailed for nearly a fortnight, during which Ralli's arrangements for the entire completion of the schooner whilst yet upon the stocks had been pressed vigorously forward, when Dickinson found himself in a position to announce to the Greek that another three days would see the schooner ready for sea, and that—a sufficient number of men being now at liberty to proceed with the work—the time had arrived for the laying-down of the ways and the construction of the cradle. The eyes of the Greek sparkled with delight. Three days!—Only three days more, or four at most, and the time for which he had so anxiously waited would have arrived; the time when he would find himself master not only of a battery which would enable him to hold the island against all comers—Johnson included—or rather, Johnson especially—but also of a smart little craft capable of sailing round and round the Albatross, and heavily enough armed to meet her upon equal terms. Let but those three or four days pass without interruption, and with what sincere delight would he view the approach of Johnson and his brig, and with what a warm and unexpected welcome would he receive them! He rubbed his hands with fiendish glee as he thought of this, and slapped Dickinson playfully on the shoulder as he bid him commence the necessary work forthwith.

Thereupon Dickinson boldly stated that he must have the advice and assistance of Captain Staunton and Lance, as he didn't know enough about cradles and ways and suchlike to build 'em properly, and he couldn't find anybody on the island as did!

The ex-boatswain's mate was in hopes that this proposition of his would load to at least a temporary amelioration of the condition of his two friends, if not the absolute establishment of a better state of things; but his hopes were unexpectedly and effectually quenched by the announcement that the Greek knew all about it, and intended to superintend that part of the work himself. The time had now arrived when a definite plan of action at the decisive moment ought to be fully agreed upon; and feeling this, Dickinson arose from his bunk about midnight that night, and lighting his pipe sauntered in the direction of the Black Hole, hoping for an opportunity to confer and finally arrange matters with the prisoners confined therein. To his great disappointment and chagrin he found the door of the place—a small low building roughly but very solidly constructed of stone, with no windows and no means of ventilation save such as was afforded by the momentary opening of the door for ingress or egress—guarded by a couple of the most ruffianly of the pirates, fellows who were completely the creatures of Ralli, and who had on more than one occasion thrown out strong hints of their suspicion that Dickinson was on more friendly terms than he ought to be with the men now in confinement. To their searching inquiries as to the reasons for Dickinson's untimely and suspicious visit to them the ex-boatswain's mate was driven to reply with a complaint as to the extreme heat and closeness of the night, and of his inability to sleep in consequence, his restlessness being such as to constrain him to rise and come outside for a smoke and a chat with somebody; and, there being no one else to chat with, he had just come to them. To this explanation he added a careless offer to relieve them of their guard for the rest of the night; but this offer provoked such an expression of unqualified suspicion from both the guards that he at once saw he was treading on very dangerous ground, and was accordingly fain to abandon his well-intentioned effort to communicate with those inside the prison door.

Driven thus into a corner, he resolved to get a word or two, if possible, with the inmates of Staunton Cottage; and he accordingly sauntered off, taking a very roundabout way, as long as he thought it at all possible for his movements to be seen by the already suspicious guards.

Dickinson's complaint as to the heat and closeness of the night was quite sufficiently well founded to have been accepted as perfectly genuine. It was pitchy dark, the sky being obscured by a thin veil of cloud which was yet sufficiently dense to completely obscure the light of the stars; the air was still to the extent of stagnation; and the temperature was so unusually high that Dickinson found the mere act of walking, even at the idle sauntering pace which he had adopted, a laborious exertion. In the great and oppressive stillness which prevailed, the hoarse thunder of the trampling surf upon the rocky shores of the island smote so loudly upon the ear as to be almost startling; and to the lonely wanderer there in the stifling darkness the sound seemed to bring a vague mysterious premonition of disaster.

Dickinson had almost reached the cottage when he became conscious of another sound rising above that of the roaring surf, the sound as of a heavily-laden wagon approaching over a rough and stony road, or of a heavy train rumbling through a tunnel at no great depth beneath the surface of the earth. The sound, dull and muffled still, swept rapidly toward him from seaward, and at the moment of its greatest intensity there was for an instant a vibrating jar of the ground beneath his feet; the next moment it had passed, and the sound swept onward toward the interior of the island until it again became lost in the hollow roar of the distant breakers.

Somewhat startled by this singular and unusual phenomenon, Dickinson hurried forward, and soon stood beneath the walls of the cottage. A light was still burning in one of the upper rooms; so, seizing a handful of fine gravel, he flung it against the window in the hope of quietly attracting the attention of the inmates. After two or three essays his efforts were rewarded with success, the window being softly opened and Bowles' head thrust out, with the low-spoken ejaculation:

"Hillo, below there!"

"It's me—Dickinson," was the equally low-spoken response. "If you're not all turned-in I'd be glad to have a few words with some of yer."

"All right, my lad!" said Bowles. "I'll be down in a jiffey. Nothing else gone wrong, I hope?"

"No," said Dickinson; "I only wants to make a few arrangements; that's all."

In another minute the ladder was cautiously lowered, and Rex and Bowles joined their visitor.

"I say, gen'lemen, did you hear anything pecoolyer a few minutes ago?" was Dickinson's first remark.

"Yes," said Rex; "did you? Unless I am greatly mistaken we have been visited by a slight shock of earthquake."

"'Arthquake, eh? Well, if 'tain't nothing worse than that I don't mind," was the response. "You see I don't know much about 'arthquakes, not bein' used to 'em, and I felt a bit scared just at first, I own; but if so be as it's only a 'arthquake, why that's all right. If anything like that happens I like to know, if it's only to keep my mind quiet. But that ain't what I've come up here to rouse you gen'lemen out in the middle watch about; it's just this here."

And therewith he proceeded to lay before his hearers his own view of the state of affairs, pointing out to them the fact—already keenly recognised by them—that the moment for action might now present itself at any time, and explaining his own anxiety for a definite arrangement of some plan of operations, together with an agreement upon certain preconcerted signals to be of such a character as should be easily understood by the initiated while unlikely to arouse the suspicions of the rest.

A long conference ensued, at the close of which Dickinson quietly returned to his hammock with a greatly relieved mind. The others also retired, but not to sleep. They felt that the decisive moment was at hand, the moment upon the right use of which depended their liberty, if not their lives, for they were fully persuaded that if their first attempt failed they would never be allowed to have another—and, though still anxious, their recent talk with Dickinson had made them more hopeful of success than they had ever felt before. Hitherto they had always been haunted by a lurking doubt; but now they began for the first time to think that there really was a fair prospect of succeeding if they faced the dangers and difficulties of the attempt with boldness and resolution. Their chief anxiety now was how to free their two comrades; and to this they were as yet quite unable to see their way. Their anxiety and distress were greatly increased on the following day by finding that Ralli had given orders that his two prisoners, the skipper and Lance, were henceforth to be kept in close confinement altogether, with a double guard fully armed at the door, instead of being released during the day to work with the others at the shipyard. To be confined at all in the noisome "Black Hole" was bad enough, and their fortnight's incarceration had already told visibly on the health of the prisoners, even when they had had the opportunity of breathing a pure atmosphere during the day; but now that they were doomed to remain in the place both day and night their friends became seriously alarmed; they felt that the sentence was tantamount to one of a slow but certain death. And the most trying part of it was that there seemed no possibility of affording any succour to the doomed men; no attempt to help or relieve them could be devised except such as must necessarily bring the party into immediate collision with Ralli and his myrmidons.

The Greek had now entirely laid aside all pretence of treating his prisoners with any show of consideration. They had served his purpose; he had made them his tools as long as their assistance had been necessary to the advancement of his ambitious schemes; but now their help was no longer necessary to him, and he felt free to gratify, without stint, the malignant and vindictive feeling with which he had from the first regarded them. One or two of them, too, notably Lance and Captain Staunton, had on more than one occasion successfully opposed him in his efforts to have things entirely his own way; and that also must be amply atoned for. So he now amused himself at intervals in devising fresh indignities, in planning new hardships, to be heaped upon the unfortunate Galatea party.

It was in this vindictive spirit that, on the second evening after Dickinson's midnight visit, Ralli walked up to the cottage, and, unceremoniously opening the door, obtruded his unexpected and most unwelcome presence upon its inmates. As he made his appearance the conversation, which had been of a somewhat animated character, suddenly ceased.

He noted this circumstance as he glanced suspiciously round the room, with his features twisted into the now too familiar malicious smile.

Bowing with a sarcastic affectation of politeness, he remarked:

"I am afraid my sudden appearance has interrupted a very interesting conversation. If so, I am vary sorray. But pray go on; do not allow my praisance to be any—what you call it—any—any—ah, yes, I have it—any restraint."

Then, suddenly changing his manner as his naturally suspicious nature asserted itself, he demanded:

"What were you talking about? Tell me—you; I insist."

"We were talking about matters chiefly interesting to ourselves," answered Bowles. "If 't had been anything we wanted you to know, we'd have sent for you."

"Ha! my big strong friend, how you are funny to-night! You want to make a laugh at me, is it not? All right; wait till to-morrow; I then shall make a laugh at you. It is I that shall be funny then," returned Ralli with the evil smile broadening on his face and his eyes beginning to sparkle with anger.

"Well," he continued, "since you will not so civil be as answer my polite question, I will tell you what I have come to say. It is this. You men are working—after a very lazy fashion it is the truth—for your living, and from now I intend that the women—oh? I beg the pardon, I should have said the ladies—shall work for theirs too. I am not any more going to allow laziness; you must all work, beginning to-morrow."

Here was an announcement which fairly took away the breath of the party. Ralli saw the consternation which his speech had produced, and laughed in hearty enjoyment of it.

"I tell you what it is, my good sir," said Rex, recovering his presence of mind. "You may say what you please as to the manner in which we work, but you know as well as I do that our services are ample payment for the food and lodging which we and the ladies get; and as to their working—why, it is simply preposterous; what can they do?"

"What can they do?" repeated Ralli. "Ha, ha! I will tell you, my very dear sair, what they can do, and what they shall do. There are three of them and the shild. One shall do the cooking for the men; one shall clean out the sleeping-room, repair the men's clothes, and make their hammocks; and one—the prettiest one—shall cook for me and keep my cabin in order, make and mend my clothes, and attend to me generally. As for the shild, she shall gather firewood and—ah! there she is. Come and kees me, you little girl."

May had, in fact, at that moment entered the room with a happy laugh; but catching sight of Ralli, the laugh was broken off short, and she sought shelter and safety by her mother's side, from which she manifested a very decided disinclination to move at Ralli's invitation.

"Come here and kees me, little girl," repeated the Greek, his anger rapidly rising as he saw how unmistakably the child shrank from him.

"You must please excuse her," said Mrs Staunton, with difficulty restraining the expression of her resentment; "the child has not been accustomed to kiss strangers."

"Come and kees me, little girl," repeated Ralli for the third time, holding out his arms to May, and entirely ignoring Mrs Staunton's remark.

But his sardonic smile and his glittering eyes were the reverse of attractive to the child. Besides, she knew him.

"No," said she resolutely, "I will not kiss you. I don't love you. You are the naughty wicked cruel man that locked up my dear papa and Mr Evelin, and won't let them come home to me."

"Hush, May, darling!" began Mrs Staunton. But her warning came too late; the unlucky words had been spoken; and Ralli, smarting under a sense of humiliation from the scorn and loathing of him so freely displayed by this pretty child—scarcely more than a baby yet—sprang to his feet, and, seizing May roughly by the arm, dragged her with brutal force away from her mother's side, and before anyone could interfere, drew out his colt and struck her savagely with it twice across her poor little lightly-clad shoulders.

The little creature shrieked aloud with the cruel pain as she writhed in the ruffianly grasp of the pirate; yet the fiendish heart of her tormenter felt no mercy, his lust of cruelty was aroused, and the colt was raised a third time to strike.

But the blow never fell Bob was the nearest to the pirate when he made his unexpected attack upon May, and though the occurrence was too sudden to admit of his interfering in time to prevent the first two blows, he was on hand by the time that the third was ready to fall. With a yell of rage more like that of a wild beast than of a man he sprang upon Ralli, dealing him with his clenched left hand so terrific a blow under the chin that the pirate's lower jaw was shattered, and his tongue cut almost in two. Then, quick as a flash of light he released poor May from the villain's grasp, wrenched the colt out of his hand, and, whilst the wretch still writhed in agony upon the ground where he had fallen under the force of Bob's first fearful blow, thrashed him with it until the clothes were cut from his back, and his shoulders barred with a close network of livid and bloody weals. The miserable cowardly wretch screamed at first more piercingly even than poor May had done; but Bob commanded silence so imperatively and with such frightful threats that Ralli was fairly cowed into submitting to the rest of his fearful punishment in silence, save for such low moans as he was utterly unable to suppress.

As may well be supposed, this startlingly sudden scene of violence was productive of the utmost confusion in the room where it originated. The ladies, hastily seizing poor little moaning May in their arms, beat a precipitate retreat, while the men sprang to their feet and tried—for some time in vain—to drag Bob away from his victim. But the lad was now a tall, stalwart, broad-shouldered fellow; his anger was thoroughly roused by the

Greek's cruel and cowardly conduct; and it was not until he had pretty well exhausted himself in the infliction of a well-deserved punishment that he suffered himself to be dragged away. And it was now too, in the desperate emergency with which our friends found themselves in a moment brought face to face, that Bob showed the sterling stuff of which he was made. Cutting short the horrified remonstrances of his friends he took the reins of affairs in his own hands, issuing his instructions as coolly as though he had been a leader all the days of his life.

"The time has come," said he. "Mr Bowles, get a piece of rope, lash that fellow hands and heels together, and gag him. The rest of you get our few traps together; tell the ladies to do the same; and let all muster down at the landing as quickly as possible. I'm off to warn Dickinson and the rest, and to release the captain and Mr Evelin. Ah! I may as well take these," as his eye fell upon a brace of revolvers in Ralli's belt. He withdrew the weapons, hastily examined them by the light of the lamp to ascertain whether they were loaded or no, found that they were; and then, repeating his injunctions as to rapidity of action, he slipped the pistols one into each pocket, opened the door, and disappeared in the darkness.

Once fairly clear of the house, Bob paused for a minute or two to collect his thoughts. Then he walked on again toward the large building in which the men were housed, and on reaching it coolly thrust his head in at the open door, and looked round as though in search of someone.

"Well, matey, what is it?" asked one of the pirates.

"Is Dickinson here?" inquired Bob boldly.

"I think he is," was the reply. "Yes, there he is, over there. Here, Dickinson! you're wanted."

"Ay, ay," answered Dickinson. "Who wants me?"

"I do," answered Bob. "Mr Ralli says you're to shift over at once."

This was simply a form of words which had been agreed on when Dickinson paid his midnight visit to the cottage, and meant that the moment for action had arrived, and that a muster was to be made at the landing-place.

The sudden summons took Dickinson rather by surprise, though he had been schooling himself to expect it at any moment; he instantly recovered himself, however, and rising to his feet with a well-assumed air of reluctance asked:

"Does he mean that we are to go now—to-night?"

"He said 'at once,'" answered Bob.

"Oh! very well," growled Dickinson, "I s'pose we must obey orders. Here you—Tom Poole, Sullivan, Masters"—and he glanced his eye round the room, apparently hesitating whom to choose, but gradually picking out, one after the other, all the men who had cast in their lot with our friends—"muster your kits and then go up to the capstan-house; you've got to turn-in aboard the battery to-night, my beauties."

The men named, taking their cue from Dickinson, and acting up to instructions already received, assumed a sulky unwilling demeanour as they set about the work of packing a small quantity of already carefully selected clothes in their bags, growling and grumbling at having to turn out just when they were thinking of tumbling into their hammocks, and so on, but using the utmost expedition all the same.

In a little over ten minutes from the time of their first being called, the men, sixteen in number, stood in the large loft of the capstan-house. Poole had brought with him the key of the arm-chest, and, opening the case, he rapidly served out to every man a cutlass with its belt and a pair of six-chambered revolvers, every one of which he had himself fully loaded only the day before, in preparation for such an emergency as the present. The chest was then relocked and left, it being too heavy for them to carry away with them, to say nothing of the suspicion which such an act would excite if witnessed, as it would almost certainly be. But Poole slipped the key back into his pocket again, knowing that the strength of the chest and the solidity of the lock were such as to involve the expenditure of a considerable amount of time in the breaking open; and every minute of detention suffered by the pirates would now be almost worth a man's life to the escaping party.

"Now, lads," said Dickinson, "are yer all ready? Then march; down to the beach we goes, and seizes the two whale-boats, eight of us to each boat. But mind! there's to be no getting into the boats or shoving off until the ladies and gentlemen from the hut's all here. Mayhap we shall have to make a fight of it on the beach yet; so keep dry land under your feet until you has orders contrariwise."

The men descended the ladder leading from the capstan-house loft, and ranging themselves in a small compact body, two abreast, marched down to the landing-place, being joined on their way by some half-dozen curious idlers who had turned out to see what was in the wind. Dickinson was most anxious to get rid of these unwelcome attendants, and did all he could think of to persuade them to return to the house; but though quite unsuspicious as yet, they were not to be persuaded; they preferred rather to march alongside the other party, keeping up a constant fire of such jests and witticisms as sailors are wont to indulge in.

Bob, from a secluded and shadowy corner, watched this party as long as he could see them, and then began to look out for his own particular friends. He had not long to wait; barely five minutes afterwards he saw them also pass down on their way to the boats.

He allowed these a sufficient time to reach the boats, and then set off at a brisk pace to the "Black Hole." He soon reached it; and on his approach was promptly challenged by the two guards, who happened to be the same two truculent ruffians who were on guard when Dickinson tried to communicate with the prisoners.

In reply to the challenge, Bob informed them that they were wanted by Ralli, immediately, at the cottage (that being the most distant building), and that he had orders to keep guard until their return.

"What are we wanted for?" was the suspicious question.

"Oh! I believe there's some more people to be locked up here," answered Bob nonchalantly.

"All right!" answered the one who had asked the question. "Come on, Mike. And you—you young swab—mind you don't let a soul come near here while we're gone; if you do, Ralli'll just skin yer. D'ye hear?"

"All right!" answered Bob, placing his back against the door; "you go on; I won't give Ralli a chance to skin me, never fear. He's a good deal more likely to skin you if you don't look sharp."

The two guards accordingly set out in the direction of the cottage; but they had not gone half a dozen steps before they returned, cursing and swearing most horribly.

"Here, you young cub, what's the pass-word? Damn me if I hadn't forgotten that," exclaimed one of them, making towards Bob with outstretched hand.

"Stand back!" said Bob. "If you advance another step I'll shoot you both like dogs."

"The pass-word; the pass-word," demanded the ruffianly pair. "Give the pass-word at once, or by — I'll split your skull with this cutlass."

Bob saw that he had not a moment to lose; that his life hung upon a thread; and that, moreover, if he allowed these fellows to overpower him, the whole scheme would probably fail; he therefore whipped out his pistols, and, taking rapid aim, pulled both triggers at the same instant. There was a single report; and one of the men staggered forward, shot through the body, whilst the other threw up his arms and fell back heavily to the ground with a bullet in his brain.

Bob remembered for many a long day afterwards, and often saw in his dreams at night, the wild despairing glare in the eyes of the dying pirate as the flash of the pistol glanced upon the glazing eyeballs for an instant; but he had no time to think about such things now. Stooping down and applying his mouth to the keyhole he said, loud enough to be heard by those within:

"Stand clear in there; I'm about to blow the lock to pieces. It is I—Robert. The time has come."

"Fire away, my lad!" was the reply. "You will not hurt us."

Bob applied the muzzles of both pistols to the lock, and pulled the triggers. Fortunately, the lock was not a particularly strong one; and a supplementary kick sent the door flying open.

Captain Staunton and Lance at once emerged from their dark noisome prison and glanced eagerly around them.

"Thank you, Robert," hurriedly exclaimed the skipper. "There is no time to say more now, I know; so tell us what we are to do, my lad, and we'll do it."

Bob pointed to the prostrate bodies of the two pirates and said:

"Take their arms, and then we must make a rush to the landing; this firing is sure to have raised an alarm, but it could not be helped. But how is this! Where are your manacles!"

"Slipped them off, my lad, the moment we heard your voice," answered the skipper. "Price—fine fellow that he is—managed that for us by putting us in irons several sizes too large for us. Now, Evelin, are you ready! I fancy I hear footsteps running this way."

"All ready!" said Lance.

"Then, off we go!" exclaimed Bob. "This way, gentlemen—sharp round to the right for a couple of hundred yards, and then straight for the landing. It will give us a better chance if the pirates suspect anything and place themselves to cut us off."

Away went the trio at racing-pace, Bob slightly taking the lead and striking sharply away to the right. It was well for them that they did so, as they were thus enabled to dodge a crowd of men who came excitedly running up from the landing on hearing the pistol-shots.

The party from the cottage had safely reached the boats some few minutes before this; Dickinson having very cleverly got them through the crowd on the landing-place by calling out in an authoritative voice as soon as he saw them coming:

"Now then, lads, make way there, make way for the prisoners to pass."

The men accordingly gave way, forming a lane in their midst through which our friends passed in fear and trembling, exposed for a minute or so to the coarsest ribaldry which the ruffianly band could summon to their lips on the spur of the moment. It was not until they had all been passed safely into the two whale-boats, and Dickinson's little band had drawn themselves closely up with drawn cutlasses in a compact line between the boats and the shore, that the suspicions of the pirates became in the least aroused.

Then there gradually arose an eager whispering among them; suspicious glances were turned first upon Dickinson's party and then toward the buildings; and upon the noise of shots being heard they all set out at a run in the direction of the sound, fully persuaded that affairs had somehow fallen out of joint with them, and that it was quite time for them to be stirring.

They had run about half the distance between the boats and the capstan-house when someone caught a glimpse of three flying figures indistinctly made out through the gloom. The alarm was instantly given, and in another moment the entire crowd had turned sharply off in pursuit.

It now became a neck-and-neck race between the two parties as to which should reach the boats first. The pirates were poor runners, not being much accustomed to that kind of exercise; but so unfortunately were two out of the three fugitives of whom they were in chase. Bob was fleet as a deer for a short distance, but he was far too loyal to leave his two friends; and they, poor fellows, weak and cramped as they were with their recent confinement, already began to feel their limbs dragging heavy as lead over the ground. The pirates gained upon them rapidly.

Presently one of the pursuers was so near that they could hear him panting heavily behind.

"You keep steadily on," murmured Bob, as he pushed in for a moment between his two companions; "I'll stop this fellow."

Then, allowing the skipper to pass ahead of him, he sprang suddenly aside, and, grasping one of his pistols by the barrel, brought down the butt of the weapon heavily upon the pirate's head as he rushed past. The fellow staggered a pace or two further and then fell heavily to the ground, where he lay face downwards and partially stunned until his comrades came to his assistance. As, fortunately, they all stopped and gathered round the man, raising him to his feet and eagerly questioning him, the diversion thus created gave the three fugitives time to reach the boats without further molestation.

Here they were, of course, received with open arms; but before their greetings were half exchanged the armed guard had turned to the boats, and, exerting their whole strength, shot them out upon the glassy waters of the bay, springing in themselves at the same moment and taking to their oars without an instant's delay.

As soon as the boats' heads were turned round and fairly pointed away from the shore and toward the shipyard, Dickinson, taking off his hat in salutation to Captain Staunton, said in a loud voice so that all in the boats could hear:

"Now, sir, we're fairly launched upon this here henterprise at last, and may luck go with us! We've all had to manage as best we could for the last few days—since you was locked up, you know, sir; but now as you're free again we wants you to understand as we all looks upon you as our lawful leader and cap'n, and that from henceforth all you've got to do is to give your orders, and we'll obey 'em."

A Night of Terror

Captain Staunton's first act, after suitably acknowledging Dickinson's expression of fealty, was to inquire how the crisis had been brought about. The explanation made his eyes flash fire; he ground his teeth and clenched his fists with rage as he thought of how he would have punished the ruffian who had laid such brutal hands upon his little pet. And when the explanation was complete, he wrung Bob's hand until it fairly ached as he thanked him for what he had done. Meanwhile poor May still lay in her mother's arms moaning with pain; and when the skipper took her on his knee the little creature once more screamed out, and complained that it hurt her shoulder. Upon this Lance, thinking that something must be wrong, made a careful examination of the child, when it was found that Ralli's brutal violence had resulted in the dislocation of her shoulder. It was of course at once pulled back into place, but the poor little creature's screams at the pain of the operation were terrible to hear; and Captain Staunton in the hastiness of his anger registered a solemn vow that if he ever again met Ralli he would make the wretch pay dearly for his brutality.

How little he dreamed of the terrible circumstances under which he would next see this miserable man.

The two whale-boats sped swiftly across the glassy surface of the bay, propelled by six stalwart oarsmen each, a little jet of phosphorescent water spouting up under their sharp stems, a long ripple spreading out and undulating away on either side of them, and half a dozen tiny whirlpools of liquid fire swirling in the wake of each as their crews strained at the stout ash oars until they bent again. The night had grown black as pitch, not a solitary star was visible, and the heat was so intense as to be almost insufferable; but the men thought nothing of this in their eagerness and zeal now that they had taken the decisive step of throwing up their old life of crime and had fairly enrolled themselves once more on the side of law and order.

In a very short time the boats had made the passage across the bay and were brought with an easy graceful sweep alongside the landing at the shipyard. The occupants quickly disembarked; and while the ladies proceeded at once under the care and guidance of Rex and Bob to safe and comfortable quarters in the schooner's spacious cabin, Captain Staunton gave orders that two large fires should be immediately lighted, one on each side of the landing, for the double purpose of affording them a light to work by and of enabling them to perceive the approach of their enemies.

"For," he remarked to Lance, "you may depend upon it that their suspicions are thoroughly aroused by this time, and it will not be long before they are after us to see what it all means."

A couple of huge heaps of shavings, chips, and ends of timber were speedily collected and ignited, the blaze soaring high in the motionless air and throwing a strong ruddy light for a considerable distance round.

Then Lance, with Bowles, Dickinson, Poole, and three or four other reliable hands armed with torches, went carefully round the schooner, inspecting the cradle. It was unfinished; but Lance thought that a couple of hours more of energetic labour expended upon it would make it sufficiently secure to enable them to effect the launch. Time was now of immense value to them; they could not afford to be very particular, and so long as the cradle would serve its purpose that was all they cared about.

They accordingly set to with a will, and very soon the yard resounded with the harsh rasping of saws and the heavy blows of mauls wedging the timbers into their places.

In the meantime Captain Staunton with the rest of the party went on board the schooner, and, after fully arming themselves with cutlass and revolver, opened the magazine, passed a good supply of ammunition on deck, cast loose the guns, and carefully loaded them, cramming them almost to the muzzle with bullets, spike-nails, and anything else they could lay hold of. This done, the skipper, unwilling to leave the ship himself, called for a volunteer to go to the battery, spike the guns there, and lay a fuse in the magazine. Bob at once stepped forward, and, being accepted, provided himself forthwith with a hammer and a sufficient length of fuse, and set out upon his errand.

He had scarcely disappeared in the gloom when Dale, who had volunteered to keep a look-out, gave warning of the approach of two boats—the launch and the pinnace—full of men.

They were observed almost at the same moment by Lance, who hailed:

"Schooner ahoy! Do you see the boats coming?"

"Ay, ay," answered Captain Staunton. "We see them, and we'll give them a warm reception presently."

"Very well," returned Lance; "we shall stick to our work and leave you to do the fighting. If you require any assistance, give us a call."

"All right!" answered the skipper. Then turning to the men on the schooner's deck, he shouted:

"Run those two guns out of the stern-ports there, and train them so as to sweep the boats just before they reach the landing. So! that's well. Now wait for the word, and when I give it, fire."

The boats, however, were meantime lying upon their oars, their crews apparently holding a consultation. The fire-light which revealed their approach revealed to them also the fact that the occupants of the shipyard were fully prepared to emphatically dispute any attempt on their part to land; and the sight brought vividly to their minds the aphorism that "discretion is the better part of valour."

At length, after some twenty minutes of inaction—during which the workers underneath the schooner's bottom plied their tools with a skill and energy that was truly astounding—the two boats were once more put in motion, their crews directing their course toward the landing, each boat having a rude substitute for a white flag reared upon a boat-hook in the bow.

The moment that they were near enough for their occupants to hear him Captain Staunton hailed them with an imperative order to keep off or he would fire into them.

They at once laid upon their oars, and a man rising in the stern-sheets of the launch returned an answer, which was, however, quite unintelligible. Meanwhile the boats, still having way upon them, continued slowly to approach.

"Back water!" shouted the skipper, seizing the trigger line of one of the guns, whilst Brook stood manfully at the other. "Back water, all of you, instantly, or we will fire."

The man in the stern-sheets of the launch waved his hand; the oars again flashed into the water, and both boats dashed at the landing-place.

"Wait just a moment yet," said the skipper, raising a warning hand to Brook and squinting along his gun at the same time. "Now, fire!"

The report of the two brass nine-pounders rang sharply out at the same moment, making the schooner quiver to her keel, and severely testing the construction of her cradle. A crash was heard, then a frightful chorus of shrieks, yells, groans, and execrations; and as the smoke curled heavily away, both boats were seen with their planking rent and penetrated here and there, and their occupants tumbling over and over each other in their anxiety to get at the oars—many of which had been suffered to drop overboard—and withdraw as quickly as possible to a somewhat safer distance.

A hearty cheer was raised by the party in possession of the shipyard. Those on board the schooner reloaded their guns in all haste, and the hammering down below went on with, if possible, still greater energy.

The boats were suffered to retire unmolested, and nothing further was heard of them for over half an hour. Then Dale, who was still maintaining a careful look-out, suddenly gave notice that they were again approaching.

The two aftermost guns were accordingly once more very carefully pointed and fired, Captain Staunton giving the word as before. But by some mischance the muzzles were pointed a trifle too high, and both charges flew harmlessly over the boats, tearing up the water a few yards astern of them. The pirates, upon this unexpected piece of—to them—good fortune, raised a frantic cheer of delight, and, bending at their oars until they seemed about to snap them, dashed eagerly at the landing-place.

There was no time to reload the guns, so, seizing his weapons and calling upon all hands to follow him, the skipper hastily scrambled over the schooner's bulwarks, and, making his way to the ground, rushed forward to meet the enemy, who had by this time effected a landing.

The two opposing forces met within half a dozen yards of the water's edge, and then ensued a most desperate and sanguinary struggle. The pirates had by this time pretty nearly guessed at the audacious designs of those to whom they were opposed. They had seen enough to know not only that an escape was meditated, but that it was also proposed to carry off the schooner—that beautiful craft which their own hands had so largely assisted to construct, and in which they had confidently expected to sail forth upon a career of unbounded plunder and licence, in full reliance that her speed would insure to them complete immunity from punishment for their nefarious deeds. Such unheard-of audacity was more than enough to excite their anger to the pitch of frenzy, and they fought like demons, not only for revenge, but also for the salvation of the schooner. But if these were the motives which spurred them on to the encounter, their adversaries were actuated by incentives of a still higher character. They fought for the life and liberty, not only of themselves, but also of the weak defenceless women, whose only trust under God was in them; and if the pirates rushed furiously to the onset, they were met with a cool, determined resolution, which was more than a balance for overpowering numbers. Captain Staunton looked eagerly among the crowd of ruffianly faces for that of Ralli, determined to avenge with his own hand the multitudinous wrongs and insults which this man had heaped upon him and his dearest ones; but the Greek was nowhere to be seen. On the skipper's right was Lance, and on his left Dickinson, the former fully occupying the attention of at least three opponents by the marvellous play of his cutlass-blade, whilst the latter brandished with terrible effect a heavy crow-bar which he had hurriedly snatched up on being summoned to the fight. Rex and Brook were both working wonders also. Bowles was fighting as only a true British seaman can fight in a good cause; and Dale, with a courage which excited his own most lively surprise, was handling his cutlass and pistol as though he had used the weapons all his life. Steadily, and inch by inch, the pirates were driven back in spite of their superior numbers; and at last, after a fight of some twenty minutes, they finally broke and fled before a determined charge of their adversaries, rushing headlong to their boats and leaving their dead and wounded behind them.

Captain Staunton did not follow them up, although the two whale-boats still lay moored at the landing as they had left them. He was anxious to avail himself of the advantage already gained in making good the escape of his own party rather than to risk further losses by an attempt to inflict additional punishment upon his adversaries. Besides, that might possibly follow later on when they had got the schooner afloat. His first act, therefore, after the flight of the pirates, was to muster his forces and ascertain the extent of the casualties.

The list was a heavy one.

In the first place, nine of the little band were missing at the muster. Bowles presented himself with his left arm shattered by a pistol bullet; Brook was suffering from a severe scalp-wound; and every one of the others had a wound or contusion of some sort, which, whilst it did not incapacitate them for work, was a voucher that they had not shrunk from taking their part manfully in the fight.

This first hasty examination over, an anxious search was instituted for the missing. The first man found was Dickinson, dead, his body covered with wounds, and a bullet-hole in the centre of his forehead. Near him lay Dale, bleeding and insensible, shot through the body; and a little further on Bob was found, also insensible, with a cutlass gash across the forehead. Then Dick Sullivan was found dead, with his skull cloven to the eyes; and near him, also dead, one of the seamen of the Galatea. And lastly, at some distance from the others, Ned Masters, with another seaman from the Galatea, and two of the escaped prisoners, were found all close together, severely wounded, and surrounded by a perfect heap of dead and wounded pirates. These four, it seemed, had somehow become separated from the rest of their party, and had been surrounded by a band of pirates. This made a list of three killed and six severely wounded.

The latter were gently raised in the arms of their less injured comrades and taken with all speed on board the schooner, where they were turned over for the present to the care of the ladies; while those who were still able to work resumed operations underneath the ship's bottom.

Another quarter of an hour's hard work, and then Lance's voice was heard ordering one hand to jump on board the schooner and look out for a line.

"All right!" exclaimed Bob's voice from the deck; "heave it up here, Mr Evelin."

"What! you there, Robert? Glad to hear it, my fine fellow. Just go forward; look out for the line, and, when you have it, haul taut and make fast securely."

"All right," answered Bob with his head over the bows; "heave!"

The line, a very slender one, was thrown up, and Bob, gathering in the slack, and noticing that it led from somewhere ahead of the schooner, bowsed it well taut and securely belayed it. He knew at once what it was.

"Hurrah!" he shouted joyously. "That means that we are nearly ready for launching."

Bob's unexpected reappearance, it may be explained, was due to the fact that he had been merely stunned, and had speedily recovered consciousness under the ministering hands of his gentle friends in the cabin, upon which, though his head ached most violently, he lost no time in returning to duty.

Lance now made a second careful inspection of the cradle; and upon the completion of his round he pronounced that, though the structure was a somewhat rough-and-ready affair, it would do; that is to say, it would bear the weight of the schooner during the short time she was sliding off the ways, and that was all they wanted.

"And now comes the wedging-up, I s'pose, sir?" remarked Poole interrogatively.

"Wedging-up?" returned Lance with a joyous laugh. "No, thank you, Poole; we'll manage without that. Do you see these two pieces of wood here in each keel-block? Well, they are wedges. You have only to draw them out and the top of the block will be lowered sufficiently to allow the schooner to rest entirely in the cradle. Get a maul, Poole, and you and I will start forward, whilst you, Kit, with another hand, commence aft. Knock out the wedges on both sides as you come to them, and work your way forward until you meet us. The rest of you had better go on board and see that everything is clear and ready for launching."

"When you're quite ready to launch, let me know, if you please, Mr Evelin, and I'll go and light the fuse that's to blow up the battery," said Bob.

"Ah! to be sure," answered Lance, "I had forgotten that. You may go up now if you like, Bob, and I'll give you a call when we're ready."

Bob thereupon set off on his mission of destruction, while Lance and Poole with a couple of mauls began to knock out the wedges which Evelin, foreseeing from the very inception of the work some such emergency as the present, had introduced in the construction of the keel-blocks.

In a few minutes both parties met near the middle of the vessel, and the last pair of wedges were knocked out.

"That's a good job well over," exclaimed Poole; "and precious glad I am now that I thought of soaping them ways this morning. I knowed this here business must come afore long, and I determined to get as far ahead with the work as possible. Now I s'pose, sir, we're all ready?"

"Yes, I think so," answered Lance, "but I'll just go forward and take a look along the keel to see that she is clear everywhere."

He accordingly did so, and had the gratification of seeing by the still brilliant light of the fires that the keel was a good six inches clear of the blocks, fore and aft.

"All clear!" he shouted. "Now, go on board, everybody. Light the fuse, Robert, and come on board as soon as possible."

"Ay, ay, sir," answered Bob from the not very distant battery.

A tiny spark of light appeared for an instant in the darkness high up on the face of the rock as our hero struck a match, and in another couple of minutes he was running nimbly up the steep plank leading from the rocks beneath to the schooner's deck.

"Kick down that plank, Robert, my lad, and see that it falls clear of everything," said Lance. "Are we all clear fore and aft?"

"All clear, sir," came the hearty reply from various parts of the deck.

"Are you ready with the axe forward there, Kit?"

"All ready, sir."

"Then cut."

A dull cheeping thud of the axe was immediately heard, accompanied by a sharp twang as the tautly strained line parted; then followed the sound of the shores falling to the ground; there was a gentle jar, and the schooner began to move.

"She moves!—she moves!" was the cry. "Hurrah! Now she gathers way."

"Yes," shouted Lance, joyously. "She's going. Success to the Petrel"—as he shivered to pieces on the stem-head a bottle of wine which the steward, anxious that the launch should be shorn of none of its honours, had brought up from the cabin and hastily thrust into his hand. "Three cheers for the saucy Petrel, my lads—hip, hip, hip, hurrah!"

The three cheers rang lustily out upon the still air of the breathless night as the schooner shot with rapidly increasing velocity down the ways and finally plunged into the mirrorlike waters of the bay, dipping her stern deeply and ploughing up a smooth glassy furrow of water fringed at its outer edge with a coruscating border of vivid phosphorescent light.

"The boats—the boats again!" suddenly shouted Bowles, as the schooner, now fairly afloat, shot rapidly stern-foremost away from the rock—"Good God! they are right in our track; we shall cut them in two."

"That is their look-out," grimly responded Captain Staunton; "if they had been wise they would have accepted their defeat and retired to the shore; as, however, they have not done so, they must take the consequences. Remember, lads, not a man of them must be suffered to come on board."

A warning shout from the helmsman of the pinnace announced his sudden discovery of the danger which threatened the boats, and he promptly jammed his helm hard a-starboard. The launch was on his port side; and the result was a violent collision between the two boats, the pinnace striking the launch with such force as to send the latter clear of the schooner whilst the pinnace herself, recoiling from the shock, stopped dead immediately under the schooner's stern. There was a sharp sudden crash as the Petrel's rudder clove its irresistible way through the doomed boat, and a yell of dismay from its occupants, several of whom made a spring at the schooner's taffrail, only to be remorselessly thrust off again.

"There is a chance for them yet," said the skipper, as the schooner continued to drive astern leaving the wretches struggling in the water, "the launch has escaped; she can pick them up."

At length the schooner's way slackened sufficiently to enable Lance, by looking over the bow and stern, to ascertain her exact trim.

"It is perfect," he exclaimed to Captain Staunton as he rejoined the latter near the companion, "she sits accurately down to her proper water-line everywhere, thus proving the correctness of all my calculations—a result which pleases as much as it surprises me, since I have had to depend entirely on my memory for the necessary formula. Well,

Captain Staunton, my task is now finished; here is the schooner, fully rigged and fairly afloat; take charge of her, my dear sir; and may she fully answer all your expectations!"

"Thanks, Evelin; a thousand thanks!" exclaimed the skipper, heartily grasping Lance's proffered hand. "You have indeed executed your self-imposed task faithfully and well. Let me be the mouth-piece of all our party in conveying to you our most hearty expressions of gratitude for the noble manner in which you have aided us in our great strait. To you is entirely due the credit of bringing our project thus far to a successful issue; but for your skill, courage, and resolution we might have been compelled to remain for years—Ha! what is that?"

A low rumbling roar was faintly heard in the distance, rapidly increasing in volume of sound, and breaking in with startling effect upon the breathless stillness of the night.

"It is another earthquake," exclaimed Lance. "Thank Heaven, we are afloat! Had it caught us upon the stocks it would doubtless have shaken the cradle to pieces, and, in all probability, thus frustrated our escape."

The ominous sound drew swiftly nearer and nearer, filling the startled air with a chaos of sound which speedily became absolutely deafening in its intensity; the waters of the bay broke first into long lines of quivering ripples, then into a confused jumble of low foaming surges; the schooner jarred violently, as though she was being dragged rapidly over a rocky bottom; there was a hideous groaning grinding sound on shore, soon mingled with that of the crashing fall of enormous masses of earth and rock, above which could still be feebly heard the piercing shriek of horror raised by the occupants of the launch. The shock passed; but was immediately followed by one of still greater intensity; the waters were still more violently agitated; the schooner was swept helplessly hither and thither, rolling heavily, and shipping great quantities of water upon her deck as the shapeless surges madly leaped and boiled and swirled around her. Finally, a long line of luminous foam was seen to be rushing rapidly down upon the schooner from the harbour's mouth, stretching completely across the bay. As it came nearer it was apparent that this was the foaming crest of a wall of water some twelve feet in height which was rushing down the bay at railway-speed.

"Hold on, every one of you, for your lives!" hoarsely shouted the skipper, as the wave swept threateningly down upon the schooner; and the next moment it burst upon them with a savage roar.

Luckily, the Petrel's bows were presented fairly to it, or the consequences would have been disastrous. As it was it curled in over the stem, an unbroken mass of water, filling the decks in an instant and carrying the schooner irresistibly along with it toward the shore at the bottom of the bay.

"Let go the anchor," shouted Captain Staunton, as soon as he could get his head above water.

But before this could be done the wave had swept past, rushing with a loud thundering roar far up the beach even to the capstan-house, and then rapidly subsiding.

"Get the canvas on her at once," ordered Captain Staunton—"close-reefed main-sail, fore-sail, and jib; we shall have some wind presently, please God, and we'll make use of it to get out of this as speedily as possible—Merciful Heaven! what now?"

A sullen roar; a rattling crash as of a peal of heaviest thunder; and the whole scene was suddenly lit up with a lurid ruddy glow. Turning their startled glances inland, our adventurers saw that the lofty hill-top, dominating the head of the ravine, near which was situated the gold cavern, had burst open and was vomiting forth vast volumes of flame and smoke. As they looked the top of the hill visibly crumbled and melted away, the flames shot up in fiercer volumes, vast quantities of red-hot ashes, mingled with huge masses of glowing incandescent rock, were projected far into the air; a terrific storm of thunder and lightning suddenly burst forth to add new terrors to the scene; and to crown all, a new rift suddenly burst open in the side of the hill, out of which there immediately poured a perfect ocean of molten lava.

In the face of this stupendous phenomenon Captain Staunton's order to make sail passed unheeded; the entire faculties of every man on board the schooner were wholly absorbed in awe-struck contemplation of the terrific spectacle.

Onward rolled the fiery flood. It wound in a zigzag serpentine course down the side of the hill, and soon reached the thick wood at its base and at the head of the valley. The stately forest withered, blazed for a brief moment, and vanished in its fatal embrace, and now it came sweeping down the steep declivity toward the bay.

This terrible sight aroused and vivified the paralysed energies of those on board the Petrel. Without waiting for a repetition of the order to make sail they sprang with panic-stricken frantic haste to cast off the gaskets, and in an incredibly short time the schooner was under canvas.

Still there was no wind. Not the faintest breath of air came to stir the flapping sails of the now gently rolling vessel; and her crew could do nothing but wait in feverish anxious expectancy for the long-delayed breeze, watching meanwhile the majestic irresistible onward sweep of that fiery deluge.

At last, thank God! there was a faint puff of wind; it came, sighed past, and died away. And now, another. The sails caught it, bellied out, flapped again, filled once more, and the Petrel gathered way. She had gradually swung round until her bow pointed straight for the capstan-house; and Captain Staunton sprang to the wheel, sending it with a single vigorous spin hard over. The breeze was still very light, and the craft responded but slowly to her helm; but at length she came up fairly upon a wind and made a short stretch to the eastward, tacking the moment that she had gathered sufficient way to accomplish the manoeuvre. She was now on the port tack, stretching obliquely across the bay in a southerly direction, when a startled call from Poole, repeated by all the rest, directed Captain Staunton's gaze once more landward.

"Look—look—merciful powers, it is Ralli!" was Lance's horrified exclamation as he grasped the skipper convulsively by the shoulder and pointed with a trembling hand to the shore.

Sure enough it was Ralli. The pirates had either not waited to seek him, or had not thought of looking for him in the cottage before setting out on their expedition against the shipyard, and he had consequently been left there. But somehow—doubtless in the desperation of mortal fear excited by the dreadful phenomena in operation around him—he had at last succeeded in freeing himself from his bonds, and was now seen running toward the beach, screaming madly for help.

The stream of lava was only a few yards behind him, and it had now spread out to the entire width of the very narrow valley. The unhappy wretch was flying for his life; terror seemed to have endowed him with superhuman strength and speed, and for a moment it almost appeared as though he would come out a winner in the dreadful race.

"'Bout ship!" sharply rang out the skipper's voice; "he is a fiend rather than a man, but he must not perish thus horribly if we can save him."

He put the helm hard down as he spoke, and the schooner shot up into the wind, with her sails sluggishly flapping. But before she had time to get fairly round the helm was suddenly righted and then put hard up.

"Keep all fast," commanded Captain Staunton, "it is too late; no mortal power can save him. See! he is already in the grasp of his fate."

Such was indeed the case. The fierce breath of that onward-rolling flood of fire was upon him; its scorching heat sapped his strength; he staggered and fell. With the rapidity of a lightning flash he was up and away again; but—Merciful God—see! his clothing is all ablaze; and listen to those dreadful shrieks of fear and agony—Ah! miserable wretch, now the flood itself is upon him; see how the waves of fire curl round him—he throws up his arms with a harsh despairing blood-curdling yell—he sinks—he is gone—and the surging fiery river sweeps grandly on until it plunges with an awful hissing sound into the waters of the bay and the whole scene becomes blotted out by the vast curtain of steam which shoots up and spreads itself abroad.

"What a night of horror! it is hell upon earth!" gasps the skipper, as he turns his eyes away and devotes himself once more solely to the task of navigating the schooner; "thank God the breeze is freshening, and we may now hope to be soon out of this and clear of it all. Phew! what terrific lightning, and what an infernal combination of deafening sounds!"

Fortunate was it for the schooner and her crew that the wind was from the southward, or blowing directly down into the bay; otherwise they would speedily have been lost in the thick clouds of steam which rose from the water, or set on fire by the dense shower of red-hot ashes which now began to fall thickly about them. As it was, though the wind was against them, and they were compelled to beat up the bay, the wind kept back the steam, and also to a great extent the falling ashes. But, notwithstanding these favourable circumstances, the crew were obliged to keep the decks deluged with water to prevent their being ignited.

Gradually, however, the Petrel drew further and further beyond the influence of this danger; and soon the rock at the harbour's mouth was sighted. Captain Staunton was at first somewhat anxious about risking the passage out to sea, being doubtful whether the explosion of the magazine had yet taken place; but a little reflection satisfied him that it must have occurred, as they had been drifting about the bay for nearly an hour, and he determined to push on.

Suddenly there was a shout from the look-out forward: "Boat ahead!" immediately followed by the information, "It's the launch, sir, bottom-up!"

Such indeed it proved to be when the schooner a minute later glided past it. But where were her crew? They had disappeared, leaving no sign behind them.

The hoarse angry roar of the breakers outside was now distinctly audible; and in another five minutes' time the Petrel's helm was eased up, she was kept away a couple of points, and, shooting through the short narrow passage on the eastern side of the rock, began to plunge with a gentle swinging motion over the endless procession of long slowly-moving swell outside.

The crew of the schooner had time to note, as they swept past the rock and through the passage, that the battery no longer frowned down upon the bay. In its place there appeared a yawning fire-blackened chasm; and the shipyard was thickly strewed with masses and fragments of rock of all sizes; both whale-boats were swamped; and a solitary gun, with a fragment of its carriage still attached, lay half in and half out of the water. The timbers of the dismembered cradle still floated huddled together like a raft, close to the landing.

"Now," said Lance to Captain Staunton, as soon as they were fairly outside of the harbour, "we are free, thank God! and, as there seems to be no immediate prospect of your further needing my help, I will go and look after the wounded and the ladies. Poor souls! what a fearful time of suspense and terror they must have passed, pent up there in the cabin, listening to all these fearful sounds, and not knowing what it means or what will be the end of it."

Lance accordingly descended, to find the ladies pale as death, and their eyes dilated with fear, resolutely doing their best with the aid of the steward to assuage the agonies of the wounded. He was, of course, at once assailed with a hundred questions, to which, however, he put a stop by holding up his hand and laughingly saying—

"Pray, spare me, and show me a little mercy, I beseech you; to answer all your questions would occupy me for the remainder of the night. Be satisfied, therefore, for the present with the general statement that we have successfully launched the schooner—as doubtless you have long ago found out for yourselves; that there has been a terrible earthquake, accompanied by a volcanic eruption which bids fair to completely destroy the island; that we are now in the open ocean, having made good our escape, and that there is at present nothing more to fear. Where is May?"

"She is asleep in that berth," answered Mrs Staunton, "so I hope the worst of the poor child's pain is over."

"No doubt of it," answered Lance; "the fact that she is sleeping is in itself a sufficient indication of that. And now, let me first thank you for your care of my patients here—to whom I will now myself attend—and next order you all three peremptorily off to bed. Away with you at once to the most comfortable quarters you can find, and try to get a good night's rest."

Utterly worn out, the ladies were only too glad to obey this order; and they accordingly forthwith retired to the cabins which the steward had already prepared for them.

The more severely wounded were then speedily attended to, their injuries carefully dressed, and themselves comfortably bestowed in their hammocks; after which came the turn of the others.

By the time that Lance had fully completed his arduous task the first faint streaks of dawn were lighting up the eastern horizon; and he went on deck to get a breath or two of fresh air. He found the schooner slipping along at a fine pace under every stitch of canvas she could spread, including studding-sails, with the breeze about two points on the starboard quarter, a clear sky above her, and a clear sea all round. Away astern, as the light grew stronger, could be seen a dark patch of smoke low down upon the horizon, indicating the position of "Albatross Island;" but the land itself had sunk below the horizon long before.

My story is now ended; very little more remains to be told, and that little must be told as tersely as possible.

The Petrel made a very rapid and prosperous passage home, and in due time arrived at Plymouth—long before which, however, the wounded had all completely recovered. Here the passengers landed; whilst Captain Staunton proceeded with the schooner to London, where the craft was safely docked and her crew paid off. The skipper then made the best of his way to the office of the owners of the Galatea, where he was received with joyous surprise, his story listened to with the greatest interest, and himself congratulated upon his marvellous escape from the many perils which he had encountered. And, best of all, before the interview terminated, his owners showed in the most practical manner their continued confidence in him by offering him the command of a very fine new ship which they had upon the stocks almost ready for launching.

I must leave it to the lively imaginations of my readers to picture for themselves the rapturous welcome home experienced by the other personages who have figured in this story, merely remarking that it left absolutely nothing to be desired, its warmth being of itself a sufficient compensation for all the hardship and suffering they had endured.

The gold which Bob's forethought had been the means of securing was duly divided equally between all who could fairly be regarded as entitled to a share; and, though it certainly did not amount to a fortune apiece, it proved amply sufficient to compensate the sharers for their loss of time.

On the receipt of his moiety, Bob gave a grand supper to all his friends in Brightlingsea, the which is referred to with justifiable pride by the landlady of the "Anchor" even unto this day.

It was whilst this eventful supper was in full swing that Lance Evelin unexpectedly made his appearance upon the scene. He was enthusiastically welcomed by Bob, duly introduced to the company, and at once joined them, making himself so thoroughly at home with them, and entering so completely into the spirit of the affair, that he sprang at a single bound into their best graces, and was vehemently declared by one and all to be "a real out-and-outer."

The next day found him closeted for a full hour with old Bill Maskell, after which, to everybody's profound astonishment, the pair left for London. Only to return next day, however, accompanied by a fine tall soldierly-looking old man, to whom Bob was speedily introduced, and by whom he was claimed, to his unqualified amazement, as an only and long-lost son. Sir Richard Lascelles—for he it was—was indebted to Lance for this joyous discovery; and it was almost pitiful to witness the poor old gentleman's efforts to adequately express his gratitude to Evelin for the totally unexpected restoration of his son to his arms.

Bob, now no longer Bob Legerton but Mr Richard Lascelles, was speedily transferred to his father's house in London; and, according to the latest accounts, he is now busy qualifying himself to enter the navy.

Poor old Bill Maskell was in a strangely agitated condition for some time after the occurrence of these events, being alternately in a state of the greatest hilarity at Bob's return home, and despondency at the reflection that henceforth the remainder of their lives must be spent apart. Sir Richard has, however, done what he could to console the poor old man by purchasing for him a pretty little cottage and garden in the most pleasant part of Brightlingsea, supplementing the gift with an allowance of one hundred and fifty pounds a year for the remainder of his life.

Some two months or so after the arrival home of the Petrel a notice appeared in the Morning Post and other papers announcing a double marriage at Saint George's, Hanover Square; the contracting parties being respectively Launcelot Evelin and Blanche Lascelles; and Rex Fortescue and Violet Dudley; there is every reason therefore to suppose that those four persons are at last perfectly happy.

It has been whispered—in the strictest confidence, of course—that there is some idea of fitting out an expedition to the South Pacific, for the purpose of ascertaining whether "Albatross Island" is still in existence, and, if so, whether there is any possibility of working the enormously rich gold mine, the strange discovery of which is recorded in these pages.

Should the expedition he undertaken and carried out with results worthy of note, an effort will be made to collect the fullest particulars, with the view of arranging them in narrative form for the entertainment of such readers as are sufficiently interested in our friends to wish for further intelligence about them.

www.ingramcontent.com/pod-product-compliance
Lightning Source LLC
Chambersburg PA
CBHW031312170626
46807CB00001B/381